# Centurion of The Boar.

## The third book of The Soldiers of The Boar.

Paperback version 2025.

Cover photo credit: Valentin Salja @ Unsplash.

The Soldiers of The Boar series consists of:

Legionaries of The Boar.

Sword of The Boar.

Centurion of The Boar.

Wine of The Boar.

Other books by Allan Harper.

The Boys from Eburacum.

All available on Amazon.

## Principal characters.

Velio Pinneius. Centurion of the Fourth century, First cohort, Twentieth legion Valeria Victrix.

Called The Boar because of its emblem.

Voccia. His young Votadini wife.

Gallus Tiomaris. Ex weapons instructor, Twentieth legion and Velio's former mentor.

Hanno Glaccus. Ex centurion and briefly commander of First cohort, Twentieth legion.

Marcellus. Velio's military secretary.

Servius Albinius. Legate in command of the Twentieth legion.

Orann. Votadini tribesman. Voccia's servant and her father's groom.

Liscus Aulus Manlio. Optio, second in command, of the Fourth century.

Civius. Centurion commander of the Delmatarum garrison at the hill fort.

Titus Vindex. Civius' temporarily attached optio, Delmatarum garrison.

Scribono. Legionary deserter from Twentieth legion.

Junius Cita. Legionary deserter from Sixth legion.

Auvericus. Lead mine operator in the hill country.

Arco. Auxiliary soldier from the Delmatarum garrison.

Drapisces. Subchief of the Carvetii tribe.

Durus Decimus. Procurator of Argentomagus.

Plautius. Tesserarius. Junior officer in Velio's century.

Losatas. High king of the Brigantes tribe.

Gramalcus. Slave merchant in Argentomagus.

Morenus. Senior centurion and commander of the First cohort, Boar legion. Velio's direct superior.

Metius. Tesserarius in Velio's century.

The year is AD 158.

In the province of Britannia, Emperor Antoninus Pius has ordered his turf and timber wall, only recently abandoned in AD 155, be reoccupied and strengthened. Control of the northern area ebbs and flows. Trimontium fort is now the most northerly occupied bastion. Further south, at Deva Victrix barracks, headquarters of the Twentieth legion, Velio Pinneius, centurion of the First cohort, is due to follow his old friends Gallus Tiomaris and Hanno Glaccus into retirement to own and run a vineyard in Gaul. He musters out in four weeks. His twenty-five years of service in the best legion in the army, The Boar, is finally over. It looks like he is free of it. His days of swords and shields are past. A profitable winemaking venture with Gallus and Hanno in Gaul beckons.

## Prelude.

## An estate in the Gallic town of Argentomagus.

He was like every other fat, bearded, Roman on a horse. He was fat. He had a beard. And his glossily coated animal possessed a noble spirit and a big heart. The slave sidled into the deeper shadows where burning shed timbers were fighting and losing their private duel with the enveloping night. Cries of pain, anguish and brutality rang out; nothing unusual in the estate, save for the time of day. Priscus had not been a kind man, but Priscus was dead and his wife, the Domina, had been less inclined to the whip these last few years. Now the old woman was lying face up in her own red puddle. The fat bearded man on the horse was enjoying the carnage he had unleashed. His men were looting everywhere. The slave slid along the warehouse wall. All the activity was centring on the house and the courtyard. The warehouse had been ransacked until even the bearded man lost interest. Laden waggons were already trundling into the profitable night. The slave seized his courage and ran into the night. He did not dare to look back.

# Part One.

## Chapter One.

### Northwest Britannia. Deva Victrix barracks. Home of the Twentieth legion.

Voccia watched him pack and kissed him goodbye, not wanting to let go. One last patrol, one last duty; that is what Velio said, before they left Britannia for Gaul and the vineyard where his friends Gallus and Hanno were waiting for them. She knew Gallus of course. The old soldier had helped liberate her from Segontio, how could she forget the language as he mixed running with swearing every step of the way as they tried to outpace the pursuing horses of the Selgovae prince and his men? Gallus was the closest thing he had to a best friend. Hanno, she did not know; she had not met him, only knowing the name from when Velio spoke about him.

Why did it have to be him? Why could the general not send someone else to do this? Velio had done his best to comfort her. She loved him for trying but nothing he could say would do except for *'I'll tell the general I'm not going to do it.'* That would have been sufficient but that was not the man she loved.

Marcellus arrived in his armour, ready for the day just as Orann led the horses from the stables. Velio was wearing his distant gaze, she saw she had already lost him; soldier's responsibilities and decisions running through his head. Orann leading the horses, Velio waiting, Marcellus giving last instructions to the house guard. The sky grey but brightening; the threat of sunshine. She held back her tears until he turned and walked his horse towards the principia to take leave of the legate. A stone turned in her heart. A horrible certainty started rising. She would never see him again. Her baby would never get to know its father. Orann, reading her distress, put out an awkward arm. Was her father's stable boy daring to offer comfort to her?

*'Make a good job of this Velio and I think your new enterprise can rely on the Twentieth legion for a new wine contract.'*

Servius Albinius' repeated message to him rattled around her head. He said Gallus and Hanno Glaccus would be delighted. What a start to their new venture. By now the two of them should have mastered the knack of the vineyard. With any luck Bacchus had already blessed them with a decent harvest, safely vatted. She pushed him and all his easy soldier's promises away and ran back into the villa.

The century was waiting for him. His new optio Liscus Aulus Manlio had them lined up. He handed the reins of his horse to Marcellus and looked at their faces. The Fourth century of the First Cohort, Twentieth legion. His century, imprinted with the pride, experience and resilience he demanded. One hundred and fifty-seven grizzled characters, double the standard century size, standing two lines deep, eyes watchful and expectant, shields clean, javelins glinting, armour buffed up to a state of insouciant perfection other cohorts struggled to match; the standard bearer in a thick wolf skin cape, his sweating features almost lost within it, company trumpeter, tesserarii and senior decorated legionaries all facing Centurion Pinneius, a Boar legend in his own way: glad it was him who led them.

Word in the barrack room was, this would be a last foray into the hills to kick arses, then he was heading off the wine trade in a couple of months. If anyone in 'The Boar' knew anything about wine, it was the legate and their centurion. At least he would not fiddle them with vinegary ration-posca, it would be decent stuff. In the background a trumpeter warmed up with husky, breathy sounds, preparing for the usual farewell.

*'This'll be the last one as a centurion with men at my back,'* Velio tried to squash the thought.

Saying 'vale' to Voccia had been testing enough. She had changed him. The baby was going to change things even more. He liked the prospect.

"We're off to the hills, lads. The legate wants an inspection of one of our garrisons. A bit of nonsense to sort out. It seems the lads from the cohort- Delmatarum might be getting too pally with the locals. Keep your wits about you and follow orders. No mavericks out there, hear me?" he said.

"Sir," they chorused along the line.

"Anyway, it'll give the girls a rest. Well earned, I've no doubt," he mocked.

Liscus' jaw worked as he suppressed a laugh. He saw them enjoying the new optio's facial gymnastics.

"Lead them out optio," he ordered.

Liscus put them into column, took his position at their head and with a brief signal moved them off the parade ground towards the Sinistra gateway and the road north. He did not move. His horse shook her head chastising his stillness and he slipped his arm under her jaw and patted her muzzle. When the last of the baggage carts, heavy with tents, was passing out the gate the trumpeter broke out 'Farewell Brother.' He saw the idlers and the off duty stopping their connivings to watch. Centurion Morenus, back in charge of the First cohort, came to see him off. They exchanged salutes and wry grins. Morenus nodding and smiling; Velio needed no advice from him.

"Mount up," Velio told Marcellus.

The watch commander at the gate was an old friend.

"Watch your back out there, centurion," he said as they passed him by.

## Chapter Two.

### Argentomagus: A town in the province of Gaullia Aquitania.

Gallus stared at the legacy of Priscus, his long lost and now late comrade of the old Second Augusta legion. This was not what he expected to find. The south facing slopes well planted with vines, yes, he expected that much. The ample supply of water from a pleasing little stream and the well in the courtyard; this was Gaul after all, not sun-baked Africa, yes that was secure. A modest villa, barns, sheds, the low building with the clay vats critical to the enterprise, yes; all of that was here, present, and correct. Some of the vats needed replacing but not all of them. There were enough intact receptacles to assess the summer vintage and gauge whether Priscus' widow had traded fair on her late husband's memory or, lined him up as a mug with capital to burn. If it was the latter, she had not an inkling of the depth of Hanno Glaccus' rage, nor his own capacity for vengeance.

He spent the day just looking, holding back the incipient anger threatening to overwhelm his self-belief. Estate slaves; forty in number, all missing. Freed men, four; winemaker and estate overseer, all missing. Carts, waggons; all transportation necessary for moving the product, gone: stables, empty. Wine in storage; none, all recently bucketed out in a hurry if the widespread spillage around the vats was anything to go by. The waste on the ground was not the work of estate slave or freed man. Implements and other assorted livestock; goats, sheep, poultry, gone. The beehives destroyed. The custom fitted wood bungs for the individual storage dolia-vats; burned in a pile in the courtyard. So, no storage of anything until a decent carpenter had paid an extended visit. The single remediating factor was that Velio was not here to see it. Blessings to Fortuna for that small exemption. A narrow-minded, suspicious man would think the estate had been turned over in the small window of time between Priscus' widow's departure and his arrival. The freedmen and the slaves should have been sufficient protection. Were they somehow party to it, or had they too been judiciously removed so they could not talk?

"Balls of Dis," he swore, over and over again at each fresh discovery.

Hanno came riding up from the bottom grounds of the estate, raising summer dust as his horse clip clopped its way along the central path. The reins bunched in one fist and the other clenched into his waist, where his gladius used to rest, he came on, head down, inspecting the ground for whatever clues might be gleaned in the dirt. He drew to a halt and dismounted.

"So," he said.

"So," Gallus repeated.

"Have we been cheated, or have we been robbed?" he mused.

Gallus rubbed his beard and cast his eyes all around the courtyard of the villa.

"The house has not been touched," he said, "damaged, I mean," he paused, "what state are the vines in?"

Hanno tied the reins to a wooden post.

"The vines have not been damaged," he replied.

He sounded surprised.

"Then we really do have a problem," Gallus murmured.

Hanno rubbed the back of his head and eased his back. The warm sun was welcome, but it was going to take time to take the chill of the north out of his bones after so many years of wearing damp cloaks.

"How so?" he asked.

"Someone wants us to fail," Gallus said, "we're going to need some reinforcements if we're going to defend this lot. We can rebuild and buy everything we need. Velio's capital will help pay for it. But leaving the vines intact means they want to know whether we're prepared to make a go of it."

"And if we are, they'll come back again to steal our wine," Hanno finished off.

Gallus surveyed the small waggon bearing their personal kit and supplies. Secreted amongst it were their sidearms plus a useful few extras he had filched from the weapons store before handing the keys to his smiling, obliging successor. Included among it all was a large sack of broken spars, rods and tangled cordage in need of serious repair. He remembered their conversation.

"That's not on any list that I recall writing," he told his replacement at the handover.

There was a knowing smile and a couple of coins.

"Not on my list either, hastiliarius, though it'll take a pile of work to get it working."

It was already lost from the legion accounting records.

"I have time where I'm heading," he had said.

"Gallus, the one-man army against wine thieves," Hanno almost smiled.

"And I thought I'd finished with the gladius," Gallus said, shaking his head.

"You Gallus, finished with the gladius?" Hanno smiled, "not in this life. Is there any wine left?"

Gallus shook his head, "only what we brought in the waggon."

"Well, it is good ground. Your man Priscus knew good ground when he saw it."

"His people were growers," Gallus replied, "he knew a lot about vines."

"And he joined the legions?" Hanno chortled.

He changed tack, "there must be a local procurator in the town, a vexillation of troops stationed nearby. We should go and register a complaint. We also have the small matter of slaves to buy Gallus. Bribes to make, remember this was always going to be a campaign not a battle. It will do no harm to have new bungs made for the vats."

"We need food first. All this will look better on a full belly," Gallus answered, "as for a local vexillation, I'm not so sure. This part of Gaul has been at peace for a long time. We can't exactly order them to protect the estate, can we?"

Hanno wiped beads of sweat off his forehead. The temperature was climbing. Now that the first shock of what they had walked into was settling down, he could feel his mood rising and improving. What was this compared to winters in Britannia?

"You're forgetting, Old Man. Soldiers and wine? I'm sure we can persuade the local commander to swing a patrol past us every now and then in return for a good price for their drink. The word will get out that we're not to be touched. And this will be an unpleasant memory. Gaul's been at peace for a long time, eh?" Hanno said.

Gallus made the stiff finger sign with his hand.

"Bacchus and Fortuna be with us," he intoned.

"A gift to Ceres more like. Out there on the estate. We must make the suovetaurilia walk around the estate and then a sacrifice. In the absence of a bull, we can use something else, whatever we can find. There must be a goose or a goat hiding somewhere on the estate we can use," Hanno answered.

He drew drawing on his centurion's experience of making propitiations on behalf of his men.

"That's what we need to do, make an offering. Stupid, I should have realised before we got involved in all this," he gestured around, "we must do it now before we take a bite ourselves."

"Aye centurion," Gallus smiled, catching Hanno's pious enthusiasm, "but there are no animals left. We will need to go and buy one in the forum. But right now, I need to eat. May Ceres be patient and merciful with a hungry man."

*

The next day they mounted up and took the road into Argentomagus, passing comfortable villas that might have been transported from the mother country itself. Neat walls and gardens, servants and slaves working in fields. The scents of flowers and the melange of sounds arising from lives untroubled by strife or fear. Worlds distant from the confines of Deva Victrix and the trumpet calls of routine tasks. In their plain civilian tunics Hanno was pleased to note they drew no attention. Their brushed and decorated horses were of more interest than the two strangers riding them, untrammelled by the weight of armour and weapons, the sweat of wearing a helmet. It was all very new and liberating.

The side road joined the army road and they picked up a little speed. They halted in Argentomagus' small forum and drank cooling water from a pretty, carved fountain. There did not appear to be any military uniforms in sight. Bustling civilians and tradesmen, animals, and children, local Bituriges people and Roman citizens. The tinkling sound of metal workers hammering the silver that lent its name to the place. Hanno spied the courthouse and a solitary legionary at its entrance. The legionary snapped to attention and gave them the full salute with a broad smile. Gallus gave him the 'down and up' inspection and nodded.

Inside, two rows of pillars defined the atrium and the pool beyond. Sunlight was streaming down. Painted walls of smooth plasterwork. Hanno breathed in and enjoyed all of it. A clerk of indefinable age approached with a polite but business-like expression. He might have been twenty or thirty, possibly even forty years of age. He declined to use words when a raised eyebrow could convey the same message. Gallus reckoned from the flowing moustaches he could only be a tamed Biturges. No Roman citizen would wear such hair without a beard. Only a tamed and Romanised Gaul would be so arrogant, as if they were the intellectual savages and he, their conqueror.

"Can the Procurator spare us an audience? We have things we need his help with," Hanno opened.

The clerk bowed and led them through into the rear of the building and the centre room. The whole layout was not much different from a standard military headquarters. A fat, bearded man rose to greet them. His fingers were heavy with gold rings and his wrists with bracelets of a native style. Gold not silver, Hanno noted.

*'Not the type to promote the local industry in the most obvious way,'* he guessed.

There was nothing foppish about his educated, judging eyes. His toga was eloquently plain and folded to perfection.

"'Salve' to the men of the Twentieth legion. A cohort commander and a renowned hastiliarius, if I am not mistaken. You are Hanno Glaccus, and you must be Gallus Tiomaris. The First cohort too I believe. This is an honour, and I never am mistaken on such detail," he boomed.

Gallus let Hanno shake arms first. The procurator flinched at the two iron grips he received.

"Welcome hastiliarius," he said, retracting his squeezed arm.

"Gentlemen please, sit, a drink of water on a hot morning perhaps? A little early for wine for me," he rattled on as his clerk settled himself at a desk and selected a pen form a small rack of them.

Hanno shook his head.

"Wine is actually our reason for wishing to speak with you," he said.

"It is always a pleasure to host soldiers of the legions, especially men of rank from a premier legion such as The Boar. You have taken over the estate of Priscus and have arrived to find it, shall we say, in less than perfect order."

The procurator's flow of buttery flim flam was like a warmup exercise before an important oratory. 'Shall we say?' had an inflection that might have been rehearsed for a court.

"Priscus and me were old comrades," Gallus said, deciding to get into the conversation, "I have the contract for the land and all fixtures including the buildings. Hanno Glaccus here is one of my partners, the other still serves but is due to discharge within the next few months," he said, "there are three of us."

The fat procurator digested this.

"Are you sure you would not like to try our excellent water?" he repeated.

Hanno read the man and allowed himself to be served with a cup of water, leaving it redundant on the table to make his point. Gallus swallowed his own cup's worth to make his own.

"We arrived yesterday to find the slaves and servants missing, the wine stolen, and a certain amount of pillage had taken place," Gallus said.

The procurator began nodding at the description.

"That is what has been reported to me," the procurator replied.

Hanno frowned, uncertain if it was their arrival or the looting that had been reported.

"It's an outrage," the official replied and stopped in his tracks.

Hanno waited for more soft, placatory words. He could feel the tension rising in Gallus without needing to turn and look. The 'outrage' did not seem to go any further than that.

He leaned forward, "it's nothing that forty slaves, a decent wine maker willing to work for good pay and the services of a decent carpenter can't put right," he purred, as though ordering floggings for acts of cowardice on the field of war: a predatory promise.

The procurator's face paled a fraction and for the first time the Biturges clerk appeared to wish he were somewhere else: anywhere else.

"You'll help us get those things, won't you?" Gallus continued.

"I, alas my dear friend, have only a squad of twenty legionaries and the same number of auxiliaries. I police Argentomagus with those slender resources. I have no cavalry I can spare."

Gallus wondered what his twenty legionaries did for amusement in a place like Argentomagus apart from drinking and trying to get lucky. Twenty auxiliaries were surely amply sufficient to keep law and order amongst the silver trade, they were hardly the most riotous of tradesmen.

"We don't want your men," he waded back in, "that's not what we're here for. We want your cooperation."

The procurator managed to look marginally insulted.

"You have a slave market?" Hanno probed.

"Monthly," the procurator replied.

"Carpenters?"

"But of course," he assented.

"Winemakers?"

"Obviously, we are a wine making province. We are known for our wine as well as our silver, I suppose. I am not in the business of making my own, so I can't make any recommendations, I regret to say," he divulged.

Gallus folded his arms.

"We have been robbed and we are reporting that fact to you as procurator. We hope you will help us bring the thieves to justice and get our business back into shape. We are not accustomed to being robbed."

He let that hang in the air.

"The local garrison is two miles to the south of us. It's only a small fort. Your kind of people, I imagine" the procurator said.

Hanno squinted at him unsure if that was another practised dig or simply a blind expression.

"Please record our complaint," he reposted, "if you are aware of any wine makers wishing employment, tell them we will pay handsomely for their services. A carpenter too. And if you gain any information about who did this, my friend Gallus and I will be generous when our first vintage comes in."

The procurator changed from pale to flushed as if the idea he needed an inducement to co-operate was distasteful. He cleared his throat, and pushing his chair back from his broad, oak desk, stood up.

"My clerk will show you out. I will do as you ask. Make enquiries and suchlike. He will show you the road to the garrison," he fawned.

Outside, they walked back to their horses.

"I'm not sure you really made a friend in there Gallus," Hanno mused, tongue in cheek.

Gallus waited until the Biturges clerk was out of earshot, fussing with the knot of the reins that really required only a tug to release.

"Strikes me we found what we came looking for," he replied, keeping his voice low.

"You think it was those two?" Hanno frowned.

Gallus swung up into the saddle and shrugged, "we know where the local garrison is. We do not need them at the moment. Let our friend run squealing to the local commander about us. Did you hear him in there? *'Your kind of people,'* the fat little runt. We have work to do. Let's check the market for the next slave dates. That one in there has 'coward' running him through him all the way to his backbone. He'll need watching," Gallus warned.

"We need to buy a bull or something suitable for the suovetaurilia, remember?" Hanno prompted.

Gallus finished with the reins, "I think we should go along and say hello to the local garrison while we are here?" he said.

Hanno shook his head, "the bull comes first Gallus," he vouched.

## Chapter Three.

## To the high ground.

After Velio got his men around the great estuary and the flood plain to the north of Deva Victrix it got easier, marching parallel to the coast, just plain old, hard slogging. Six days later they entered the beginning of the high country and its lakes and rivers. According to his map, the Iter X road led in towards Cantiventi fort at the head of one of the great lakes. He read the milestones. The worst was over. They just had to get to Cantiventi, and the string of forts helped to break up that journey. He would rest the men for a couple of days and gather what intelligence he could to assess the local attitudes. After that, the local auxiliary commander would point the way.

Standing on a high ridge he saw the problem in this part of the province; hill passes and long pieces of water. Before leaving Deva, he had taken an afternoon with the legate's librarian going through information carefully and bloodily gathered over the years. The Carvetii people were a reportedly passive sub tribe of the Brigantes; that was not good news.

*'And they have renounced their war god Belatucadrus? A bit unlikely I think,'* a guard dog growled in his head.

Belatucadrus' name was occasionally heard around the legion. This local god was attracting interest from the ordinary fighting legionaries. It was only fear and respect for the supreme power of Mars Ultor that prevented them adopting Belatucadrus. Besides, Belatucadrus was not winning the war with Rome. It rattled around in his head. Passive tribe with a popular war god? Hardly convincing intelligence but, he supposed, it might be true. Looking at the rise of the hills and the likely obstacles of rivers, forests, and marshy ground, taking a hundred and sixty men up there in search of trouble was the easy bit. Getting a hundred and sixty of them back out again, quite a different thing.

Yet another river tried to block their westerly path. A well maintained stone bridge defeated it.

After Galacum it was an easy march to Cantiventi. It was pleasant country, and the lads were chirpy enough. Getting away from barrack tedium was the tonic to their morale and brought a spontaneous song. He joined in, grinning.

"Optio Liscus Aulus Manlio, you will sing. That is an order," he said

"I can't sing sir," Liscus grinned back.

"Well neither can they, you should be in perfect harmony."

He glanced back at the century whose step clicked from the temporary respite of walking at ease back to legionary marching pace. He nodded to his trumpeter.

"Announce our arrival," he said.

His horse's ears pricked to the trumpet sound, and it turned its head towards Liscus' mount as if repeating his own conversation. A miasma of amused delight flooded his heart. He was going to miss all this.

They marched up to Cantiventi's stone walls, through the vicus road, creating precisely the sort of stir he wanted. Let them feast their eyes on what a First cohort looked like at close quarters. Let the auxiliary know their place. The lads put on the swagger. The standard bearer wore his 'face' signalling the implacable destiny of Rome to conquer the world. Tesserarii bawled the commands from Liscus. Pila were grounded, shield rims hit the ground, crunching into gravel. Silence greeted them. A dog barked and two small children picked their noses before running off to play.

He eased around in his saddle, the view down the lake was truly impressive. Moreover, it was peaceful. The fort gates opened in welcome. Their trumpets began sounding. An optio came rushing out, halted under the nose of his horse and gave him a breathless salute.

"Salve, soldiers of The Boar. The Second cohort Morinorum greets you," he spouted in a spume of enthusiasm.

Twenty minutes later he was strolling down to the lake with the fort commander, leaving Liscus to sort out camp-lines, supervised by an audience of the local children. The civilian vicus stopped short of boggy, flat pasturage by the lakeside. It was larger and busier than he expected. They took seats on a convenient oak trunk washed up on the gravel beach. The bright reflecting sunlight on the rippling water and the cacophonous sounds of birds seemed a thousand steps from the duty he had come to perform. There were men out fishing from boats.

"Your men?" he asked.

"Some are," the praefectus replied.

He was not a full status Roman officer, detached from one of the legions to command. Most likely he was a Belgica auxiliary commander, from the same region as his men, if Velio was any judge. Whatever his origins in the empire, he was wearing a beautifully intricate and burnished cuirass. Velio withheld judgement of the capability of the auxiliary command. He had not crossed paths with this cohort before.

"Tell me about the Delmatarum cohort," he said nodding at the hills.

The Belgica centurion huffed, "it's both complicated and highly unsatisfactory. They are not part of my overall command, incredible though that seems given the short distance that lies between us. They serve a different function. Their job is to keep the hill passes open for trade to and from the coast. Ours is to ensure the transport from lead and slate-stone mining in this area carries on without interruption. Not everything goes out on the Iter X. We get it brought here and send most down the lake to a depot at the southern end. The rest is waggoned out by road in both directions. Have you any idea of the amount of lead the army uses? Frightening, truly frightening quantities. A lot of it comes from the hills around here. We are also the general supply point for all troops in the region. If your men need wheat for making bread, we can supply it," he smiled as if he deserved credit.

"So, what is the complicated part of that?" Velio asked.

"The Delmatarum garrison is not a cohort, I mean there is no longer a need for a full cohort up at the fort. It's only a maniple garrison. Just the two centuries and they report to the praefectus of the Third cohort Aelia Classica, at the port of Iuliocenon. The rest of the Delmatarum are scattered across the region in various locations."

He pointed to the west, as if it would be helpful for Velio to understand where west and the ocean lay.

"They are within direct signalling distance of each other. It's a straight valley down to the sea. 'Aelia' gives it away, one of the

Emperor Hadrian's units, as you probably gather. Makes perfect sense I suppose but still, I find it an unnecessary complexity. What comes in from Uiliocenon is supplied to the forts in this area, including us, and the garrison on the Stones."

Velio nodded, feeling a tad confused. But it was all boiling down to a single question.

"So, if there is, or should I say was a problem at the hill fort? What do they call it?" he paused, diverted by his own diverging lines of fact gathering.

"There are various names for it. And that's another problem. No one seems to know what to call it, so the name changes every so often. It just baffles me, I can tell you." the praefectus shook his head in mock horror.

Velio decided to continue, as he was not much wiser on the point.

"If there was a problem the commander up there cannot handle, it would be the responsibility of the Aelia Classica commander to deal with it, I presume?"

"Exactly," the centurion smiled for the first time with any degree of warmth, "they are not my problem. Though you should know, there are rumours of problems up there. Quite why Iuliocenon has not stamped all over it escapes me. The senior centurion over there is 'a man of the sea' so to speak and his opinion of the Auxiliary as a whole is less than polite. We are lesser animals apparently. We don't correspond much."

*'Sarcasm?'* Velio wondered, *'clumsy humour, or a soldier really pissed off with all of this legion-versus-auxiliary snobbery? Mithras, he can see I'm legion. Thanks be to the gods it was not like this up on the emperor's wall. Hanno Glaccus would have had foam coming out of his mouth.'*

"Unfortunate," he agreed.

They contemplated the view. Hunger began gnawing at his stomach. The praefectus got to his feet and brushed the back of his tunic below his armour free of bark and dust.

"You'll eat with me tonight, your optio too?" he offered.

"My gratitude to your cook," Velio answered.

*'My guess it's going to be fish, that's why you've got some of them out on the lake,'* he calculated.

Together they meandered back through the vicus. He tried to absorb the mood of the local tribespeople. The faces were friendly, their Latin was decent. The women smiled with an openness he wanted to think reassuring.

"It all seems very peaceful," he said as they entered the fort.

The praefectus surprised him.

"Well, you can never take these people for granted. They have old gods for the land and the earth. What they really feel about our mining their hills is not something they have told us. Not that we give a toss, but it would be useful to know. I can believe general surface mining might not annoy their ancestors too much, but there are independently run sites around these parts with tunnels, ladders and scaffolding going down deep. Just because they do not fight does not mean they can be dismissed like servants and slaves," he opined, "if anything they are too compliant for my liking. It's as if they do not care. And somehow, I don't think that is the truth of it by a long shot. The Carveti are not to be dismissed," he tightened his mouth.

*'You are a wiser man than you look,'* Velio conceded.

## Chapter Four

### The fort in the hill pass.

"You won't believe this, but I've heard the emperor has ordered the legions to go back north and reoccupy the turf wall."

"Sounds like our emperor needs to wear a hat when he's out in the sun."

"Wants it rebuilt in stone now too."

"First it was, 'build me a wall,' then it was, 'we're going to retreat back to the Stones of Hadrian, and so now it's, 'go back and built it in stone now.' Are you kidding me?"

"He needs to make up his bleedin' mind if you ask me."

"Who told you this?"

"I got it from one of the waggon guards the last time through."

"You believe him, Arco?"

"I'd believe anything of this army," Arco replied.

The duty optio paused at the foot of the rampart steps and kicked the toes of his boots to clear the accumulation of mud. His two watchmen went silent. Clearly the duty tesserarius was off the rampart attending to something else. He climbed up and scanned the pass down to the far away coast.

"There's a waggon convoy coming up sir. Down there, about three or four hours away. They've not reached the rising ground yet," they informed him.

He followed their pointing, screwing up his eyes to a better focus. It made no difference; he still could not see it down in the meander of the bottom lands of the valley.

"Three or four hours, eh?" he said.

They nodded. He knew what they were angling for at this time of day.

"You'll stay on duty until they're past and over the summit," he said and watched their faces fall, "and do not mock the emperor if you want to keep your backs intact," he said.

"As you command, sir," they crashed out salutes.

He nodded and left them to mull over his warning.

"Bastard," Arco hissed at his departing back, "it's going to piss down, just look at those clouds. Once it starts, they might not even try to get over today."

"Where did he come from, Arco?" the other growled.

Arco scratched his neck until he worked out what it was his comrade was really asking.

"He came over from the legion. Came to tell us how to do it. The centurion's pet enforcer. I think he might have an accident one dark night. All these slippery wet steps. That's what I think," Arco replied, snickering.

"Come on, you bastards, get a move on," his mate yelled down at the waggons, miles off in the distance.

The optio halted and looked back at the two of them. For a moment Arco thought he might have overplayed things. The officer sent them his most baleful, leaden stare and turned away.

"You need to keep it down," Arco hissed.

Giving a new optio a reason to hold a grudge was in no one's interests.

## Chapter Five.

### The road to the hill fort.

Velio dismounted, forcing Liscus to do the same. The men behind him were beginning to straggle as the zigzag winding of the road got progressively steeper and steeper. It was a torrid section, worse than anything he had seen before in the north. It felt like the mountain was rearing up like a stallion with its hooves searching for a victim to kick. Constructing it must have been a nightmare. If this was the best route through to the coast, it must have been surveyed and decided. It left little doubt about the impassibility of the others. He doubted whether Hannibal himself had faced traversing over a worse piece of hillside in the Alps. The lack of alternatives was militarily troubling.

*'Hold the road and you hold everything,'* he noted, *'and if you do that, you control access to the hill fort and if you are a Carvetii or Brigantes, the hill fort guards nothing without your permission. But, sleep easy centurion, the Carvetii people are a passive sub tribe of the Brigantes. It says so in the legion library. Remember Velio?'*

He smirked to himself and choked back the vernacular dismissal favoured by the men.

He took the horse by the bridle, waiting for the column close up. Marcellus dismounted alongside and gazed up at the unforgiving hillsides around them.

"Quite a haul up here, isn't it sir?" Liscus offered, "getting waggons safely down this must be as hard as getting them up and over it."

"Good place for an ambush," he replied, "basically indefensible if you were surprised. So, let's not be surprised. Send out six men on up ahead. I want to know what's up there. Eyes, right and left on our flanks," he ordered.

He pointed at the overshadowing hillsides. Hostile bowmen could rain havoc on them. They were an easy target.

"Is it much further?" Liscus said.

Marcellus grinned back and Velio shook his head at them both.

"Let the men have a drink from their bottles. We will halt and reorder the ranks at the summit. I'm told the fort sits on a west facing slope. It can't be much further. We're nearly at the top of this beast. Whatever else happens, when we get sight of it, we are 'parading for the emperor.' Got that?" he said.

"As you command centurion," they replied.

"Ensure the men know. I'll have no excuses," he ordered.

He glanced at Liscus' earnest young face. He could tell his optio was about to make an unnecessary comment, then changed his mind, giving him a half salute in reply.

'*He learns,*' he mused.

At the summit of the pass, the three of them remounted. Liscus paraded his mount back down along the column, talking to the men, encouraging them. They did not need it, but Velio let the young man practise his authority. This was his first real patrol. He wondered what the men said about him, what happy or grievous nickname they pinned on his back. Whether they rated him. When all this was history and he was out and making wine in Gaul, another centurion would take over and Liscus and the junior officers would all have to learn a new commander's ways. They might even miss him.

He snorted at his own foolishness and told himself, *'miss me, they'll be glad to see the back of me.'*

Liscus brought his mount back into place and waved the order to begin descending. Velio rode alongside, parallel, so that Liscus was the officer visibly at the head.

*'Time to relax a bit, Velio,'* he told himself, *'two or three days here will tell me all I want to know. Take them back to Deva, report to Servius and say 'Vale' to the lot of them.'*

The fort caught his breath. Lying on the right-hand side, at the upper reaches of the pass, the legion had put it on a natural promontory, so it rested like a stone guard dog. As perfectly positioned as a fort could be, just as long as you were not one of the unlucky sods who had to serve here, year in year out.

*'Good job for the auxiliary,'* he reckoned.

He had no idea what Dalmatia was like as a place. Whether it was warm or cold, parched or swamp ridden. The Delmatarum were its contribution to the empire and Antoninus Pius sent them here, as far from home as he could arrange. Their gods must have deserted them. He smiled at their appalling luck. Sunlight was hitting the fort's walls and rooftops, bathing it in glory. A splendid sight. Except for a wind that came driving inland with a ferocity to match the dog.

"Pity them in winter," Liscus murmured.

"Good enough for them," Marcellus opined.

From the higher altitude he saw the uneven lie of the ground inside the walls, even stark outcrops of un hewn stone chewing up through the thin soil and grass. There would be no problem with drainage, that much was for certain. He decided they would march down the crest and shoulder of the hill in silence and suggested Liscus give the order.

The Praetoria gate swung open as they arrived. Liscus marched them in and halted in front of the two long horrea for the grain stores. The maniple of Delmatarum auxiliary paraded their nearly matching numbers. The two bodies of men eyed each other in silence. This was a full-sized fort intended for a cohort. With this small holding force, four of the barrack blocks would be empty. That would cheer up the lads. No one would welcome a billet in an army tent up here.

The centurion in charge stepped forward and Velio took an instant dislike to him. He felt his hackles rising.

"Hail centurion. My name is Civius. This is my command," the man said.

He was no more a son of the Delmatarum than Velio, Liscus or Marcellus. Velio could see he was a Narbonii from lower Gaul and by his uniform he had been seconded from the Second Augusta legion. He shook his head in awe at the army's perverse way of complicating the simplest of arrangements.

At Cantiventi, the command of a full auxiliary cohort was safely entrusted to a commander who was an auxiliary officer himself. Here, a two century auxiliary command had a regular legion centurion in charge. Not one sent all the way from the legion's base in the south at Isca Augusta. No, that would have been overtly perverse, instead and indeed worse for Civius, he had been despatched overland as the Second Augusta retired back south to its base years ago, after its major part in the construction of Antoninus Pius' turf wall. Except, he had lost direct oversight of four centuries of his cohort under a further realignment of the province's ever shifting manpower.

The rankling injustice had put a lingering tightness to his features. This was not an Augusta centurion's post and he did not care who noticed his displeasure.

*'Punishment by exile. Shades of Tiberius,'* Velio nearly felt pity for him.

Someone in the Second had decided to punish Civius by sending him to this valley. He doubted it had been for a minor transgression. What had the man done to deserve this posting? Offended one of the tribunes perhaps? Laughed at an ill thought out suggestion? It made him grateful for the good relations he held with the tribunes of the Twentieth.

And then he remembered it had not always been that way: no indeed it had not.

*

It was getting late in the day. He ate with Civius and his officers and felt a weariness growing on him after the day's ride up the long valleys and passes. A temporary room in Civius' own relatively luxurious praetorium residence was apparently not going to be offered and part of him did not mind. Any bunk calling his name would do. The headquarters, with its wooden window shutters, bereft of the sophistication of glass, summed the place up. Better to keep his distance until he decided whether his dislike of Civius mattered in any way to the inspection.

He took the room normally allotted to the centurion of the first century. Less spacious than barracks for legionary troops, auxiliary soldiers made do with what they were given. His men split themselves across two blocks. Marcellus, the standard bearer and the trumpeter were among the men in this same block, Liscus had taken the obvious decision to use the centurion's room in the second block. Marcellus had laid out his travelling kit. There was a low buzz of discussion across the bunks from the men. They checked his reaction as he entered, and he waved his hand to let them know they could continue. A solemn game of dice had drawn a cluster around it. Their heads stayed bowed as he passed to his room. He did not mind.

That night the heavens opened, and a torrential noise hammered on the roof. It went on for hours until it was impossible to sleep. He listened to it for a while, pleasantly warm under the blankets and realised he was not going to slide back into sleep. His brain was churning. It was going to be a long night lying here without Voccia for company. He got up and found his boots and cloak. Marcellus was on the first bunk outside his door. His standard bearer was sound asleep opposite, no longer sweating in his wolf-skin. The wolf skin seemed to have been given the honour of a bunk to itself. Marcellus raised his head and he flagged him back to rest. At the barrack room door, he lifted the latch and peered out a gap at the hissing venom coming out of the skies. Cold air flooded in. The grass outside was thickened with it. The smell of earth and timber. The gush and hiss of water draining. He peered towards the ramparts where miserable sentries should be hiding in their cold stone turrets and rooms by the gateways. The walls were black. Not a solitary torch burned up on the walkways. Utter silence prevailed except from the sound of unrelenting rain.

*'Go back to your bunk, Pinneius,'* he told himself.

The voice in his head was nagging again. To treat this fort the way he had Trimontium, as a place where nothing happened outside his direct knowledge. Officers might bring explanations, but he preferred to already know what they were reporting. It had not always worked that smoothly, but he liked the sense of awe it inspired in his men that 'Centurion Pinneius knows before it happens.' A fallacy of course but he liked to encourage it. The damned voice was berating him to go out in the black, cold rain and find out what the night watch was doing. It never let him rest. Why was it always Servius Albinius living in his head? He went back to his room, lifted his helmet off the small shelf and went back to the doorway, vine stick in his hand. Marcellus watched him pass by. Velio buckled on his helmet. The crest of a First cohort centurion was more impressive than that of an ordinary centurion. It was more impressive than the one Civius wore. The comparison warmed him to the coming trauma of facing the divine Tempestates at their worst. It was a fearsome night. The goddesses had chilled the temperature and racked up the wind and rain; the change smacked him in the face. He yielded to their displeasure, lowering his head, his cloak flapping like a demented hawk, making his way through the torrents they were sending, for the closest rampart stairway. He reached the main walkway only to be greeted with an extra degree of chill and violence that made him gasp. He peered out over the stone wall at the night. There was only darkness and the malevolent, primitive sounds of a river running in spate somewhere down in the cleft of the pass. Turning his back to the worst of it, he saw the tower at the corner junction of the walls, rapped the door with his vine stick and barged in without waiting for an invitation.

Inside an optio gazed up at him from a stool that almost dwarfed the only source of heat, a small fire. Two guards stared at him as if he were Jupiter himself: their faces aghast. The flames of the torch lamps danced in alarm at the gust of wind he brought with him. He closed the door and felt the small room's surge of heat.

"Titus Vindex, sir, welcome to the lands Jupiter has misplaced I fear, and all of us into the bargain," the optio said.

Vindex got up gave him a confident salute and offering his stool by the fire. The two guards saluted, retreating like mice around the walls of the turret room, seeking escape from the cat that had just found their nest. The optio glanced at their awed faces. Velio's feather crest was cowing them. Velio took off his woollen cloak and shook the worst of the water from the lanolin coated fibres.

"Hang that up for me," he told one of them, taking command.

"Go and circuit the wall. Report back when you are satisfied there is nothing to see," the optio ordered his two soldiers.

They took the order and the hint and slipped out of the door taking the last of the room's carefully accumulated warmth with them. Titus Vindex produced a small flask of wine from the floor.

"Something to keep out the cold sir?" he said.

Velio took stock of the younger man before him. He had an honest, willing look: eagerness mixed with ingrained professionalism. The optio could have left this hour of the night to one of his tesserarii to cover, but here he was, keeping the men on their toes when it would have been so much easier and popular to let them sit, reasonably dry and warm, letting the hours pass until dawn and the 'Alert' sounded. Velio took a shine to him.

"My gratitude, Titus. Is it always like this?"

He gestured at the noise of the storm that was not much reduced by stone walls and an oak door.

"Ever since I arrived sir. Disrupts the transportation of stores from the harbour. The road up here is treacherous even when it's dry. In this," he gestured, "it is impossible. Which can be a blessing sometimes," he added, watching Velio sip the wine flask.

The fire had warmed it to a temperature that brought pleasure as it went down. Velio handed it back and ventured a thought.

"It was you who raised concerns about this garrison and their relations with the locals?" he posited.

Titus Vindex weighed the flask without thinking, judging how long it would last. Velio remembered the times when the price of another flask of wine mattered enough to cause him pause for thought.

"When those two 'lights of the Delmatarum' report the 'all clear,' I'm going back to my bunk. I can't keep this up all night, every night. Centurion, this is a rat's nest. They're on the take, from Civius down. There are Carvetii brigands and a smattering of deserters out there. They know more about what's on the waggons coming up the pass than we do. This is dangerous country to move supply waggons through. I have never been so glad to see regular troops marching down that slope. A soon as I saw you, I knew my message had got through to Deva. Keep your men alert sir, these Dalmatians can be adept with a dagger when they want to be. They need cleaned out and honest troops brought in. The whole lot of them," Titus said.

"You are Second Augusta too, are you not?" Velio queried.

"I am sir, recently arrived to replace an optio who I believe was sent to his ancestors before he was ready. That's what I meant about Dalmatians and their daggers," Titus expanded his previous comment.

Civius was Second Augusta legion. Presumably Civius had requested Titus? It did not quite sit straight the way it should. The Second Augusta barracks were much further south than the Twentieth's. If Civius needed to replace an officer, why had he not sent a request to Servius Albinius who was much closer?

*'Perhaps he wanted an officer he already knew he could rely on, or thought he could rely on?'* Velio wondered, *'but that officer was too alarmed by what he discovered to go directly to the closer legion for help? No wonder Civius is less than welcoming. What happens in the legion should stay in the legion, common knowledge only to those in the know. And you and your letter broke that trust.'*

The implications came thick and fast as he weighed it up.

"Titus, have you any evidence I can put before my own legate? He is not going to thank me for bringing him a tale without any facts," he replied.

"You have set the dogs loose with these allegations, you understand? Widespread thievery, condoned by officers? This is not even the frontier. There can be no mitigation of the allegation if you are wrong and on the other hand, none for the perpetrators if you are correct," he summed up.

Titus took the brutal, stark truth, as Velio delivered it, on his chin. He put the wine flask down by his stool. He straightened up and Velio saw there was an angry fire burning in those eyes.

"Evidence? There is evidence in plenty. Evidence of thievery with the stroke of pen. The largest waggon convoys carry manifests because they drop off part loads at various forts along the Iter X. Single waggons are less likely to carry paperwork because they carry fewer and less valuable things. Nothing odd in that. You know how the army likes reports and lists. I believe it works like this; everything that can be amended, is amended downwards. Every manifest item that numbers in fives or tens gets a single stroke after it leaves the port; a fresh hand," the optio divulged.

Velio took a moment to understand what a single stroke achieved.

"Ah, so, V becomes IV and X becomes IX, is that it?" he mused aloud, not wholly certain he was following.

This sounded far too simple to escape detection by the average quartermaster clerk who was adept at fiddling wet and dry stores and records to a higher standard than the average army 'mule.' The only thing they could not renumber was the armour and weaponry which fell under the remit of men like Gallus Tiomaris and hastiliarii throughout the army. Titus nodded. The fire in his eyes was not quite so fierce now that Velio was listening and thinking.

"Five can become four and ten becomes nine, just so centurion," he answered.

"Clever thievery. Not too much to be noticeably greedy but still, a hefty percentage," he frowned.

Titus stooped to gather the wine and surrendered his flask again. Velio moderated his swallow of the comforting liquid. This was a much faster validation of the rumour he had come to check than he was expecting. The drenching from the weather goddesses to get here did not seem so unpleasant now.

"You will not credit me with this truth, but I can tell you, I believe the ink used by the harbour superintendents is shared with whoever it is does the fraud up here. There are documents where you would not see the X or the V has been altered. That's the praefectus and his officers. The Decumana gate gets busy the night after a convoy passes through. The ground is steep all the way to the valley floor. The booty gets left out or tossed down the incline and by dawn you would never have known anything had occurred. Tidier than brazenly having the local brigands hauling entire waggons away," Titus went on.

"Forgive me Titus but what do they do with the pilfered cargoes?" Velio pushed, thinking of how this would go on paper.

"What is left out is taken by the local Carvetii. Perhaps even their overlords, the Brigantes too. I should not be surprised," Titus whispered.

He kept a wary watch on the oak door for his auxiliary guards.

"Quite an enterprise," Velio said, "and how is payment made?"

"It's subtle and occasional. Silver, sometimes gold. Native worked, exquisite jewellery that can be sold for fortunes in the fora in Londinium and elsewhere. Every legion town has seen the payment even if no one really understood what was behind it. And it's not all the time. It depends on what the ships at the port are landing. No arms or weapons. They're not that stupid, but everything is fair game," Titus went on, hot faced again, "if they traded fairly for it, our coins for their silver and the like, but they are stealing from the emperor," he trailed off.

"How long have you known?" Velio asked.

Zealous young officers were not uncommon, and the emperor could certainly afford the losses. It was army discipline that could not stand the price.

Titus Vindex scowled, "I had my suspicions. They're too damn lax. Civius is no soldier as far as I can see. I'd string the lot of them up if it were up to me or throw them down that gorge. Hear the water? That's it building up, coming off the hillsides. It's going to run like that for two or three days. It's a steep drop out there. Almost a Tarpeian plunge, you might say," he smiled.

A dour crease in his lips showed his frustration. Velio sat back. His cloak steamed on its peg. His boots were soaking wet, and his tunic was damp where the cloak had not held back the rain. He got up.

"My gratitude for your honesty optio Vindex. If I have anything to do with it, you will be rewarded by the emperor for this service. Stay safe. It may not be only me they fear."

"Good night, sir, I will," Titus replied.

"I'll leave you to the joys of the Delmatarum," he commiserated.

"I need to buy better dice," Titus replied, deadpan.

*

"Trouble, sir?" Marcellus whispered from his bunk.

Only the upper half of his face was exposed to the wash of cold air Velio brought in to the barrack block. Velio unclipped his cloak and removed his helmet. He bent down to speak, keeping his voice low.

"Unexpected gifts too easily given. Makes me suspicious. We'll talk tomorrow with Liscus."

Marcellus saw the centurion's door close. There were scant hours of sleep left to catch before the dawn trumpet.

## Chapter Six.

### Argentomagus: Gaul.

Hanno walked along the row of vines. He halted and took a tiny bunch of grapes in his fingers, ignoring Gallus' plea not to touch the fruit as it was growing. It was bad luck, so he said. If there had been forty slaves on the estate, what had they done all day when it was not harvest time or selling time? Feeding them all would have taken a hefty cost out of Priscus' profits. There were kitchen gardens so they must have been given permission to grow vegetables. Beehives to tend. But, a half-century's worth of labouring muscle? Ten slaves he could understand, fifteen would be better, but forty? It was a conundrum. Gallus had struck a bargain with Priscus' woman when he bought the place, and forty slaves was what she pledged. Where had they disappeared to?

Seventeen new ones, fresh from the forum market, had arrived yesterday. The men looked strong, the women, healthy. They were going to have to be, because there was much clearing up to be done. Seventeen felt about sufficient. Gallus, after a bit of hot irritation last night had relented: for now. The slave merchant's deputy had taken details for another twenty three, price to be agreed as and when they became available and had passed inspection. He put his hands on his hips and took in the view. The estate sprawled from the road up to the crest of a long south facing, shallow ridge that stretched its arms out on either side of the villa and the estate buildings. The buildings lay approximately one third of the distance from the eastern boundary. Beyond that were several miles of pleasant rolling land before Argentomagus made its strategic presence visible up on the plateau protected by its rivers, ditches and walls. The Bituriges had picked a strong site for their town. He wondered if it had resisted the great Gaius Julius Caesar, or, looked at his legions and yielded the gates to him.

He saw a half-troop of sixteen military horsemen with a decurion at their head, riding past the small stone mausoleum of Priscus on the roadside and entering through the estate gates. They trotted up the lane between the fields. Heads rose from the task of weeding amongst the vines. Remembering that Gallus had gone into town, he walked back to the central yard area to greet them. They were dismounting by the time he arrived. They were not auxiliary and therefore, he deduced, not part of the procurator's assignment. They must have come from the fort.

"May I assume you are Centurion Hanno Glaccus," the decurion smiled and saluted.

"Well, I was, once. No need my dear boy, but my gratitude all the same. Always good to get a salute," he replied, "come, let your men have water. I'll get them some bread. Join me for wine. You have news for me?" he replied and waved his hand to his closest servant.

The decurion passed the reins to a trooper and followed Hanno to the shaded table and chairs that saw fortunes won and lost each night. A small set of dice lay in a small wooden cup to the side. The decurion smiled. He removed his helmet, laying it on the table next to the dice cup. Hanno poured wine and gave it to him. The man was older than he expected. A soldier who had reached his career limit, perhaps? It was no disgrace to command a troop of legion cavalry; not at all. The furrows around his eyes and the thinness of the close-cropped beard spoke volumes.

'Dear boy,' now felt a tad presumptuous, but not insulting. No insult to be addressed as 'dear boy' given their relative circumstances.

"So, my friend. What legion are you?" Hanno refined his greeting.

"We are detached from the Eighth legion: the Octava Augusta. Two troops and four centuries. Not that we are overworked around here, though I shouldn't say it. It's been peaceful for years. The procurator has got it all under control. We are his town guard I suppose in the unlikely event that something happens. The silver trade, the metal workers, it is important business, valuable, if you understand me? Silver blanks are sent to the mint at Lugdunum. The army, the emperor himself, relies on towns like Argentomagus to help pay the troops, even if he has never heard of it. And then there is the wine trade and the farm estates to keep an eye on. There are good horses to be got around here too. The grass is good and the water is clean," the decurion averred.

Hanno nodded at the little lecture.

"The Octava Augusta. A fine legion. Well-spoken of. I was in The Boar, as was my partner Gallus Tiomaris who is not here at the moment," he replied.

The decurion smiled and drank a sip.

"Believe me centurion, everyone knows who you are," he replied.

"Do they?" Hanno said, the wary dog inside him pricked up its ears.

*'First the procurator and now the regular detachment from the Eighth. Why is everyone so interested in Priscus' successors? Just being nosey?* He wondered.

That he and Gallus might be a local source of gossip and interest had not occurred to him. Perhaps it was not so surprising. He tried to stay relaxed.

"Centurion, this is prized land, coveted even. You will have noticed the soil and the water. Old man Priscus, I knew him, picked this ground out when he discharged. His wines became the stuff of the gods themselves. And when he passed to Elysium, his widow got good offers in hard gold for it. She refused them all. She wanted to keep her husband's memory alive, I suppose, and keeping the estate going was her way of doing that. They had no sons to pass it to, they were not blessed. By and by, the years passed and when she could not make a go of it, she chose your partner Gallus, so I hear. It raised a little feeling in the district. Ruffled the goose's feathers a bit. And it's a big estate. There is more to it than the slopes you can see here. There's another, bigger parcel of vines in the next valley. Obviously, it can't be seen from here. Priscus created quite a spread over the years. Centurion, the wine from this estate is considered so good it's worth a bit of bloodshed to secure it. That's the local opinion," the decurion explained.

*'Forty slaves, a bigger parcel of vines in the next valley? Does Gallus realise? I don't think he knows how big this place really is?'*

Hanno clicked the pieces into place, and rolled the dice.

"It's always difficult to keep a big estate safe I imagine, much like a marching camp. Needs a lot of digging and guarding day and night, but if the boundaries are well marked, all citizens can see and choose when they step over the line? They make that choice. We both know every soldier knows the kind of transgression that risks a flogging and the ones they can get away with, it is exactly the same with civilians," he lectured, "any man who steps on another's land and says he did not realise his error is a liar and as for bloodshed, we did not come here to shed blood. We did that on the emperor's pay. This is for us," he said spreading his arms out.

The decurion sat back in his chair.

"I heard you found items missing when you arrived?" the cavalryman probed, "no wine in the vats?"

Hanno looked at the decurion and considered whether to be open with him or not, '*trust or don't trust, which is it to be Hanno?*' he asked himself.

He saw the soldier was having what might be similar thoughts.

'*Let's keep Velio's name out of this for now,*' he decided.

"My partner Gallus thought he was buying a simple vineyard for us to make a decent living in our retirement. Have we bought our way into a local feud?" he said, keeping it innocent.

The decurion finished his wine and checked what his troop were doing. They had polished off the bread from the house and were sitting about talking, checking their mount's coats for insect pests and looking at the nearby vines with interest. Four had removed their helmets though he had not given permission. With their long cavalry swords, slim shields and shining lances they looked very capable. There was a charm about the estate. It had a good feeling. A man could settle his debts to the gods in such a place.

"The old woman made the mistake of trusting the overseer that Priscus kept his thumb on for years. Once Priscus died she tried to keep up the quality of the wines and the profit, but he milked her like a cow. Eventually she had no choice to sell up. Her last independent act was to sell it to a man her husband remembered and trusted from the times they spent in the Second legion," he paused and stood up, "a man who would know how to fight back if it came to that," the decurion explained.

He scowled, "the poor woman went missing shortly after. I am ashamed to say the Eighth legion did not look after an old comrade very well. Whatever you decide to do here centurion, my conscience will be clear. Call it a warning, call it advice, a bit of scouting intelligence, call it whatever you want to. I have given you what I know," he retorted.

"It's going to come to that?" Hanno said.

The first real pangs of unease began taking hold. He had not retired here to fight. Fighting was for Britannia and those days were past, Gaul was for civilised folk.

"Don't trust the Biturges, they're all crooks. Don't trust the procurator," the decurion added, making amends for the intemperate moment.

"Leaving whom?" Hanno asked, unfazed.

"Everyone else you know and have served with," the decurion raised his eyebrows and cocked his head.

"The Twentieth legion are not exactly handy," Hanno replied, "Gallus was only briefly in the Second for a time when he joined up. He is a Boar man through and through. We all are."

"For the Senate and People of Rome, centurion," the cavalryman quoted.

"You have a point; he was Second before he was Twentieth. Knowing Gallus, he'll have a scar somewhere to prove that," he grinned, "never let a comrade down," and finished off his wine.

"Not if I can help it. May Fortuna know you are here, centurion," the decurion replied.

He swung back up into the saddle and with a raise of his fist led the half troop back down the dusty track to the road leading to Argentomagus.

Hanno watched him raising dust until they were out of sight, hurried to his horse, and spurred over the rise in the direction shown by the decurion. At the top of the rise was a splendid view of another larger valley, its south facing slopes redolent with vines which so far had been left untended. Doubtless some judicious weeding would be required to bring it into trim, but the sheer scale of it cold-clutched his chest.

"Forty slaves? Now I get it," he said.

The home slopes were less than half the size of what was lying before him.

"Balls of Dis Pater, you played a mean joke on us, Priscus," he called out.

He felt angry and frustrated by the sudden turn of events. The decurion had been careful not to smile when mentioning this further piece of land. Small wonder: if there was to be defending to be done, this second valley would spread them too thin. He had not come here to fight over grapes. He was here to laze his old bones in the sun, play dice and drink wine whilst Gallus and Velio did all the work running the estate.

"Balls of Dis Pater," he repeated.

Forty slaves. They were going to need forty soldiers if there was going to be a fight.

'A fight? What am I thinking?' he tried not to laugh.

## Chapter Seven.

## The fort in the hill pass.

Velio stood on the ramparts and admired the fort's commanding view and wondered, not for the first time in his career, if the Tempestates really had abated, or were they playing a game? If the rain had come as winter snow, he would have been cut off for days. His precious intelligence voided by a choked landscape. Instead, blue skies and warmth reigned: the ground steaming and drying out underfoot. The road to the bathhouse was awash as the fort drained itself after the deluge. Almost shaking off the water like a sopping dog. A little gushing stream no thicker than his finger left a tiny cleft in the wall and got swallowed up by the road's deep drainage layers.

The men of the protection detail from the harbour about faced and made ready to march back west down the valley, their part finished. The new escort of auxiliaries were in place and Titus Vindex was making ready to lead them off. Today's waggons lurched forwards as the horse-trains took the strain. He wondered if the poor beasts ever raised their heads to look up at the rising pitch of the road and felt their hearts quail.

By the Porta Praetoria a work squad was hard at work shifting the freshly delivered stores. From what Civius had said they received their wine and vittles from the port. Their reciprocal gift was lead, stone and timber for transportation by the coastal fleet. He turned back and went to the principia and the meeting he dreaded. They had not sounded 'Farewell Brother,' to the departing convoy. He shivered, even auxiliary trumpeters should know that; it felt unlucky.

Later he took his horse from Marcellus without a word and headed up the pass to clear his head and cool his temper. The meeting had not gone well. He had allowed Civius to get under his skin. Too many numbers. Too much obfuscation. Too damned smug. Some things that were not quite right. It felt as though he had enough to condemn the Delmatarum but not the evidence that Servius would demand. Was it the lack of evidence that was making Civius so smug, or the imprecision of his questions? If it had been Deva Victrix, he could have hauled Titus Vindex in to give evidence, but as was becoming abundantly clear, this was not Deva.

The road from the Praetoria gate to the top of the pass reared up over him in a series of wicked turns and zigzag dog legs. The horses and the men who had sweated to put the Iter X over this pass had his admiration. Thousands of cartloads to drag tons of stone. He considered dismounting and leading the horse on foot as it topped the summit but held back, testing its mettle. The beast plugged away and triumphed. He halted and looked back down at the lop-sided fort on its plateau, lying perfectly placed to control everything transiting the pass. Putting in the fort would have been plain sailing after putting in the road. He grinned at the irony. Bringing waggons through here was a job for heroes, and well-fed animals. Somehow serving time up in Trimontium and the turf wall, seeing off the Selgovae, the Caledonii, and their like did not seem quite so bad. The doubts voiced by Cantiventi praefectus sprang into his head. Had the Carvetii stood back and watched, uncaring, while all this was happening across their lands, right in front of them? Perhaps they had no stomach for facing up to an army capable of engineering such feats?

He took the horse off the road and drew his water flask, gazing down on the next valley lying before him before swinging eastwards in the direction of Cantiventi. Titus Vindex and the convoy were out of sight, lost somewhere in the myriad folds and dips. It was pretty country all right, down there on the bottom lands. Good water supplies, thick green grass for pasture, the greenest grass imaginable and lush as a woman's hair. Carvetii livestock were grazing in the lee of towering bare hills. The upper slopes were devoid of soil and vegetation. It was quite a contrast. It reminded him of the high mountain passes in parts of Gaul to the north of Rome.

The conversation with Civius, allied to what Titus Vindex had been so keen to divulge, rankled. It smelled like they were on the take: he had no doubt of it. He could either take that at face value and trot back to Deva with his mission accomplished and a recommendation for a change in command of the fort. Servius Albinius would surely believe his word. Or, he could stay longer and try to weasel a confession out of Civius. Getting a confession was more appealing. If Civius had any honour he might take a stroll, pull his pugio from his waist belt and finish the business.

He held the reins back to pull the horse to a standstill and began to dismount. A convenient rock looked a likely enough place to sit and take a drink of water and get the mechanics of the larceny clear in his head; how did they actually work the fraud? Uiliocenon would have reprimands and queries to deal with if they routinely shipped quantities in fours and nines. Rough sea passages and shipboard breakages might take a cull of the amphorae, but dry food and materials losses could not be explained away. It was too obvious. And then, were the waggoneers in the know too, and what about the men and officers of the escort? They would have to know? So, keeping that quiet was impossible. So then, were the two forts in on it, their commanders and their officers? He doubted it could be on that sort of scale. Much more likely it was a rogue officer in charge of the escort knowing which particular waggon in which particular convey was carrying something worth pilfering. By deduction, not every convoy would be of interest, depending on what was discharging at the port. Which meant it could only be a crime of intermittent theft at best. Not so exciting. Servius would not thank him for it. But Titus Vindex implied it was worse. If Civius was going to be unhelpful, his counterpart in Uiliocenon might be more forthcoming. An unannounced visit to the port, march the century down there for a bit of exercise, keep the locals guessing, apply a bit of pressure, ask to inspect the inventory and see who cracked? He liked the plan.

Something hit him, bursting past the edge of his cuirass, catching him just under the ribs. He tumbled sideways out of the saddle and hit the ground with an overwhelming burning pain. White heat flooded through his side and chest. It rose up, filling him like Hades' breath and it went dark.

"He's not dead. Junius, you missed."

A voice broke in through the darkness. Pain was pinning him down as if he had been nailed with a hot poker. He dared not move. He opened his eyes. A bearded man in his late thirties, possibly older, it was hard to say, dressed in a mixture of legionary tunic and leather leggings, topped by a cloak was stooping over him, blocking out the sky.

"Well finish him off Scribono and let's get after the waggons," an unseen voice shouted.

There was irritation in the words.

"Junius, you might want to take a look? This is not your centurion pal from the fort. It's someone else. You've shot the wrong man."

Velio heard the jeer of sarcasm through the hot pain. He saw a sword rising, held vertically in a meaty fist. The muscles in the forearms balled tight for the downward strike.

"Be quick you bastard," he snarled up at him.

A thousand ways to die and it was going to be by murder on the side of a road in the middle of nowhere, from a man he did not know. Morta was going to snip his thread. It was over. The man called Scribono made to plunge the point into his chest.

"Unlucky mistake my friend," Scribono replied.

He took a second look, surprised, "I know you," he said, sounding baffled.

"Kill him Scrib, take what he's got and catch us up," the Junius voice pressed for action.

"Who are you?" Scribono asked, looking less and less likely to plunge the sword into his chest.

"I'm Centurion Velio Pinneius, commander of the Fourth century, First cohort, Twentieth legion. Now if you are going to kill me, just do it," he spat in defiance.

To his surprise the sword was sheathed. It was an army issue gladius, in an army scabbard, the detail stuck.

"The same Pinneuis who was a weapons instructor in the Fourth cohort? Long-time past?" Scribono said.

Velio nodded, wondering if this was a set up for a dagger through the eyes instead. Not a way he fancied dying.

"I was in the Eighth cohort, before I got tired of all this," his assailant waved at Velio's armour and helmet, "I had a cousin called Brutus Carruso. Remember him? You should do. Velio Pinneius, well, well, well. Lucky dogs and dice. Not so good with arrows, eh centurion?" Scribono jeered.

He stood back and shouted.

"Junius, this one is worth more alive. I'm taking him back to the camp."

A distant voice shouted what sounded like agreement. The two of them were alone. Scribono reached down and took Velio's sword and pugio-dagger, tucking them in his belt.

"I can get that taken out," he offered, gesturing to the arrow.

His fingertips strayed to the fletchings and waggled the arrow a tiny bit. Waves of pain rocketed through Velio. He gasped in agony.

"Are you going to behave for me centurion? Or else I will have to finish you here and leave you for the hawks and wolves," Scribono taunted.

Velio could feel sweat on his forehead. He hated arrows. A weapon you cannot see or defend in the heat of a fight. Scribono's fingers closed in on the end of the arrow again.

'*A man from the Eighth cohort might still have a shred of loyalty somewhere in him,*' he calculated, nodding assent.

"Good. I can't be doing with killing a brother of The Boar. Didn't plan to do that today. Some things count in this miserable fuckin' life. I'll leave murder of a wounded brother to Junius Cita and these Carvetii heathens. But, if you'd been one of those Delmatarum scum, you'd be at the gateway of Elysium already. Not that they go there anyway. A heathen shit-bog more like. Got me?" Scribono warned.

"How do you know about me and Brutus Carruso?" Velio gasped as Scribono dragged him to his feet.

Scribono held him upright while he sucked in air before making him walk uphill. He clutched his horse's saddle with his right hand and tried to stem the blood, pressing his left hand against his armour. Every step was a fight for air even on the smooth surface of the road. The arrow point was nailing him. He was frightened to breathe lest the stabbing pain cut deeper. He gazed up at the summit of the road and feared he would not last. Scribono waved his free arm, making the horse toss its head. More pain surged in response.

"He was my cousin. I used to be in the Eighth cohort before I saw the error of my ways. He was Fourth, right? We always kept apart, kept our heads down so no snotty officer could know we were kin and use that against us, you understand me centurion? There were those who would do that for spite. And Brutus wasn't too bright. He was a big dumb bear. Brave as shit, but not too bright. He came to see me and asked for my help once. Took me to the Fourth's camp and pointed you out," Scribono divulged.

"Why did he do that?" Velio wheezed, coughing blood that spumed into the air.

Scribono let him rest for a moment. Velio wiped his mouth and tried easing the arrow but took his hand away. Scribono shook his head.

"I took an arrow once. Best leave it for a calm head to get it out. You'll only make it worse," he cautioned.

Velio nodded, "I need to sit down."

"Just keep moving centurion. I've not reached the best bit. Then you might want to sit down," Scribono cackled.

"So why did Brutus point me out to you? I gave him sword lessons once and then he tried to kill me in the middle of a patrol to confront the Votadini. Why?" Velio said, trying to divert his mind from the pain.

'A fight with the Votadini' sounded about as ridiculous as fighting your grandmother, and less dangerous into the bargain.

Scribono smiled a tight little victory.

"Because centurion Hanno Glaccus told him to."

Velio stopped in his tracks. Scribono was grinning like a wolf. He thought fast.

"I can't keep going uphill with this arrow. Let me get back on the horse," he said.

The deserter cocked his head.

"Centurion you disappoint me. You think I'm as stupid as dear old Brutus? Keeping holding on to the saddle. You can manage that can't you? See that ridge?"

Scribono pointed away from the road to the right hand side of the valley.

"You are going up and over that. Set your mind to it, or I will have to obey Junius for once and kill you here."

*

Marcellus found Liscus on the rampart by the Praetoria gate, looking out over the narrow funnel of the gorge where the river was running in fury.

"It's getting a little late, don't you think sir?" he ventured.

"He's probably caught up with Titus Vindex and is going with them to Cantiventi. Seeing how long it takes, that sort of thing," Liscus replied, "depending on time he might stay the night. I can't see Titus trying to get the waggons back up the pass today."

He continued with his contemplative scanning of the hillsides that seemed to produce so much water.

Marcellus bit his tongue. It did not seem likely, nor useful to know how long a waggon convoy took to reach the supply hub on the lake. How did that resolve whether Civius' men were on the take?

"It will be getting dark soon," he replied and kept it neutral.

The young officer gave him a direct look. Marcellus thought for a moment he had crossed the kind of respect-line that would never have bothered the centurion. The optio was raw but he was not stupid. Velio had a good opinion of him, he had said as much when signing the appointment order.

"If his horse does not go lame, he should be back tomorrow with Vindex and his men. And if he is not, then you can worry Marcellus,"Liscus said, "we both can," he added.

Marcellus waited, sensing there was something else coming.

"Look around Marcellus. They did not choose this site on a whim. The road needs security. This is not an area to go out searching with a single century and no cavalry support. Once you take men off this road to go chasing Carvetii, they'll be like deer, in these hills, you'll never catch 'em. Only likely to get your men isolated and killed. We have no choice but to wait for the centurion," Liscus stated.

*'And pray that the Delmatarum are still soldiers at heart,'* Marcellus hoped.

It began raining again.

## Chapter Eight.

## The lead mines at Cantiventi.

Auvericus stared at their emaciated bodies. Seven dead slaves, gone in the night, a mixture of the young and not so young, local tribal and Germanic Gaul. The miserable brutes were dying on purpose.

'*What is the point of my bothering to feed and water them?*' he raged.

Cattle in the pastures were more resilient than these men. Criminals, cheats and murderers, these ones were not going to make a further contribution to meeting the quotas: contract quotas that would not fill themselves. This area of the province was littered with the stuff. You could practically pick loose ore up from the ground. Children could do it. And the abundance of water to sluice it was surely sent by Jupiter himself. Yet these slaves persisted in denying him a useful return on their cost. Seven in one night. He nodded to the guard to get the corpses out of here before they added to the ungracious stink. He rubbed the back of his neck. He would have to get younger fitter ones in future or decide much earlier when they arrived whether they were going to be worth feeding at all.

Small scale mining was not proving the noble profession he had hoped it would be. He could admit it to himself. It was grubbing for sesterces and pitching for the chance of a larger follow up contract. More sesterces, bigger contracts, gaining a reputation for reliability and timeliness. That was how nobility was going to be gained. That was how hard it was going to be. The long game. A bigger mine and a better contract, something to match the ones in the south, now that would be noble. Owning more than one mine would be noble. But then again, with the paucity of quality convicts and criminals, the army was making things difficult. And what was so especially noble about slaughtering naked tribal savages in comparison? Or humping stones to make roads, or building walls of turf in the far north? Useful though they surely were. Every time he appealed for labour the local commanders said their gaols were empty. It might be more efficient to just enter the slave business himself.

Owning and running a mine in Hispana, where the ore was purer quality, now that would be noble and a great deal more agreeable. It was only the thought of owning a mine in Hispana where sesterces and cheap labour were more fecund than goats and cattle that made this current aggravation bearable. He stood back, watching the bodies getting loaded onto a cart by his guards and chose not to ask where they were intending to dispose of them. So long as they did not pollute the streams or offend the local sensibilities of the nearby vicus, any hole in the ground would suffice. Fifty waggon loads of galena ore per month, come rain or thunder. Fifty waggon loads per month was what he wanted in order to make this work. It was high time the army marched back up north and hammered the tribes.

*'And bring me back seven more cheap slaves,'* he fretted. '

*'Seven in a single summer's night, what's it going to be like in the winter? Auvericus, you are far too soft,'* he chastised himself.

If they were determined to keep dying rather than filling his waggons, they would do it on fresh air and water. He whistled for his chief overseer.

"Stop the food ration, it's costing too much," he sighed.

His man's face creased in a form of joy he found repulsive, turning to shout the news. He reached a decision. In an odd way the seven dead slaves had helped him make it. Perhaps he should be grateful to them? Pah. He snorted. There was no money to be made in digging the ore. He would have to smelt it too. Give them the end product instead of watching it get floated down the lake for someone else to profit. The idea heated him, his imagination began flowering with possibilities. A 'metals' contract might run in tandem with the ore quotas or, and he licked his lips at the very sweet possibility, supercede it entirely. He might not have to rely on his own mine and slaves to produce sufficient ore. What if he could make deals with the other small operations and smelt theirs too? Doing both parts of the dirty work would push the value up tenfold, perhaps higher? And with enough profit those smaller operations could be his too. Various small mines feeding a smelt works: that would be noble.

He looked around. There was a bit of unused, flat stony ground that would be suitable for the site of a new furnace and next to it was a slope of rock that could be chiselled and gouged to make a drainage channel running down to receiving troughs. Various shapes and sizes would be needed. It would require fencing to keep out intruders and accommodation of sorts. No one stole raw galena but finished lead was a different proposition. He would need more guards. Perhaps ex-soldiers? Tomorrow, he would get stone workers up here to make a start. He felt his spirits rising. An offering to Vulcan would be in order and a visit to the praefectus. He would need to get down to the bottom end of the lake and make fresh deals, research the prices. It felt such a natural development of the business he wondered why he had not thought of smelting before. He would commission his own stamp for the metal. Something with his name. Something Britannic and noble. His product would cross the sea to Gaul and beyond, bearing his reputation with it. He would become the father of top quality lead in the province, surpassing the southern mines: Auvericus.

## Chapter Nine.

### A Carvetii enclave not far from the hill fort.

Velio awoke with Vulcan's fire seething in his side. Biting his lips, he got himself up into a sitting position and checked his wound with his fingers. The arrow had taken him low on the left side between the first and second straps of his metal lorica as he began dismounting the horse. The plates of armour must have opened a fraction as they flexed with his torso. It must have been a soldier's arrow. Hunting arrows had long, thin heads, to better pierce the animal. This one felt like it was probably a heavy gauge, man killing, tip. Sweat flooded into his eyes, stinging and blinding him. The arrow was out. Blood had saturated a bandage in a deep ruddy red stain. An army capsarius would have changed it for him by now, put pressure on it, worked to stem the flow. A wave of hot dizziness hit him, and he turned to vomit. Darkness. In an unseen corner of the Carvetii hall, a woman watched and did not speak.

Later, he woke with sunlight streaming down from the smoke hole in the roof. A small bowl of porridge and a wooden spoon lay beside him. Steam was still rising from the oatmeal. The bandage on his ribs had changed colour from the vibrant alarm of fresh blood to the rusty tinge of an old dried wine stain. He reached over with his arm to take the food and a predatory snap of pain nipped him, ready to use its teeth if he provoked it again. He eased his hand to the food and brought it close. Swallowing was easy enough. The thought of needing to cough or a sneeze frightened him. When the food was gone, he looked for water. A cup of fresh milk caught his eye. How could he have missed it? He lay back once more and breathed slow exploratory breaths, seeking the edges of the pain; and there it was, waiting for him, licking its lips.

The old woman came toward him, taking small steps, wary as a deer, as if he were fully armed and capable. He found it incongruous. She must know he was incapable of resistance. Every muscle felt tightly knotted as though he had marched from Eburacum to Deva in a single day. He felt knots in places far from the site of the wound. She could not know he was left-handed, but it did not matter, she could take him with kitchen knife.

She knelt and raised the edge of the compress from the arrow wound. He did not want to look. Her fingers assessed the exit hole and he winced. She raised her fingertips to show him. They were clean, there was no blood.

"It has sealed," she said in her own tongue.

Velio got the gist of it. A gnarly old fist waved, inches from his face.

"Don't move, keep it sealed," she warned.

He had seen it happen before. A man takes a simple battle wound that seems to clot and heal. He does not sweat much. Aesculapius seems willing to aid him. But then reversal; the god changes his mind, an offence taken perhaps, sending a sudden red swelling that grows into a volcanic protuberance. Delay and heat before explosive excrescence. Another opening and sweat, fever and death. The Fates nod, their work fulfilled. Aesculapius moves on, he has others sending him their prayers.

He kept watching the wound. The blood he coughed up was more spray than flood. He did not vomit. Death's red herald was not coming, he had taken a lucky one. The old hag knew her mosses and tree barks. He felt the wound sealing up inside, getting itchy and a slow purge of returning strength pushing against the pain. And, he reminded himself, he was not getting any younger. Forty-two was not old, but the arrow had shaken him: surely it had. Inches higher and he would have been in Elysium with old Marcus Hirtius. Voccia would be a widow with an unborn child on the way, thrown out of his house in the barracks, left stranded in a Roman garrison vicus where she knew no one. Would she travel back north to find some kind of sanctuary with the Votadini, carrying a dead Roman soldier's whelp in her belly? What kind of welcome would she get at the farm she had left to come and find him? And as for Gallus and Hanno, they would never find out what happened to him or why he did not keep the bargain.

*'Blood of Mars Ultor, you and me Marcus. Arrows for both of us. You can take a friendship too far, you know,'* he grinned a crooked grimace.

Talking to Marcus never hurt nor made a bad situation worse.

*

Scribono came to shed where they were holding him and sent the old woman away. Another man was there. Another deserter by the look of him.

"Junius Cita. This is Centurion Pinneius," Scribono played host.

Junius Cita was maybe forty years of age, he reckoned.

"A centurion of The Boar, my, we are going to fetch a pretty bag of coin for you," Cita said.

He pulled up a stool and Scribono did likewise.

"The question is, centurion, are you going to live? Have you survived the hag's medicine? I'm afraid trained capsarius are a bit thin on the ground around here. Never mind though, it looks like she has kept you from the claws of death for the moment, eh? The porridge hasn't done for you. The question is, what are we to do with you? Scribono here gets all sentimental about the Twentieth and says he's not going to kill you. Me, I'm Sixth and I'm not sentimental about centurions. It's my experience that most of you are bastards," Junius Cita said.

He scratched the side of his mouth with the nail of his fore finger.

"Got nothing to say centurion?" he speared.

"Kill me and get on with it you treacherous bastard," Velio snapped.

Scribono grinned.

Junius Cita smirked back, "that's more like it, centurion. I thought I was boring you."

He paused again, drawing it out. Velio got himself up on his good elbow.

"Kill me and hang for it later Cita, it's all the same to me. I don't bargain with cowards and traitors," he reposted.

"Oh, I don't think we'll be killing you just yet centurion. Where would be the fun? Rest, get strong and then we'll find a way of killing you," Junius Cita promised.

He rose up off the stool.

"Guard him well Scribono. Don't come and tell me he has escaped, or you know what I'll do."

He towered over Velio. There were scars on his legs, arms and face. None of them were fresh. Velio could not help noticing both men were still wearing their army boots. The clearest possible symbol of their desertion. Junius Cita had either been ferocious in battle or deficient with his sword and shield. Velio read his eyes. They were not those of an untrained man. Brawling scars from the backstreets in Eburacum? Was this a man who could not walk down a street past other soldiers without wanting to show how tough he was, that he was top dog? Did he have a back decorated by the lash? Such scars healed just the same an any other.

"I'm keeping your sword centurion. Rather splendid, I think. And Scribono is keeping your pugio. Your breastplate is outside on a stump for arrow practice. Let's the local lads see what Roman armour can withstand," Junius said, matter of fact.

Velio tried to not react.

"And your pretty feathered helmet has gone to the Carvetii chieftain whose shed this is. He is very impressed. He's never seen a First cohort officer's helmet before. All in all, centurion, you have your tunic and the caligae on your feet, be grateful for that much. The hag will look after you and once you're fit, we will see whether this nickname of yours is really true. Scribono remembers Swords Pinneius quite well; you're the man who got his cousin killed if I'm not mistaken."

## Chapter Ten.

## The hill fort.

Liscus stepped up to the small stone dais on the parade ground. The Fourth century looked at him in total silence. The fort was agog at the wild-fire news. Titus Vindex and his auxiliary had returned.

"It appears that centurion Pinneius is missing. We are going to find him," he said.

He did not know what reaction the news was going to generate, and the words sounded flat in his ears as he announced them. The parade ground was solemn as a grave side. Cloak tails flapped, feathers in junior officer's helmets dared to bend in the breeze instead of standing upright. There were no voices, nor murmurs, no sarcasm under bated breaths, no smirks, no covert malicious delight for prayers answered. They stared back at him. His confidence soared like one of the ravens wheeling around the crags. The Fourth century were already accepting they were going out to retrieve their commander. In an ordinary century he supposed Velio would have had about a third of them devoted to his word. Another third would have obeyed because they had no choice excepting the lash, and a final third forming the disgruntled and the mouthy. These divisions did not exist in the First cohort. Velio Pinneius would be cremated, if necessary, but he sensed the centurion was not going to lie out there unmourned. The faces staring back at him were telling him, '*we are not returning to Deva Victrix without him.*'

The relief of it warmed him. They had taken the order as if it had been Velio himself speaking. For two months he had been wearing the feather crest of an optio, a full optio of the legion. The centurion had warned him about the step up, the loneliness that would come with it and sit on his shoulder. Warned him about the former comrades and brothers who would become reticent to speak freely. Or even joke in front of him in the barrack block. The tesserarii would look to him for guidance and leadership. So far it seemed to have gone well. Life in Deva Victrix had been routine. The centurion had made his choice. All was well. And now, within days, his first patrol out of Deva, Velio Pinneius had gone missing leaving him in command of the century. No wonder they were quiet in the ranks. But did they think he was already dead? He turned to his senior tesserarius.

"Take the left-hand side of the Cantiventi road and search it until you can swear on the altars of Mars and Fortuna that you cannot find him or his body. I will take the right-hand side. Meet me at the bottom of the pass when you are certain," he ordered.

The tesserarius saluted.

"Well?" he allowed the question he could see in the man's eyes.

"What about the other side of these two hillsides sir? The valleys beyond. Do we cross over?" the tesserarius queried.

He assented, nodding his head.

"I want to be certain he is not lying dead in this valley before I take the men up into the higher ground," he replied, "and doing that will make it impossible for us to support each other if we run into a trap."

"As you command sir," the tesserarius replied, still waiting.

The parade ground was engineered out of a favourable, low step in the hill. It loured over the heights of the pass and the fort below. It seemed to him a much more likely place to find a lost man.

"Tesserarius?" he said.

The centurion always allowed reasoned questions from his sub officers. He kept his nerve. Now was not the time to get shirty before deploying the command.

"You think this is a trap sir?" the tesserarius asked.

"Take half the men and comb this side of the road up to the summit and beyond it. I will take the other half over the river and do the same. Keep me in sight at all times. I will do the same. We will meet at the bottom of the pass," he repeated and pointed for emphasis, "then we will decide how to tackle the high ground. I am not dividing the century any more than I have to, not here," he said and avoided the question.

'*Where in Dis Pater are you sir?*' he fretted.

The tesserarius' eyes widened, and he nodded. Liscus wondered if he had actually said it aloud. The north side of the fort sheered down into a gorge, making that side effectively impregnable. Velio could not be down there if he had ridden up the road. Besides, searching down there would require all the men that he had here.

"Continue tesserarius," he said, wanting to end this discussion.

He changing his mind. Getting the tesserarius on his side would ensure the others were in line.

"Tesserarius, the centurion is probably the last man in the Twentieth legion I would expect to fail to return from exercising his horse. Something has happened, and a trap with him as the bait is exactly what the local heathens might try."

"And the Delmatarum sir?" the tesserarius dared a final question.

Liscus looked him in the eyes.

"I think we'll leave the Delmatarum to count waggons for now, now get your men organised and moving," he said, ending the debate.

The tesserarius saluted and turned away. Marcellus stood waiting next for an order. Liscus outranked him, despite his status as the centurion's military clerk.

"This does not look good Marcellus," he said keeping his voice down, "you will stay here on the off chance the centurion turns up, though for the love of the gods I can't see how that's going to happen. I want you to start drafting a report of what has happened since we arrived here. And pray the centurion himself is able to tell you to tear it up and start again."

"Aye sir. And I'll keep my ear to the ground with the Delmaratum. Just in case," Marcellus added.

Liscus raised his eyebrow in disbelief. He took stock of the other side of the pass beyond the gushing black waters of the river. The hillsides were scrubby with straggling thickets of bushes, stretches of bare rock and scree, except for a small stand of trees that must have found sufficient soil to flourish. They made him uncomfortable, and he expected they were probably making the men feel the same. In fairness, they were too far away to conceal attackers, yet the primitive, wary part of him felt they bore an elemental, watchful disapproval of the fort and its environs. He checked his weapons, pushing the feeling away and decided to lead his men on foot. It was irrational but he was tempted to split out a squad of men to start felling the timber.

*'It can wait until later, Liscus,'* he promised himself.

Civius approached in his full-dress armour. He raised his hand in greeting and got straight down business.

"Salve, optio. Titus tells me your news. Do you wish my men to scout for you?" he said.

"You have my gratitude, centurion. I am going to search the road and the low ground. If we have to search higher, then a couple of your men would be welcome to guide us," he replied.

Civius nodded and straightened the sword hanging over his shoulder.

"Well, I hope you find him. He may have got himself lost. I will send a rider back to Cantiventi in case he has arrived there in the meantime," he said leaden faced.

'*Velio will love that news getting out,'* Liscus bit down on the words.

He saluted and nodded. There was nothing else he could do. Civius outranked him.

"Well do carry on, optio. Don't let me detain you and your men," Civius spouted behind him.

Feeling he had been dismissed with a certain degree of unwarranted curtness, Liscus waved the second part of the century out of the gate and strode after them, fuming. Civius watched as they filed through the Praetoria gateway and turned left on the roadway.

"Thank you, Jupiter, thou best and greatest," he said.

Titus got them over the river at the point where the mountain stream was not much more than a narrow shallow step of silver water and polished stones. They spread out and began combing the rough tussocky ground. The line of men doglegged on the higher slopes as they struggled to keep footing. He took position in the middle and drove the line. On the far side of the valley the senior tesserarius and his men were ahead of them. They had the trumpeter with them. Three hours later they rejoined the road. The tesserarius had his men lined up. His face told Liscus all he needed to know.

"So, it's the high ground?" he said.

The tesserarius nodded, "we could climb up from here and work our way back towards the fort. It would save time, sir," he suggested.

Liscus put his hands on his hips and took a long look at the hill on this side of the road. He shook his head.

"I don't think he's up there," he said, "he would not have ridden up there voluntarily and I can't see any caves up there. Take the men back to the fort and search the hill above the parade ground. You will get a good view down the high tops of the valley from there. If you find nothing, take the men back to the fort and wait for me there. Keep them in the barrack blocks for now. Let them eat. Tell the praefectus nothing but tell the centurion's secretary what is happening. Do you understand?"

"These Carvetii are supposed to be the compliant tribe in this area. Not warlike like the Brigantes," the tesserarius responded.

Liscus shook his head, "they are allies of the Brigantes. There will be blood links and oaths between them, you can depend upon it. If they have managed to capture the centurion, it might not be too good. I don't want the men getting stirred up. You know what they are like. Keep them focussed on finding him."

"They will follow orders, or I will be recommending the skins off their backs sir," the tesserarius answered, scowling at the unspoken idea there could be indiscipline among the First cohort.

Liscus lifted his hand knowing Velio's century was as likely to disobey an order as snow falling at harvest time.

"Gently tesserarius, go gently," he coaxed, "we did not come here expecting to have to fight our way back out. I do not think that was our centurion's plan and it should not become ours now that he has gone missing. Keep it that way until I order 'swords and scuta'."

*'Swords and shields, perhaps, but who would have imagined it might be for such a reason as this?'* he thought.

"As you have commanded me, optio," the tesserarius replied.

Liscus watched the other half of his command go marching back up the hill road towards the summit. Turning to his own tesserarius, a younger agile man, he pointed at the slopes.

"We're going to sweep along the crest back towards the fort. If the centurion is not here, we are going to have to widen the search further tomorrow, so I want you to take two squads to the top and tell me what is on the other side. Do not take the men down there. I just want to know the lie of it. Keep a sharp lookout for Carvetii. I will get the rest of them moving," he said.

They reformed four hours later.

"No sign sir?" the other tesserarius asked after making his report.

"None. He must have been captured," he said.

"Then it's going to get a bit bloody, one way or the other," his young tesserarius responded, matter of fact: dispassionate.

"March them back, I'll be along shortly," he said.

He stood on a rock and rotated around three hundred and sixty degrees, trying to summon up Velio by force of willpower alone from the upland moors and hillsides. The trees he had been watching earlier were now shaded as the sun descended towards a horizon far beyond the port of Iuliocenon, and its Aelia Classica garrison. That Velio could have vanished off the face of the land within sight of two forts, which were themselves in close communication of each other was beyond fathoming. He looked back at the black shaped trees and spat.

## Chapter Eleven.

## Argentomagus.

The bull groaned and sank down onto its knees. Gouts of its life's ending sprayed Gallus across his face, chest and legs. It moaned a long, horrid sigh of defeat to his razored-edge sword blade and fell onto its belly. The shining eye transfixed Gallus with an oxen stare that was both reproving and resigned. He kept well out of reach of the horns, stepping away from the head. The halter rope tightened and pulled the wooden post askew as the animal fell. A shiver ran through its body, and it made a last, futile complaint, blood spumed out of its throat in outright mockery of fountains in every forum in the empire. It crashed over onto its side and lay, hindlegs kicking, at the invisible feet of the divine Ceres.

"Excellently done Gallus. That must surely find favour. As clean a despatch as the priests could manage in Rome," Hanno exulted.

Gallus stepped aside from the twitching bull and the puddling stain growing on the earth at the side of the vineyard. It ran over the dry earth, pooling small stones into miniature islands, thickening in the heat even before it had time to drain into the ground.

"And one bull will be enough for the whole estate? We shouldn't repeat it on the other side to be sure?" he asked, frowning.

Hanno knew he meant the newly discovered slopes in the next valley. He shook his head.

"I think this is the best place Gallus. The sacrifice is for the whole estate. Ceres will understand our prayer," he judged.

He stepped in and patted the animal's flank. A simple act of consolation, gratitude and respect. Gallus waited. There would be good eating tonight.

"I'd thought I was done killing things," Gallus murmured, "but there is always another reason to shed more blood. Lovely animal though. Pity we could not tan the hide, it does seem a waste."

*'You need a drink, my Stoic friend,'* Hanno sympathised.

Ceres could not be cheated of the whole animal. It would not be seemly to flay the bull for leather.

"Gallus, come and drink some wine and toast our offering. You'll feel better," he said.

Gallus wiped the blade clean of blood and bedded it back in the stained leather sheath. Unlike Velio and Hanno with their swanky officer's gladii, he had worn this one on his hip for more than thirty summers, and always kept it always sharp to shave his chin. Velio had a bit of a penchant for old swords too, he recalled. He had even owned one from the late, but unlamented, Ninth Hispana legion for a while. He was a man with an eye for a sword, was Velio.

Velio: it would be good to see him here, free of the army. It would strange too, to set their own pace of working, bound by the vines and harvest times. Their worries no longer centring on their small parts in keeping the peace in a distant province. Instead, it would be about selling good wine at favourable prices. That was more like it. The three of them, free to make a good living under a warm sun. He looked at the young brown bull. They would cut enough beef for the villa and the rest would lie there until tomorrow and be burned. It would need a fair-sized pile of wood to dispose of the body. As things lay the bull would need hauling further from the vines. He should have thought of that before tethering it. He brightened at the thought he would not be the one doing the manual labour.

"Coming centurion," he said.

"We need to choose house slaves from the ones we have. Ones we can depend on. Four or five should be sufficient. And we need to appoint an overseer for them," Hanno said.

The villa needed cleaning. They needed a decent cook for themselves and another to feed the slaves.

"Are we going to let them sleep in the house?" Gallus queried.

Hanno stopped.

"It would make sense," he said, "the small room beside the kitchen. It's big enough, I think. But all the rest will sleep in the long barn. Best keep them shackled at night until we are sure of them. Just suggestions Gallus, you bought the place. It's your decision. There may be bad eggs hiding amongst them. We will need a firm hand from the overseer to weed any out."

"And we need find a winemaker," Gallus replied, moving on.

"We need to repair the fences in the other valley," Hanno counted the tasks on his fingers.

"And we need more horses. Hanno write a list. This will take time. Priscus' woman told me everything we needed would be here. I wish I could get my hands on her," he raged.

"I was coming to that little nut. I think we should try and find out what happened here, Gallus. Perhaps she has followed Priscus to the afterlife, sooner than she expected?" Hanno posed, "perhaps she is not the one who cheated you?"

"I paid in gold," Gallus railed.

"Well, look on the bright side Gallus. The vines are healthy, we have sufficient slaves to keep the weeds down and work the fields, the kitchen garden, the fruit trees, mending trellis, and pruning. Not to mention general repairs. We have made a sacrifice. Now we have time to get the estate organised before harvest time. Not long though. And it looks like there are no presses in the sheds. Your friend Priscus must have used his slaves to tread the grapes. Makes the best wine that way but it is an expensive waste not to use further pressings," Hanno expounded.

Gallus felt his eyebrows rise at Hanno's newfound and undeclared knowledge of wine making.

"Perhaps that where his reputation came from. I say we set to it and concentrate on that for now Gallus," Hanno continued.

"We'll make a decent posca for honest soldiers and the ordinary folk. Then sweet Falernian white for the nobs to pay a premium. If it's good, we'll limit how much each customer can buy. Create the demand. Come to that, we want customers to sell to," Gallus replied, thinking he had missed the absence of wine presses.

Hanno was marching ahead of him in that respect.

"Well then, some good red, some premium white and a fair priced posca: that's sufficient for now," Hanno replied.

He paused, afraid his uppermost thoughts were going to upset the old wolf-wrestler.

'*What is the point of friendship if you can't speak the truth?*' he decided.

"She did let the place run down a bit Gallus," he ventured.

"And charged me a hefty price for the chance to buy it before anyone else could bid," Gallus growled.

"Nothing that three men of The Boar can't put right in a summer or two," he replied.

"There's not a single amphora left. Even when we have a harvest fermenting in the dolia-vats, we have no storage vessels," Gallus said.

He stayed calm and pragmatic.

"So, this place was cleaned out by men who know the trade. That's not so surprising," Hanno countered.

"They bothered to take the key to the lock of the storage hall after they cleaned it out. How determined do you have to be to remember that kind of detail? And how about all the waggons to move the wine?" Gallus spat.

"You don't actually know how much stock was left?" Hanno pointed out.

Gallus rubbed his chin, "that's true. But think of all those villages we burned over the years Hanno? It takes more than a single torch, that's all I'm saying," he said.

"Your friend the procurator?" Hanno offered.

"Has men enough to take this place apart. This took organisation and many hands," Gallus summed up.

"Perhaps our wine is lying in another man's storage hall?" Hanno said.

"He took an opportunity when there was no one strong enough to stop him. He can't do that again now that we are here. I won't let him, Jupiter hear me. And what about the missing slaves?" Gallus grumbled.

Hanno leaned forward. Gallus was getting het up about something that was past. If their fox was the procurator, there might be another way to trap him but brooding on the injury done to their business was not going to help. Gallus needed to put this behind him.

"Do you think he would be stupid enough to sell them back to us?"Gallus speculated.

Hanno marvelled at the old wolf-wrestler's ability to see things in a different light, just when he had convinced you otherwise. It was a hope inspiring idea. Slaves were generally faceless. Their life histories of no interest to their new owners, except for their health, experience and any skills they possessed. It would not take an owner long to forget the detail of how he acquired a common field worker he had never actually set eyes on.

"He has to make the mistake of selling one back to us for the truth to come out," he breathed, "and that slave would have to speak Latin for us to know, but I fear whoever did this is not so stupid a man, Gallus," he murmured.

It stuck in his head for the rest of the day.

## Chapter Twelve.

### The smelting works, Cantiventi.

The first of the grey gold flooded down the stone runnel into the holding trough, bubbling and alive, released from its prison in the ore, smoking and hot; like the blood of mother earth herself. The thought troubled him. Vulcan had had his prayer and sacrifice but what about the native goddess? It would be folly to offend by not giving her, her dues. His foreman stirred the cooling metal with an iron spoon and scooped a sample, laying the spoon on the wet ground to cool. A skin formed on the metal, changing and dulling its colour. The foreman waited before measuring the heat with delicate touches of his filthy hands and prising out the spoon shaped ingot. Auvericus held out his hand, but his foreman shook his head. It was still hot. He waited a little longer until the urge to touch it was too much. It was heavy and tactile in his hand, with something almost feminine about its shape, seductive to the rub of his thumb. He felt himself getting aroused at the amount of the money that was now lying in the piles of raw ore. He slipped the shining ingot into his pocket and stared up at the sky where rain clouds were hanging low.

"See how much you can produce today. I want to know how much metal I can get from how much ore and how longs it takes. Understand?" he ordered.

The first drops of rain started.

"We will begin a roof tomorrow. I want this furnace burning every daylight hour. Get waggons out for timber. I want this furnace running hot. I want moulds for water pipes, three different sizes. Square plate moulds and rectangular ones," he said.

*'At last. This is what I left Hispania for. At last, Fortuna you smile on me. You know my name: I am Auvericus. Hail and blessings to you Fortuna. Tonight, I feast in your honour. One day I will return home and buy the finest mine and raise a statue to you at its entrance. I swear this,'* he prayed.

He gazed at the furnace and the steady trickle of molten metal draining over the lip of the collecting trough as it began to overflow. His heart was racing. The trough was full to the brim. It must be high yielding ore. He got back on his horse. An empty cart was already leaving with two men. He could see the wood saws and axes loaded in the back.

"Bring me the driest dead wood, all you can find, and you will be well rewarded," he said, "no wet wood."

His foreman began to whistle, oblivious to Auvericus. A tune of noise and little melody. He smiled. This was going to work out splendidly. The foreman had the look of a man inspired by an unspoken bonus.

## Chapter Thirteen.

### The Carveti chieftain's hall.

A week after Junius Cita's taunt about making him fight, Velio's legs were chained and they brought him to the chieftain's hall and pushed him down onto the rushes on the opposite side from the door. The pain inside was fading and he could feel his body healing. He made himself calm and rolled sideways and up to a sitting position. Checking he was alone in the hall, he got to his feet, the warning pangs nipping in his side. His head felt clear. The hall was circular, timbered, high roofed, with the usual exit hole for the smoke and a solitary doorway. The family sleeping quarters were on a platform elevated up from the ground space. Down below was the kitchen, fire and the meeting area. Fresh meat was hanging from hooks. There was an oven. A bench with cheese. Milk churns. Vegetables in baskets. Water pails. A cask that might have ale in it. The chieftain's hunting spears were displayed on a rack. The heads ranged from the slenderest of leaf profiles, ideal for a long-range throw, up to an array of battle spears. Each spear head had been burnished to maximise the shine of the iron. Next to them was his own immaculate, polished helmet, dominating the display. He made himself look away. Whatever happened in the next few hours was going to decide whether losing it mattered a jot, in the great scheming of the Fates. He pushed aside the fear he might never wear it again. Several shields were hanging on the walls: one made from woven pliable withies, another made from block-oak and the third, a bronze masterpiece of repoussé decoration, all swirls and curling motifs. He reckoned it must be the Carvetii equivalent of a parade shield. He touched it with his fingertips and without thinking lifted it off the peg on which it was hanging and hefted it with his right arm. It was balanced and comfortable to wear and lighter than he expected. He turned about to face the hall. The door was open, and he realised his mistake.

A Carveti, Scribono and Junius Cita were staring at him. At their back two young men, not much more than boys, sons rather than servants of the Carveti perhaps, tried to peer past their elders. Velio slung the shield off his arm and held it out to the Carveti. The deserter's faces were everything he hated in soldiers who conflated the concept of courage with the mindlessness of casual brutality. Scribono started forward, his hand reaching for his sword. Cita just glared. The Carveti ignored them, taking his shield back from Velio's outstretched hands. A swathe of excuses, pleadings, compliments tumbled around his tongue.

"I apologise," he managed, in Brigantes.

*Why did you demean yourself?'* he scourged himself, *'I'm a dead man anyway.'*

But he knew why. He and this Carveti had more in common than with either of the deserters. There was in the man's almost placid acceptance of his offence, a whisper of mutual understanding, of enemy to enemy.

*'Time to take position,'* he decided.

"I am centurion Velio Pinneius, of the Twentieth legion," he said.

The Carveti was shorter than he was in height but square shouldered. A scar ran laterally across his face, making what was left of his nose a notched bump in a torrid landscape. Up close he saw moustaches and beard hiding the gap of missing upper teeth.

*'Is that from a sword slash? A blow deflecting off the shield? That shield? A full force blow would have taken your head off at the eyes. You must have bled like a pig. You were lucky not to be blinded. Lucky to survive,'* he assessed.

It was an old scar. The more he looked at it the more obvious it became. The chieftain let him look, with the composure of a man who accepts he will be examined. Velio's own sword arm bore a healthy decoration of crisscrossing scars that he had accumulated over the years but nothing like the one he was looking at now. Was this wreckage the only father's face his boys had known? There must have been a different face before battle took it away? Something less hideous before they were even born? Did they shrink back when he tried to smile, shrink from the monster? Or did they revere his mutilation as the sign of a formidable warrior?

His rank did not appear to be eliciting much of a reaction. Not that he expected it. What threat was he to these men? Scribono must have filled the chief in when he brought him here. That part of this nightmare was a little vague. The Carveti knew who he was alright.

"Tie him up Scribono," Junius ordered.

*'So, you command Scribono, do you Junius?'* he sized up, *'I wonder how you manage that?'*

Scribono was the more soldierly looking of the pair of them. Junius Cita was the weaselly, barrack block kind. Another Rugio from his distant past. Better he was out of the legion than contaminating it from within. He hated the type. Instinct said Junius Cita had been a deserter for longer than Scribono. His wood was rotten. The Carveti placed his shield in the hands of the taller of the two lads.

*'Definitely his son,'* Velio decided.

The shield was very carefully put back in its place.

*'A special shield, a totem?'*

His interest got going as Scribono pulled his arms behind his back and applied the rope. The lad's father kept his silence. Cita took a pace forward, his grimy thick beard and blue flashing eyes, giving him the look of an Aventine assassin with a grudge.

"Put him back in the shed, make sure the rope's right. Now that the old woman has worked her magic. We need to decide what we're going to do with him."

"When I decide," the Carveti spoke at last, in Latin.

"That's what I meant," Junius Cita did not skip a beat.

"Sit him down. I want to look at him," the Carveti said, "my boys have not seen a Roman up close. It is time I showed them, the Romani are not so brave without their armour and their war machines."

"Drapisces," Scribono began.

Velio started, surprised. The Carveti lifted his hand ending whatever argument Scribono planned.

"So now you know my name Roman. Tell me yours again," Drapisces said.

His voice was surprisingly clear through his missing teeth. Junius Cita scowled. Scribono stepped back from the knots he had tied. Velio was kneeling with his arms behind his back. Nothing he had faced north of the wall, with Marcus Hirtius or Gallus had ever felt more dangerous. Drapisces waved his sons forward. They hesitated as if he was a venom spitting snake. He straightened up and stared at the two of them.

*'Decent enough lads,'* he gauged, *'is father going to let you stick a knife into me? Give you your first Roman to kill so you can be a man and hold my head up outside. Show the real warriors you have become men? Win your manhood? Is that what this is?'*

The whirring in his head was at odds with the fact Drapisces must have ordered he be kept alive after the arrow wound. He clutched at the logic that Drapisces would not have wasted his time. The boys could have finished off a wounded man and achieved the same purpose. Neither lad moved to draw his horn handled knife from his belt.

"I am centurion Velio Pinneius of the Twentieth legion," he repeated.

Drapisces glanced at his sons.

"The new helmet I have on my wall tells me he is a chief, boys. Do not be fooled because he kneels here tied like a goat. This is a great chief within his army. The helmet tells me that. A soldier of great power. A dangerous enemy. To kill him in battle would bring great honour to you, either of you. But you are not old enough or skilled enough to fight him even though he is wounded. He would cut you down in a stroke. But I look at him now and I do not have a reason to kill him. I will need to speak to Caturiges. Perhaps he will find a reason," he said.

He turned to Junius Cita and Scribono.

"I wish you had not brought him to my hall. You have brought me a problem that needs careful considering. Before today this man knew nothing of me or my hall and now, he does. I have no choice but to sacrifice him. I cannot release such a deadly warrior."

Scribono made to speak.

"Now you can take him away," Drapisces cut across them both.

## Chapter Fourteen.

## The hillfort.

"It's been four days Titus," Liscus complained and wrapping himself deeper in his cloak.

Titus did likewise, turning a shoulder and bending his head away from the breeze. The evening was cold and getting colder. The rain feeding from the west was coming in, incessant and determined, but it was easier to confide out here where no other ears could hear his concerns. Admitting his fears out loud to someone else made it all the more certain something had gone horribly wrong. His fellow optio was wearing a sympathetic look.

"And there is no sign?"

Titus repeated the same question he had been asking on each of the prior days. Liscus shook his head. Titus was older and senior to him. It was obvious to him Liscus was still feeling his way with his men at times.

*'Best not to underestimate him Titus,'* he told himself.

His sole meeting with centurion Pinneius in the watchtower left no doubts the men temporarily stationed in the barrack block were the best in the legion.

Liscus opened up a little, "I have seen bands of Carvetii moving in the distance when we've been searching, but we can't get close up to them without cavalry and even if I had them under my command, what use are horses up here? They just keep trying to draw me deeper into the hills, but I'm not going there."

He gestured at the wet hills surrounding the fort.

"My men were of no use?" Titus queried.

His best trackers had spent the last two days aiding the men of the First cohort. Liscus shook his head and tugged his lip frustrated.

"I expected to search the local tribal villages and whatever passes for a stronghold in this area. Your men seem to have lost their memory of those locations," he barbed.

Titus kept nodding. The performance of those men was typical of the quality he had found in the garrison.

*'Best not to underestimate him,'* he reminded himself.

"I told your centurion of my concerns about the looting of the convoys, how it was done. The men I ordered to help you are good men but, they are at the mercy of their superiors," he said.

"You are their superior," Liscus reminded him.

Titus heard a hint of unexpected venom in the words. So, Liscus had teeth. It was his turn to make a little admission.

"I am an outsider. Oh, they follow orders when my shadow touches them. Out of my sight I doubt their worth," he confided.

It was a glum truth. Liscus thought about offering encouragement, but Titus swept on.

"We are here to harry the proud and console the compliant. The Delmatarum have forgotten their purpose. I am ashamed to be in their company."

Liscus considered the words. It was all well and good, but it did nothing to locate the centurion. It was Titus Vindex' job to make the Delmatarum better soldiers than they evidently were now. If he could not or would not do that, he was no better than them, despite his rank and fine talk. Civius, was all ineffectual bonhomie and good intent. Thank the gods he did not depend on Civius to guard his back in a battle. He was no closer to finding Velio than he was on the day he went missing.

"I am taking the century back down to Cantiventi, right now Titus. A messenger will ride to Deva Victrix. The legate must be told one of his most senior centurions has been taken," he declared.

Titus raised his eyebrows.

*'What will Civius make of that?'* he wondered.

"I think Velio Pinneius is alive. I think he is being held captive. If it's the Carvetii who have him and they do not return him by the time I return, I think Servius Albinius will unleash The Boar. Mark my words, Titus. The time for this foolishness is running out. You might let that thought do the rounds of the Delmatarum. Just in case any of them are withholding information," Liscus warned.

Titus felt his face getting hot despite the foul wetness whistling in the air. Was Liscus accusing him of complicity? On the facts so far, the lack of a corpse did make Liscus' summary quite likely. The horse he had been riding had not been seen either. If he had fallen from it, surely the beast would have been found or at least seen by now?

"They've not seen what 'harrying the proud' looks like until they see what the Twentieth can do when they get into their stride, Titus. When Albinius sends more troops he will want heads to be taken, slaves to be taken, crops destroyed, cattle appropriated, huts and halls burned. He won't care who is innocent. If you are a Carveti living in these hills you will feel his wrath. And as for Civius, who has done nothing to remedy the problem, it will not surprise me if he gets a summons to appear in Deva Victrix. Not in the least. You may never see him back here again,"Liscus concluded.

Titus smirked, "then it's not all bad Liscus," he said.

Liscus took a final look at the latest manifestation of the Tempestates and stepped towards the rampart steps. A thought struck him.

"Has Civius told the praefectus down at Uiliocenon the centurion is missing?" he asked.

"I don't believe he has,"Titus conceded.

He made a dismissive toss of his head.

"Why not, in Jupiter's name?" Liscus said.

"He has not considered it necessary to involve the garrison at the seaport in any search, given his own century were here," Titus answered.

Liscus could hear the words drip with sarcasm and disgust.

*'Except he is not searching for our centurion, is he?'* Liscus looked at him and did not reply.

For a fleeting moment he felt sorry for Titus, marooned in this awful posting with men he did not trust and a commander he clearly despised. To try and console him would be patronising and given their respective seniorities, inappropriate. He shied away from the gruff humour friends might exchange. In time they might get to know each other better.

"Vale," he said.

Titus nodded and watched him descend the rampart steps and go striding off to his barrack block, the cape whirling at his shoulders, fist on the pommel of his gladius: the attitude of an angry man. The centurion's man Marcellus was bound to include the omission of Uiliocenon in his inevitable report. The thought of a dry bunk suddenly felt like a refuge from this bloody mess. He was scarcely off the walls heading back to his room when Arco came running up to him bringing orders. The auxiliary saluted and blurted it out.

"Centurion Civius wants to see you sir."

*'The man is a spider,'* Titus muttered to himself.

"Very well," he acknowledged.

Arco's pinched little face suggested he had been ejected from a cosier billet to come and find him. There was a vapid stupidity of bovine intensity about him. The guarding of a rain cursed hill pass was all he deserved. He was just like the rest of them, Civius too if it came to that, content to be part of an underperforming garrison, cheating the emperor of petty cargo. And when it came to matters of importance like helping find an officer who had either been murdered or captured, they were totally bloody useless, making him look bad into the bargain.

"You have to get out of here, Titus" he breathed, "get yourself back to the legion before they drag you into their crime."

Civius was working late. Titus nodded to the guard standing just under the shelter of the principia entrance, avoiding the worst of the incoming weather and chose not to rebuke him. This rain might last for hours. He saluted the open doorway of the Aedes room. A solitary lamp burned within, holding back the vapours of darkness and keeping the garrison imago signum and the two century standards protected. In here the comforting aura of Rome's power was tangible. The Tempestates might whistle and rage outside but within these walls the sense of order provided by Roman stone and tiles prevailed. In another room he heard low voices discussing the quantity of the grain rations newly received into the warehouses. A fug of warmth from the burning fire smacked him as he entered the commander's office. A plinthed bust of the emperor, Antoninus Pius squared him in the eyes, and he glanced down out of respect. The room was small, almost claustrophobic. Like a summer's day when you could lie on your back in the grass and reach up and touch the passing clouds, here it felt like a tall man might spread out his arms and touch opposite walls with his fingertips: both were illusions. Civius was sitting at his desk, surrounded by paperwork.

*'Warm and dry and safe. Probably the safest place in the empire,'* he jeered to himself.

"Sit down Titus. I've been reviewing your last report, your opinion of the men. You have my gratitude for the promptness. I like to get an outside view occasionally. It's easy to take your men for granted. They get sloppy, stuck up here with no active duties to perform. Sloppy and bored. There are times I think peace is not the friend of soldiers. And yet Pax Romana is what we bring, what we want to instil, is it not?" Civius began.

Titus absorbed this philosophical lecture and wondered where Civius was going with it.

"I think it's time I let you into my little secret. You are to be stationed here for the foreseeable future and you can take that to mean until the year turns at the earliest. Not an appealing thought? Your face betrays you, Titus. So, something to make your duties here more palatable, more profitable, shall we say? It's only fair. We tend the emperor's road. Occasionally things get dropped by passers by. Things they hardly notice have gone missing at all. The other centurion and optio both take part in my secret so it's time you did too. But before then, we really need to get rid of the

Twentieth. Get them marching back to Deva. Can you find a way to do that for me Titus?" Civius smarmed a sudden bonhomie.

Titus felt uncomfortable. It felt as Civius had just placed a noose over his head, and it was resting on his collar bones. Dealing with him would be so much easier if he understood what rules Civius was playing by. He decided to spit it out and see what Civius made of it.

"I told him," he said.

"You told what, to whom, Titus?" Civius said.

Civius' expression darkened.

"The Boar centurion Pinneius. I told him all about the fives and the tens, the changing of the inventories," he confessed.

"Why would you do that, young Titus?" Civius purred.

A clear warning.

"Because it's wrong. It's stealing from the emperor," he said, glad to tell the centurion what he really thought about this sordid, squalid thievery.

"Don't be a fool optio. The emperor put me here. To guard his road. He has not said I should not profit a little for my dedication," Civius snapped.

"Even so, every five and ten?" Titus jousted.

His cheeks felt hot. The feelings of disappointment and outrage that the honour of the greatest army in the known world could be suborned by such petty stealing appalled him. He felt sick in his belly.

"Titus, you disappoint me," Civius paused, "so, the centurion knows the secret? How foolish of me to think a smart young optio, a man like Titus Vindex, would not work it out for himself. Well, what am I to do with you. Titus? Can I trust you?" he posed.

It sounded like a threat.

"I am loyal to my legion, the emperor, and the people of Rome," he said.

"You have not ever been to Rome, Titus," Civius sneered.

"I have not," he replied.

"Then I can allow you two out of three. Can I trust you, was my question?" Civius repeated.

"To do what?" he fenced.

"Get rid of the Twentieth. I cannot order them away without arousing suspicion. They had orders to come here, and those orders had a purpose," Civius explained.

Titus had an uneasy suspicion he was being walked into a trap.

"And if I do?" he asked.

"If you do, I will reconsider my opinion of you. I have you for six more months optio. You will be here into the winter. Has anyone told you we hear wolves up here in winter? They are in these hills. Take it from me optio, when you stand night guard up on the wall and wolves are calling in the darkness, they can sound very close, extremely close. It's an effect of the hills around us. Magnifies the sounds. Makes it unpleasant. Makes the hairs on your neck stand up and the chills run down your back, doesn't matter how brave a man is, how civilised Rome has become, the reaction is the same. These ones are not descended from the kindly animals that suckled Romulus, you understand me? They are beasts of the Britannia mother goddess, and she does not want us here. You don't think much of the Delmatarum, I can tell, don't bother trying to deny it. Well, let me tell you, they stand just as well as any soldier does in the daylight against mortal men. I can make those six months unpleasant for you Titus," Civius' mouth tightened, "it does not bother me either way, but I hope you will see sense."

The warning was stark enough.

"I will get rid of the Twentieth legion, for now. How will we keep them away?" he replied.

*'We? Good, he commits himself.'*

Civius breathed a little easier. Titus had worried him with his blind honesty.

"That depends on the missing centurion," he continued.

"Optio Liscus Aulus Manlio assures me the legate will send a vexillation to punish the Carvetii if Centurion Pinneius cannot be found," Titus said.

He tried to hide the chaos pumping in his veins, tightening his chest.

"Anything that assures the Iter X remains open to the emperor's traffic is to be welcomed," Civius answered and smiled.

The mouth creased but eyes did not warm. Titus found it a rather baleful attempt at intimacy.

*'There really is something untrustworthy about you, Civius'* he thought, *'I am right.'*

Civius raised his hand in half salute. He returned it and got out of the room. He was thoroughly confused. Talking to Civius was like conversing with two- headed Janus. Which head was he to believe? With one tongue he plotted systematic pilferage from the convoys and with the other, the idea of Servius Albinus sending retribution upon the Carvetii disturbed him not one whit. Whose side was he on?

*

Titus found his bunk and lay down weary and confused. The barrack block was quiet. In the very short time since the bustling Twentieth had left, the isolation was far worse, far more obvious. The legionary voices had cheered the place up until the centurion went missing. Then the chatter and humour went flat. The barrack blocks were now silent, the way they were when he arrived, as though the fort's ghosts had stolen the voices and put them in a sack, and it was only the memory of the living that lingered to unsettle him. He made the stiff finger sign under his blankets lest ghosts were lurking at his bedside. Getting back to his friends in the Second as soon as possible was all that mattered.

The next morning Civius called his fellow centurion from the other Delmatarum century to his office.

"Did he buy your apples?" the soldier said.

Civius smiled.

"I think he is suitably confused," Civius grinned.

"Ah. So, he is yet to prove himself?" the centurion assumed.

"Let the next few convoys pass. This fellow Pinneius is a damn distraction. Put feelers out. I want to know if he is dead or not. Have the Carvetii made a mistake, I wonder if they have not overstepped?" Civius said.

"Better that he is dead," the centurion opined.

"Actually, I disagree with you. But he will report his suspicions if he turns up. Close down our little tolls, let the waggons through," Civius replied.

"That will show up unchanged V's and X's on the manifests. That will raise questions about what Uiliocenon is playing at. Can they not count to five and ten? The baggage masters at Cantiventi will have to be stupid not to notice," the centurion replied.

"Or too busy to worry about it," Civius said.

His comrade centurion raised his eyebrows disbelieving that such an obvious change in pattern would not betray itself to even the most casual eye.

Civius raised his hand to calm the fears.

Have faith brother, and say a prayer to Jupiter. Tell Arco. Make sure he does as he is told. No mistakes, no foul ups, no one is to get greedy, this will blow over. Centurion Pinneius will turn up suitably embarrassed at having fallen off his horse and getting himself lost, cold and wet and our optio Vindex will see where the best interests of his career lie. All will be well. A bit of restraint and calm heads is all that is needed," he ordered.

"As you have commanded me," the centurion acknowledged.

Civius was the senior ranking centurion between them, and he commanded.

## Chapter Fifteen.

## Cantiventi.

Caturiges sidled his way through the throng that had gathered at the quayside eager to see what treasure the Hispaniard's waggon held. Treasure that required an escort to see it safely transferred to the cargo boats. The sight of his priestly robes opened a gap for him, dispensing with the need for polite words. He was young, untested in some of their eyes, but there was not a single soul who would dare to impune his druidic lineage. He eased his way to the front, taking cover behind the local men.

The waggon trundled to a halt at the dock. The soldiers from the fort stood around watching as usual, choosing not to help. The wharf men got up from their tables and chairs, at pains to signal their displeasure at the interrupted game, pocketing the gambled winnings before pilfering hands in the crowd passed their way. There was a murmur in the crowd, and he strained to catch it.

"Auvericus has started melting the lead stone," a man told him, "he is pulling out the metal now."

He tried to judge the mood. This was a step Auvericus had not taken before. It brought possibilities to mind. The wharfingers had the first slab of lead off the waggon and hefted onto the quayside. It shone in the sunlight, like a great flat pike. They unloaded a slab for each of his fingers. The locals murmured. He kept his opinions to himself. In his opinion, shared with Drapisces, the people living under the fort's walls were drifting too easily into becoming little Romans. They had softened. The guttural words of the soldier's tongue as noticeable as Carveti. Mixed phrases that began in Carveti and ended in Latin. It was the same thing each time he came to Cantiventi. Slowly the Romans were turning his people into servants and sellers. They had been conquered by wealth. They were blind. They were lost.

The stone quarrying had been tolerable because in the beginning, when they first built the fort, the Spaniard and others like him, had only been doing what his own people did, gathering the gifts Borwenna left for mortal men to take. A goddess' gentle mercy. It was hard to blame the Romans for doing what the Carveti did too. She left the lead stone on the ground, in little pockets. But then they built the wharf and ships came sailing up the lake to ferry Borwenna's stone away. The Romans were quick to trade and their goods more than made up for grousing over the quantities they took. Why should they be upset? The hills were unconquerable. There were mountains made of lead stone and men could never cut down a mountain.

Except, within a twinkling of time, the Romans had mopped up all the easy to reach stone and had begun to dig down. Down into her flesh. Under the ground where the spirits rested. Making caverns and wooden walkways, bringing oil lamps, buckets and ropes, slaves brought in from foreign places whose tongue no one understood, though their sad, pathetic faces spoke all that was needed to know. They had sown and reaped defeat in distant forests. They were digging into Borwenna herself. Sometimes they went too far, and she breathed death at them, sending corpses to the surface for the miners to think about.

It was not simply about the digging and the taking. Heating the stone for the metal left an unusable residue. The miners cast it aside in heaps as though it did not matter. He wondered at the waste to make these ten slabs of lead. It was only a solitary waggon, today.

Auvericus was doing his best to remain aloof from the heaving and hauling as the lead disappeared into the bowels of the ship. His horse pranced at the landward end of the dock. He waited and watched as the ship's ropes were cast off and coiled up by the sailors. The crowd dispersed, fun over. The wharfingers were back at their table. He followed the crowd back to the vicus still trying to gauge their temper. The Spaniard was just one of them beginning to systematically rape the land. This was beyond taking trees for timber and stone for forts. This was turning into the evisceration of her heart and loins and Borwenna could not defend herself. She would not be here to protect future generations of his people if the Carveti did not take a stand to protect her now.

He found Auvericus settled down to eat and drink in a tavern while his waggon and its guard headed back to his mine up the valley. Caturiges marked him down. He sat and took the ale brought to him without charge by an anxious landlord.

*

Liscus stole a piece of Marcellus' bread and took it outside to think. His messenger was on his way to Deva Victrix. The century was eating. For the present there was only the uncomfortable truth that the centurion was out there somewhere and he, Liscus Aulus Manlio, had failed to find him. He dreaded to imagine what the men might be thinking. Discipline was holding tight, but he could feel a tension, an expectation that his next order would be coming soon. The expectation that as an officer he knew what to do next and worse still, he would be correct in that decision. They ate quietly. Marcellus appeared philosophic; they had done all they could for now.

A waggon trundled through the vicus with an unusually large escort, drawing a crowd along in its tail. A lead waggon most likely. He chewed the fresh bread with its delicious hard crust. There was a posturing trader riding alongside the waggon. He took a dislike to the man.

## Chapter Sixteen.

## Drapisces' hall.

Velio woke up on his bed of the straw and waited for the pain in his side to begin cutting him. It did not come. Daylight filtering through the woven walls brought a brightness that could only mean the sun was shining out there, in the world beyond his cage. He got into a sitting position. His insides felt strong for the first time since the arrow was removed. Optimism pumped like an eager dog. He quietened it down. His legs were still chained to the post, the way they were last night when he fell asleep. The gods had not rescued him. He was going nowhere in a hurry. Raising his left arm, he made dummy strokes with an invisible sword testing the limits of his wound. He stood up and tried with more effort. The wound curled its lip, bared its teeth but did not bite. The 'hammer-blow' attack would be impossible, but if he really was going to have to fight Scribono, defensive parries would serve to keep him alive, except, what if Scribono used that same hammer-blow attack on him? Not having a shield would expose him but be less draining on his slender strength. He would have to outwit the deserter with faster, close in, swordplay. There might only be a couple of openings before he was worn down.

*'Shouldn't be difficult,'* he snickered to himself, *'he's Brutus Carruso's cousin. Probably the same sort of block head.*

And then what? Junius Cita stepping in on his blind side to finish what Scribono had started? He spat into the straw and kicked the phlegm with his boot. If it went that way, then so be it. The Fates would either cut his thread in this heathen place, or he would get out. Voccia's face, in tears at the news of his death, flashed in his head. He pushed her away. This was not the time for sentimentality or softness.

*'Why did you order Carruso to kill me, Hanno? I thought we were friends? Over all these years you kept that secret. We have a partnership in Gaul with Gallus. Why Hanno, why?'*

He mourned the cold sick feeling that he had lost a friend. There was no answer to that one, not in this place.

*'Hanno Drusus Glaccus Ticinus, you owe me an explanation. Or it's just a lie to bait me,'* he considered, and like that alternative better.

But the cold, sick feeling remained. Somehow, it did not feel it was a lie. Scribono's face had been triumphant when he spoke. Footsteps crunched outside the hut. He hunkered back down, hoping it was the old woman with food.

*

Drapisces beckoned Caturiges to come closer to him. Caturiges bowed to him before taking the seat offered. He listened to Caturiges' tale of woe, keeping his face as still as he could manage. No good would come from inciting the priest into white mouthed foamings. Rather, it was about choices. Scribono and Junius were keeping their opinions to themselves for once. The prisoner appeared to be absorbing their attention. 'The brave soldier,' as he was beginning to think of him, was a useful ally of sorts, unforeseen, unexpected; ultimately doomed, but useful for the moment, nevertheless. The trouble with young Caturiges was, he wanted to kill every Roman, he lost sight of the strength of their legions. Still, the news that the mining was developing into melting the ore into pure metal was insulting, and he would have to act on it. Perhaps he should let Caturiges fight the brave soldier and make Scribono watch. It would do the Romans good to see it was Drapisces who decided who lived and died under this roof. He looked into the fire chewing its way through the alder logs and hid there for a while to think and let Caturiges fret.

*'Caturiges kills the soldier and dedicates his body to the mother goddess for her desecration by the Romans. Thereby Scribono gets revenge for the family insult he speaks of, and I can use all of it as reason to attack the mine and kill them all. Word will spread that we will not tolerate anything more than the gathering of the ore. More mines will be attacked. The Brigantes will hear that the Carveti still have balls to fight. They will send emissaries and together we will join to destroy the fort on the lakeside, taking back control of the hills, fort by fort.'*

It pleased him to think the dream. Taking back hills that had been lost. Caturiges coughed. He looked up at the twenty-six year old man. Caturiges was tall and strong. He could have been a natural fighter had he not been drawn to the gods and spent so little time practising with weapons.

"Caturiges, son of Hanarval, get your sword and you, Scribono bring the Roman. Caturiges is going to show us the power of the gods and take his anger out on the Roman."

Scribono stared at Drapisces, anger flashed in his eyes.

"He is mine to kill. For Brutus. My revenge," he snarled.

The word tumbled out. Drapisces stood up from the fire.

"I have made my decision. I want to see the Roman go down to Caturiges' sword," he said.

Junius laid his hand on Scribono's arm.

"Let it go this time brother," he hissed.

Drapisces was too powerful to disobey. The look of those eyes over that disfigured face was enough.

He whispered another thought, "give him his own sword to fight with. Do that last thing for a former brother. You will get it back when he dies."

"Going soft Junius?" Scribono snapped.

Junius bared his teeth and pulled his comrade away from Caturiges who was now beginning to square up to the two of them.

"That's right, I'm going soft," he pretended.

Velio was waiting as Scribono opened the hut door. Scribono took a key from his belt and showed it to him.

"What's this?" Velio queried.

"Don't get your hopes up centurion. The chieftain wants you to fight his priest. Don't expect another meal. He is young and strong, and he hates us Romans."

Scribono knelt and unlocked the shackles. Velio fought back the urge to kick the deserter in the face. Looking outside the hut he could see Junius Cita holding his sword by his side.

"And if I win?" he said.

"You won't, but if you do then I'll kill you for Brutus," Scribono retorted.

"I'll look forwards to you trying to do that," he jibbed.

Junius handed him the sword. Their eyes met and the shade of something akin to encouragement flitted across Junius' face. A quick inspection told him his gladius was undamaged. He hefted it and rolled his wrist re-engaging the weight to his arm. The wound stayed silent.

'*Perhaps there is a chance,*' he dared to hope.

A crowd of Carvetii began gathering in the space between Drapisces' hall, the hut and other smaller halls of his warriors. Women and wide eyed children peering past and through the gaps in the assembling circle of men. Drapisces and the man he was going to fight entered the ring. The priest was exactly as Scribono had described; young, fit and strong with the familiar madness of his creed filling his eyes. Filled with the simmering anger of the righteous. He stood bare chested, covered in a myriad of intricacies; blue circles and spirals signalling the cultural rejection of the blood stained, toga wearing, man before him. The skin was tanned and the muscles solid. Fastidiously combed long dark hair, beard and moustaches touched his shoulders and collar bones. A twisted rope torc of silver gleamed around his throat. Thin braids of woven hair were decorated with what looked like slender tubes of the same rolled metal. His leather woollen trousers fastened at his waist with a broad leather band that was part belt, part armour rising up to defend his midriff. The leather itself was embellished with repeating designs of serpents and spirals. Everything about him spoke of prestige and nothing of a warrior trained in killing.

Velio felt the first positive flicker of hope in his chest. There were probably umpteen men standing behind him who would be far more deadly to his long-term survival than this one. If the wound behaved, he was in with a chance; this was possible. It would have to be done quickly. He had no time to waste in prolonged combat. Without a shield to block his right-hand side, all the impact would be coming at his injured left flank. He doubted the wound had been healing long enough to withstand what was coming at it. Anything more than a couple of flurries of the sword arm and he knew it would bleed. He resisted the desire to nurse it. If it opened up, then it opened up. If he was beaten, it was not going to matter. He went on the offence, looking for weakness in the priest's head.

"For the Senate and the People of Rome. For the glory of the Valeria Victrix, The Boar legion. The best legion in the army of Rome," he called out saluting his sword to the sky, hoping his braggadocio would rile Scribono and Junius too.

Anything to foment unplanned reaction. Anything to seize an advantage. There was an answering growl from the more mature warriors of the Carvetii, but he did not care. He was not fighting them, yet. Stepping into the centre of the circle he began circling the priest.

"Kill him Caturiges," Drapisces said, "and show us the power."

Velio sensed a flicker of support but also an understated challenge from chieftain to his own man. But there was something else in there too. A tinge of unease, uncertainty, perhaps, now that Velio had a sword on his hand? Or fear that the gods might not be listening? The Carvetii warriors at his back went very quiet but he could feel their hot breath.

*'He's not certain he can do this.'*

He concentrated on the man in front of him, grasped the thought and held it like a rope.

*'Aesculapius be with me. Touch my wound with your healing fingers and lend strength to my body. Mars stand at my back, and I will honour you with this fool's blood. Jupiter thou Best and Greatest, I honour you now and always,'* he sent his own prayer to the gods.

Caturiges was armed with the kind of long slashing sword he had seen many times before in the years up at the wall. All the tribes favoured longer blades than the gladius. They never seemed to learn the superiority of a short sword and a big shield over a long sword and small shield. The priest had no buckler. Evidently, he did not own one or was not going to be lent one. It was going to be an initiation of man on man. He was right-handed which suited Velio.

Caturiges had never seen a Roman centurion up close. This one was not a tall man. Perhaps in his early forties, not much more. Still a fit fighter. The head was once brown haired. A mid brown, not the dark colour of the north, but now greying at the temples and retreating from the forehead. The eyes were hard. A nondescript colour under brows lowering for battle. They were also assured, calculating, capable of transmitting forgiveness for an offender's honest contrition. The eyes were a warning. The straight nose was undamaged by service in his army or by war. The lips were thin and determined, hiding the teeth from sight. The heavy stubble on his face gave him the animal intensity of a poised and calmly waiting bear; secure in its place under the skies. The shoulders were thick on a lean frame. The forearms well-muscled. There were none of the serious scars a soldier would be proud to show off on those forearms, only a couple of faded worm-lines. The hilt of the short sword seemed to nest in his paw. The dirty tunic did not hide the bearing of a soldier inured to hardship.

Caturiges licked his lips, ignoring the signs, seeing instead the sort of glory and praise names for killing such a man. He was still enjoying that thought when Velio jousted his left hand blade out and flicked the end of his sword. The blades chimed. A murmur rippled through the crowd. Caturiges realised the odd grip was something new. His blade moved a fraction at the impact. Velio smiled at him.

"Come and kill me boy," he challenged in rough Brigantes, "before your breeches stink more than they do already."

The crowd growled at that barb. Caturiges took the hook and swallowed, wading forward with high angled, head swipes. Velio deflected them relying on the superior power of his wrist, smiling to provoke Caturiges, stepping back to draw him forward, trying to fight with his elbow steady, not moving his arm too much, waiting for the tearing of the flesh and muscle. If he could make the priest rush, he might lose balance. The faster he came on, the wilder and less co-ordinated his attacks would become. It only needed a single opening, and it would be over. That was all he had the strength for; enough to work a single opening. The longer this went on the weaker he has going to get. There was no time for the usual 'Pinneius' élan and dash. Soon the wound would begin fighting him too.

Caturiges was a swift learner and sent his blade in at knee height, seeking to inflict a crippling leg wound. Velio blocked and feinted a counter jab, but it was only a threat. The Carveti was not quite close enough. A shield would have allowed him to step in, absorbing the blow that would leave the body open for the killing strike. Caturiges halted, his alarm flashing on his face as he almost danced out of reach from the point of the gladius. Then he inched backwards. Velio fixed him with a stare, testing whether the priest could be conned into forgetting his guard. He beckoned him with his right hand to attack. Caturiges stopped to consider. Velio decided it was time to finish it. He stepped forward and closed the gap to the distance he wanted and began flicking his blade against the tip of the longer weapon, pushing the blade repeatedly aside with the outside edge of his own, as if it was annoying him. Tapping the iron like a steel woodpecker. The hard, unfriendly clashing sound had an unsettling timbre. The priest began defending. Velio sensed his poise had gone.

*'Enough of this nonsense,'* he snarled in his head.

He smiled his dourest, wolf's welcome at the priest, and in a flurry too fast for the young druid to react to, disengaged the sword tip and buried the gladius just above the top edge of the protective belt. A frightening, huge wound. He pulled it out so fast, blood took a heartbeat's delay to follow the blade, spilling down the priest's belly and onto his clothes. Velio did not have to do any more, the boy was but short steps from death, but he pushed the tip of the gladius past Caturiges' head, and ripped back, severing the major artery in his neck and stepped away. His favourite stroke. Achilles himself might have applauded.

He turned around as Caturiges collapsed in a welter of blood, seeking the face of the strongest warrior he could find to challenge. All his earlier restraint and concern for the arrow wound fled his control. The man he wanted was standing only a scant few paces from him. The fist on the shaft of his hunting spear was white knuckled in fury and disappointment. The eyes bored back at him, almost glassy with intent. Velio spread out his arms, fingers stretched on one side and sword pointing on the other.

"Roma Victa," Velio told him

Suddenly, he had the strength to kill another Carveti while he had the chance. His own tell-tale signs of battle rage murmured in his ear, and he pushed the siren enticements aside. He could not fight them all.

*'Let them make the next move,'* he coaxed himself to stay alive.

Caturiges was face down on the grass, twitching and bleeding. The silence around the space was like a cloak. Drapisces stared at the young man lying at his feet and then lifted his gaze to Velio. He waited for Drapisces to give the signal to end this charade. His side rebelled and the wet sensation returned.

*'What now?'* he wondered, *'are they going to fight me like a gladiator until one of them kills me? Balls of Dis, I will kill every last one of you. Hear me Mars.'*

"And you said Brutus Carruso was going to kill him?"

Junius Cita turned and mocked Scribono. The deserter folded his arms.

"That boy was no legionary," Scribono replied.

He glared at Caturiges who was still twitching on the grass.

"True," Velio answered.

"Put the sword down centurion," Junius Cita said.

The tone of voice betrayed him. Velio heard it distinctly. Spears were pointing at him. The soldier stepped forward within striking range. His own traitorous gladius strapped to his belt, hands hanging loose by his side. Velio turned and looked at Drapisces. The chieftain's face was stony and calculating.

"The sword, centurion. Please," Junius repeated.

"If I am going to die, I'll do it here and now with my own sword in my hand," he bit back.

"I'm happy to oblige you, centurion," Scribono pulled his sword.

"Scribono, you will stand fast. I have a feeling the centurion has not even warmed up. And even with an arrow hole in his side he is faster than you are," Junius ordered.

It was the same tone. Velio felt sure of it now, Junius must have been an officer of some kind, perhaps a tesserarius or a signifer, a cornicen maybe. Possibilities beckoned: perhaps the former Junius

Cita could be reached. The Junius Cita who had achieved a degree of rank and knew how to order men and follow orders.

"I'm going to kill him for Brutus," Scribono snarled.

His face worked up in a mask of rage now that blood had been spilled.

"Did you ever fight Brutus?" Junius asked Velio.

Velio saw the curiosity behind the question. Scribono halted to listen as well.

"I gave him some lessons to speed up his hands. We did not bout," he replied.

A soldier should know instructors rarely bouted swords, even practice ones, with common legionaries. Far too tempting for a soldier with a grudge to take it too far. Except most instructors were too adept to take a blade from a legionary. In the back perhaps, a coward's blow on a dark night in the tent lines perhaps, but never in the belly, fighting one on one in daylight.

"I am not Brutus," Scribono persisted.

Junius ignored him and put his hand out for the sword, trusting Velio would not take it off at the wrist. Velio ran it flat across his forearm, leaving a smear of Caturiges' life there for everyone to see. He raised the arm to the crowd to show them the blood, to rub in his victory. They tensed like wild cats, barely holding back from the provocation.

"Take him back to the hut. Chain him up. He will be sacrificed to the earth mother. The gods have judged Caturiges. I must consider their message to us. It is not a good omen. He should have killed the Roman," Drapisces intervened.

Velio smirked in Scribono's direction.

"You and me. It will need to be another day, mule," he flyted.

Scribono glared back daggers but dared no more than that. It was obvious Scribono was, like his cousin, a humble legionary.

Velio decided he could work on Junius Cita. Cita must have guilt buried in that head of his, it was bound to be there. The Sixth were a good legion. Desertion was a huge step for an officer of any rank. Particularly when there was no real fighting going on. It was not like the country north of Antoninus Pius' wall. Down here it was peaceful. So, what had driven him to throw away his pension and the chance of a decent piece of farmland? Junius Cita might be worth saving. Junius Cita might be his road out of this.

## Chapter Seventeen.

### Deva Victrix barracks.

Voccia called Orann to her side. As usual he was smelling of horses. The 'smelly horse fool,' they used to call him at home. Happier sleeping in the stables with the horses for company than under father's roof. Not so stupid though. He had evaded death at the hands of her assailant Segontio, the man who raped her. A point she had not missed.

He did his best to wipe his boots clean of the hazards from the stable, but he could not wipe the Votadini in him away. The guard at the entrance held him there until Voccia supplied the required permission. She sent a servant to relay it, in deference to Velio's instruction that servants do these tasks. She was 'Domina' to every slave and servant in the house. Well, Domina was pregnant and Domina wanted warm reassurance and care, not power to make his servants happy or miserable. Orann, even if he was not aware of the fact, was the closest link she had to her old life. Soldiers tended to be denied permission to marry. She could see the reason for that even if it seemed abnormal for a warrior not to live with his family close to him. In this strange Roman world many things were wrong. And neither was she a citizen of Rome. So Domina, was Domina under sufferance. Not quite the real thing: tolerated because Centurion Pinneius said so. And the servants loved her discomfort. All except Marcellus, his soldier servant. He accepted her, but then he had known her from the fort they called Trimontium. He knew she was a woman of status in the Votadini world.

Three days after Segontio, the brute who raped her, was hung up outside the gateways at Trimontium for his tribe to see, Velio came to visit her. She knew the soldiers were leaving because he had already told her so, and she had rebuked him, leaving him sitting, ashen faced in his office in the fort. He came this time with a contrite face. Their last embrace became a kiss that became this growing child in her belly. And then he marched away exactly as he said he was going to. Back to his beloved legion.

Her elder brother Tianos returned from service with the war leader Asuvad to take over the farm she had been watching grow increasingly unkempt since the murder of their parents. Segontio's uprising, though it had failed, had led to the destruction of Trimontium's sister fort in the west, Blatobulgium, and it had also served to put Tianos and her on opposite banks of the same stream. Or, perhaps, if she asked herself truthfully, was it her love for Velio which had put them there? She did not care either way. Besides Tianos had the right to farm father's land and would never yield. Her other, younger brothers would do whatever he said, until they drifted away, or he drove them. The swelling evidence of her condition prompted bitter arguments with him and one day she could stand no more. She told Orann to ready horses and without much affection, left Tianos to the fields, the cattle and the politics of a land where the legions had weighed the balance and decided to pull back to their stone wall. The hostile tribes further north celebrated whilst her own pondered a future without Rome's casual affluence.

Orann guided her south. She was glad to go. She expected emotions to get the better of her as the home valley disappeared behind the folds of the kind green hills but when Orann gave her the chance to stop and take a final look, it was a pretty view but the cord had snapped. Perhaps the different man Tianos had become, and the graves of her parents had cut it?

The Roman road led them down past empty forts and empty signalling turrets to the stone wall. They passed through with the soldiers mistaking them for a couple, which was not so strange for their ages were similar. Then they passed through a thick network of outposts lying south of the wall. Enquiries brought them to Deva Victrix. Six and a half and a half months after she thought they had said their final goodbye she told Orann to knock at the gateway to the barracks on the river and ask if they had heard of Centurion Velio Pinneius.

Orann answered his summons and paused at the villa entrance while a distinguished looking officer left in a hurry. The legionary guard crashed out a salute which the officer acknowledged but did not halt to return. He left, swishing his cloak tails back to his domain in the principia. A servant coughed. He turned.

"Domina will see you," she said.

He followed into the atrium. Voccia smiled with her lips, but her eyes were worried. She beckoned him to sit beside her. Immediately putting him on edge.

"That was the centurion in charge of the headquarters," she opened. He was no wiser as to what that meant.

"He is the legate's hunting dog. When he barks the soldiers jump," she enlightened.

*'Everyone jumps when anyone barks here,'* he wanted to joke.

"He is a friend of my husband," she went on.

That part stuck in his throat. He liked the centurion. The centurion was kind and honourable, would have helped him join the legion as he wished, except she commanded he was her servant, and he was to do what she said. He was not free to act like a Votadini warrior and serve the legions. That had been her final word. In return for faithfully guiding her to this place through hostile Brigantes territory, her sole concession was that he could don a Roman style tunic as a symbol that he was a friend of Rome.

Thankfully the centurion had four horses of his own plus those of Marcellus to keep him occupied. She called him husband but there was no wedding ceremony, no invocation to gods and ancestors. No public declaration of any kind. Without it, they were as married as two horses in the stable.

"The headquarters centurion had told me my husband is missing," she got the words out and clenched the knuckles of her hands.

"But I am not to worry, he said they will find him. The legate himself commands it," she forced bright words, "Orann, I want you to go back with the soldiers who brought the message and help them look for my husband. They are soldiers. They know how to search but they do not know how to look. I have asked for you to be allowed to join the riders back to their fort at Cantiventi. It was somewhere near there my husband was last seen. It has been agreed. You will be allowed to take a spear and shield to protect yourself. You will leave tomorrow. You make take a horse from the stable only if you swear to bring it back unharmed."

*'How can I do that?'* he wondered.

"Yes, my lady," he replied.

*

Marcellus gave a low whistle to draw Liscus' attention. The optio came over so they could speak in private. The camp at Cantiventi had grown more gossips and fox-ears than he believed possible due to too much time sitting on their arses watching cargo boats plying up and down the lake.

"The messengers are returning from Deva. They have arrived at the head of the lake, should be up here once they have watered the horses," he said.

"I wonder if Servius Albinius is going to march or whether he will leave us to sort it?" replied Liscus.

"I have four asses that say he sends men to help. A torture detail at the very least," Marcellus speared a tiny bet for fun.

"Your bet is covered. I think old Albinius is such a ruthless old dog he will only march if he finds out our centurion has been killed by the Carvetii. Their gods will be of no use to them if that happens. He will paint the grass red with them," Liscus said accepting the bet.

"A dedicated torture unit is useful, don't you think? It takes a certain kind of soldier to do it I always think," Marcellus mused, "chopping heads and nailing them up is one thing but prolonging it so they can tell you something useful, that is quite a skill."

Liscus licked his lips, "careful Velio does not get to hear you have an unfulfilled ambition."

"Me? A torturer? Never, Jupiter be my judge. I was just saying, that is all," Marcellus backtracked.

He sniggered.

"You could read them one of the monthly reports to headquarters. We would have the centurion back like that," Liscus clicked his fingers.

Marcellus halted at the invisible line betwixt the second in command of the century and a legionary with special privileges. It was time to surrender with best grace possible. He signalled defeat.

Liscus winked.

"Tell me when they arrive. The camp praefectus over there will want to hear what they have to say. Four asses, Marcellus, I hope you are good for it?."

*'The centurion would kick your arse. He signs off those reports as his own'* Marcellus breathed inside, *'optios, nothing but errand boys masquerading as centurions in waiting, the whole lot of them, they think they know it all.'*

The couriers reported to Cantiventi headquarters building. Liscus and Marcellus and the Morinorum commander waited for the message from Servius Albinius.

"You are telling me the legate's instruction boils down to 'get on with it?' Am I correct?" the praefectus spat.

He puffed his cheeks, dissatisfied. The junior officer adjusted the lower edge of his lorica armour, Marcellus reckoned it was a purely nervous gesture. The tesserarius was a seasoned veteran of the century and despite the commander's huffing, Liscus as a legion optio was the officer to whom he was charged with making the report. He flicked his gaze to Liscus and the praefectus and nodded affirmation.

"What did he say exactly Plautius," Liscus coaxed.

Plautius bit his lower lip for a split second and stood taller in his boots.

"The legate said, and I am ordered to quote him verbatim, 'in the old republican days, the Scipios would have decimated any unit that returned without their commander for cowardice,' sir," Plautius said, keeping his expression as stony as he could.

The Morinorum fort commander pursed his mouth and kept his counsel. 'Getting on with it' sounded infinitely preferable to the solution preferred by the Scipios.

“In those words, Plautius?” Liscus said.

“In exactly those words, sir,” Plautius replied.

“Anything else Plautius?” Liscus probed.

Plautius swallowed before answering.

“I don't think the legate was pleased at the news, sir.”

“Well, I think he has made that clear,” Marcellus chipped in, unable to resist.

Plautius flicked a panicked glance at Marcellus.

“Marcellus, this is not the time,” Liscus warned.

“You may stand down,” the commander intervened, and took back control of the room.

The tesserarius left the three of them alone.

“He really does value Centurion Pinneius doesn’t he?” the commander mused.

Marcellus reckoned it was possibly the most, detached, inane remark he had ever heard.

“We will return to the hill fort in the morning,” Liscus replied. Servius Albinius did not make idle comparisons and Plautius’ worried look when Marcellus made his fatuous remark only emphasised the gravity of it.

Outside the fort Marcellus ran into Orann standing by a horse he recognised as Velio’s.

“My mistress Voccia has sent me to help you find the centurion,” he blurted out, “I will do anything I can,” he promised.

“Good Orann. Things are looking serious, and a good Votadini like you will help.”

Marcellus clapped his shoulder and took him over to the marching camp where the century tents stood in serried lines.

Liscus was going to have to sort this out with or without the help of the Morinorum. He felt his spirits climb. Orann was a good lad. And he spoke the tongues.

## <u>Chapter Eighteen.</u>

### <u>Argentomagus.</u>

The procurator had to read the note several times before the gist of all the repercussions hit him. The game was up. The unthinkable had happened. The new owners of Priscus' estate had struck a supply deal with the centurion commanding the local vexillation of the Eighth legion, Octava Augusta. If those two old soldiers managed to get a harvest off the vine and into storage, the army would have a very good and selfish reason protect their own interests. And his chances of running them off their property diminished. Besides, these two were not ordinary dog-faced legionaries. The local centurions would rally to help comrades from the old Twentieth. He scowled at their damnable bonds.

*'May the barbarians rape your womenfolk while you are tied to burning posts,'* he fumed.

He sat back in his chair pondering the difficulties. The obvious way out was, inevitably, poison. Short and simple. If a doctored mushroom was good enough for the Empress Livia to send Augustus to his ancestors, it was good enough for him. Poison it would be. There was sufficient hemlock and alternatives to hand to do the needful. This army contract was the second time they had surprised him. If nothing else, they were proving to be stubborn and quick footed. The first nasty surprise had been acquiring the services of a local winemaker. One who was too good in his art to be bribed into joining his net of retaliation, unlike his delightfully deceitful brother. But this needed careful planning and preparation.

*'My friends,'* he would say, *'we have begun with a bad start, mea culpa.*

*Let me make amends. Come and be my guests for an evening feast.'*

He practised how the invitation might go. The ideas came thick and fast.

*'How about a note of invitation before the harvest, Durus? Do it before they bring the crop in,'* and in his position he was well placed to step forward in the guise of concerned benefactor to administer the estate and its reputation.

*'Isolate the honest winemaker. A small slander might help. It's small apples if there are peripheral casualties, better so in fact, to hide the true targets. Word has it one of the decurions from the vexillation is on friendly terms. Why not roll him up in it too? Spread the target wider than the obvious. If the estate has debts, get in early and offer a loan. Recouping it after their unfortunate demise makes everything sound legitimate. Oh, indeed Durus, oh indeed you can.'*

He rubbed his hands together, feeling his mood perk up. The note was troubling, but he had a solution and half the problem already resolved. He stood up and admired himself in the mirror. Procurator in a small town. Smoothing an eyebrow, he would stay on after the deed was done before he sought a move.

"Durus Decimus, you are wasted here," he said to the mirror.

His mildly distorted image leered back at him.

"And now, the Procurator of Argentomagus shall eat," he announced to the room, "there is much to do."

It could all have been so different. The gods, the Fates, had given him a left leg that was prone to weakness. He could never have made it in the legions. Even an 'eques' has to get off his horse and let it rest at some point. Cavalry troops must walk sometimes. It was a sour thing to swallow. His grandfather, Gaius Decimus, had wanted him to serve: Father, not so much. Politics was father's calling. They used to argue and bicker.

"Durus must train for the army. He can overcome his leg," Grandfather's war cry.

"Durus will do better if he gets into the administration," Father's inevitable counter.

His teenage development decided his path. The leg was a liability to a budding warrior. It always would be. No amount of training and running could make up the shortfall. It was always going to limit him. No soldiers would follow a man who never knew when his leg might lose strength and make him fall. And he could not keep up with marching men on foot. It required only an interlude in the villa gardens speaking openly to Grandfather to set his path straight. The leg, he said, would lend character to a budding politician and servant to the people. Grandfather Gaius was no fool. He was disappointed but he had eyes in his head and could see the way the wind blew through the orchards. The storm of anger Durus expected never came. Grandfather put his hand out and rested it on his shoulder.

"Then we must make you the best horseman you can be. You come from a long line of equites. You will master horsemanship. The knees are what counts on a horse. How you use it remains with you."

Thirteen years old and he dared to make his first peace treaty. The old grey man of the garden put a gold aureus in his hand and sent him off to the stables to choose a pony. Old man Gaius had no intention of giving up on the lad. Young Durus would, in time, have authority to order legions and armies even if he could not serve in them. In that, both he and the boy's father, Baculus, were at one.

That winter, when Saturnalia was beginning to fade into a warm memory, and the oil lamps in the villa were still fighting battles with early dark evenings and poor weather, Gaius went to the ancestors and took with him the spirit of the last of the real soldiers in his family. Durus got his bequeathed cavalry helmet and sword and a personal letter. Things that had lived on pegs on Grandfather's bedroom wall suddenly lay on his bed now. After the funerary rites Father buried himself in politicking.

He drifted within himself, uncertain what to do now that old grey beard was no longer present in the gardens. Horses seemed to be the answer and he took to them every waking moment, becoming adept and at ease in the saddle. The empty space left by Grandfather was filled by the thrill of strong, beautiful horses that took him flying to the limits of his skill. They seemed to understand his pain and carried him away from it in warm afternoons of exertion and fun. The diversion did not last. On a rain swept day, when his friends left and his mount was dried off and stalled back under the care of the grooms, he felt something inside him change, the moment so clear, like a fever that releases its victim, lifting and departing in an instant. The spark left him. What use are the varying forms of power Father and Grandfather argued over if they cannot hold back time or death, bring happiness, wealth, and villas in the country?

He tried the normal period of military service because, after all, he was an eques and Grandfather had always wanted him to serve under the standards. But a kindly tribune who remembered Grandfather took him aside.

"My dear boy, you are not cut out for the Germania frontier. The emperor thanks you for your desire to serve Rome. Best leave the fighting to others. I will write on your record that you are fit to serve the people."

And he was allowed to 'retire without serving,' his honour intact. A kind act indeed.

Baculus sent him to Gaul. To learn the basic arts of administration before he tried to rise up the class to higher honours. The senate was not an impossible dream though it was a distant peak. Procurator of Argentomagus would be a short, useful, stepping stone to positions in wealthier towns. But against Father's well planned out strategies he rather enjoyed it. The silver trade was blossoming, and profits were abundant. The armies needed coin. At least they needed silver bar for the mint in Lugdunum to issue coin to the army. Even the generals issued coin at times to their men: especially the army of Germania. Then, Baculus passed: he returned home once more and found the villa and gardens even emptier than before. He swore not to return to this place where every sight brought him painful joy. Mother wept but he refused to bend. When he came back to Argentomagus it seemed fresh and unblemished by unhappy memories, empty gardens and the ghosts of the past. He dallied with women of suitable class, and others less so, but chose none of them. He decided to make it his town. In every sense of the word.

*

After he had eaten, he called for his most placid mount and set off for the estate of Priscus with a four man auxiliary escort. The road west led down into the valley, through the town's double wall and ditch. He let the men talk as they travelled, dropping in and out of their predictably women centric conversation. The ridge above the villa came into view. Keeping the mounts to a walk he took his time to check out the state of industry as the entrance gates drew closer. There were slaves working out in the vineyard, two men on horses nearby talking together, a hum of insects, the colours of the early flowering grasses and plants and the recumbent, benevolent peace of a place where all was as it should be. It was not what he hoped for at all.

He passed Priscus' roadside tomb before turning in through the gateway and the long ascent up the estate road to the villa. The villa's shutters were open, the adjacent buildings, the storage and maturation barns were tidy and their doors wide open to the warm day. Voices were raised: he listened to the tone, it sounded good-natured bantering. A whistled signal announced him.

*'Soldier's habits,'* he assumed.

An enormous, shaggy deer hound came from the nearest barn, its head up, ears pricked forward, tail wagging in placid, slow waves. It looked a young dog, eager to make friends with strangers coming to its yard. He took a look at the maw and dismounted, holding out his ring bedecked hand. His horse, less wary, dropped his head down to commune with a brief touch of nostrils on nose. The dog sniffed his hand and gazed up at him, tail still batting back and fro but giving no closer affection. He lifted his eyes from this brown descendant of the wolf. Gallus came striding out following the dog. Hanno arrived from another direction. Together they bared their own teeth in careful, diplomatic smiles. He handed his reins to his closest guard.

"Hail Gallus Tiomaris and Hanno Glaccus," he called, "you have been busy, I see."

"Hail Procurator," Gallus replied.

"Procurator," Hanno chimed.

Decimus waited to see whether the secrets of the villa were to be revealed to him. The wafer thin moment of invitation passed; evidently, they were not willing to let him inside. They took him instead to a table set in the shade with an excellent view of both the road into the estate and the close fields of vines where the two mounted overseers and the visible slaves toiled in the morning's rising shimmer. The passage of a few weeks had apparently done something to temper Gallus Tiomaris. Yet Decimus wagered in that demeanour lay a fighter and brawler best avoided. The marginally younger of the two, Hanno Glaccus, had a great deal more polish about him. The acquired calm of an officer no doubt. All those years of authority impregnated themselves into the way he conducted himself. Talking inside would have been preferable. He rolled the way the dice landed. He smiled, it was time to make the pitch and sell the lie.

"You know, I do not want it said that as procurator I do not do my bit to support the local businesses of our noble veterans. New ventures take time to grow. You are your own legion now, finding your feet in the ways of commerce. It can be a skirmish, let me tell you both. But hopefully one without the need for bloodshed."

He pretended a fraternal laugh and hoped they would join in. Hanno gave him half a chuckle. Gallus' eyes wandered to the dog lying at his feet. It raised its eyes at him and beat the earth with its tail. He ploughed on.

"My spies tell me you have agreed a contract with the local garrison even before the grapes are picked. Congratulations. The reputation of these fields goes before you. I worry you will think we got off on the wrong foot. About the slaves and the state of the villa when you arrived, and so forth. I have men making enquiries about who committed the looting and the theft of slaves. Please let me assure you there will be heads on poles, if necessary, skin laid bare to the whip if that's what it takes to return citizens' rightful property."

Hanno glanced at Gallus, *'are you buying this bull?'* he wondered.

The old hastiliarius was wearing his usual phlegmatic expression, the one for passing or failing recruits under training. Hanno gave up trying to guess what Gallus was thinking. Velio was much better at working out what was going on behind those eyes. The procurator was oozing charm and tact from his pores. He wanted to vomit.

*'Sleazy, little fat vermin,'* he adjudged.

He sipped from the cup of water, letting Durus Decimus chunter on with his attempt to build a stockade out of sand.

"I came to invite you to come and dine with me. I can see the grapes are colouring up nicely. It will not be too long before you will be too busy for socialising. I know it well. Priscus was often a hermit here on the estate at picking and crushing time. The best sign of the quality of the harvest was his face when he finally did ride into the vicus for a chat," Decimus prattled.

Gallus stiffened.

"You and Priscus were friends?" he queried and folded his arms.

Hanno bit his tongue. Gallus was never more dangerous than when he spoke this way, bringing you on as if you had a great wisdom and he considered himself privileged to receive it.

"Oh indeed. We debated the empire over many a flask of his most excellent wine. I offered to buy the estate, did you know?" Decimus affirmed.

"Did you?" Gallus smiled his executioner's smile.

Hanno sat back and watched Gallus sizing up this fat little rat.

"Indeed, I did. There are other well-established estates around here. Plenty of good vines to be had and the like. But," Decimus wagged his finger, "I took a fancy to Priscus' estate and once it was in here," he tapped his temple with his forefinger, "well, you understand, I could not get the idea out again."

Decimus paused, "it is such pretty ground."

"It must have been a shock when he died," Gallus sympathised.

Hanno covered his mouth, smoothing his face with his hand.

*'Really Gallus, you're taking the piss now,'* he tried not to laugh.

"I was relieved he passed it on to his wife. A good woman but she could not keep control. Her overseers took her for a ride. She had to sell. I made her a very, very good offer and she turned me down. Really, I was generous to her. More than if it had been Priscus himself," Durus Decimus admitted.

He drank, gathering his thoughts, recalling his outrage that the woman had the temerity to reject his bid. He could feel heat warming his face. He swallowed more water to keep calm.

"And then you heard she had sold it to me?" Gallus intervened.

Hanno watched intent.

"It was very frustrating. I do like this land. But now that I have met you both, I can see it is good hands. So come and dine with me. I want to buy the best white and red you produce each year," Decimus declaimed.

Hanno leaned forward.

"I am sure we can reach a mutually acceptable price, Durus," he said.

Gallus nodded, keeping his counsel. Decimus got up, ready to leave.

"I will send a messenger nearer the time," he said.

He fiddled with his toga, "if you two gentlemen ever decide to sell up and move on, perhaps you will be good enough to let me make the first bid. I promise you, you would not be disappointed."

"There are three of us," said Gallus, "our brother Velio still serves but discharges in the next month or so. I expect we will be in Argentomagus for a while, Durus," he replied.

Durus Decimus nodded. He made firm arm shakes and took the horse reins back from one of his men.

"Such splendid country, don't you think," he said.

He waved his arm around at the scenery, and spurred out of the courtyard. His four men followed sending up the dust in a tiny cloud.

"Eat his food, sell him wine but never turn your back on that one, Hanno," Gallus said.

"He wanted the estate and she turned him down. Sounds like a freely made admission of guilt to me, Gallus," he replied.

He stared out at the fields and the rows of heavy foliaged vines.

"Do you know where she is Gallus? Where she went after she sold you this place? Was she going to move into the vicus and buy a nice villa with servants to look after her? See out her days tending her flowers, making pots of honey?" Hanno asked.

Gallus sniffed at Hanno's pleasant fiction.

"I think she's dead Hanno. I think that bastard had her killed because she rejected his offer," he answered.

"You think she could be lying out there?" Hanno asked, nodding to the vineyard.

Gallus shrugged and walked away leaving Hanno surveyed the slaves working, oblivious to their conversation, and made the stiff finger sign to counter whatever evil Durus Decimus had sown. It was not too late to search for her body and perform the rites:

appease her spirit. They had made the suovetaurilia sacrifice honestly, with open hearts and more reverence than either of them had felt in many campaigns, but if there was an unhappy ghost present in the ground it probably had not been accepted. A piaculum prayer might put the mistake right. But only if she really was lying out in the fields. Gallus might be wrong. But if she was, the thought she might raise a curse on the crop gave him the shudders.

## Chapter Nineteen.

## Auvericus' lead mine.

The oil lamps flickered. The slave inhaled: the moving air was still stifling and hot, but it was a tiny bit fresher. He fixed his gaze on the dance of the farthest little flame as it bowed and bobbed and settled once more to become a yellow spearhead and decided it must be blowing up top for the effect to reach down the gullet of the beast to where he was working. The Beast was their name for her, and they feared her. If there was a scrap of food, from the scraps they were fed with, they took turns to leave it when their shift was called to the surface: anything to placate her. The mine guards knew and said nothing. Sometimes they could hear her breathing in her sleep, making the dark caverns murmur and sigh, softer than the sound of autumn wind in pine trees but similar and yet slower and deeper; more measured, more intimidating. A sound to make the blood run cold. And when the Beast breathed her fetid warning on a puny lamp, they froze in mid stroke and crept silently back up the shafts, huddling at the first lamp still burning and waiting for the guards to notice the sudden silence and come bawling down the galleries with their bright, tar fuelled torches. Days could pass, the moon could fall and rise again, and she would slumber in complete silence, they could work untroubled, the baskets full, and the pulleys humming. And then she would open an eye and breathe on a lamp to remind them.

Her flanks were made of galena seams running horizontally and also downwards in steep slopes and pitches. The easy to reach ore was long cleaned out by the ancients, leaving their tool marks of antler and stone, iron and blood. Marks of the long dead. The Beast's primary opening was horizontal like a cave or a lair: just one reason for its ill-gained name. Not especially appealing to look at, it had the visage of a mouth opened for feeding. The mouth's tongue was a bed of galena walked over each day by every man who worked there, untouched by pick or shovel out of fear and superstition. The Carvetii, in the safeness of their halls, called her Borwenna, the mother of the earth. The toiling slaves preferred the Beast.

Auvericus set out his stall early by digging downwards. Ladders and wooden walkways, ropes and buckets led down into the gloom. Down in the galleries oil lamps took over from the rows of pitch-soaked torches in the entrance hall. He learned from experience that the smoky torches chewed up too much air down below. Oil lamps let men toil and sweat. Twenty three slaves, convicts in the main, chained in shifts, day and night. He had no need of sunlight to make him rich and neither did his slaves.

He knew what they called the mine and he rather liked it. There was something elemental and noble about conquering the Beast. The mouth of the Beast was almost toothless, like the great gums of a giant hag except on each side two small extrusions of stone resembling like nothing else than stumps of broken teeth. The slaves touched them at the start and end of their shift.

He never went down into it after the day he bought it. Let the slaves face the Carvetii earth goddess and take their chances with her mercy. They might last a few weeks before the lack of food made them too feeble to work. The attrition rates appeared to please the commander at the fort as evidence of justice delivered. He did not consider it was justice delivered, more like profits delayed. His overseer reported daily production in bucketloads and casualties from the vapours as they occurred. The Beast showed no clemency. He saw no reason why he should anything other than feed her fresh slaves in return for her ore. Just so long as he did not have to go down there.

*

Drapisces chose to wait until after Caturiges had received his funeral dues, using the time to appoint a new priest to his family. The stark wound in Caturiges' belly was a reminder of the potency of a Roman sword. The old pains from the wounds in his head bubbled up. His head throbbed, his jaws ached. He took a potion and waited for his body to release him. The new priest tried a different infusion and earned his instant gratitude. Perhaps Caturiges could have learned from this man.

The Roman centurion was a problem. He was too powerful to be wasted in a common sacrifice. Killing Caturiges had strengthened the Roman's value. The gods would more inclined to grant a prayer made with this man's blood. His new priest seemed to share Caturiges' anger at the growing rapaciousness of the Roman mining and timber felling and also his own opinion of the prisoner's blood value. He took stock of his people's temper at Caturiges' demise. There was anger and appetite for revenge. He let it simmer and consulted with his highest warriors. Together they forged a plan and let the new priest guide them. The Roman was the obvious offering for success but he resisted their pressure. He was not going to waste him. He was going to strike when he was good and ready.

*

Drapisces held his men back until he was sure they were all in place. This was going to be a clean smite and he wanted it done quickly before the soldiers at lakeside could be alerted. The approach to the mine was a narrow pass between high rocks. It was more a cleft or passageway than a gully or valley and it opened out below him into a wider space with huts and sheds and a smelting furnace. The cave entrance to the mine was at the foot of the far wall of rock. He sent men to seal off the upper and lower ways out and a thin screen to marshal the steep sides in case any slave tried to climb their way out. The steepness of the rocks made it unlikely, but he was taking no chances. Junius Cita and Scribono were further to his left at the head of a goat-path. The sun was rising. The changeover was going to happen soon. When the two shifts met, he was going to strike. The main slave compound was in open ground lower down the hillside below the start of the defile and beyond that, closer to Cantiventi, Auvericus' house enjoyed a pleasant view. Auvericus and any potential rescuers were now cut off by his warriors blocking the defile.

The minutes drifted by. There was movement in the shadows of the entrance, rough voices breaking the silence. One by one the nightshift began stumbling out of the mine entrance, groping with eyes screwed tight in the strengthening sunlight, tossing their handpicks to the ground, a bunch of ragged, stooped and broken men. In the distance from the direction of the compound, he could see the head and shoulders of a man on horseback: the day shift was coming. Below him exhausted slaves were drinking from a trough of water they shared with the horses. He lifted his arm up to get the waiting warrior's attention. The rider passed below his hiding place and circled the horse around to face the slaves behind him. The man was not wearing any armour. His six other guards shepherding the slaves along on foot were clad in leather armour and carried whips and swords. None of the arriving slaves looked up. He raised his hand again to signal Junius Cita.

Cita sent an arrow from his bow and hit the horseman in the small of the back. He tumbled off the horse which reared and flailed its forelegs sending the closest slaves stumbling back out of its reach. His warriors surged out of hiding, hurtling down the goat path. The slaves seemed transfixed; the other armed guards were stunned. Cita fired off more arrows. It was quick and bloody. Borwenna was avenged.

"Run," he stood up and barked down the startled miners.

One of them took his time to rifle the body of the mounted overseer, taking his dagger, and cloak. He looked up at Drapisces then stuck the dagger into the chest of the dead guard, before cutting the leather purse free of his belt. Draspisces' own men were too slow to do it. The slave stood his ground with the dagger and money bag. He hesitated and then raised his hand offering the pouch to Drapisces. Drapisces shook his head.

"Keep it my friend, come with us if you want to," he called out, "bring them all if they can keep up."

"You want to feed them, Drapisces?" a warrior called.

"I'll feed them all if they want to join us," he said watching the other guards' corpses being similarly ransacked.

He wondered how long the slender amounts of coin would remain in their possession. They were in no condition to keep it against his well-fed men.

"Check inside, see if there is anything worth taking," he ordered.

"There's nothing worth taking in there," the slave said.

"Can it be burned inside?" he asked.

The slave shook his head. Drapisces saw Scribono enter the mine and left him to it. He stepped onto a suitable rock and claimed victory. Around him newly freed slaves were climbing up out of the defile towards him. His men were helping the weaker ones. He made a throat cutting gesture for the guard's heads. Scribono walked back out, empty handed. Drapisces watched the dead guards' mutilation and knew how to appease Borwenna. The lead guard's horse was defying attempts to capture it. Ten or more of the freed slaves were coalescing into a separate knot. They looked stunned by the flurry of killing and the sudden decision by the others to join the warriors.

*'They do not wish to come with us,'* he realised.

They had no chance of surviving the inevitable Roman backlash that was going to start as soon as the nightshift did not stagger back under guard. Perhaps an hour of time, no more, before Auvericus sent someone to find out what was happening. His own men regained the height over the defile. He stared at the band of hesitating slaves and waved his hands apart at their predicament, leaving them to decide.

"Scribono," he called," throw the heads down the mine."

## Chapter Twenty.

## Drapisces' hall.

Velio could hear movement outside the hut a little before daylight. The voices told him a raiding expedition was going out.

*'Where?'* he wondered.

There were farewells being made. He peered through a gap in the wattling of his prison and could just make out the upper lines of the earthen parapet encircling Drapisces and his people. It would not survive ten minutes against a determined assault by his century. It was astutely positioned, on a steep slope with one entrance to defend. No obvious means of escape if needs be, but there must be secret fox path out of here. Excepting its height, it was little better than an overnight marching camp in terms of military resilience.

*'Perhaps they have sighted Liscus and the men? They must be searching for me. No it can't be that. This lot are not strong enough to take on the century. Unless there are more of them nearby,'* he chewed it over.

If it was Liscus, Drapisces would probably order him killed before his mules had time to get up and over the earthworks. There would be no gladius put in his hand for a noble fight to the death this time.

*'If it's you Liscus, Mercury lend you speed my friend,'* he prayed.

He strained at the manacles around his ankles, testing their strength, hoping for a different result this time. They remained as unbreakable as the last time. The crude lock was pickable but not without a spike or a nail for a key.

*'It's now or never, Velio,'* he told himself.

He sat down. Whoever came next to the hut with food for him was going to Hades. It was them or him. He chewed his lip and reconciled a heathen's death against the lives of Voccia and the baby to come. There was no contest.

Twenty minutes later the sun was fully up, and light flooded through the gaps in the walls sending shadows and splashes of cheering light across the straw. He heard the footfall and choked down the faint remorse as he guessed the identity of his likely victim. The hut door creaked open and then closed. A wooden bar snibbed in place.

'Voccia, Voccia,' he told himself.

He knew the familiar scent, of herbs and cooking and feminine musk. Pretending to be still sleeping he let the old woman come close and lay the bowl of hot cooked oat porridge at his side. He grabbed her arm without opening his eyes and yanked her off balance and before she could protest broke her thin old neck, like snapping a goose. A horrid, loud sound: he tensed as she went limp. He opened his eyes and saw the light dying in her face. On her waist belt was a key. There was no need to use a knifepoint or an iron pin on the lock, she had brought everything he needed. With his fingers, he touched her eyelids closed and laid her on her side facing away from the doorway. He took a knife and the key from her, setting himself free before rubbing heat into his feet with his hands.

"Thank you," he said.

For her ministrations of his wound, he was rewarding her with death. Carvetii heathen or not, she had not deserved this end for her skill and care.

"You saved me. I am sorry to do this to you, Grandmother," he whispered.

*'Don't go soft, you stupid bastard,'* the soldier in him woke up.

He slipped out the door. The layout of the hilltop was a mystery except for the fact Drapisces' hall was now at his back and the shed where they had kept him was off to its right-hand side. The earthen wall was the only marker that mattered now, he needed a section as far away from the watchers at the gateway as possible. He hunched low, nerves screeching at the terrors of getting captured and slid his way along the outside wall of the first hall in front of him holding the old woman's knife ready by his side. There was a soil pit of excrement behind the hall: unoccupied, one less fool to kill. He darted across a frightfully exposed gap between homes that was only a few paces wide. He checked his back, his heart pumping. There was no one there.

*'Don't hang about, get out of here,'* he told himself.

Two more house walls shielded him from the inner face of the rampart. Close by a woman was singing to her baby, a warm peaceful lullaby. He pushed forward to the last piece of cover, a low lean-to sort of shed for goats. The bleats of kids greeted him. He took a moment to assess the odds of scaling the wall, and what might be likely to be waiting for him on the other side? Not all the men would have left the fortress. Drapisces and his warriors had womenfolk to protect. He took a long scan on all sides, telling himself he was in a quiet part of the citadel. There was nothing to be gained from being cautious now. He put the cold blade of the knife between his teeth and threw himself at the single slope. There was an outer defence ditch on the far side, and he dived down into it for cover. Still no voices of alarm, the singing woman was still crooning. The ditch had a twist where bedrock broke through the soil. He eased along to the rocks, knowing the grip would be better than damp earth, counted to three and wriggled up and over the rock letting himself tumble into the grassy slope which fell away in a steep descent. His side flared hotly but there was no time to do more than press the palm of his hand on the dirty tunic and carry on. A gorge of rock and trickling water lay in front, plunging towards a tree line. A javelin's throw of coverless hillside separated him from sanctuary. He took a hurried drink at the stream, checked his side, and found there was no blood. He made himself breathe and calm down. His dirty army tunic was good camouflage. There was a chance he could do this. He craned his head to take another look at Drapisces' stronghold, but the tilting shoulder of the hill was hiding it. Attackers would find that false summit an unpleasant welcome. If he could not see them, they could not see him. He drank more water and scurried for the trees, praying like he had never prayed before. The branches raked and scourged his arms and legs as he plunged deeper into the safety of the trees. The sweet stink of forest and rotting vegetation was intoxicating. He swallowed it down like sweet wine. At a spot where a rock jutted up in a small plinth, reminding him of the platform he used to address the troops from in Trimontium, he jumped up to check the surroundings. Trimontium; so long ago. Before Voccia, before Scribono told him Hanno Glaccus ordered Brutus Carruso to murder him. Blood was running down his forearms and shins, the wounds nipping now. He smeared the worst of it away, leaving red war paint on his skin, wiped his blood coloured hands together on his equally bloody tunic and took stock.

"Could be worse Velio," he said, "could be a Carveti sword in your guts before they stick your head on the branch of a tree."

He smiled. He was not done for yet. The priest of Drapisces found out the hard way. He wanted food for his belly and a clean tunic. Best to clean the wound and keep the hot red swelling away. The old hag had served him well with her potions and mosses and he had rewarded her by breaking her neck. He frowned and made the sign.

*'At least I gave her a quick death,'* he consoled himself.

Up there in the hilltop they might not have even discovered her body.

"Get off your arse Velio, there is no time for this," he barked at himself.

The gorge struck down through the forest at a fearful rate. One slip would be the end of it. At the edge of the woods the water splayed out into a pool and rushed on to the lower ground that seemed to flatten out very quickly, thick bushes on both banks concealing its course. The thought of being clean once more was overwhelming. He waded into the pool and sat down. The cold water took away his breath but the aches and pains in his sides and his limbs went with it. It was not the soul consoling warmth of the end of day caldarium at Deva with oil and a strigil, but it felt good. He stripped off and gave the gory tunic a cursory rinse, wringing it out as best he could and put it back on.

*'You've got to be alive to feel cold lad, so stop complaining,'* he once told a young legionary not long after he took up his centurion-ship.

*'Where in Hades' Arse am I? Which way is north? Where is Liscus and the hill fort?'*

None of the hills looked familiar, they all appeared barren, not that he had bothered to study them much since marching up from Cantiventi.

"Fuck," he muttered.

The bark moss on the pines told him where north lay. But it did not tell him anything more. He sat down to think. Food, a horse and a sword were the minimum requirements for staying alive out here. Now that the Carvetii wanted him dead, as did Scribono and probably Junius Cita too there could be no mistakes. North felt like the wrong direction. West should lead to the coast. South was where Deva Victrix was, though it must be miles away and eastwards, once clear of the Carvetii lands, lay the unfriendly Brigantes. He rubbed his hands over his wet hair and beard. His skin felt better. He was cold but his fighting spirit was returning. It was too early in the year for nuts to have ripened on the trees. There might be mushrooms but that was another risk. There might also be wild boar roaming the forests. A tiny knife and a stick off a tree were not going to give him protection against a wild boar. He stood up feeling uneasy. The pugmarks of a bear lay within arm's reach of where he had been sitting, deep and clear in the soft ground. The sides of the prints had begun to fall into the centre: not wholly fresh. He touched one with his fingertips.

*'That's a bear Velio, and it looks quite a big one. Oh shit. Time to go, Velio,'* he told himself, holding down a sudden nervy flux in his gut.

It was far too early in the day to consider resting up. Now the thought of doing that in this wood that appalled him. Even more reason to get clear of Drapisces' clan before the warriors returned. He chose west, hoping that if he could get to the sea somewhere on that coast, he could find Uiliocenon and its allegedly intemperate marine centurion-commander. A bit of intemperate anger was precisely what was needed right now.

Going west soon became impossible. The local gods were lining up the hills to thwart him. Crests rose up with skirts of treacherous shale and scree, inviting him to dance. Boxed in at one point he trekked back out the way he had come through the hills and tried to work his way around the canyon. Now the hills were running north to south, the gods were playing with him. His side started playing up and he sat down to rest by a stream, feeling hemmed in and trapped. It was past midday. The old woman must have been found by now. Perhaps Drapisces had returned? Were they searching for him? Junius Cita and Scribono would not let him go so easily. One whiff of deserters hiding in the hills and the forts would have to respond. Perhaps southwest would do? Strike the coast further down? Uiliocenon might just as easily be southwest as west or northwest. Fearing he was stiffening up, he got to his feet and pushed on, sticking to the valley floor instead of trying to fight his way over the high tops. He started making better progress. In the distance he saw smoke drifting up in a lazy cloud.

"Weapons and food Velio," he said aloud, "weapons and food."

*

Cattle were grazing in open pasture along the riverbank. It ran a modest course, winding among and over rocks, past eddies and scours in the riverbanks where sand and shingle lay exposed by winter torrents. He kept low and used the river as cover. The hall was palisaded and set up on a very modest hillock less than half a bowshot from the stream. A crowd of goats were cropping flowers.

'*Bound to be horses,*' he breathed.

All these people had horses. He stalked closer. A burst of male shouting made him freeze. A man and two burly younger men, sons most likely, were having an argument. Flattening down, half in the water and half pressed against the grassy bank, he tried to make himself invisible. The three men got heated, something about the cattle. Payment maybe? He could not tell, the accents too thick and too rapid to untangle the exact words. There was the unmistakeable sound of a slap of hand on flesh. He risked lifted his head up and saw the older of the three towering over one of the others lying on the ground. The other young man had his hand on the pommel of a sword that for now he was not yet ready to draw.

"Fool. You are a fool, boy,"

The father's tongue lashed the words.

Velio winced at a memory of Misenum and his own father stepping off a boat buoyant with captured fish. The last day he spoke to Father before the legions marched past and he ran to join them. He held his breath. If the other son pulled out the weapon, taking their horses was going to get much easier.

*'Go on lads, do it. Kill your Pa and give me your horses,'* he hoped, *'I'll leave you the farm. Just one horse, that's all I need.'*

It was too much to hope for. The other son's hand did not move on the pommel. His father stepped forward and jabbed his forefinger into his chest. He could feel anger flowing one way and hatred flowing back between them. They looked like they were ready to go to war themselves. Something inside turned like a screw. Was it self-contempt or a glimpse from the past of the young weapons instructor he had once been?

*'Call yourself a centurion of the First legion? Cease hiding and go and take what you want.'*

The two Carvetii lads were cowed by their father but did not back away. He rose up from his cover and with the knife in his hand hanging by his side began walking towards the three of them. The words in Carvetii were evidently hot and well baked because they were burning weals onto their faces. Whatever the cow had meant to the three of them, something about it had unleashed this reckoning. He came on toward them. The hall had a barn. They might be keeping the small goats and the geese in the hall for safety but not the horses. He halted and waited, keeping his knife hand by his side. If bluff failed, he was going to kill the three of them.

*'Mars hear me and be patient with me. I ask too much I know but I will make them bleed in return for your blessing,'* he vowed, *'Holy Mothers of the Parade Ground, stand with me. Epona lend me a horse.'*

The word for horse in Carvetii escaped him. Was it the same as Brigantes, he wondered? Centurions did not give orders in Brigantes or any other barbarian dog-language.

"I need to borrow a horse," he said, interrupting their argument, hoping the surprise might goad them into complying.

Sometimes the bald and unexpected stunned people into acts they would normally refuse. They turned and stared, each of them taking in the message from his tunic and his soldier's stance. He saw his Latin was too complicated for them to follow. The son with the sword did exactly what he hoped and drew it. Velio stepped in close, slashed his lower forearm open to the bone and ripped the sword from his grasp, pushing him away with his other hand. The father screamed in rage at the crippling of his son and lunged forwards bare handed. Velio put the point of the sword out and fended him off.

"Equus," he repeated, keeping it simple and his voice low.

This man did not appear to understand the danger he was in.

*'Not that you want to co-operate even if you do understand,'* he suspected.

The man charged with a shake of his head, snarling. Velio scowled a warning and raised the palm of his right hand to halt the attack. The worked up Carvetti hurled himself at Velio. He had no choice but to cut him down. One dead, one with the strings and muscles of his sword arm forever crippled, the other, the one who had been lying on the grass, now up on his feet and blazing with frightened eyes at what was happening.

"Equus," Velio repeated, letting impatience get the better of him.

*'Last roll of the dice lad. Where are the damn horses?'*

The lad got it and pointed to the barn. He checked the condition of the man on the ground. He was clearly dead. The wounded son was white faced with pain and shock, gripping the wound closed, tears of agony forcing their way in the corners of his eyes. Man enough not to cry out in pain. He beckoned the other lad to lead the way. Were there servants, a mother, sisters? Why did neither lad try to raise an alarm?

*'Because in this valley there is no one close enough to hear, no mother, no sisters, cousins, uncles to help,'* he suspected.

There were five animals stalled in the barn. He chose the best and found himself up on the animal, surprised he managed the leap without pain. Flicking the point of the sword at the lad to move him out of the way, he kicked the horse into a trot. Outside the scene had not changed except the wounded lad was cradling his father's head in his arm. He shouted defiance and his brother burst into galvanised action, seizing a hayfork from the wall of the barn. Velio took it in with a glance and spurred the horse. A man could throw a hayfork and make it fly straight like a javelin. But a one off, unpractised hurling was not likely to be successful. Not even he or Gallus could do that trick.

'You forgot the food,' he cursed.

Stealing the animal had put it out of his head. Going back meant he would have to kill the lads, no way around it. Killing the old woman in the shed still troubled him. Velio Pinneius did not kill old women skilled in healing, regardless of whether they were a true born Roman citizen or a heathen Celt. It was not who he was. Aesculapius was probably raining furies down from the heavens upon his head at the murder of a healer. He snarled at himself and accepted hunger as atonement for her death.

Following the river would inevitably take him to the sea. Heading back inland to the hills might get him back to the hill fort and Civius, or in touch with one of Liscus' patrols. They must be out searching for him, getting frantic at the thought of finding his body. On the other hand, this morning's sally by Drapisces and his men had not been on horses. He was certain of it. The warriors had left on foot. If he ran into them the speed of the horse would be his shield. He tugged the reins and headed back the way he had come towards the high ground, striking to the east.

The farmer's uninjured son picked up the wayward pitchfork, feeling useless now that it was all over. He had failed completely. Father was dead and his older brother badly wounded. The thief was escaping back up the valley to the hills from where he must have come, otherwise, they would have noticed him coming from a distance. His older brother rolled himself upright. Blood was coming from his lips where he had bitten through them in pain, it was running down his chin into his beard and he was white faced. He stopped and bent over, vomiting into the grass. He lifted his head, spitting bile into the grass, afraid to look at his wound a second time.

"Don't just stand there, get Pa's horse, take a bow and a spear and get after him," he barked.

"I can't kill that man," his younger brother replied.

Horror and fear filled his stomach.

"You can't kill anything. You can't even protect the cows. He did this to us. Get after him. Find out where he goes, where he makes camp. Don't come back until you know. He's going to die for this. I'm going to put his head in an oak tree. The Roman pig."

## Chapter Twenty-one.

## Cantiventi.

Liscus digested the Plautius message back in his tent. The reference to Scipio and decimation of ranks did not feel like Servius Albinius indulging them with an idle lesson in history. Servius Albinius commanded the legion, and he was master of their all destinies and careers; their leader in battle and interlocutor with the gods. He was something bigger than merely the legate of the Twentieth.

Something stored away in the back of his mind said Servius and the centurion had long service together and the legate held Velio Pinneius in high regard. Servius had given a command:

"Go and find him."

"Well, that's it then Marcellus, we're going back to find the centurion. Best keep the decimation remark to yourself. I expect Plautius is too wise an owl to go blurting it out. It's time to sweep the Carvetii villages and see what we can find. Someone must know where he is," he said.

"You believe our centurion still lives?" Marcellus asked.

"You know him better than me Marcellus. Swords Pinneius is not going to be slain by some dirty little Carveti. The gods will not allow the man who found what was left of the Ninth to die in such a manner," he replied.

"Ah. You have heard that little tale? He does not tell it very often. Rarely, if ever in fact," Marcellus confided, "I'm not sure he likes it. It cost him a friend into the bargain. The fame is not something he enjoys," he went on.

"I did not say he told me directly," Liscus answered.

Marcellus saluted the optio.

"As you command optio. Will you notify the camp praefectus we are leaving or, shall I?" he queried.

"Marcellus, if I tell him, the word will race ahead of us. Through the fort and the vicus and out beyond. No, I think the century needs exercised. They are getting old, fat and lazy, wouldn't you say? We will head down the Iter X to the tail of the lake and sweep west and around to the Delmatarum. That way we will have a clear sight of any followers and we will have a better feel for what is out there. Let word of the exercise get out, but nothing else."

"Old, fat and lazy. The lads will love that," Marcellus grinned.

Liscus knew it was cheeky to call Velio's men that but not finding Velio during the first sweep of the hill pass could only mean he had been taken prisoner and the absence of a ransom demand was compounding his growing concerns. Why had no one come forward to try and negotiate with him? Fear of losing their heads was one obvious reason but still, the Carvetii were keeping awfully quiet about it. As though it had not happened at all.

He ordered a complete breaking of camp, packing the tents in the carts for a full exercise with three days rations. They stepped off two hours later, which pleased him. The wolfskin standard bearer scowled as he fell into step behind Marcellus' horse.

He had other ideas.

*'This is no way to leave Cantiventi, tails between our fucking legs. The centurion would never do this if it was the optio that was missing. Not until he was certain he was dead. And even then, there'd be blood on the grass and howling women.'*

Liscus could feel the simmering in the ranks. They did not much like the order to march south. That was not where the centurion was, was it? But they were marching and that was all he cared about. Discipline was the only thing that mattered. The local garrison kept their trumpets silent.

*'Don't know whether blowing Farewell Brother is appropriate boys? Good, best you know nothing for now,'* he decided.

At the last minute he chose not to take the Iter X because its path would take him away from the water. Instead, he led the century down the side of it. Narrow tracks and stony lakeside beaches helped hide the deception but it was slower going. Halfway down the lake he decided to stamp his authority, calling the junior officers, tesserarii together to a meeting under a convenient tree. He had them form a semicircle facing him while he saw past to the waiting ranks of legionaries at their backs, watching and murmuring.

"We are going up into the hills and we are going to find the centurion whether I have to butcher every village and hall between here and the coast," he said.

Plautius was the first to grin.

"I don't want to hear another grumble," Liscus hissed, "and I don't want to have to tell the centurion I had to flog some of his men to obey me in his absence. Neither do you."

Plautius could feel the stoat's grin on his face and did not care. Somewhere in the night Optio Liscus Aulus Manlio had stepped out of the shade of his promotion. His alter ego was wearing an implacable face.

*'Now that's a proper warning. This is more like it,'* he wanted to say.

"Let's get moving before the word gets out that we are not taking the Iter X south," Liscus added.

He remounted and nudged the horse into a walk. The word appeared to like be wildfire in the ranks. There were people in this life who only sounded happy when they were offered the chance to go killing and slaughtering.

At the foot of the lake, he took them over the river, towards a valley, ignoring the friendly shouts from the detachment at the docking area. If it looked like an exercise march, then that is what would be reported. Word of their movements would be back in Cantiventi with the next boat. It was not that he mistrusted the commander of the Morinorum. Velio had spoken favourably of him on the way up to the hill fort. Unsurprisingly Velio preferred him to the greasy smear of humanity that called itself Civius.

Orann was enjoying himself more than anything else he had done since coming south from Trimontium. Caring for the centurion's horses had been one of the happy times. Living and working in the huge Roman fortress was beyond anything he could compare it to at home.

Marcellus put him charge of his spare horse and the optio's and told him to take a place at the rear of the waggons. The few legionaries who looked at him seemed friendly enough, teasing him about his slim, 'pig-sticker' Votadini spear. The column cleared the tail of the lake, crossed the bridge on the river and began a long wending up to the higher ground through a valley. The mistress' orders rang in his ears.

*'I want you to bring him back to me Orann. Do that for me and I will let you sleep in the house.'*

Liscus sent a detachment of six contubernia, forty-eight men, and a tesserarius to search the first homesteads in lower section of the valley. From the shrieks and squeals emanating from the buildings the locals were not expecting such robust treatment. He waited until the squad set fire to a couple of houses and returned to report the negative fact. They headed further up the dale and did it again, and again. Native horsemen appeared moving ahead, spreading the word. He did not care and took the men deeper into an area none of them knew. In the distance a stark mountain reared up forcing him to detour.

*

Drapisces heard a horseman arriving outside his hall. The voice of whomever it was had a loud message. He laid down the centurion's helmet by the side of his chair and went to the door. A crowd was already gathering around the rider; a farmer from down the valley. He raised a hand in salute to Drapisces.

"The Wolf Soldiers are coming. They are starting to burn houses. The word is they want their soldier chief," the farmer cried above the hubbub breaking out.

"How many of them?" he shouted back over the noise.

"Enough to be dangerous. This is no little patrol, Drapisces. They are looking to fight," the farmer said.

"Their soldier chief has escaped. He killed my best healer this morning, stole her knife and escaped. Is he among the soldiers coming?" he replied.

The farmer shrugged. Drapisces hoped the soldier was with them. Revenge for killing Caturiges and the woman would be sweet today.

"How far away, how long?" he demanded.

The farmer dismissed the relevance question with a flick of the reins. There was almost a lack of courtesy in the gesture that brought home the danger coming up the valley.

"Drapisces, they are going to attack this fort. These ditches won't hold them back for long. Take my word, get your women folk and children away from here. My family are taking to the hills for a while until this passes. You had better hope they get him back alive Drapisces, or else they will kill everyone in these valleys," the farmer spat.

"Then we must get word to our friends in the Brigantes . They will not stand aside," he answered.

"That is all as it should be my lord, but we will be dead before they have time to come to our sides," the farmer said.

Drapisces waited as the farmer brought his horse under control, thinking of the Roman feathered helmet lying on the ground only steps from where he stood. The old anger started rising in his chest, the throb in his head, the searing desire to spill Roman blood. He ran his fingers over his broken features, watching as the farmer watched him.

"I did not seek this face to frighten my wife and children. I got it defending what is mine. My land and my cattle, my people. I got it standing in the battle lines beside our brothers the Brigantes. If you are going into the hills, send word to them and tell them Drapisces did not run," he replied.

"As you wish, my lord, but consider your women and children. There is time to get them out of the small gateway to the forests."

"Out there, I cannot protect them. If the sons of the wolf discover them, they will be lost to me. It is better they stay, so their husbands and fathers, and brothers fight."

The farmer raised his eyebrows a fraction.

"You do not have long to rally your men, Drapisces," he said.

"The gods reward you for bringing me this warning. Ride safely or die well," he said, turning back to his hall.

Junius Cita was blocking his way.

"Where is your comrade from the legions?" he asked, and tried to mask the irritation of having his own doorway effectively barred to him.

"He's gone to try and follow the centurion. It's personal, you understand? He had his cousin killed. Scribono has sworn the centurion is going to die. Caturiges could not kill a weakened man and he's mad now. You should have let him fight the centurion. Caturiges had no chance."

The words tumbled out of Junius' mouth.

"I suspected as much. But if Caturiges wanted power, then the gods should have protected him against a wounded man. What use was he to me if he could not kill a weak and wounded enemy? Why would I listen to a weak man?" Drapisces asked.

He lifted his hand to his face drawing attention to it, though it was unnecessary. Junius found it hard to argue. Centurion Pinneius might have been wounded and weakened but he was not weak. The Carveti continued.

"This is what can come from following a weak leader."

Junius stepped aside. If the news was true, the centurion's company were coming for vengeance or as a rescue mission, perhaps he was no longer safe here, Scribono too? So far, Drapisces had been amenable to their presence, even welcoming their prowess.

Drapisces grimaced his wrecked face, the closest thing he could manage as a smile.

"Junius, remember the day we found him holding my war shield. It was fortunate he was a wounded man. Otherwise, he might have fancied his chances fighting his way out. Not that he would have beaten me, but you and Scribono, I'm not so sure. I have his helmet and its pretty feathers in my hall. If the Romans get in here, it will tell them all they need to know. I'm not giving up the trophy. If they want it, they will have to fight me for it. If you and Scribono decide to stand with me today, you will be welcome in my hall, and I will make sure all my people will know it. But if you run, never come back," he said.

"They used to be our comrades, fellow warriors, but now since we came here, they have become our enemy too. I did not fight alongside the men who are coming to attack you today, but Scribono did and if they capture us, we are dead men. Make no mistake lord Drapisces, we have nowhere to run," Junius replied.

Drapisces looked at him and for a second Junius had a flurry of anxiety. Had he got Drapisces wrong? The Carveti turned his back saying nothing and went to his defences.

Junius went to the small hall he shared with Scribono and checked his weapons. Drapisces did not have sufficient men to hold off an attack for long and the longer he held out the more determined the legionaries were going to become. The bloodshed there was going to be. He saw Scribono in the doorway.

"You've heard?" he asked.

Scribono nodded, "I've seen them. it won't be long."

"Who are they?" he said, knowing already he was not going to like the answer.

"They," Scribono emphasised, "they, are carrying First cohort, Boar shields Junius. Looks like a single century. So, nothing to worry about," he replied, deadpan.

Junius sucked in his cheeks.

"This lot won't stand for long. We need to decide how to play this Scribono, my lad."

## Chapter Twenty-two.

Liscus called Plautius and Marcellus aside. Together they stared up at the shoulder of the hill masking the Carvetii stronghold. He pointed to the curving contours.

"They must have seen us coming and if they didn't, the word will have spread ahead of us. If the centurion is up there, they will kill him as soon as we begin the attack," he said.

Plautius nodded. The odds for Centurion Pinneius surviving his rescue were slim to non-existent. Attempting a night attack would be hazardous beyond reason.

"He is a soldier sir," he muttered.

'*He knows the risks. He could be dead already,*' he dared not say aloud.

Marcellus frowned and folded his arms.

Liscus read his thoughts. The century was standing waiting. Their faces hard and fixed. After all he had told them the single purpose of the expedition. Plautius' expression brightened. He eased the chinstrap of his helmet aside and scratched his chin.

"You could send his servant up there. The one that's eating our dust. He's a Votadini isn't he? He might be able to get in and find out whether the chief is there."

Liscus considered it for a moment. It was far from the worst suggestion he had ever heard. The Carvetii were not likely to be stupid enough to think handing over the centurion alive at this point was going to prevent them getting chopped in retaliation for taking him in the first place. The Votadini might be allowed to ride the hill path and bring back news. But then, that was going to leave him waiting for a native servant to dictate his tactics. His choices would be limited, and dependant entirely on the accuracy, honesty and truthfulness of Orann. Hardly an appealing proposition. Using him at night to smuggle a message over the walls to tell the centurion they were coming might be one thing, but this: the men would think he was weak. And night was just fanciful wishing right now. If the Votadini did not return at all, the tribe up there would know for certainty what was coming. He shook his head.

"Split the men into two. We are going up that path, through or over that gate and we are getting Centurion Pinneius out of there. The first half century will come with me up the path. You will take the other half around to the far side of the hill and attack the earthworks. Get in behind them Plautius and we will crush them in a vice," he decided. Marcellus nodded approval.

"As you command me, optio," Plautius replied.

Orann sat watching the soldiers and wondered what they were about. One group began making its way around the base of the hill and it was obvious. Going with them without being in a friendly uniform was likely to get him killed. Once they got up there, the Carvetii would fight to the death. Mistress Voccia had told him to find the centurion. She did not say to get himself killed. He turned his horse and led the two spare mounts back down the path and paused to watch the optio's preparations for a frontal assault. The Carvetii must know resistance was going to cost them dear. He did not want any part of that. Being a soldier was fine as long as it meant working with the horses. Killing Carvetii womenfolk was not palatable. He was not a murderer. He retreated a short distance back from the preparations. There was a small side valley. He waited for Marcellus to order him to stay where he was, but Marcellus was out of sight and the optio was too busy to notice. He led the horses into it, dismounted and let the animals drink their fill from a stream. After a time, they lifted their heads and looked at him. He laughed at them waiting for their next order and let them graze. Instinct, more like an itch than a certainty, made him mount and take the horses deeper into the valley. The cleft in the hills was as rocky as all the others but the bottom land had been smoothed out by streams into a passable route. He pushed on and left the soldiers to their work on the other side of the hill, hidden from sight and sound, and prayed they would show mercy to the women and children. Knowing what they were likely to do drove him deeper into the peace and silence of the valley. He doubted the sounds and screams would be audible here.

At the head of the valley, he had the possibility of bearing left or right. He chose right. The path took him into a softer greener valley. The whole area was a mass of interconnecting gorges, valleys, and corries. This one had the softness more like the lands around Trimontium, good cattle country. In the distance a Carveti man was riding towards him with an urgency that would wear out his horse before long. He pulled up and let the rider come close, leaving the shield Mistress Voccia had lent him on the saddle thong. He rested his spear against his shoulder and waited.

*

Velio pulled up and checked around for any sign he had come this way after escaping this morning. He was lost. The excitement was over. Now he was tired, and it was getting to all look much the same. His side was hurting from the hard riding. He touched the wound and checked his hand for blood. So far, the wound was staying closed. The old woman's magic potions had been powerful. It was a pity she had had to die. Somehow since leaving the farm he had drifted into a different valley. This was not the one he thought it was, this one was turning into unrelenting rock, hillsides, woods and streams. He spat in frustration. It was now midday. Which way was Cantiventi? The alternative was to try to reach Civius and the Delmatarum garrison. The direction of that was equally mysterious. The horse was giving him pain and he had no food and no bow to shoot anything. Pushing on without a clear direction was only going to wear out the animal. He might snare trout in the stream but how long would that take? The boy he had spared at the farm was going to raise an alarm. There was no time for dithering to go fishing. His belly was going to have to be content with water. He kicked the horse.

*'Jupiter do not desert me in such a place as this,'* he fought down the panic that was telling him he was lost.

*

The rider slowed as he approached Orann, eying the spear and the extra mounts in front of him. He was not a Roman auxiliary, not a Carveti, but he was of the tribes, more a farm lad, if anything, like himself.

"Greetings, friend," he said, inspecting Orann.

Orann nodded back, hoping the spare horses with legion markings would not be noticed.

"Greetings," he replied.

"What tribe are you?" the rider enquired.

"I am Orann of the Votadini," he answered.

"I have heard of them. In the far north beyond the wall. You are a long travelling from there," the rider suggested.

Orann nodded and decided not to add anything more. The young Carveti was about his own age.

"I am following a murderer who has killed my father, wounded my brother and stolen a fine brown horse," the lad said.

"I have seen no one," he replied, "when did this happen?"

"Not long ago. He sneaked up on us and surprised us in the early morning. He was a Roman. He spoke their dog tongue."

*'The Master, I've found him Mistress Voccia,'* Orann rejoiced.

"He was alone?" Orann said, trying to keep calm as happiness surged in his chest.

"Yes, he was. I am tracking him," the lad answered.

*'You're not a very good tracker then,'* he mused.

"Where are you going now? I can tell you he is not behind me. It will save you the trouble."

The Carveti tugged his nascent moustaches, not replying, too interested in Orann's spear and the shape of the shield pegged to the saddle. The game was up.

"I am going to our chieftain Drapisces for his help to hunt him down," he said and lifted his head.

Orann lowered the tip of his spear and laid it crosswise over his horse's neck.

"I can't let you pass my friend. By the sounds of it your enemy is my master," he said, "and if your lord Drapisces has his hall behind ramparts on this hill beyond, I fear he has worries of his own this morning."

He let go the reins of the two spare horses. The shield on its peg was too far to stretch. The Carveti would close the gap before he could use it. The young man's eyes narrowed.

"Let me pass Votadini. He killed my father. You understand blood honour. You are of the tribes. Our cause is closer than our horses. There is no need for us to raise the spear against each other," he pleaded.

Orann switched the spear point to aim straight at the lad's chest.

"Go home and prepare your father for his journey. Go home and grieve friend. I won't let you pass," he said.

The Carveti kicked his horse forward and thrust out with his own spear. Orann fended the point aside and swirled his mount around. They circled, jousting and lunging at each other with the spears, the horses neighing and invigorated by the sudden outbreak of the fight. The slender blades of steel snaked out as they clashed and turned. One touch in the belly or chest would decide. Orann's horse was bigger and stronger, giving him a slight height advantage. He stared into the Carveti's face and saw a young man both afraid and proud who was not going to give way. He used the trick he had seen the auxiliary cavalry use in training and dipped the spear, sticking it into the opposing horse's shoulder. It snorted and reared in pain, and he twisted the blade before pulling it out, drawing a rising crescendo of agony from the animal. The lad tumbled off its back, landing helpless, as his wounded brother had been earlier that day; his spear arm out flung, his belly undefended. Orann looked down at him on the long grasses and prodded the injured and bleeding horse away. The startled outrage on the young face changed to pleading up at him. Mistress Voccia was not going to believe he had done this. The smelly horse fool had fought a combat and survived.

*'They won't call me that anymore.'*

He raised his spear and finished it.

"Carveti, this is not what I wanted," he said and dismounted with his knife.

## Chapter Twenty-three.

Liscus tightened the helmet strap before turning to his signifer.

"Men of The Boar are you ready?" he bellowed.

"Ready sir," they answered.

The signifer bared his teeth, resembling the wolf cape and its gaping maw atop his helmet.

"Forward," he ordered.

The path wound up to the Carvetii gates in a series of bends. He could see defenders on the earthworks and a prickle of spear heads showing. He was most obvious target they had.

*'Mars be with me and if I die, I ask it be quick and I show no weakness in front of the men,'* he prayed.

He unsheathed the gladius at his side, raised it and took off, loping up the path, determined not to be distracted by looking around. If the men were not following, he was a dead man. But the chances of that were good anyway. At the first bend a warning spear flew past his head. Native horns started booming and he heard echoes from the valley sides. A brief glance out of the corner of his eye on the bend told him the signifer was with him. All was well. The signifer never charged alone. The path crooked its way up the hill. The ruts from wooden wheels told him this was the main approach. The next spear missed his boot by the narrowest of margins. He hoisted his shield, turned and called out the next order.

"As Testudo," he boomed it out.

There was no room for a proper formation. It was going to look more like an armoured snake than a block. The shields swung up with commendable precision. He waved them on, staring at the worn path as he jogged on as hard as he could, his lungs beginning to complain, his mouth feeling dryer than grain. A missile jolted his shield so hard it pushed him back onto his heels. Swiping the gladius over the outside he dislodged a spear. He stooped under his shield and threw it off the path to prevent injury to the men coming on. Another spear struck. Its narrow point burst through to the back of the shield and nicked his forearm. Removing it was impossible. It would be suicide to try. Shame at his cowardice flooded his head. Rage and aggression followed too. He halted, the signifer bumped into him, halting as well. He glared at the century spreading out underneath him.

"Run you idle bastards, call yourselves the First cohort? If Velio Pinneius dies, I'll have you digging latrines for the Tenth," he threatened.

A howl of protest broke out from the men. Behind him the unshielded signifer was chanting a litany to himself as he waited stoically for an arrow to end it.

"Hail Jupiter thou Best and Greatest, hail Jupiter thou Best and Greatest, hail Jupiter thou Best and Greatest."

His chest was on fire, his thighs aching in pain, the weight of enemy spear had unbalanced his shield, making it both heavier and awkward. His arm was protesting. The temptation to dump it and charge on was only cautioned by the fact he was at the mercy of the defenders above him. If he could get up to the walls, he might be able to risk it. A mocking voice in his head told him he was a lying bastard; if he got to the walls there would be a spare shield or two from his own men.

"Fire at someone else you heathen bastards," he complained.

A guttural laugh at his back surprised him and gave him courage. The gates of the earth fort were heavy beams of local oak. He dared not look up for fear of an arrow in the face. The signifer joined him and then the first rank of four legionaries crashed headlong into the gate testing its strength. It shuddered, which was more than he could have hoped for, but it did not give.

"Pila then up and over the tops lads, it's the hard road today," he waved them on with his sword and then ditched his damaged shield, beckoning them to the sloping banks of earth. A veil of spears from above took out at least ten of his men. There was no time to count how many were dead. The single return volley of javelins had some effect but giving the Carvetii free pila to throw back down was a calculated gamble. Climbing the defences bearing a large shield was well-nigh impossible. Without waiting for his order, the men began discarding their shields, attacking their way up the rampart with one hand for grip and the gladius in the other. Long spear thrusts took out the first legionaries gaining the top. He saw a young lad hurl a rock at their heads. The lad caught his eye and snarled down at him like a treed wildcat. His half century spread along past either side of the gateway and its curtain rampart like liquid. He doubted the chieftain here had ever imagined and planned for sufficient spears to withstand a legionary assault. But there were bowmen up there too as well as stone throwers. His proud legionaries were falling in numbers, taking a beating. The signifer had an arrow sticking out of the chain mail on his shoulder. He was holding the signum upright as if he was on the parade ground at Deva under the calculating eye of Servius Albinius himself. His stream of invective was goading his comrades to maximum effort, but Pinneius had never ordered Liscus to get them slaughtered. How would Marcellus write that up?

"Up lads, get up, we have to get in there. Plautius, for the love of the gods where are you?" he implored.

The horns booming from the stronghold were everywhere. His own trumpeter was blowing manfully.

*

Drapisces strode along the defences watching the single officer leading the assault. The man had courage. The sooner he was dealt with the better. He raised one of his three spears, taking aim and sent it flying down through the air just ahead of the running soldier. It stuck into the path close to the Roman's boot drawing calls of praise from the warriors around him.

"I missed," he growled, "and I have wasted a spear. Do not waste yours my friends. They will be among us soon unless we kill them all."

"They have us on all sides Drapisces," shouted a warrior.

Scribono and Junius Cita stepped back from the edge and tried not to draw attention to themselves. Cita kept his bow by his side and an arrow in his hand looking as if he was seeking a target. Scribono had his spear pretending to cover Junius Cita. They acted for their lives.

The Romans were surging up the path covered by their shields, Drapisces knew what was coming. The old battle fury exploded in his chest. Scribono and Cita appeared unwilling to fight now that their old comrades were right below the ramparts. He snorted: he should not have taken them in to his stronghold in the first place. There had always been the stink of betrayal about them. The sole consolation was they were going to have fight for their own lives just as much as his own people. If there was time, he would cut them down with his own hand before the Romans took him.

*

Plautius felt a nudge. Not a polite tap on the shoulder or a salute. He turned his head. The nearest legionary was pointing to the hillside. He bit back the rebuke that was on his lips and followed the finger. Where the hill tumbled in a steep fall towards trees and a rocky gush of water, three men were running down off the defences into the cover of longer grass.

*'Cowards, the rats are starting to flee already.'*

"Let them run," he said.

Eighty men was all he had to storm this place. It was going to take more than salty determination to get in there with such slender numbers. Diverting men to chop those three was a luxury he could not afford. In seconds they had disappeared down into the ravine. It was too late to change his mind now. The loud piercing sounds of horns must mean the optio had begun the main attack, drawing all attention from this side. He could not tell whether the horns were the enemy's or their own. There was no obvious weak point but anything he could do to draw men from the main gate was going to help the optio. And now the barbarians had made him the gift of showing him there was a second entrance. A wicker water-gate down to the river below. The hilltop itself was too small to harbour a spring. They must take it all from the river or the highest spring. The path from the water-gate was well worn but it was narrow. It did not look a serious obstacle, but it was so narrow it might only allow one man through at a time. If it was defended, it would get bloody. A necessary distraction to the wider assault.

*'Oh, for scorpions to throw some bolts up there,'* he fretted.

The centurion had not considered bringing a couple of scorpions was necessary for an inspection of a hill garrison. This was only supposed to be a final patrol for him. Plautius supposed it was the legate's way of keeping the centurion occupied as the days wound down. Now look what it had turned into, and the means to sort this out was sitting safely tucked up in the weapons store in Deva Victrix. He scratched his chin. The horns were calling to him.

*Time to go, Plautius, boy,'* he told himself and lifted up his shield.

"For the legion, for Centurion Pinneius, he's up there watching us lads," he cried.

He drew his gladius and strode forward. The men were arrayed in a long line on either side that would compress as the advance developed. They would become progressively easier targets the closer they got to the walls. Shouts high above signalled they had been seen.

They struggled to keep an orderly line as the gradient increased. Men began climbing in small echelons, stepping into formations behind each other as the frontage narrowed. It was a pig of a slope. It was like trying to fight underwater against a tide.

*

Drapisces felt the momentum change around him. Resolve was everything in a battle. The two Roman deserters had vanished from the ramparts and more and more soldiers were getting up over the earthworks and fending off his people's frantic attempts to dislodge them. He caught sight of a boy lying with his chest pierced by a javelin, the clutched rock he had intended to throw testament to his courage. He was not more than ten summers old. A child: a child of his clan, a likeable happy lad. He tore his gaze from the child. The screams of women burst into his head. Why had he not heard them before? He tried to rally his own courage, but it leaked away through the noise and the sight of the boy and his pathetic rock. It was one thing for men to die fighting for him, but this was too much. His eyes refused to leave the sad little bundle lying spread out on the grass. A cold flood of remorse chilled him to the bones.

"Enough," he shouted, "they have beaten us. Open the gate."

His nearest warriors stared at him. He threw his last spear to the ground. His father's bronze shield refused to leave his arm and he let it hang down touching the grass. It was over. The Carveti were not strong enough to resist the sons of the wolf. He felt shame at his own weakness. His ancestors would shun him. He was unworthy to bear the chieftain's shield. But the boy had spoken more eloquently than all the battle speeches and boasts he had ever made in his life.

"Enough," he shouted again.

They began to obey. The sound of weapons falling to the ground was a taunt to their independence. The gates began to open. Legionaries flooded in. He felt the rebuke of his men on his face. Was this what he really wanted? Then why fight at all and waste the lives of so many brave men?

*'What am I doing? Has the boy died for nothing?'* he stormed.

He stooped down, gripped his spear and shield again and lunged forwards. His men followed suit. It was too late to get the gates closed again, but he only felt an unquenchable madness screaming defiance and death in his head. The second surge caught the Romans by surprise. They yielded ground. He saw the confusion in their faces. Liscus waved his sword arm in a backwards motion, pulling them back to reform. He held them in a shield line. Behind the Carvetii Plautius entered the opposite side of the compound.

*

Liscus got the surviving Carvetii herded and penned until they were no longer a threat. Now he was up here the hilltop was not a large compound. He sheathed his sword as Plautius restored order and sent pillaging parties through the houses. The few last cries of defiance told him they had control. He put out his hand for a flask from his nearest soldier. The legionary gulped and relinquished his water. He knew from its weight there was not enough in it to quench his raging thirst. But it might still quench the legionary's. He handed it back unbroached. His soldier's grateful face said everything. Within moments another flask appeared from another hand. He swallowed it down to the last remnants of liquid and was still thirsty as he wiped his mouth with the back of his hand.

"Thirsty work," he commented.

"Sir," various voices agreed with him.

The search parties were beginning to produce things of interest. He looked at the pile of trophies being laid for his inspection. Marcellus was doing the rounds counting the casualties, checking the wounded.

"You should see this sir," a tesserarius said.

He produced Velio's helmet from behind his back. Liscus took it. It was clear that it was undamaged.

"Any sign of the centurion?" he hoped.

"No sir, only his helmet and these two jokers," the tesserarius replied.

"Jokers?" he quizzed.

Scribono and Junius Cita were propelled against their will through the assembled men of the First cohort who had already considered, judged and decided punishment.

"Legionary Scribono, sir."

"Legionary Junius Cita, sir."

"What are you two doing here?"

He stared at the two men dressed in a mix of legionary tunics and native trousers.

"They took us prisoners sir," Scribono blurted.

Liscus doubted that was true. They looked well fed for prisoners.

"Four years ago," Junius embellished.

Liscus pulled his helmet off and handed it to a legionary. This was something for Marcellus to check when they got back to Cantiventi. Marcellus read his look and shrugged a noncommittal, *'I'll do that,'* message.

"Is there a centurion here. Centurion Velio Pinneius?" he said.

Scribono shook his head. Liscus smelled the lie.

"What Legion, Cohort, Century are you?" he barked.

"Second," they lied together,

"He's third cohort, I was sixth, second century, centurion Mucianus, proper tyrant, sir," Junius said.

"I hope so, or you'll be flogged and hung for desertion," he said, "four years here and you never managed to escape?"

Scribono shrugged.

"We tried to, sir. But they kept us chained up at night and in the day, well just too many spears around to get off the hill in one piece."

There was a rumble of contradiction around him from the watching legionaries. He shared their disbelief, but it might be true they had been captured.

"So, you managed to get loose right now when we attacked? That's a bit convenient. Are you sure you have not wandered from the standards?" he queried.

Junius Cita stepped forward and saluted.

"With respect sir, it wasn't like that," he said.

"Oh, was it not, soldier? Tesserarius, take charge of these men until we return to Cantiventi. I want this whole place searched for the centurion. And I want it burned. I want the body count and the wounded. Find carts to get them off the hill. Put their chieftain in chains. Plautius, come with me," he snapped.

## Chapter Twenty four.

Orann held up the severed head and held it out admiring his victory. It was much heavier than he expected, and it was leaking blood and gore. The features had gone soft. The lad's angry face now reposed, the eyes stilled to winter ice. This was the first man he had ever killed, and he felt strange staring at the flaccid features quickly turning to the colour of wax. He had butchered animals at Eidumnos' hall to feed the family. Boar, deer, geese and the like. Blood had never bothered him. Hanging up a deer to drain was messy but it was not anything much more than cleaning a fish from the river. Oftentimes the womenfolk did not even ask for his help, which was good for the horses. No smell of blood on his clothes to alarm them. Just more of it on the ground, the deer innards more edible than fishes. But this was different. This was a man, like himself. One he had fought to overcome. A man he had conversed with before they set to. And his head bled and dribbled more gore than any boar or animal he had slaughtered for the master's table. So, this must be what it was to be like, being a warrior, taking your enemies' heads as trophies, the best of their weapons for your own, choosing to disregard anything inferior that diminished your status?

He tied the head to his saddle using the man's hair for fastenings and arranged it so that the face was on the outward side. His horse, one of the centurion's, must have had the scent of a man's blood on its coat before. The centurion was a mighty warrior. It must have experienced a head hanging off the saddle, resting a dull weight on its shoulder. It seemed unfazed by what he had done or the blood dripping down its flank. It was sure to draw flies. The hardest bit of the whole thing had been ignoring the lad's short mute pleading as he lay spreadeagled and defenceless on the grass. That was the moment he understood what being a true warrior of the Votadini was going to be like. He congratulated himself on not being weak and letting the lad go.

He took the new horse into tow with the others and enjoyed the warm smugness of what the soldiers would say when he returned with the head. Perhaps the optio or Marcellus would reward him? Make him an official scout? Except, he did not feel ready to go back and see the carnage and murder they had committed inside the Carveti hillfort. There would be nothing useful he could do, and the sights would be pitiful. The Carveti were not his enemies, he had no feud with them, nor did he know much about them beyond the fact they were allies of the Brigantes. The latter were most definitely enemies of the centurion and his men. That tribe was still defiantly butting their heads when the opportunity arose. Thus, the Carveti had brought all this upon themselves by abducting the centurion. He kneed the horse forward and went exploring the valley in front of him. Before long he wished he had returned to the soldiers. The hills were much bleaker than those of home and he had gotten himself temporarily lost. There was enough daylight left, time to about turn and retrace his steps. Three figures on foot caught his eyes darting at speed over the rough ground. Locals: they gave the appearance of knowing where they were heading and then, they caught sight of him and changed direction.

Three against one would be an altogether different affair from the little combat he had just won and the horses he was leading would lure them to attack. He turned and put distance between the men and himself. He paused on a low rise of grass and looked back. The men had gone. Or at least, he could not see them. He spurred on unconvinced he had shaken them off or that they had given up on his horses. Bending up into an eastern leading corrie he kept his animals moving. When he paused again, the distinct shapes of the men were framed for a fleeting glimpse against the rocky backdrop of the hillside. He pressed deeper up the inclining valley. So long as he did not need to dismount, he could stay out in front of them but if the valley closed up on him, he would have to turn and face them. A roil of nerves began knotting in his stomach. His earlier jubilation evaporated.

Up ahead a horse caught his attention. A man was lying at its feet and like a faithful dog, the horse was waiting and cropping at the tough grass beside him. He got closer. The horse was held by its reins to the fist of the man on the ground. At his back, was it his imagination tricking him or could he really hear their voices calling to him to halt and speak with them? Offers of friendship floating in the wind? He looked down at the man on his face in the grass. Army caligae on his feet; a bloodstained dirty army tunic. A crisscross spider's web of small white scars on his left forearm.

"Centurion sir? Master?" he queried.

The man moaned something incomprehensible, and turned his head to the sound of Orann's voice. It was the centurion. He slipped off his horse with his own reins clamped between his teeth, gripped Velio under the armpits, heaving him over and then up into a sitting position. The centurion looked exhausted. Lines of weariness gouged his face through a new beard that was dirty and uncombed. He was not the same master he knew from Deva Victrix. What would the mistress say if she saw him in this state? He took a water skin off his horse and fed the liquid to him. Velio gulped, his hands shaking, spilling water down his tunic. Orann let him drink his fill, with his back uncomfortably exposed. His nerves shrieked at him, every instinct screaming danger. Velio handed the skin up to him, nodding his thanks. Something of his old warmth touched his expression as he wiped his mouth with the back of his hand.

"Please, we must hurry centurion. There is no time to explain. Let me help you up. There are men coming and they want the horses. Can you ride if I get you up?" he implored, pointing to the three strangers who were now closing in fast.

Velio focussed, nodding in recognition. Orann propelled the older man into his saddle with a sudden strength that surprised himself. He smacked Velio's horse on the rump and herded it away from danger. Velio began coming to his senses as the peril loomed.

*'How long was I lying there?'* he wondered.

It did not matter now. Somehow, he had managed to keep a hold of the horse.

"It's good to see you Orann, let's get out of here," he said, "lead on if you know the way."

"I'm lost centurion," Orann replied.

"No more than me. Let's get away from those three. There is much to do," he said, "that way," he pointed to the higher ground.

Orann frowned, the lower ground would be better for the horses to outrun their three protagonists, but he obeyed the order. There was not a word about the head hanging off his saddle. He swallowed his disappointment and presumed the centurion had not noticed. The centurion was making heavy weather of riding the horse; sweat began running off his forehead and his face went pale.

The harder ground was only making things worse. Checking to their rear the men were still following.

"Centurion, perhaps we should fight them while we have light. If they come at us after dark, it will be difficult," he said.

Velio did not answer.

"Centurion, we cannot take the horses much higher, it's getting too steep," he reasoned.

Velio turned in his saddle.

"The higher we get the less they will want to press an attack uphill. It's hard to climb and fight, believe me, I've done it. There's a spot up there where we can tether the horses and see if those three still fancy it. I see you have a sword on one of the saddles Orann. You'll need to give it me and use the spear. I only have this useless knife," he said.

Orann pulled the reserve gladius from the optio's spare mount.

"Are you well enough to fight master?" he asked.

Velio grimaced a little.

"I've been better," he paused and saw the farm boy's decapitated head.

"But you have been busy too I see. Getting used to soldiering, eh?" he twitched a smile.

Orann shrugged, now that it had been spoken aloud, he did not know to answer. What would a warrior say? Eidumnos had not been one for taking heads. Chasing cattle thieves did not call for that at Trimontium. The Selgovae were the ones who went in for that. He nodded back.

They reached a tiny ledge of hillside with the slenderest of stances for the horses. He tethered them to a large rock and took the Carveti boy's spear off the back of one of them. His own spear was a superior weapon.

"They can have Votadini or Carveti iron in their ribs," he announced holding one in each hand.

Velio chuckled. Below them the men had halted. Without asking Orann stepped to the lip of the edge and shouted down, brandishing them.

"Carveti or Votadini?" he taunted.

Velio weighed the sword in his hand. A flurry of challenges passed between Orann and the men. He recognised Votadini getting repeated, but the words were too fast for him to follow. But the tone told him all he needed to understand. They came up slowly choosing the footholds, their heads so far beneath Velio and Orann's feet, they were utterly exposed to Orann's spears, showing their contempt for him. If it was not for the fresh head hanging from his saddle Velio might have shared that low opinion. If the lad could hit two of them, he could deal with the last one, if it came to that, but the ground was so unfavourable it should not take much to make them move on, he reckoned. It sounded like 'Romani,' they were repeating, gesturing at him. Orann became more vociferous, shouting in Votadini, shaking the spears. The Votadini were renowned as a peaceful tribe. He wondered if they even had a war cry.

"Just kill one of them Orann and I'll take the other two," he called out.

The three warriors stood staring up at them and the horses. Orann slid one spear into the crook of the other arm, reached down and picked up a sizeable stone. He straightened up, tossing it and catching it in his hand.

*'Now that is good thinking lad. None of them have shields. Throw it and they will come. No warrior is going to run from a lad throwing stones. Let's get this over with,'* Velio thought.

The three Carveti looked at the stone in Orann's hand and the ample reserves at their feet.

*'Three against two, uphill, I don't think so lads,'* Velio guessed, *'but you can keep us pinned here for a while. That could get difficult. Better to do this now.'*

"Throw it Orann. Let's get them stirred up. Get them to come at us," he ordered.

Orann grunted and flung the stone down at the three men, not choosing any of them in particular. He missed them. They shouted up at him. Orann selected a bigger rock and hurled that. They began spitting back curses at him. Velio liked the reaction and joined in. Anything to provoke a rash attack. Orann hit one and drew blood. They were standing taking the punishment, put off from climbing higher by the steep gradient. They began stepping back as Orann maintained his volleys of rocks. Velio heard insults, but Orann was laughing at them, making provocative gestures with his hand.

*'If they go back down and wait for us, we'll have trouble getting down,'* Velio decided.

"Orann, is there food in the saddle bags?" he called.

"No master, I did not bring any. I only intended to walk the horses while your men attacked the hilltop," Orann replied.

"Liscus has attacked a hilltop?" he queried.

"Yes master."

"Can you find your way back?" he said.

"Not while they are here," Orann stated. "I have been up and down many valleys since leaving your men. I'm not sure how to get back to them. I'm sorry master."

It was not what he wanted to hear but Orann was at least honest with him, he could not be faulted for that. He was as lost as Velio in this damned confusion of hills.

"We can't stay trapped up here Orann. Are there any more weapons on the horses?" he asked.

Orann shook his head. The optio's spare sword had been the only one.

"Give them the spare horses and see if they leave," he ordered.

"Lord Liscus told me to guard them," Orann said.

"Let them go Orann," he said.

"One of them is mine. I took it today," Orann pointed to the prize he had won.

Velio saw Orann had crossed the invisible bridge from servant to Votadini warrior, albeit inexperienced in war but he had survived his first one-on-one encounter and come out the other side alive.

"Very well, release the two Liscus gave you to hold. I will explain everything, you will not be in trouble," he said, "we can't get trapped up here. If more of them come, we'll never get out. It's time to pay, Orann."

Orann looked at him confused, "and if they don't go?" he asked.

"Then we go down there and fight," Velio replied.

Orann untied the two cavalry mounts and pushed them to the edge. They looked down and shied back unwilling to go down by themselves. He tried coaxing them with his voice, but they refused to budge.

"I'll have to lead them down," he said.

Velio shook his head. The three Carvetii grinned up at them.

"Fuck," he said.

There was no alternative to fighting now. Getting down there was as treacherous as the Carvetii trying to get up to them. Whoever stayed put was going to hold the advantage.

"Yes master," Orann answered.

Velio put his hand on his side checking his wound for the umpteenth time, pulled it away and saw there was no blood. Orann realised what was the matter and looked in through the torn tunic at the wound for him.

"It's nearly healed master," he said.

Velio gave him a thankful pat on the shoulder.

"Then if we have to go down there, we will send those dogs running," he replied, "but first, you are sitting on one of my stable horses. And I have a Carvetii horse. You are going to give me my own horse back, you will keep the one you won, and the rest of them we will release. If we wait for night those three will be up here. This is no place for a fight."

Orann's eyes brightened, "you think they will accept the horses?" he asked.

The Roman looked tired but he had found fresh strength. Velio snorted as he waited for Orann to sort out the reins and tether the horses they were keeping.

"It's what they want, but it's dangerous. Once they are mounted, they are a harder proposition."

Orann did not know what that meant but Velio's grim face brooked no dissent.

"I will lead them down master," he offered.

"Good lad, leave me your spears and I will cover you," Velio replied.

He paused, "Orann, if this goes wrong, jump on one of the horses and get out of here. Go back to Deva, tell my wife what happened. Don't argue, there is no time."

He made it sound like a command. Orann thought about arguing but quailed at the idea of disobeying the Master.

"I take my spear, I think. You have the sword," he replied.

"Very well," Velio sighed, "one last thing Orann. When you get down there, scatter the horses, don't hand them over. Give them something to think about. Let's not make it easy for them."

Orann liked the thought of not surrendering the horses after all and began comforting them as he sidestepped his way down the slope using the butt of his spear as a staff. The reins tightened as the animals baulked and as he kept the pressure on, one made the first tentative step, its forelegs stiff, haunches bunched up, head tossing, but surrendering to the entreaties of his voice. Velio saw straight away Orann would not be able to defend himself. All his attention was fixed on keeping his balance and guiding the horses. An opportunity blossomed in his mind. A quick look confirmed their own horses were still secured to a rock. He forced himself to wait. The three enemy warriors were watching him, reckoning the next play as this game unfolded. If he threw caution to the winds and risked everything, he could scramble down to the bottom in seconds. He clamped his hand on the sword pommel watching and waiting for Orann to reach the bottom. Halfway down Orann halted and made a show of patting their muzzles. Now that they were over the lip and descending, they were more willing to be led. The three Carveti were almost licking their lips. Orann got down the last part of the slope, smiled at them and slapped the rumps of the uneasy Roman horses. Then, he screeched in the ear of one of them. The horse reacted as if he had branded it. They bolted as one and careered towards the Carveti who jumped aside to avoid a trampling. Two of them darted after the horses, the third came at him. In his ear he heard another roar. The centurion surged past him waving the sword. He met the Carveti head on. Orann moved aside raising his spear. It was enough to distract the Carveti who flashed a sword blow at the spear tip. Velio closed in. The Carveti recovered and parried. Orann felt his blood get up and jabbed, catching their opponent on the hip. The sword flashed at him again, but the spear gave him a better reach and the sword tip whizzed past his stomach leaving him unharmed. Velio pushed in and ended it. Orann drove his spear in too, making sure. The Carveti sank to his knees.

"You are not taking my horses," Orann promised.

Velio stood back, it was over. The warrior buckled as Orann wrenched out his hunting spear.

"You should know my name is Orann of the Votadini. And I send you to your dreaming," he said.

'*A little presumptuous,*' thought Velio, '*but you did help.*'

He wondered for a moment if Orann was going to take the man's head. The lad looked as though he was debating that very point with himself.

'*If the roles had been reversed,*' Velio mused.

He touched his side. It was still dry despite the wild plunge down the hill. The other two horses were leading the remaining Carveti away from them. The danger was over.

"Time to get on our horses, Orann""

He pointed at the dying warrior, "if you are taking his head, get on with it."

He climbed back up the slope and brought the two mounts down. Orann was holding the severed head. Velio sucked his teeth and decided to say nothing. He got up into the saddle, glad to be riding one of his own horses on a decent saddle. His side did not feel too bad, all things considered. Mars and Jupiter were due a sacrifice of thanks. Orann took his time tying the second head on the other side of the saddle. Two heads in one day.

## Chapter Twenty-five.

### The hillfort; the next day

"Hey, Arco, there's strangers at the Decumana asking for you," a voice called out.

Arco swung his legs off his bunk and sat up.

"From Iuliocenon?" he asked.

His mate smiled a twisted grin.

"Best you go and look for yourself, Arco, my old cock. Don't let that grumpy, whore's son Vindex catch you. Oh, and by the by, they look like 'old mules gone astray in the night, slipped their ropes,' if you get me, so be careful, eh? They must be fuckin' mad coming here in daylight," his mate said.

The alarm bell started ringing in his head. There were only two people he knew that could possibly meet that description. And if his mate could tell they were deserters, everyone else would see it too. He kept his thoughts to himself, clipped on his cloak and left the barrack block, pretending there was nothing on his mind. Outside the wind was blowing as usual, like a fierce trumpet call up the valley. Up on the parade field their sister century was hard at it, drilling, voices lost in the perpetual gale. The hill glowered behind them, its notches and ridges reminding him of giant or, godlike, axe strokes. The Dextra gate on the seaward side took the prevailing wind and its guard were never happy. The Sinistra gate was just as bad because the dopey tribune, or whoever it was that chose this site in the first place, ignored the steep slope of the ground. The interior lines were laid open like a tilted plate to the prevailing wind. Of all the guards to be endured in this sodding place, the decumana was the best sheltered but the least profitable. He doubted it was a coincidence that whomever they were, the two mules had chosen the best of the four available gates to come knocking.

Scribono was leaning with his back against the outer wall, arms folded, looking like he would rather be anywhere else than here. Junius Cita turned his back to the ramparts, hiding his identity as best he could. He spoke first.

"The game's up for now, Arco. That stray centurion we shot instead of the one from here, the one Scrib decided to take back to Drapisces? Well, he fuckin' escaped. Just to really fuck things up, his century stormed Drapisces' walls yesterday looking for him. You'll need to lay off the waggons for a while until we can work something out," he said.

Arco looked at him. Dishevelled and unshorn he could pass for Carvetii at a distance but close up, he looked like what he really was, a deserter in an army cloak. A mule that had gone astray, on purpose.

"So, if Drapisces has been captured how are you here?" he snapped.

"Easy, my friend, there's no need for that tone," Scribono scowled.

"We're just letting you know there's no customers until we get this sorted. No need to fall out," Junius continued.

He raised his hand at Scribono. He looked up at the fort's wall. The duty sentries had read the signs and moved along, leaving them to talk, keen not to get involved. Arco shook his head.

"Don't worry, they're not listening. But you haven't answered my question. How are you here?" he said.

"After it was over some green optio gave us a couple of cloaks. He had them to spare, if you get my drift. Drapisces did not go down easy. Well, he did not go down at all. As soon as I saw the shields coming up the hill, I knew he was fucked. They were First fuckin' cohort, Boar markings, clear as day. He had no chance. They were taking us back to Cantiventi. Didn't believe our story. We escaped last night. We reckoned the game was up and talked our way out past the guard and came here. No chance to pick up a couple of swords or anything. It's lucky dogs and dice they didn't put us in chains like the rest of those dumb Carvetii. And they found the piggin' centurion's helmet, so Drapisces is definitely for the old chop. Look, we haven't got a pugio between us Arco, no silver, nothing. You've got to get us some kit," Junius said.

"And a bit of bread," Scribono muttered, "I'm bloody starved."

Arco pulled his pugio from the sheath and handed it over to Junius under guise of shaking his arm in greeting.

"You two, who are you? What century are you? Who is your centurion?'

Titus Vindex peered over the wall down at them'

"Arco, bring those men in," he ordered.

"Fuck," hissed Scribono.

"Play along, Scrib," Junius Cita hissed.

Arco looked up at the optio and saluted, "as you have commanded me, sir," he replied.

"Don't run, for Mithras' sake do as he says," he added under his breath.

"Fuck it," Scribono replied.

He bolted for the beginnings of the hilltop where the escarpment fell away to the steeper ground below. Junius Cita swung his fist. Arco fell back.

"Get those men," Vindex shouted, "guard get after them."

*'If you'd killed him this would never have happened. Only the gods know why you kept him alive and took him to Drapisces. Chop him, rob him, hide the body, perhaps, but keeping him alive, madness. This will end badly,'* Arco fumed

"Run, you stupid bastard," he said, clutching his split lip, surprised by the forceful blow.

Junius pursed his mouth in regret and took off after Scribono.

"Arco, get up man and get after them," Titus Vindex shouted.

He took his time getting up. Scribono was already out of sight, below the eye line of the ridge. Junius Cita's cloak, flapped like a sail as he followed. Arco turned and opened his arms wide. He had nothing to use against them. He had been off watch. The pugio had been his only weapon. He delayed for the guard to come rushing out of the gatehouse room and pointed the way.

The escarpment was an ankle breaking nightmare to run over. Rocks, tussocky coarse grass, hollows and thin gravels made it easier to ascend than to get down. Scribono ran for this life, prepared to break a leg in order to escape the flogging and worse up waiting up there in the fort. Junius Cita might have a chance of talking his way out of it, but he knew he was doomed if they caught him. Arco would disavow any knowledge of him. All deserters were executed as a deterrent to the others. The only question was, would praefectus Civius do it here or send him to Cantiventi to die?

It was a long slope down. A pilum whistled past him and hit a rock, clanging as it skittered sideways, bent by the impact. Another followed. He dodged and changed direction. The bastards were trying to kill him. He had no idea where Junius was and cared even less. At the lower slopes he took a glance back. Arco and four of the Delmatarum were hounding Junius. Even at a distance Arco looked like he was trying not to be involved.

He turned and kept running, leaving Junius to his gods. There were shouts. He paused once more. Junius was surrounded. They had him pinned. The pila were not for show. He had a surge of dread for his companion.

"You poor bastard Junius, they're going to chop you for sure," he cried and kept running.

When he checked for the final time, they were dragging the Sixth legion man back up the slope. No one was interested in him now they had Junius Cita.

## Chapter Twenty-six.

Junius stopped protesting and banging on the door. There was little he could say to talk himself out of it. He did not speak the tribal tongue fluently enough to hide behind the language and he was still wearing his old tunic and much repaired caligae. Nothing betrayed him more eloquently than Roman army boots, despised by the natives. He did not have the complexion of a native. And his lack of woad marks and arm rings gave him away. He had thrown his old legionary ring away long ago as an act of severance. He thought there was nothing left that marked him as a deserter and yet the optio had taken one good hard look at him and said:

"What legion?"

He was screwed. Had Scribono gotten away or was he being held somewhere in the fort as well? He was parched and no one was paying him any attention. The only light in the tiny storeroom was coming through the gaps around the base of the door. It took time to adjust to the gloom. There was no water in here. It was built into the north wall, small and cramped: a hidey hole for sentries to sneak down off the wall and take a breather from whatever watch they were supposed to be on. He could just make out the small graffiti of bored and powerless men scratched into the stone. Phallic gestures to ward off the local evil of the place, insults against junior officers and one telling plea on a north facing wall:

*'Boreas have mercy.'*

But the cold winds still blew.

Arco had tried to distance himself when they dragged him back up the hill and through the gate. Shooting the centurion off his horse had been a mistake but Scribono letting him live had been far worse. He slid down the wall and sat on the stone flagged floor. The centurion had escaped Drapisces' fort. The way he had despatched Caturiges the priest, despite his wound, was ample evidence he was a dangerous opponent. He clenched his hands in tight balls. There was nothing in the small cell he could use for the tiniest of sacrifices. Not even a beetle. Nothing he could offer the gods to act on his behalf. Nothing to pay for his earnest prayer the centurion was dead out there in the hills.

## Chapter Twenty-seven.

### The hill fort.

"How much further is it Orann?" Velio gasped.

His side ached. This wound was not letting go. It should be healing better than this. All this horse riding was not helping.

*'Where in Hades arse is Liscus?'* he railed at his junior's incompetence.

Orann stuck his hand out and steadied his master in the saddle.

"Not much further master. I can see the fort. I'll get us down onto the road and then it will be easier for you," he replied.

Velio lifted his head. There it was; the same sight he had seen when he brought the century up to inspect the Delmatarum. How long ago was that? Two, three weeks ago: longer? He held it in his eyes and did not let anything distract him, like a drowning man with the rope that would save him just fractionally out of reach. If his horse stumbled, he was going to get off and keep walking. Voccia and Deva Victrix had never looked so wonderful as these oak hewn outer gates. The smell of cooking floated up the road towards him from invisible fires. Legionary bread, a spot of porridge, a handful of olives, a cup of ration posca, sometimes a thin share of rabbit stew. He saw the day watch on the wall had spotted their approach. Two dishevelled riders walking their horses down the road, up past the garrison bathhouse, right to the walls towering high overhead. He could imagine what they were thinking. Not much of a threat. The trumpets were silent. The off duty men at the bathhouse doorway stood intrigued by their appearance. Under the Praetoria gateway they halted. He looked the duty tesserarius in the eyes.

"I am Centurion Pinneius," he said, "open the gate please."

"Sir," the man snapped.

Willing hands helped him down.

"He is one of my household staff, he is not to be touched," he said, pointing at Orann, "he needs food and a bed just as much as me."

The two Carvetii heads bought Orann immediate friends. The gate guards' attitude improved.

'Will you speak with the commander, sir?" the tesserarius asked.

By his look and general smartness, he was another legion regular detached to the auxiliary.

"I suppose I had better. Are any of my men here?" Velio asked.

The soldier shook his head.

"No sir. Your optio took them back to Cantiventi. I hear they are out looking for you further south. They searched the hills around here for you. Where were you sir?" he said.

Velio smiled.

"I don't really know but I'm glad to be back," he said.

The tesserarius saluted, "the Delmatarum welcome you back into the light sir. The gods have delivered you from those heathen scum."

...He paused, smiled and scratched the corner of his mouth, "the commander is down in the bathhouse. He may be a while."

Velio digested the inferences of that plus the tesserarius' bemused grin. The post's most senior officer was sitting in a hot bath right now while he, a centurion of the First cohort was just back in the gates, from Mithras knew where, with blood on his tunic and heads on his servant's saddle.

“Well, he must know I’m here. I’ve just walked past it,” he shook his head.

The pain in his side seemed less but waves of exhaustion were rolling over him as he began to relax from the strains of getting here.

“A bed and some food will do until the commander is ready,” he said, “if my men are back in Cantiventi I need to get there as soon as I can.”

“With respect sir I think you need some rest, that wound needs the medicus, and a new tunic would not go amiss. We have no seamstresses up here, so repairs like that don’t happen. Let me see what I can do,” the tesserarius pointed to Velio’s bloodstained tunic.

His broad competent face spoke volumes. The thought of ladies with sewing needles patching soldier’s tunics at a little booth in the camp was so out of place he nearly laughed.

“Perhaps you are right. Lead me to the infirmary, and feed my servant, he is the reason I am still alive,” he conceded.

## Part Two.

## Chapter Twenty-eight.

### Argentomagus, Gaul.

Gallus stood over the shallow, exposed grave. She was lying on her side, as if she had been tossed in like a sack.

"What are we going to do, Gallus?" Hanno asked.

Gallus looked back at him, "give her a decent burial," he retorted.

*

A little eddy of irritation managed to ripple the decurion's temper. He sucked through his teeth to get the clerk's attention. The officers of the Octava Augusta were not used to being kept waiting by civilians, no matter how exalted their master's rank. Durus Decimus was a pain in the proverbial, but he was the procurator. Lord of Argentomagus and all its environs, right up to the walls of the legion's gates and not a damn step further. The Bituriges clerk heard the oral rebuke and said nothing. The procurator's door was staying closed until he had digested his midday meal and was not going to open until he was ready. The soldier had mistimed his arrival. He offered the soldier a cup of water, to placate him.

"Call me when he is ready," the decurion said.

It was hotter outside than in the civic building.

Argentomagus dozed in the heat like a well-fed hound. The forum stalls were busy but in a slow, sedate way, butterfly voices murmuring at the food vendors. Trusted slaves were running errands, a cart was unloading empty amphorae to the oil seller. A dog was sniffing a spillage, uncertain whether to taste or not. The silversmiths were silent, taking their ease like the procurator. A mason was eyeing up the entrance to a nearby house; it was a hot day to be wielding a hammer on stone. The decurion finished the water and decided enough was enough. The news could keep. He was not standing waiting on a civilian any longer. So much for his routine liaison visit; Hanno Glaccus and Gallus Tiomarus had found a body in a shallow grave in the most distant of their fields. Their faces had been expressionless when they told him. They both had that contemplative, pre-battle look. He was horrified for her and for the sort of retribution those two were capable of unleashing. Durus Decimus should be appalled. But feeding his belly was apparently more important than hearing a decurion's news. The information could wait.

Back at the fort his commander listened while he reported and said, "it's purely a civilian matter."

The decurion regarded his sharp, young, senior officer.

"There are only two of them over there sir," he said, "and they're getting on a bit, no disrespect to either of them. If this turns into trouble they won't survive, Twentieth legion or not," he observed.

"Hmmn. You have a point," his commander replied.

He stood up and pacing around his office. The officer's clerk and decurion swapped looks and bided their time. The centurion folded his arms, digging fingers into muscles.

"I have agreed we will take some of their next vintage, to help them get started. We could argue that gives us an interest in their wellbeing," he posited.

He paused and chewed his bottom lip, "a vested interest, so to speak."

He took his seat once more.

"And this wasn't just some slave they found? One that keeled over in the fields?" he asked.

The decurion shook his head.

"Hanno Glaccus is fairly convinced it must be the wife of ex legionary Priscus. Said it was clearly an old woman. The ground has been dry recently, so," he paused at the edge of the pit.

'*So, she's not had much chance to rot is what you are trying not to say,*' the commander guessed.

"He may be getting on a bit but Gallus Tiomaris is not a man you would choose to face when he's angry. Sir," the decurion said.

The centurion quelled his urge to smile. Gallus Tiomaris was a hastiliarius. He doubted the old boy's rage would amount to much more than a finger snap of thunder and rain. Glaccus was the old centurion; he was the one that might require diplomatic handling.

"Durus Decimus, what have you done? Why couldn't you take 'No' for an answer?" he muttered and drummed his fingers on his table.

"They are good fields sir, valuable. Priscus worked wonders but the ground is exceptional, blessed, you might say" his clerk ventured.

He did not like the sound of that thought. An immortal interest in the estate skewed the scales. He weighed his options once more.

"Keep an eye on them. I'll alert the other officers. Make sure the death is reported to the procurator. I want you to go back today and do that,"he ordered.

"As you command, sir," the decurion replied.

"And ask Hanno Glaccus and Gallus Tiomaris if they want any help from us," he continued.

"I have already told them I will swing my troop past their property on a regular basis," the decurion replied, "anything more would be tricky," the decurion suggested.

The centurion nodded back: tactically, the sight of patrols visiting the estate regularly should suffice to warn off potential troublemakers.

"Very well, that will do for now," he acknowledged, "there's no need to be heavy handed. Argentomagus is not at war."

His clerk beamed at the very idea.

"Begging your pardon centurion but what is the procurator going to do?" the decurion said.

The centurion commander clasped his hands behind his head and decided to explain the situation better.

"He wants those fields. He has always wanted them. Make no mistake on that. As to what he will do, frankly I have no idea, but a little night time sabotage to get them is not impossible by any means. He comes from good family. His grandfather was a soldier. Have you noticed his leg? It stopped his career before it started. I suspect our procurator is a man of frustrated ambitions. I've seen their type before. They are dangerous men. Of course, the old woman's death might be nothing to do with him and a decent burial is all that is needed. Tiomaris and Glaccus will put that to rights. Dismiss decurion, I'm sure you have other duties calling for your attention, as have I. Look after our interests over there. Do what is needed. Remember, I want my wine," he glanced to his clerk, "and if you do find out who killed Priscus' wife, bring them here to me."

## Chapter Twenty-nine.

## Argentomagus procurator's office.

Durus Decimus held his breath, listening to the voices outside his door. He understood most of it, but it was a little muffled. Then it went quiet. He restrained the urge to go and see.

"It sounds as if the body of old man Priscus' woman has been found,"his pet Bituriges reported a few minutes later.

"Oh, well put it in the register," he instructed, "and close the door."

Once the clerk gone, he put his head down into his hands. The plan to invite Hanno and Gallus to dine now seemed fraught with danger: redundant. He had already divulged his desire to own the estate.

*'What a fool I've been. Grandfather would have cuffed me for stupidity. What kind of soldier tells his enemy his plans of attack?'*

He cursed his big mouth. And now her body had been found they would be correct in putting the dice side by side and thinking he may have had an involvement. A vested interest in her demise. An interest he had advertised to their faces. How could he have been so stupid to open up and say so much?

He made himself calm down and breathe deep long breaths. It worked, he felt his heart slowing. Blind panic was not going to help. He needed to think. The invitation to come and dine with him could still stand. It had interesting possibilities. Poison them and get them off the scene? No, that road was now closed. It had been a stupid notion in the first place. If he made good on the invite, it would be to tease out what they knew from what they suspected.

To bring them closer. He cursed his own greed. It was beyond the bounds of public credibility that the owners of the estate could keep dying so regularly. Argentomagus was sleepy but it was not comatose. The Eighth legion were certainly not the kind of men to miss the link. And to think, he had tried to inveigle with the commander to turn a blind eye. Well, that plan was in ruins. What to do, what must one do?

## Chapter Thirty.

## Cantiventi.

Auvericus left the praefectus' office clutching his bag of compensation and a script for the free provision of twenty healthy slaves to replace his losses and first pick from the next consignment. Given that his mine was within four miles of Cantiventi, the losses had succeeded in both embarrassing the commander and serving as a tart reminder that this part of Britannia still harboured dissidents and peace was a fragile thing. Commerce could not prosper unless the praefectus exerted some proper control. He had done better than expected out of the meeting, although he sensed the commander was curter on his departure. The money had been placed on the table for him to pick up, not handed to him as courtesy might have demanded. But better than all of that, there was an opportunity for a juicy bit of revenge.

The headquarters duty officer escorted him out to his horse.

"Get what you wanted?" he said as they were about to part company.

Auvericus gazed at the outer encampment where the newly returned soldiers of the Twentieth had set up tents. He was hearing good rumours that all had not gone well. It was tempting to make a snide riposte about the presence of so many soldiers and his own misfortunes, but it he held it back. A Roman centurion would not care in the slightest that his operation was effectively stymied until he could drum up more slaves. He concentrated on the question.

"That Carvetii leader they have just brought back in: Drapisces. Your commander said he might have led the attack on my mine? Can I have him as one of my slaves? It would be amusing to put him in chains at the site of his misdemeanour," he said, surprising himself at the unheralded idea, "your praefectus has given me a promissory note for twenty men," he flourished the scroll.

The centurion's face betrayed no emotion.

"Personally I don't give a toss, it's all the same to me, but as a rule we don't put slaves to work in their home area. Gives them hopes of escape. Slaves should not have hope," he said, "it's either the mines down south or the chop for him. Though I think the men over there, might be taking him back to Deva for punishment. They lost good lads in the hills, so I hear. And strictly speaking he is a prisoner of the Twentieth legion, so neither I nor the praefectus can interfere, whether he attacked your mine or not," he said.

"Who do I ask?" Auvericus persisted.

He doubted the praefectus was completely unable to intervene in any way. That was just the centurion playing little games. In Cantiventi he was all powerful. It was more likely he just did not want to get involved now that the Twentieth had Draspisces.

"I'll take you over there and see what they say," the centurion replied.

They walked in through one of the four gaps in the little ditch demarcating the camp from the civilian settlement. The locals were conversing with soldiers across the gap, dallying the time of day. They had relaxed faces, smiles flashed. It had the feel of a place that welcomed the army and the money it brought. The duty guard saluted the centurion and let them pass. The headquarters tent was conspicuous in the midst of twenty or so others all neatly lined. Auvericus saw it had two legionaries standing guard on either side of the entrance. The mood was different here: tenser. Groups of wounded men were sitting talking. A group of Carvetii men were sitting in chains on the grass. Another group of women and children further away looked like they had been tied up. The children looked overawed and scared.

*'As well they might,'* he considered.

Both groups had half a dozen gaolers watching them. A glance told him they looked fit and strong, perfectly serviceable for digging galena. By the side of the headquarters a man was pegged out like a starfish on the ground. He did not need to ask the name of that one. The smell of baking bread hung in the air. No doubt to torture the Carvetii as much as to feed the legionaries. The centurion halted at the headquarters tent flap and saluted the officer surveying his command. Liscus saluted him back. He had a venomous look about him that Auvericus did not much like.

"How are your wounded, optio?" opened the centurion.

Liscus gave a non-committal shrug of his shoulders. The Cantiventi medicus had still to walk the few hundred paces from the garrison infirmary and take a look for himself. He was not much impressed by the delay.

"I await your medicus, sir. If you could remind him, I would be grateful. My capsarius believes they should all live. My dead will be buried here with your praefectus' permission. I can't keep the bodies until we leave for Deva," he said.

The centurion waved his hand, "I can guarantee his agreement. We would not insult them. There is a pleasing spot overlooking the lake where we put our men when we have to. How many did you lose?"

"Eleven," Liscus said.

Auvericus saw raw anger in the soldier's face.

"And I did not get my centurion back, and I've got twice as many wounded," Liscus said.

The centurion nodded.

"It was a tricky operation, optio. But I am hearing your men cleared the hill and sent a warning to the tribes in these parts," the centurion replied.

Liscus took scant comfort. He hooked a thumb at the prostrate prisoner.

"We are going to make this one and the rest of them pay. Jupiter hear me."

The centurion nodded for a moment and blew out his cheeks as though he had suddenly remembered the reason he had come to visit.

"This is Auvericus. He owns some of the local mines around here. We believe your man Drapisces launched an attack on the most important one. Killed the guards and set all his slaves loose. He has a note from the commander to cover his losses in manpower. He wants Drapisces."

"Well, he can't have him," Liscus snapped.

The centurion smiled a thin, joyless acknowledgement at Liscus' sentiment,

"Optio, it's not your decision to make," he said.

Auvericus kept quiet. Liscus pulled out his best argument.

"Drapisces is a prisoner of the Twentieth legion sir. I don't have authority to hand him over. My centurion would have to order it."

"That's rather the point though optio, is it not?" the centurion purred.

"Look sir, your miner can take as many of the others as he wants but Drapisces is going back to Deva Victrix with us as soon as we get our centurion back," Liscus fenced, "we found the centurion's helmet in his hall. He knows what happened to him. And he is going to tell us one way or the other."

The centurion considered it.

"And if you don't get your centurion back optio, what then?"

Marcellus coughed behind Liscus. A discreet, *'I'm here if you need me,'* message. Liscus raised his hand a fraction at his side.

"We are not going back without him," he vowed.

The centurion's eyes warmed.

*'Was that a test?'* Liscus wondered, *'because I'm only an optio?'*

The centurion demurred, "fair enough, optio. Auvericus, the optio here says you can fill your quota from these prisoners, but not Drapisces. I would not argue if I were you. This is a First cohort century, and they will not take kindly to it. And frankly you are rather outnumbered."

He turned and left Auvericus to make the best of it.

"Thank you, sir," Liscus said to his back.

"My pleasure optio, take no offence, I had to ask. I hope you find your centurion," he replied, raising a hand in farewell, "don't be deceived by the locals down here, these are not good hills to get lost in."

"He does not help you?" Auvericus queried.

Liscus faced him and breathed out a bullish snort of air. A variety of replies ran across his tongue. He discarded all of them.

"We have not asked for help," he replied.

*

Velio rolled off the bunk in the centurion's room, wondering what time of day it was and where his tunic was, certain he had crashed onto the bed fully clothed. Was it the same day? Orann appeared at his door with water. The barrack block was quiet. This must be one of the unoccupied ones.

"Better, master?" he asked.

"Better Orann," Velio answered.

"The wound, master?"

"It feels a lot better too, not so hot," Velio said, rolling his eyes.

Orann saw Velio's tongue flick his lip as he gave a wry smile.

"Mistress will be pleased," he said.

Velio swallowed the water and held the cup out for more.

"Yes, she will Orann, she will. How long did I sleep Orann?"

"Since yesterday. The commander came to see you as soon as he heard you were back safely, but you were asleep. You should not have been put in here. The commander was angry, very angry but they decided not to move you. He said talking could wait. A senior soldier came and dressed your wound when you were sleeping."

Velio touched his side and realised his tunic had been replaced. His side felt much easier, his breathing was much less painful. The tightness that had been keeping him on edge, bordering torture riding on the horse, had mysteriously gone and he ventured a deeper, careful breath to test today's limits. Though he knew it was now mostly a pain of the mind. Aesculapius had watched his actions and been merciful. He would need a small offering.

"You are to rest for two days master then the wound will be better. Riding a horse will be easier," Orann instructed.

"I think I'll stay off horses for a while Orann. Walking is safer. Two days Orann," he chaffed.

Orann brightened up, "perhaps a walk down to the bathhouse master, make you feel better, some hot food, and then you should rest some more master. The commander is sending word to Cantiventi that you have returned safely. The century is there," he chattered on.

He went back out into the main block and returned with a clean cloak and a beautiful mail shirt of chain link squamata, like fish scales, which seemed alive as it folded down on itself, like a burnished snake. He saw Velio's eyes widen.

"Whose is that?" he said.

He had never owned one. This was a masterpiece of craftsmanship and expensive, to boot. He got up and touched the scales with his fingertips. To be lent this was far beyond reasonable expectation. A spare, standard issue, lorica segmentata would have been quite acceptable until he got back to Deva. He slapped his forehead and pretended to turn it into a rub of his forehead. Orann was looking perplexed. This was an auxiliary cohort. There was no store of spare lorica segmentata; except for the officers' cuirasses, they all wore chainmail. But this, this loan must be from: from Civius himself? A standard gladius and pugio came next. He grinned at the definite message. No one was parting company with their personal weapons for him.

"Helmet?" he asked.

Orann shook his head.

*'Perhaps that is just as well. No spare First cohort, centurion, helmets lying around, eh, lads?'*

"When you are ready the commander wishes to speak to you, master," Orann prompted.

'*So much for the bath house, Orann,*' he mused.

Civius rose as he entered the principia. He was convinced the man was as crooked as a vine stick, but at least he was polite and had the military graces: a professional serpent. The other centurion, whose name he could not recall, and Titus Vindex, rose to greet him.

"I see the armour fits," the centurion began, "I thought you and I are about the same size."

He inspected the fit on Velio and nodded approval.

'*Ah, so it's yours. Makes sense. Didn't really think Civius would have done it,*' Velio thought.

"I will return it at the first opportunity," he said, and tried to dodge the social embarrassment of asking his name again.

He hoped the smile of gratitude would suffice for the moment. He took his time shaking their arms in turn, weighing up the atmosphere in the room. Titus Vindex gave him a coded look. The plan to call Civius out for his dealings evaporated. Now was not the right time, besides something else must have happened in his absence.

"Is there something I need to know?" he asked and took the offered seat.

Civius cleared his throat. The centurion was giving him a fraternal smile of uncommitted friendship. Titus had his fingers clasped on his lap like a child instructed to listen and not fidget.

"The lead mines are under attack by Carvetii brigands and production is to all intents down. Mithras only knows what has set them off. Years of relative peace and no suggestion this was coming. Our intelligence reports are worse than useless. Someone should be made to pay for this. Bloody embarrassing: looks like we are sitting in the latrines all day. I can only imagine what Servius Albinius will say when he finds out," Civius spouted, "as you know the Brigantes are their overlords so we can expect an escalation across the mining region. If they come in support in any great numbers, then the Uiliocenon – Cantiventi road is going to become a target and thus compromised," he halted and waved at the stone walls around them.

*'You're not seriously worried about beating off an attack here, even if you are a bit light in numbers. It's that you won't be able to pillage the waggon convoys until this is over. That is what you mean,'* Velio translated.

"It's all started without any warning; we do not know what sparked it off, but it appears to be co-ordinated," the centurion intervened.

Civius took a drink of water.

"We will need support. I do not have sufficient men here to safeguard the road. And Cantiventi is split cavalry and infantry. It does not have sufficient infantry to lend us manpower either. Same situation at Uiliocenon though they are full strength. And they have their ships I suppose. Centurion, I must ask you to keep your century here until this all settles down. We need your men. The auxiliaries need reassurance that the legion is supporting them," Civius implored.

"I do not see that will be a problem," Velio replied, "have messengers been sent to Deva Victrix?"

"Not yet. At least I have not sent any. Cantiventi may have," Civius checked with his centurion.

The centurion shook his head.

“Best we get messengers away today. I can give you a week and then I must return to Deva. But I need to let my men know I am alive. They can march here, and I can arrange fresh troops to come up from Deva if the situation requires and Servius Albinius agrees,” Velio asserted.

“A week will be a help,” Civius replied.

Velio nodded and got up. For now, the Carvetii had bought Civius a little respite from the censure coming his way. Now was not the time to get back into it in front of his officers.

“Hmmn, actually I think it would be best if I go down to Cantiventi and rejoin my men,” he said, “I can’t do anything from here.”

“We will give you an escort, Centurion Pinneius,” his opposite number vouched.

He decided not to argue.

“So, in the circumstances we find ourselves in, am I to assume your inspection of the Delmatarum garrison is over?” Civius licked his lip.

Velio listened: if the Carvetii and Brigantes were going after the lead mines then a bit of lightweight local pillage from the waggon convoys was galling, but weighed up by someone like Servius Albinius, was neither here nor there. Let some other mug sort it out if the legate was really that bothered. He had taken an arrow trying. Hanno Glaccus’ well-known distaste of arrow wounds made perfect sense now that he had taken one. His first one ever, and his last if he had anything to do with it. Gallus and the vineyards in Gaul, Voccia and their unborn child were beckoning.

*‘Time to get out Velio,’* he told himself.

He saluted them and left Civius' needy question hanging. He went to find Orann. They would leave tomorrow. He frowned: Orann was going to have to give up his trophy heads. This was going to require diplomatic words. But riding into Cantiventi with two Carvetii heads hanging on his saddle was hardly going to endear him to the locals. The Morinorum commander would not thank him for stirring things up. Outside the pleasure of cold fresh air hit his cheeks. He was famished. Just the smells of the garrison cooking fires alone were driving him to eat. Orann would take the order better on a full belly. A little posca might soften the blow with perhaps the additional promise of a military pugio for his belt, or his own gladius with the promise of lessons. As soft bribes went, it was an easy one to arrange, provided Orann played ball and threw the damn things over the gorge before they left.

"You did not mention our deserter," Titus Vindex said.

Civius compressed his lips, "no, I didn't, did I?" he replied.

Titus had a cold clamp of foreboding in his gut.

"I would be honoured to lead the escort tomorrow," he rallied.

*'Centurion Pinneius get me out of this serpent nest,'* he prayed harder than he had ever before.

Even harder than he had to win this posting away from the legion and what felt like suffocating rules and strictures.

"I don't think it requires an optio. A tesserarius will be sufficient," Civius said.

Titus felt his resolve crumbling. Tomorrow, when the centurion left to rejoin his men, he, Titus Vindex, was going to be isolated; more isolated than ever.

*'That's the kind of thing that makes men run from the standards,'* he realised.

The men in this fort did not have his back and he had no bond of brotherhood to cover theirs. Just the discipline that good soldiers did that for each other.

*'Take my sword and throw it over the ditch. Caesar bled on the floor of Pompey's Theatre surrounded by allies and his friends.'*

"As you command," he acknowledged.

The other centurion put his hand to his mouth, hiding his distaste. He could read a face better than any man in the fort.

## Chapter Thirty-one.

### The Halls of the Brigantes, to the east of the Carveti lands.

Losatas listened to the tale of resistance told by Drapisces' men. He did not care for the Romans ripping stone from the ground and trees from the forests. He frowned; this was not good news. His distant cousin had acted while he sat by. Even if they had suffered defeat they had stood and fought.

*'Drapisces, you always were a man of solid shoulders.'* he admitted.

If he did not act his men would soon be at his door. It was not a question of making a decision. There was no decision to make.

Afterwards, he chewed an apple and watched the constant movements of the flames in his fire. What if Drapisces was already dead? The Carveti would return with requests of honour to support them. Drapisces' death would draw the Brigantes into an unplanned war. If the Romans had taken him and his people as prisoners, they would execute him as an example and send the rest to slavery over the seas. Thus, the Carveti would in their defeat, and without intending to, remove his right to wage war at his own pleasure. He flicked the apple core into the flames, hearing it hiss. It protested its immolation and then, in a finger-snap, went quiet.

*'Like a dying breath. There's a black raven's thought for so early in the day Losatas. Even for you. Strange, dark thoughts,'* he chided himself and shivered. *'Where do you get them? From the gods?'*

Were they in this old hall right now, lurking and whispering at his shoulder, prompting, urging, silently beseeching him to act in the name of his people?

*"Take the Carveti messengers at face value, Losatas and raise your spear. Stand with them."*

Words in his ears. He glanced behind himself and was glad to find there was no one else in the hall, feeling foolish for doing so, glad no one else was watching. They did not come very often, but these moments spooked him. He took them all as proof he did not act alone, unguided and blind. The hall's old wooden timbers, the blackened roof rafters, the smoke vent in the high pitch, light dappling down in a bright arrow on to the fresh sweet rushes spread below: none of it was strange, or worrying or hiding at his back, whispering. If he did not fight, would all their dying breaths be like apple cores tossed into the fires of the red-cloaked wolf?

*'You spook yourself like a child,'* he warned himself.

That old maverick, Orgidor had preached defiance right in this very room to all his young men. He had slept under these very rafters, welcomed to the end of his days. He went down fighting rather than living with dishonour and the silent condemnation of their shared forebears. What kind of man could sleep in peace under the deerskins when so many ghosts howled for attention in his head? Orgidor: a warrior cousin with the balls to resist the Romans and kill them. He had been an inspiration. But Orgidor was gone now, dead now without a doubt. A memory and a song, sung in his own halls.

"Orgidor, is that you?" he asked, clammy at the possibility.

He closed his eyes and listened.

He spent the day pondering his choices. The day after, he awoke and told Drapisces' messengers the only thing they, and his cousin's ghost, wanted to hear.

## Chapter Thirty-two.

## Cantiventi.

Liscus permitted Auvericus to inspect Drapisces, more to wind the mine owner up than to do him a favour. Drapisces' bonds were tight giving him no slack. He motioned the guards to step aside whilst Auvericus got down on his haunches to speak to their prisoner. Marcellus came out to watch, interested in this small diversion from writing the report of the last few days' actions. Velio's helmet, cuirass and sword had all been recovered. The chest armour had taken punishment from target practice. It was not going to be any use until it was repaired. A bit of elbow grease had restored the proper amount of shine to the helmet and gladius. Seeing the equipment gave him confidence the centurion was out there, alive and kicking. The weather was turning for the better. Liscus had done pretty well in his first independent command attacking the hill fort. Velio's servant had vanished taking the two spare mounts. He doubted it was desertion. Velio's man was not going to go back to his own kind in preference to the life he had chosen. Velio spoke too highly of him for that to be likely. And he had built up credit playing his small part in the ultimate defeat of Segontio and his Selgovae at Trimontium. The men liked him, and they were good judges of character.

*'Balls of Dis-Pater, where in Hades' arse are you Velio?'* he fretted.

"So, what's this performance about?" he asked Liscus.

The optio grinned back The miner was nose-to-nose with the broken face of Drapisces hissing vengeance for the loss of his livelihood, which Liscus reckoned was putting it a bit strong, it was more like a temporary disruption, and it was never good practice to tell your enemy he had hurt you.

"He wants our man for one of his slave quota," Liscus explained.

"Fat chance," Marcellus retorted.

"That's what I told the centurion who brought him over," he said.

"So, you're just pulling some of his tail feathers out for fun?" Marcellus queried.

"No, it's the Carvetii who's doing that. I lost eleven men to catch this bird and I'm not setting it free to the first businessman with a complaint," he jibbed.

"Not a good career move," Marcellus agreed, "well, must get back to work, can't stand here, the legate's report won't write itself."

"Let me know when it's ready to sign," Liscus said, "do you want me to check it when it's ready? Does he check them or ever change them?"

"Just my spelling, sir," Marcellus replied:

Liscus chortled.

Towards late afternoon Marcellus was putting the finishing touches to the patrol report while Liscus checked on the wounded. Distant cheers caught his attention. He cocked his head and listened, trying to gauge the likely causes. A patrol up from Deva perhaps? The cheering grew louder. The century trumpeter broke out Stand to the Eagle.

He leapt from his stool, grabbing his sword and helmet and surged through the tent entrance. Both headquarters guards were standing with unsoldierly grins on their faces and pointing. He followed their direction. No one appeared to be Standing To.

*'What the hell is going on, why is the call sounding? On whose orders?'* he bit his tongue.

The trumpet call was sounding now in response inside the main fort. The automatic assumption of danger. Two horsemen were approaching on the Iter X road out of the hills into the camp. They were being mobbed by a growing clump of off-duty legionaries. It could only be one man and his servant. The trumpet ceased. The camp was in an uproar. He had never heard the century cheering so loud as they were now. The horses clip-clopped their way through the throng of men to the headquarters tent. Liscus was hurrying to get there. Marcellus beat him to the salute.

"Salve. Welcome back centurion," he said.

"Salve and my gratitude Marcellus. We are glad to be here," Velio replied.

Orann slipped from his horse to help Velio down. Velio straightened up, turned, and looked Liscus in the eyes.

"How are my men? How many have I lost?" he demanded.

Liscus saluted again, out of habit and for something to fill the gap between hearing and answering.

"We took the hill fort where you were held. Near a fifth are dead or wounded but we have the man who held you and we have your armour,"he said.

"A fifth?" Velio challenged.

"It got a bit brutal sir," Marcellus chipped in, "we thought you were in there."

"I'd like some wine and some bread that's hot from the oven. I can wait," Velio replied, "now take me to my wounded."

An hour later he had reassured himself the standard was safe and had dictated a report for Marcellus to polish up as best he saw fit.

Marcellus would play with the phrases he had dictated anyway and he had long since given up on expecting any final report to resemble the pristine original. Orann was lost somewhere in the camp getting drunk with the men; promoted by them to honorary legionary of the Twentieth. Liscus and Marcellus stood in front of his tiny desk, so recently theirs, and waited for judgement. He lifted his head. All pleasure at seeing them again washed out by the losses of his beloved century. Hanno Glaccus had not given him command of a First cohort century to waste it in the hills of nowhere important.

"It's time I spoke to the prisoner," he said.

Drapisces glared up at the three of them. He was calm in his head and felt grateful his heart did not pound like a hammer. Death was coming for him soon. He could feel it. He had done all that he could for his people. Someone else would have to lead them, but it would not be his sons. They were trussed and bound like goats, too far away to speak to; too far way to offer his last advice, too far away to say he loved them more than any man had loved his sons. This single son of the wolf had not only laid his hands on the Great Shield and survived. He had beaten Caturiges in the duel and slain his best healer, Agata. He had been a fool to risk her. He had never expected a wounded man to kill the old woman who tended him. What kind of a warrior did such a thing? He hoped the Roman gods would curse him for it. Now, because of all these mistakes the Roman was in complete control. He wondered if they would drown him in the lake, inflicting dishonour or whether they would give him a fighting chance to go out with pride: like Caturiges.

"Where are the two Romans?" Velio said, he knew Draspisces understood whom he meant.

"Your men captured them when they took my home from me," Drapisces snapped, "Roma Victa," he sneered.

Velio bit his lip. The broken faced man was going to fight him to the end. They were foes in name and cause. He deserved to be chopped. But then, for different reasons so did Civius.

"Rome always wins," he replied.

Drapisces turned his head away, refusing to say more. Velio stepped back and shook his head at Marcellus and Liscus. There was no point in wasting further effort. Torture was not something he liked inflicting. The application of hot burning irons, or the fists of angry legionaries might drag the truth out, but the Carvetii had no face left to lose and he had no stomach to see a man branded. He toyed with a final question. The names of his soon-to-be-slave sons?

"Marcellus, go to the bathhouse. Tell the orderly I want hot water, steam and a plunge pool that is colder than the lake. I want the sharpest razor in Cantiventi, a barber, a flask of wine."

"Do you require a good whore, sir?" Marcellus queried.

"That won't be necessary," he replied, "but decent a strigil and oil from the olive will do splendidly. And one more thing. Tell this dog what I am enjoying. Tell him he and his sons will never be warm ever again," he decreed.

*

The camp was quiet that night. Liscus told the men to respect Velio. Their centurion needed rest. The Cantiventi praefectus urged Velio to take a bed in the comfort of his home in the fort. For the moment he was content to keep the kind wishes of auxiliary commanders at bay. The sight of his small travelling altar, set up in his tent for him by Marcellus, brought a lump to his throat. He knelt down and gave thanks to his gods they had not forsaken him. They had summoned his rescue through the unlikely frame of a Votadini stable hand. He had his helmet and his sword back but not its leather shoulder strap. Which was a pity; it was the parting gift from a comrade leaving the legion. Plautius had asked for the privilege of making him a new one. His breastplate was irredeemably punctured from Carvetii spears and arrows. He did not feel it would be lucky to ever wear it again, even if the cohort smiths could repair it. Would the centurion in the hill fort let him buy the chainmail he had been loaned? The breastplate could hide under a piece of cloth on the floor for the time being.

From his camp bed he could hear owl calling in the adjacent woods. Orann was well fortified with wine and asleep under a cloak like a hound, with a new gladius and scabbard tucked in the crook of his arm, oblivious to the eerie, fluting sounds. Marcellus had offered him a proper bed, but Orann refused with unexpected bashfulness and a smile. Had the lads been joshing him?

Civius' request for a week's support rolled around in his head. A messenger would have to go with the reports to Deva Victrix at first light. He got up, stepped over the sleeping Votadini and put his head outside the tent. His sentry saluted.

"Salve," he murmured in reply.

"Salve sir. Bloody owls, what a racket," the man joked.

"Scorpion practise, tomorrow," he replied, "a flagon of posca to the man who nails it."

The soldier's eyes twinkled in the gloom, "good to have you back sir."

"Thank you," he replied and retired back to his bed to think.

Drapisces' capture was likely to draw in the Brigantes just as Civius surmised. One hundred and twenty fit men and a dozen on the quick mend, the others would take longer. Get this right, snuff out the resistance, and the lead mine harassment would be over. Get it wrong and Cantiventi would have the Brigantes pounding at the walls. Somehow the local praefectus did not inspire entirely him with confidence, despite his undoubted intelligent understanding of the local situation. He lay back allowing the problem to roll around in his brain. He could feel his eyes tiring. The warmth of the army blankets was wrapping him in happy fatigue. This mining entrepreneur Auvericus was the key. He just did not know how it would work yet.

*

Auvericus laid siege to the camp gateway until Velio relented to speak with him. He took him for a stroll down to the lakeside close the wooden quay where the ships were loading galena, timber and slate stone, like every other day. Except there was none of Auvericus' valuable smelted lead ingots.

"I know it was Drapisces' men that attacked your mine, Auvericus," he opened, "but the praefectus here has compensated you, and you have first choice of slaves until your numbers are restored. He has played fair with you, Auvericus," he probed.

The Spaniard was about the same age as he was, tall build but portly, with years accustomed to food and good wine, not a man who worked with his hands or sweated when he could buy men and women to do it for him. Auvericus possessed a certain authority and presence, Velio could admit that much. In a senatorial toga, if you did not know to the contrary, he would pass first inspections. His close-cut black beard was tinged with red. An affectation of henna perhaps? The hands were meat slabs and had he been younger, leaner and fitter, he would have made a stolid legionary or officer. He walked with a certain grace for such a big man, standing fully a head height taller than himself. He could see Auvericus was being very careful not to appear dominating, walking several steps to the side of him and he noted the small courtesy. Too many times grievances started because a big man thought that physique was enough to get him what he wanted. Neither was he ostentatiously dressed or jewelled. Velio found he was warming to his company.

"Centurion, it is the only mine I have, though I have interests in others and plans to expand, and until I get hold of enough slaves and better guards, I cannot reopen. I hear my rivals have also been attacked north of here. If they succeed in halting the mining, what will be next, the stone quarries? If the Carvetii start fighting with their heads it will get expensive, trust me centurion. This Carvetii fellow has stirred something up, more than just our mining. It could be the beginnings of another rebellion. He has much to pay for," Auvericus replied.

"Indeed, he does, eleven legionaries to be exact and I'm going to make sure it hurts," Velio said.

Auvericus lifted his hand like a supplicant.

"I am glad to hear it. If I may, centurion, whether you nail him up or flog him to death I can assure you I can supply a longer and more miserable life and end for him. Something your men can savour. A revenge that lingers for days, weeks, perhaps even years."

*'I'm sure you can,'* Velio guessed.

They walked up onto the wooden quay and strolled past the ships and the labour gangs to the end of the pier. In the water of the clear lake Velio could see trout resting in the shade, their gills beating as they moved in calm serries between the oak posts. He looked out across the quiet expanse. It was so peaceful, a world away from the mountain stronghold and the sword fight with Caturiges, or the farm with the angry father and two weak sons, or the sloping hill where Orann bearded the Carvetii warriors and they traded horses for their lives.

"I'm going to let you borrow him to use as bait," he said.

Auvericus raised his eyes and folded his arms, putting his weight back on his heels as he processed the idea.

"Bait?"

"I want the Carvetii, and the Brigantes if they are coming into this, to attack the mines around here. I hear what you say about the potential for this to spread to the quarries and a general rebellion. A war of destruction instead of a war of open battle is not their style. They are too hot headed, no discipline, no command structure. And I happen to know Drapisces' chief priest is dead."

He decided not to explain how he knew as Auvericus' demeanour changed.

"I am not going to chase around after them like a scalded goose. I am going to load these mines with legionaries, and we will put an end to this. And then quite frankly, I can go home. But I want him back. He is going to be executed in Deva in retaliation for the lives of my men."

He pointed to the trout, "bait and a hook, is all that is required."

Auvericus nodded, chewing it over. He could still get to keep Drapisces if the dice rolled his way.

"I'll need the rest of his people too, to make up the quota," he brogued.

"No, no other local slaves. These people are going south to the slave markets at Londinium. It's never a good idea to slave them in their own country. You should know that. Slaves and criminals should not have hope. Those who dare to kill Roman soldiers are criminals and deserve to be treated so," Velio over-ruled.

Auvericus knew that was true.

"I can't open the mine with only him," he reasoned.

"Couldn't you though, for now? Let the word get out that no tribal leader is going to prevent Auvericus lawfully digging his mine," Velio plotted.

"Ah I see now: bait," he said.

"They will not know which mine he is in, and we can spread the rumours of his capture. I'm not lending him to you so he can dig the ground," Velio went on.

"Apologies centurion. I am being very slow. Can I buy you wine in the tavern?"

## Chapter Thirty-three.

## Argentomagus.

Durus Decimus watched Gallus Tiomaris' new overseer dig into the leather purse on his waist belt and pay for three slaves. Words passed between them before they thrust their hands forward and the manacles opened. They climbed onto the waggon bed exchanging glances with each other. He watched spellbound: these were not the ordinary, scruffy, half-starved remnant of tribal unrest, full of self-pity, and trying not to draw attention or the whip to themselves. Around the market honest citizens were doing exactly that; ignoring the purchase of slaves by one of the local vineyards. Was this evidence of Gallus and Hanno bringing their workforce back up to strength? Or were they increasing it? Gallus' overseer had two new mounted guards to help him. They had the unhurried aspect of competent men. The three slaves were blond Germans by the look of them: young men, tall and clean limbed, with surly dispositions. He kept in the shade waiting for the waggon and the overseer to leave. When it did, he let it trundle out of the forum square before sidling across to the slave pens.

Gramalcus saw him approaching and smiled.

"Salve procurator, may Jupiter and Fortuna be with you today," Gramalcus greeted.

"Thank you, Gramalcus, that is most kind," he returned, "business continues to prosper for you?"

"Indeed, it does procurator, and we need not ask too closely why, need we? Slaves coming and going from one estate in particular. By night in covered waggons, some by day, what?" Gramalcus said as they shook arms.

"They are safely away then?"

Surely, Gramalcus was teasing him?

"Oh yes, procurator I had them all away that same night. Discretion is something we understand in this business," Gramalcus confided.

He nodded back, walking along the perimeter of the now empty pens; the steaming smell of human ordure, worse than lions for the games, surely a call for a bucket and shovel. On cue another of Gramalcus' staff came hurrying to clean the cages. It hit him with a jolt that he did not know how many men worked for the slave merchant.

"They were a special delivery?" he recovered.

Gramalcus stood close to him and took an almost comedic look around for eavesdroppers.

"Well that you ask, procurator, well that you ask. They were auxiliaries from the Germania frontier, Mattiaci, these ones, don't see too many of them. Good soldiers usually. Got a little fired up about their conditions up at the defence wall, apparently, began talking sedition, mutiny, that sort of thing. We don't normally get the chance to buy from the army as such. They deal with it themselves, as you might expect, you know? For reasons known only to the gods, the local commander put a parcel of them 'to the chains.' Sent them to different markets. Must be someone's new thinking up there. Used to be, their mates beat them to death with clubs in front of their regiment. Now it's slavery. Personally, I don't agree with it. Keeping an angry ex-soldier, a man who's trained to kill, in domestic service is not going to end well. I'm glad to be shot of them. Cash out, cash in, move on. If this is the new way, it won't last long. It will only take a few innocent civilian domina to get robbed, raped and murdered when their husbands are away, and the army will go back to the tried and tested. But while the opportunity is there, I would not be doing service to the good name of my ancestors not to make the best of the opportunity," Gramalcus professed.

"Do Gallus Tiomaris and Hanno Glaccus know this?"

Decimus dared to hope the opposite.

Gramalcus nodded, "absolutely, seemed quite keen to have them when I mentioned I was going north to collect them. That whole thing was another affair entirely, let me tell you."

Decimus quashed the unwanted anecdote.

"Really, that is where they are going to?" he feigned.

*'How on earth did they know you were sourcing convicted soldiers? Did you tell them? How long has this being going on? How is it even possible? Mutineers sent to the chains? Careful, don't let him know you are bothered. Close this conversation down.'*

He breathed in a long lungful.

"Well, those two are not going to stand for any nonsense, are they?"Gramalcus replied.

Decimus beamed every grain of insincerity he could muster and patted Gramalcus on the shoulder.

"I mustn't keep you Gramalcus, really I mustn't. the emperor waits for no man," he replied.

He worried and fretted about it the whole day. Those two old foxes were unlikely to have former soldiers picking their grapes. They had the ordinary type for that menial work. It hit him. Gramalcus had not actually said whether those Mattiaci were the first or indeed the only consignment for Gallus Tiomaris and Hanno Glaccus. He could not prevent any more being bought. Not unless he could manufacture a reason. The worst interpretation must be their defences had effectively doubled and the Mattiaci were going to be offered mercenary terms in return for compliance. What a dangerous game. The game of desperate men. That's what Grandfather would have said. The whole scene at the forum had been a sham. Those two old fools were getting ready to make a fight of it and that simpleton Gramalcus was too stupid to see he was abetting them.

*'The crafty bastards.'*

He felt an uncomfortable roiling sensation in his stomach. He took a sip of watered wine, but it did not help. He called for his cook and surrendered to her suggestion of a little fresh milk, so warm it fought to stay in his throat and not go down. One thing was becoming clearer by the day. Waiting until the harvest was in and the young wine was in vats, was no longer going to work. Tiomaris and Glaccus would be too strong. It was going to have to happen sooner. He would offer a sacrifice to Miseria and ask her to fill their cups with sorrows.

*

Gramalcus checked his site. Everything looked in order for tomorrow. The pens were locked and clean, the water troughs full. It was enough for one day. He went to the tavern where the soldiers from the fort roosted in the evenings before the recall trumpet sounded. Argentomagus ordered its day to the cycle of the fort's trumpets. It did not object to being a soldier's town. Young men enjoying fighting with the legionaries on feast days, fists in the yard at the back door of the tavern, nothing too malicious, no pugios or blades: just bits of horseplay, point scoring, 'who's got the bigger balls' contests. Sometimes 'call outs' in the forum, upsetting the stalls, getting Durus Decimus off his arse until his town guard restored order.

The tavern was busy, legionaries outnumbering the locals. It was all quiet for the moment. The last fight had led to a broadcasting of dire warnings to all and sundry and notices pasted up on the forum walls. The procurator had given a final word: desist.

"Legionary Gramalcus, how goes it?"

"Gramalcus, you old wanker."

The usual greetings.

"Good evening children, landlord my usual please," he raised a hand in good humour and headed to the nearest vacant table.

His usual service was wine, bread and olives and it arrived as if it had been waiting under the counter for his benediction. He smiled at the innkeeper's daughter.

"Are they behavin'?" he asked.

She flicked her hair back as she straightened up.

"Like little lambs, I think I might keep one as a pet," and swirled away in a swish of her dress, drawing the glances she wanted.

"Little lambs," he gurgled as he swallowed.

The bread and olives were gone. The empty platter had only crumbs and oil left for evidence. He had devoured it and not even noticed. So many things to think about. He tapped his knuckle on the wine jug, it chimed the right tone. The door opened and Gallus came in, his eyes searching the room for him. Gramalcus noted the fast looks Gallus attracted. One of the two new men of mystery in the town and a tavern always loves a mystery. The crowd parted to let him through, inspecting, assessing, evaluating, reckoning. He arrived at the table, and they shook arms.

"It's been a long time. I never thought I'd forgive you for leaving us and going to the Boar," he said, trying to moderate the smile he wanted to crack.

Gallus shook his arm and grinned back.

"The Second was a good legion, it still is. But you know how it was," he replied.

Gramalcus settled for that. It did not matter now; it was all ancient history.

"My boy tells me you've been busy buying the best of my slaves. I did not realise it was you until I got back from the Germania front. Those three today for instance, keep your pugio handy, just in case Gallus, that's my advice at least until they've settled down, you understand? There's hard fighting going on up there at the moment, you know? And many captives are being taken. It's getting a bit rough. My kind of place. Who's this partner of yours? I hear he's a real lemon-face," he quizzed.

Gallus laughed, "ex centurion Hanno Glaccus has done it all my friend. A soldier of the old days, not one of these modern pups. Got to command the First cohort," he said.

"So, his shit shines, well that you ask, well that you ask, but seriously, you can trust him?"

Gramalcus did not much like centurions as a breed. Gallus felt an odd wave of surprise that Gramalcus cared either way.

"Gramalcus, he did fifteen years on the wall of Antoninus Pius and commanded the withdrawal, didn't leave a single man to the enemy," he lifted his cup.

Gramalcus nodded.

"I heard. I still listen to the news that comes our way," he flicked a look to the men from the fort, "they're sending them back, did you know?"

"To the turf wall?" Gallus guessed.

"Word is, the emperor wants it in stone, to rival Hadrian's Stones. Sheer fucking vanity if you ask me," Gramalcus sneered.

"Good because they'll need decent wine and that's what we're here to provide," Gallus returned.

He kept the truth a secret.

"So, my spies tell me Gallus, so they tell me. And you've bumped into the local opposition?" Gramalcus prompted, filling another cup for Gallus.

He lifted the empty jug up to the landlord who tilted his head in reply. His daughter smiled.

"Durus? Don't make me swear Gramalcus, there are ladies present," Gallus grinned.

"It's not taken you long to work that out. I'll give you that. Yes, he is one of those all right," he answered and lowered his voice, "you will need to kill him, you know? *'You can't negotiate with the Carthaginians'* as both Scipio and my old man were fond of saying."

"We're to going to kill him. Don't you worry. We found Priscus' wife lying in a field, what was left of her," Gallus hissed.

He sat back on his stool and rubbed his knuckles into the small of his back, stretching his neck to the left and right.

"Well, that settles it, I suppose," Gramalcus hunched forward, "you'll let me know if I can do anything?"

Gallus waited for the landlord to deposit the fresh flask on the table, offer to fill their cups and be dismissed with a casual wave from Gramalcus.

“He used to buy from Priscus. He is on your side even if you don’t know it,” Gramalcus whispered, swallowed and set the cup on the table.

Gallus nodded. This all felt very convenient. He decided to change the subject.

“Thanks to you for the note with the names of those three slaves” he said.

Gramalcus nodded, “Nahan, Eudo and Bodusio. I hope they serve you well and the whip can stay on its peg,” he replied.

“They’re soldiers, they’ll soon know what the game is,” Gallus opined.

## Chapter Thirty-four.

### The vineyard, Argentomagus.

"How exactly are we going to do this?" Hanno asked, "a bit of bloody revenge is all well and good but how, I say again, are we going to do this exactly, Gallus?"

Gallus raised his head from the last of the vat lids specially carpentered to replace the ones that had been burned before their arrival and chose not to hear the question. The wooden bungs were cut precisely to each vat, each marginally different from its neighbour. Hanno seemed indifferent to the fact he had an audience listening. The storage building had been one of Priscus' innovations, turning an old stable into a vat shed with the huge clay vessels, part buried to help keep the temperature of the liquid from wild fluctuations each day and night. The reason for ignoring Hanno's question took the shape of the new winemaker standing at his side. The fruit was close to ripe, if not already waiting for the human hand to pluck it. The wine maker was champing to get going. He was a half Bituriges, half Roman, from a family of local wine makers. Gallus ran his hands around the rim of a vat and replaced the bung, bumping it home with the flat on his hand. It sat like a hen on its eggs. He gripped the lid and tried to twist it. The friction of the clay held it fast. He scratched the back of his neck through his grey mane and nodded.

"This is the last one? You are happy with them?" he asked.

"We need to pay for them if you are satisfied," the winemaker reminded him.

"Indeed, we do. The price is fair?" he said.

"The price is robbery, but our Balisca grapes produce a rich wine. It will be good no matter if all you do is the basics, but I am going to make it magnificent and these bungs will last forever," the winemaker replied.

"You can assure me it will be magnificent?" Hanno intervened, abandoning Durus' possible fates for another conversation.

The winemaker pulled at his pleated moustaches.

"We have been making wine here since the gods gave us breath," he replied, "before the legions came, before Caesar and his armies," he expounded.

Gallus sensed an impending tirade of Gallic pride and stepped in.

"That is why we wanted you to be the one who made our wine," he soothed.

*'Gallus, you're becoming a politician in your old age,'* Hanno smirked.

"When should we start picking?" Gallus went on.

The Bituriges recovered his decorum, "we can begin picking and treading as soon as the vats are washed out and dried. In this weather they should be dry in a day. If we start today, we can pick tomorrow," he said.

"Are all the vines ready?" Hanno asked.

The winemaker smiled.

"The vines over the hill will be picked last. An extra day or two will make the difference. These fields have ripened quicker this year," he said.

"Have you worked on this estate before?" Gallus asked, realising he had never asked that question before.

The Bituriges smiled back unflustered.

"No, I did not deceive you, if that is what you are asking? We share the knowledge," he replied.

Hanno glanced at him and let the obvious question pass.

*'Some sort of guild,'* he decided, *'not so unexpected.'*

"Tomorrow, Gallus. Let's get the men working on sluicing out the vats," he said.

"The skies are gentle," the Bituriges prompted Gallus.

He surveyed the serene blue sky over their heads. It was finally here. They really were going to do it. After all that had stood in their way the grapes were ready and his man was clearly itching to start.

"Very well, set them to work." he ordered.

*

"How are we going to do it, Gallus?" Hanno persevered.

Gallus looked at him, and gave him the puzzled look.

"Durus Decimus, our little pal, remember?" Hanno said, keeping his rising irritation with Gallus' bull-headedness in check.

Gallus rattled the dice in the cup and played to annoy him.

*'Balls of Dis, not again,'* he tutted as Gallus swept the four asses from the table top across into the pile on his side.

"Our little pal," Gallus replied, handing the cup over for Hanno to make his next doomed, unlucky throw, "is going to get an invitation to come and sample the wine when it's ready and then I am going to take him on an evening tour of the estate that he's not going to return from."

"And you don't think anyone is going to suspect you have adjusted his ribs with steel?" Hanno hedged.

He could see no difference in Durus Decimus giving an order to one of his men and Durus wielding the dagger in his own hand. He still did not fancy having to draw out the gladius. His old bones were enjoying the hot sun of Argentomagus, getting used to the constant heat, but he could feel laziness creeping up on him; his fighting days were over. Whereas, the old wolf-wrestler beside him did not want to accept the Veniconii, the Damnonii, the Selgovae were battles in the past.

"I don't care if they suspect or not. Durus Decimus will be with his ancestors, his body will be left out for the boars to eat, quite fitting, eh? The Boars will eat him up. And no one will care," Gallus said.

"And the local commander, the Eighth legion, our friendly decurion, what do we tell them?" he wondered.

Gallus seemed to have settled on a plan without discussion.

"Without a body what can they do? We just have to say he went for a walk to aid his digestion after a good evening with us and, so far, he has not returned. We will search for him everywhere except where I put him and co-operate with the Eighth," Gallus scooped up the dice.

"They will suspect," Hanno pointed out.

Gallus snorted, "perhaps. My money says they will say '*that's justice for Priscus,*' and do nothing more than make a show of searching for him."

He broke off. The slaves on the treading tables were beginning to chant. Hanno watched his friend's eyebrows rise in astonishment.

"Our slaves are singing," he said, "don't let Gramalcus hear about this. He'll say we're feeding them too much."

The dice clattered on to the table. Hanno listened. The chant was low and soft, not quite half hearted but wary, apologetic.

"There are worse places in the empire to be a slave I suppose, Gallus,"he said.

He voiced the question that had been niggling him.

"The three you brought back the other day, the convicts from Germania, what are you going to do with them?"

Gallus frowned, "remember when we arrived here, and I said someone wants us to fail here? We know that someone is Durus and maybe others with him. We will need swords if they decide to steal the vintage. Much as I want to take Durus for a long walk in the evening, we may not get the chance. He might launch a bit of sabotage on us and if he does, we'll need every sword."

"You're going to offer them freedom if they agree to fight for us?" he divined.

Gallus bit his lip, "look, it's just the two of us until Velio turns up. Plus, the kit I pinched before we left Deva. Three more swords would help even things up," he replied.

"Three more swords might be a bit much to handle on our own, if they suddenly decide to chance the game" Hanno growled, feeling uneasy.

"They're auxiliaries, they'll do as they're told. I've seen the looks in their eyes. Frightened men, glad to escape the death they expected up on the Germania lines. They'll do as they're told Hanno, if the option is a sword in the gut today or the chance to walk away as free men tomorrow," Gallus retorted.

"That's very poetic, Gallus," he said.

He decided that reminding Gallus he had commanded an auxiliary cohort for fifteen years on the wall before rejoining The Boar to take over command of the First cohort was unlikely to make a snot of difference. Yes, auxiliaries would follow orders, particularly coming from a legion officer, but this was not the army, and these men were disgraced scum, consigned to slavery. They had no reason to rediscover their former discipline and zeal.

"When they see us with Boar shields and armour, they won't be able to help themselves. Leave it to me Hanno. They'll see the bargain, besides what German auxiliary did you ever meet that did not want to join in a fight?" Gallus smirked.

"Gallus, may I just point out there were no Mattiaci in Britannia, these are the first ones I've ever seen," Hanno grinned.

Gallus dismissed it with a wave.

"Just throw the dice and surrender your money, I'm on a streak today," he chirped.

## Chapter Thirty-five.

### The vineyard, a week later.

The wine master thumped the last wood bung into place. The evening light was beginning its drift toward darkness, taking the heat of the day with it. The whole of the estate stood watching. They did not quite cheer but waited for Hanno and Gallus to signal food from the kitchens before they believed the toil was over.

Later, he felt a bit more like talking. The two soldiers were not so bad for ex-military types more used to ordering people about than taking advice. He considered whether to speak out about the thing that was bothering him. He waited until the slaves had been dismissed and the guards herded them back to the barn for the night before accepting an invitation to join them in the villa for food and wine. Gallus sat upright instead of reclining and rabbited on about the successful first stages of the harvesting and offering thanks to Bacchus tomorrow. Nataseulta would be more deserving, but he kept the goddess' name to himself. The Romans could pray to their gods if they liked, and he would make the real offering, the one that counted, to her.

Hanno reclined, nodding agreement. It was all very sociable. A first harvest safely gathered was no small thing. The opportune gap in the conversation arrived and he decided to take it.

"Priscus was noted for all his wines. You know all this. I was told that there was no wine left in the stores when you arrived," he began.

Hanno nodded a slow acknowledgement. Gallus decided it was time to lie back and rest on his elbow.

"His Falernian was always treated with respect. Only the best amphorae were used to sell it. All his wines were stamped with his mark of course, like all winemakers, he advertised his wine, but in a subtle way. He only used the best amphorae he could get hold of," the winemaker said.

He checked to see Gallus was paying attention too.

"Priscus put a lot of wine in small amphorae. Every winemaker stamps their own wine. Priscus stamped his with -*'Priscus made this wine'* – and he had to put his Falernian out in several sizes, because it was so expensive. He wanted it drunk but understood ordinary people might not be able to afford to buy large amounts. He had a big need for quality amphorae for a quality wine. His lora and posca went out in regular sizes," he explained.

Hanno shook his head, and sent the briefest of messages to Gallus. The wine master saw he had glimmerings of interest in his eyes. Lora, posca and Falernian: wines that drove the empire and its citizens. The wine master licked his lips and pressed on. In too far to hold back now. He was committed.

"Erm, I was told that when you arrived all the dolia had been emptied, some of them smashed, which must have been a great shock. You must have thought you had been robbed blind, I imagine, but that would not have been where Priscus stored his Falernian. It would all have been in flasked up in amphorae, hundreds of amphorae," he said.

"And they're all stamped *'Priscus made this wine,'*" Gallus twigged.

"What was in the dolia was probably the last remnants of his posca waiting decanting into amphora. It was not the Falernian.

No, Priscus had that safely stored. It takes years to reach maturity. It needs additives to sweeten it. Imagine the value of a couple of dolia filled with aged Falernian? You could name your price. What I'm trying to say is, no one would have destroyed Falernian wine. You gentlemen know the tavern price, I am sure. Destroy the ordinary posca and the lora, yes possibly, to create the illusion of destruction and also a local shortage to push the price up, if they were smart. If you ever find someone with an excess of Priscus' amphorae in their villa that are still full of wine you would have good grounds for suspecting them," he finished.

"How much wine?" Gallus queried.

"It has to be stored for ten years or more to reach its best. Priscus would have had a growing stock set by from each harvest. If all that was taken, then someone must have hundreds of jars of it," he answered.

"Too expensive to all be drunk here I would have thought," Hanno murmured.

The wine master assented.

"It may be spread to the four winds of the empire by now, as far as Rome itself perhaps, but my guess would be there is still a lot hiding in cellars in Argentomagus," he vouched.

"Do you mean there was a plot to rob Priscus' wife and the estate?" Hanno grunted.

"Did you find hundreds of smashed clay storage jars when you arrived?" the wine master said.

"Not exactly. We found the place ransacked. Wine on the ground, burned dolia stoppers, general destruction," Gallus chipped in.

"Mindless looting, made to look like a bit of 'harrying' as you soldiers like to put it?" the winemaker teased, "oh, I think it was anything but that."

"What do you know about harrying?" Hanno growled.

"And why does it matter so much to you?" Gallus rejoined.

Where was this going?

The winemaker took his own cup to his nostrils and inhaled.

"Because they showed no respect for the man, his wife and his wine. Or, the years he devoted to the land and the vines. He was good to his slaves you know, better than most I would say. As long as they put in the work and did not steal too much," the winemaker eulogised.

He drank his wine and stood up.

"We have just begun the task today. The gods have smiled on us. There is still a long way to go. You need to decide what the mark for your amphorae is to be. The local potters are waiting for the orders I can assure you. I have them on high alert. In four weeks' time we will have done the defrutum and be ready to fill the amphorae. In four or, five weeks' time you can start selling the posca and the lora though, I would hold it back a little longer. Drum up the local enthusiasm. Keep them keen. No one is running dry quite yet," he smiled and felt better now that it was off his chest.

"And then we must pay you," Gallus smiled.

"Master, I hope you will need me for many years to come," he replied.

Hanno stood too.

"So who was Priscus' winemaker?" he asked.

The winemaker gave a hesitant little twitch of the mouth.

"You mean who was the one who took advantage when Priscus died and rooked his old wife? That I regret is an affair of family dishonour. One that I put right when I heard," he replied, "he will steal no more."

A cold flat finger touched Gallus' spine.

"You came to us to make that right? To make amends?" he accused.

"Why should we trust you?" Hanno barked, louder than he intended.

The wine master blanched at the parade tone erupting from calm features.

"Because I have told you it is a family dishonour I am putting to rights. My family have been winemakers without our own ground for generations. Well, we have a small bit of a hillside, but it hardly counts as land in these parts. We sell our services rather than grow our own vintages. Our reputation is all that matters to get us full plates and employment. Every family has a soul that's been touched by badness of some kind. Mine is no different. I had no choice in the matter, he had ruined things for all of us. That's why you can trust me, centurion," he replied.

"Then there is no need for you to return to town this evening. You can sleep here under our roof if you wish," Gallus said.

He offered his arm, and they shook. Hanno did the same.

"My servant will show you to your bed," Gallus went on.

It sounded strange, Hanno thought, to be landowners, winemakers and owners of servants in an estate villa in Gaul. *'This legionary will show you to a tent,'* would have sounded so much more natural. Gallus called his servant's name and the winemaker left them to ponder.

"It's been quite a day," he said and sat down again.

*

Trajan rumbled a growl in his young throat. Gallus opened his eyes. The villa was silent except for the occasional creak of oak timbers settling in the cooling night air. He was not used to the villa's strange night music, and he had been sleeping on the cusp, off and on for several weeks, never far from waking but always resisting the comfort of deep sleep. The young dog rumbled a second low, rippling warning, like the trundle of cart wheels on gravel.

"Trajan, ssshh," he chided.

He put his hand out from the blanket, clicked his fingers and called him to the bedside to settle him down.

It was dark outside, too early in the night for barking dogs to be wakening up the entire household. Trajan stood by the closed door, the low growl like a music note, sustaining and echoey in the room. Gallus whispered to him again, but Trajan refused to budge. He sighed and got up hoping that a quick check outside and a chance to pee would settle the dog down. Out in the atrium the night torch kept the nocturnal spirits at bay. The Mattiaci, Nahan, raised his head from his straw filled mattress in the shelter of the wall. This one, Gallus was certain, was trying to make amends. All three Mattiaci had seemed quick on the uptake. They had fallen under the roof of hard old legion men who had no scores to settle.

Hanno had taken one look at them and said, "you speak Latin and nothing else or I'll have your tongues out."

Their reaction had been interesting.

Gallus shook his head, and the disgraced soldier laid his head back down. Something about it pleased him. He lifted the torch from the iron stand and took it with him. Outside the night air was cold and thick with invisible menace. The hairs on the nape of his neck rose in the old familiar reaction. Here it was once again, the onsetting sensation of danger.

*'Balls of Dis, what's this.'*

He held Trajan back with a finger through the rough rope collar, realising bringing the torch was a mistake; he had made himself a target. An arrow hit the tamped down earth at his feet. He dropped the torch to the side. Trajan snorted and stepped sideways, wriggling and wresting to be free, twisting his powerful neck at the collar: his ears up and his teeth bared. A second arrow hit him. Trajan barked, demented and whining as he crashed to the ground. Nahan came stampeding out at the noise, barehanded. He released the dog to charge before the burning pain swept over him and things went completely black.

The archer moved back to where his accomplice was holding his horse. The dog was hurtling toward them, a blur in the darkness. He mounted his horse and kicked it hard into a gallop. Together they escaped the onrushing hound. Trajan pursued for a while and then gave up in a sudden protest of barking at the point where the accomplice was ready to draw his sword and swipe him.

"Did you hit him?" he shouted to the archer.

"I hit someone, one of them perhaps, that fuckin' dog got in the way," the archer snapped.

"We need to kill it, or we'll not get the job done," the accomplice bayed.

"Easier said than done. Bit tricky in the dark, eh?" the archer snapped.

They pulled up under a stand of trees.

"The dog will have woken the place up. That's screwed it for tonight. We'll need to let it calm down a bit. Durus ain't going to like it," the accomplice complained.

"Well Durus can come and do it himself," the archer grunted.

## Chapter Thirty-six.

## The Procurator's office, Argentomagus.

Durus Decimus listened to his two saboteurs' report and grew despondent. In the distance he could hear what he liked to call the town's 'music,' the sound of hammering from the closest silver shop. The sweet sound of money being made. It was the best sound in Argentomagus. Its answer to the incessant trumpets and bugles from the fort. The saboteurs waited for his reaction, both of them truculent and hot faced. They had made a future attempt to destroy the new wine impossible. It appeared these two oafs had achieved little except raising the general state of alert on the estate. He listened to their fatuous promise to go back after the furore had died down and destroy the precious dolia. He watched them wriggle before his eyes. Nothing short of an infantry assault was likely to make that work. All that was needed for a full-scale disaster was for Gallus Tiomarus and Hanno Glaccus to recognise either man in broad daylight. He decided to cut his losses. Perhaps there had been a touch of misfortune attached. It had been naïve not to think Tiomaris and Glaccus would have bought a watchdog. But his men were certain they had landed an arrow on someone, but they could not say more

He tapped the tabletop with the back of his fingers, rapping his rings on the wood, hoping the arrow had hit one of the two prime targets. An arrow from out of the night was still a uscful threat. A wounded man raised the stakes. They would be on high alert, knowing they were not welcome. The more he thought about it, the more positive he began to feel. Perhaps it was not the worst outcome? He folded his hands into a clasp and dismissed them with a nod to his secretary to pay them off. The Bituriges clerk raised his eyebrows and said nothing. He confirmed the change of tactics with a weary nod and bit off a rebuke to 'get on with it.'

The wine was untouchable now. It was on its way to flasking and sale in the forum. With hindsight, he saw the idea had been less than perfect, unbecoming even, for a man of his status to stoop so low. There had to be another way. Besides neither Gallus Tiomaris nor Hanno Glaccus had sons to take over the business from them. Time and Jupiter's mercy would eventually put them in the ground like all men and he would get what he wanted in the end. He would have to be patient, but even if he moved on to a higher post in another town, this estate would be his in time. Outside the procurator's office the men pocketed the money.

"The one you said you hit," the accomplice accused, "we don't know who you hit. He thinks it's one of the soldiers. It could have been anyone. I thought we weren't supposed to kill anyone? Just do the mischief and scarper."

"Old habits," the archer sneered, "the bow made me do it."

## Chapter Thirty-seven.

## Cantiventi.

Velio awoke feeling sweat running like ice and rivers down his back. He rolled over and tried to dry the chill into the fabric of his woollen blanket and get warm again. He was freezing cold all over. It did not work. He shivered: worse still, in his dream Gallus was dead. How did he know that, how could he know that? For whatever reason the gods must want him to know. Had they woken him to make sure he remembered the dream? Why? If it was true Gallus was gone, there was nothing he could do to change things?

*'Poor Gallus. How did this happen, my old friend? Hear me Mithras, let it not be true. Let it not be true.'*

He swung his legs off the bed and sat up.

*'If it is, I hope it was quick and clean, Gallus,'* he hoped.

The guard outside his tent moved at the sound of the camp bed creaking. He swept cold sweat off his face and reached around in the gloom seeking a towel and dried himself off, then made himself lie back down. The rustle of the guard carried through the goatskin walls of the tent. He debated whether to light a lamp and make prayer to his gods for Gallus' safety. Doing that would wake Orann up. The lad deserved a night's sleep. If Gallus was dead, prayers for him were already too late. So strange it was only Gallus he feared had been killed, Hanno's face did come to him in the dream. It must be a sign from the gods.

He lay, wide awake and troubled. Maybe they were merely cruel and evil humours of the night. He made the sign and warmed from the towelling, felt drowsy. The next thing he knew was Orann shuffling around moments before the first trumpet call of the day.

Marcellus was the first to arrive as he dressed followed by a legionary bearing a large bowl of steaming hot jentaculum porridge. Marcellus waited as he prowled around the confines of his tent blowing on every volcanic spoonful.

"Orders for the day sir?" asked Marcellus.

Velio was in middle of swallowing. He laid the bowl down to cool and waved the spoon.

"Release the Carvetii leader into the custody of the mine owner Auvericus and send Plautius and eight men to escort them back to his property. Plautius is to remain at the mine. They will need rations. Tell him he may expect a reaction from hostile warriors and is to defend the mine, Auvericus and Drapisces from capture. We will support him from here if he comes under attack, so I want line-of-sight signallers between us and the mine. I'm not sending men out there to die, Marcellus. Send other detachments to the four nearest mines with prisoners that look most like Drapisces. From a distance they all look pretty much alike. I want signal lines put in place with them too. Get word out in the village that Drapisces has been condemned to the mines in his own lands as a new punishment. But I don't want the enemy to know precisely which mine he has been sent to, understand? And I want the rest of his people on boats down the lake today. Get rid of them to the markets and make a show of it, lots of noise, understand?" he ordered.

"You think they will believe we are keeping him here in his own lands instead of exiling him? We are provoking an attack sir," Marcellus warned.

"That we are. If the Carvetii and Brigantes are out there planning disruption to the mines, as my dear friend Civius believes, we need to deal with them quickly. Otherwise, we will be stuck in these hills defending the Iter X until next winter. And I for one have better plans Marcellus. Oh, and I also need to tell the Morinorum commander what's happening. His patrols are likely to come under attack too. Send for Liscus, I want a word with him."

"Covering five mines with so few men will leave us a little stretched out there, sir, and there are the signallers to add in," Marcellus dared to use his privileged opinion.

Velio picked up his porridge.

"Indeed, it will, but I need a big enough reserve to deal with the Carvetii and Brigantes if they do show their hand, and I'm hoping eight-man detachments will appear weak enough to tease them enough into attacking," he explained.

"What if they really come in numbers, sir?" Marcellus said.

Velio spooned more food into his mouth and swallowed.

"That's why Liscus is going to hand pick the men," he said.

Marcellus saluted and left. Later, at the Morinorum commander's suggestion, he reduced his plan down to Auvericus' mine and the two nearest ones as the traps. The map on the table was clear, the fourth and fifth closest mines to the lake were too far away for any support to arrive in time if an eight-man guard came under prolonged attack, signalling lines or not. He took the advice and returned the camp. The commander was non-committal about the plan but offered no alternatives. If he had local intelligence to offer, he kept it to himself.

That afternoon, Velio had Drapisces brought in front of him. Plautius stood off to the side. Auvericus was early and stood with his horse reins in his hand and the other on the animal's muzzle. He appeared to have sparked a look of malevolent determination in the tesserarius. Plautius brought gifts.

Velio's helmet had been re polished to the way it had been prior to his capture and a new shoulder strap secured his sword. The borrowed squamata mail shirt glittered on its own. Drapisces fixed his eyes on the helmet that had adorned the wall of his hilltop home. Velio swithered whether to put on the helmet, to rub in the point that the tables had been turned and fortunes had returned to the correct order of things. He tucked it under his arm. The legionary squad assigned to Plautius came to efficient attention. Plautius saluted, he nodded back. The feather crest transfixed the Carvetii's attention. This was the day, he decided for Boar Law, whether the Carvetii, the Morinorum or Delmatarum liked it or not, they would all taste Boar Law. He did not give a damn either way. His patience had run out.

"See that face, tesserarius?" he said to Plautius and his men.

"Indeed, I do sir," Plautius replied.

He raised his voice so the century could hear him.

"This man wants you dead. That face hates you. It hates your legion, and it hates Rome. He is a barbarian. Make no mistake tesserarius and guard him accordingly. And bring him back. He and I have unfinished business. Take no chances at the mine. Signallers are in place but if you consider you are going to be overwhelmed, get out and bring your men back here. I want to draw the Carvetii and Brigantes out into the open. If they choose to attack us here, that will suit me well. Good luck tesserarius, Fortuna march alongside you," he said.

"As you command centurion," Plautius answered.

Auvericus had a jaundiced look on his face as the squad marched Drapisces past him towards the small sinistra exit. He made ready to mount.

"I want him to suffer, centurion," he said.

"You don't get to decide," Velio snapped.

"And you do?" Auvericus challenged.

Liscus stepped forwards, like a good second in command and ushered the mine owner away.

"Just get on your horse, Auvericus," he suggested.

"How long do we wait sir," Marcellus asked Velio.

"Have the other two squads left, Marcellus?" He asked.

"They have sir," Marcellus replied, "they have further to go."

"Good, our hooks are in the water. Let's see what bites," he replied, "sound the call for 'General Inspection'. After that, tell Metius I want those prisoners down to the dock and on boats sharpish. I want them out of here."

Marcellus glanced at the empty quayside and bit his tongue.

*

Arco paced along the rampart with Scribono in his head for company. In his head and in his face. His two 'fences' for moving the spoils were locked up in the fort or out in the wilds with no arms to defend themself. It was all down to the bloody Twentieth legion and their interfering bloody centurion. Drapisces should have killed him when he had the chance. Mithras knew what Scribono had been thinking when he decided to make him a prisoner in the first place instead of killing him on the road? He could have even stood back, let him ride past and join the optio and the convoy. The upshot of Scribono's botch-up put the entire enterprise in danger. Why had Junius not stepped in and pulled rank?

*'Scribono: where are you, you useless fucker?'* he fumed.

He was the wilder of the two. You could reason with Junius. At least it used to be that way. Now, Titus Vindex was pushing for his execution. He paused at the turn of his section, nodded to his counterpart on the nearest wall and about faced to re-pace the two hundred and fifty-eight steps to the edge of the Praetoria gateway. If Vindex got his way, it would make his own position safer. There would be no one with reason to save their skin by exposing his part in the waggon looting. Provided Scribono stayed out there at liberty, Junius' death might help calm things down. It was a shame about that, he was not so bad a brother, for a deserter. Civius, would cover his tracks. And who up here had not thought similar things at one time or another?

The next morning Arco watched in line while they tied Junius to a post on the parade ground, next to a pile of broken and reject javelin shafts and an ominous pile of stones. The ranks on either side of him murmured and judged. He wondered what last regrets were passing through Junius' head.

*'Getting caught, probably. You stupid bastard, why did you come to the fort?'*

He tried to dismiss Junius as a misguided fool, but he came bringing a warning, for which he was now tied to a post. The last act of an honourable soldier, no more, no less. Down below in the fort, Civius in his full-dress uniform was mounting his horse. As always, an auxiliary was detailed to hold its reins, lest the act be less than gracious. The other centurion mounted with perfunctory efficiency once the commander was secure and seated on his mount. Together they clip-clopped their way through the fort, taking their time, inspecting the century lining the route as though the set of their uniforms mattered on a day like this. It was all part of the psychological punishment. Junius Cita would not remember this in the afterlife but every man of the Delmatarum present would carry these moments with him. Out the Sinistra gate and up the well-trodden incline to the parade ground. 'Clip clop, clop clip,' they came on, so slow and unhurried, the horse's shining coats brushed to perfection and in step, like a wedding dance. Junius did not have long left now. He stared at the two officers bearing the unwelcome gift of death in their faces.

*'Steady Junius. Do this for the Sixth. Die like a soldier,'* he implored.

The trumpets kept blowing 'Punishment' until the two officers arrived in front of the waiting century and dismounted, then ceased in practised unison. The dramatic cessation echoed and bounced off the surrounding hillsides. The Delmaratum had seen plenty of floggings but never a stoning. He swallowed and suspected the jitters he was feeling in his belly, the pounding beat in his chest were mere flickers to what was happening inside Junius. He tried to catch his eye, but Junius had retreated to a stockade within his head. Civius took his place on a stone rostrum. Arco stared at the ground for the indictment.

"Junius Cita has been identified a deserter from the Sixth legion. He has disgraced his legion and the standards he vowed to serve under. He has betrayed our beloved emperor Antoninus Pius, Father of our Country. Punishment is due and the legate of the Sixth has honoured the Delmatarum cohort by permitting us to deliver punishment here, today, at the hands of you men. He instructs me to remind you the legions are bound by the same discipline as you are. There can be no favouritism. The punishment is equal for all soldiers of Rome. Desertion is a crime against the Senate and People of Rome. It is a crime against the emperor himself," Civius proclaimed, letting it sink in.

Arco saw Junius was now standing with his head held up, eyes fixed on a distant place. A girl, his mother, the first time his father sat with him in a tavern and bought him a drink?

'*Steady Junius,*' he breathed.

Civius stood back and nodded. The centurion stepped in front of them, his eyes glittering with the anger of a regular soldier betrayed by desertion. The message clear and unequivocal. He pointed to the first eight men at the end of the row.

"Put down shields. Ground your pila. Pick up those staffs and beat the prisoner," he ordered.

The eight men dug the butt ends of their javelins into the ground and rested the rims of their shields against them. One by one they picked up the wooden staffs and stood in front of Junius Cita. A communal reticence seemed to seize them.

"Here," the centurion barked.

He stood in front of Cita.

"This is for all the men who stay faithful and do their duty," he snapped and swung his heavy vine stick into Junius' lower ribcage.

The noise of breaking bone brought a grunt to Cita's gagged mouth. The centurion stepped closer and pulled out the gag.

"It's a bit too late for 'sorry centurion' now, my lad," he hissed, "continue with the punishment," he barked to the eight soldiers.

In a flurry of blows Junius Cita crumbled, blood streaming from his face and ears, down onto his knees. The centurion let them continue the beating until Cita had stopped moving. He stepped forward and put his vine stick on the earth for a moment, before hauling Junius Cita to his feet, gripping his bloody tunic in his fists. Bubbles of red breath foamed in the gore. He took a piece of rope from his belt and tied Junius Cita across his chest upright against the post. Junius' face was hidden by the forward loll of his head. The centurion stepped back, picked up his vine swagger-stick and dismissed the eight men back to their ranks. He felt his legs tremble. It was not over yet.

"Every man in the front rank will file past and take a stone. Administer the punishment on the prisoner. The punishment is death by stoning,"the centurion commanded.

At the end of the front line a tesserarius pointed the queuing men to the pile of stones. One by one they picked up a missile and stood in front of Junius Cita. For a moment his chin remained pitched down on his chest. Slowly, he raised his blood-pulped face. Only his eyes fought back; his loud rasping inhalations a final exhortation to end it for him. His eyes sought the stone in the leading man's hand. The auxiliary whipped his hand back and fired the missile, striking him in the middle of his chest. Junius grunted and his head slumped again. The soldiers ranked themselves in small clusters and took fearsome aim at the shortest range. The first flurry brought three misses and a reprimanding bark from the centurion. Thereafter the sharp-edged slate stones lacerated his bare shins and knees to ribbon. The stones pounded and tore open his tunic, splitting flesh until the entire front rank of the century had passed before him. By then Junius was a broken, grisly doll of a man, a child's nightmare. He was hanging from his chest rope, legs lost, head burst open, clearly dead. The silence across the parade ground was broken by the idle sough of the unrepenting wind and the slight shake of Civius' horse's decorated harness ornaments, the one sound complimenting the other. High overhead, clouds came drifting in from the western sea. The hills and grasses noted the moment for a second and then discarded it, letting the spirit of Junius Cita depart: all debts paid.

"Next rank," the centurion ordered.

Arco felt his guts churn. He was not going to escape the duty. What did it matter now, throwing rocks at a dead man? Friend or no friend? Civius motioned the centurion to check Junius Cita. The centurion raised his vine stick to halt the second rank and strode to the prisoner to make the briefest of checks, lifting Junius' chin up with the gnarly end of his swagger stick before standing back and nodding in satisfaction. Civius nodded.

Arco breathed out. He could not have thrown a rock in any pretence of intent at Junius, dead or alive. There were things a soldier could not do, no matter what threat of punishment held over his head. He would have thrown wide.

*'Like a coward?'* he berated himself.

Junius had stood and died like a man, and it was, had been, his duty to help him out. Had Junius even seen him waiting in the ranks? Had he been steeling himself for the moment the two of them faced each other for the last time? Would he have looked up at him and forgiven him? Had it all been worth the silver? Living life as a renegade, hiding under the noses of the closest auxiliary garrison, biding his time for the next opportunity to sell plunder to the Carvetii? Had he ever looked down off the hilltops down to the sprawl of the hill fort and wished he could simply march back through the gate and report to the duty officer?

He bit back a womanly surge of feelings, the truth was an unremitting 'no.' By the time his turn was due the poor sod was already dead. He had been excused duty and a part of him felt dirty, lessened. Civius remounted his horse. He waited for the command to take the body down. Civius let his second in command mount and together they returned to the fort where the other century still stood lining the route. In front of Arco's row, a younger soldier vomited at the sight of Junius Cita.

*'Just you wait until he's been hanging there like meat for a couple of days, and he starts to stink,'* he fulminated and spat onto the grass, *'that'll fix your appetite.'*

"Are they leaving him there?" a voice whined.

He exchanged a glance with his mate beside him. It was clear Civius did not possess a merciful temper today. Nor did he have all the facts. How could he, he had never bothered to ask the identity of the other party to the illegal trade from the waggons. He had left Arco dealing with such tawdry details. The tesserarii gave the orders to about face and march back to the fort. Without Junius and Scribono on the outside of the wall the skimming off from the waggon convoys had ceased. Civius must have guessed there were deserters in the mix. Surely, he must have done: or had it been the opposite? He had executed Junius purely because he was a deserter, little realising the man he had just ordered stoned to death was his primary dealer on the other side of the wall.

*'Perhaps this is it,'* Arco thought, *'it was good while it lasted but Civius is going to call it quits now that he's covered his tracks. The centurion from the Twentieth sniffing around has put the wind up him. A clear warning. Someone has blabbed and word has leaked. And, Junius, you paid the price. Thank you, Jupiter, Best and Greatest, you have not deserted me,'* he breathed inside.

He marched back down the incline to the Sinistra and cursed Civius every step of the way as a brutal old fox.

*'But he's not covered all his tracks, has he? If he did not know about Junius, then he knows even less about Scribono,'* he realised.

Crows began clustering around the stake.

## Chapter Thirty-eight.

### Losatas' hall, Brigantes territory.

The same two Carvetii messengers were waiting before him once more. Borwenna had been on his mind. His priest did not like the idea of warriors invading her domain and fighting within her flesh, even if they were doing it to kill Romans. But the mining had to cease, likewise the felling of the trees and carting of stone from the hills. Brave men told him the deep shafts underground sometimes sighed and murmured, when she was displeased, such things were true. Perhaps they were taking her too much for granted? Small tributes of food and drink left at night were all very well, but it was hard to know whether she felt any less different towards them than she did the Roman invaders. He knew what his priest would say: *'she wants blood.'*

The same predictable answer to all questions concerning the gods and their tempers. But one day the Romans would be gone and Borwenna would still be there. So too would the Brigantes and Carvetii and every other tribe brave enough to carry on resisting. When that time came peace would have to be made with the goddess or no man would ever be safe to venture into her again. And now this news the Romans were trying to taunt them by sending Drapisces' to the mine nearest to his home. Perhaps Borwenna would intervene and save him? Or perhaps she would eat him and take his flesh as her sacrifice? Out of the corner of his eye he saw the messengers growing restless. He had kept them waiting. He signed his priest and his senior counsellor to come and stand at his side.

"We are going to help you in your battle against the mines. But we will not attack them directly. I leave that to you, the Carvetii, to defend your homes. Sniping at mines is easy work for small war bands, it does not need the warriors who will rise for my spear. Instead, we will destroy the waggons and men they use to transport the stone. Borwenna will have no cause to turn her face from her people. The Romans will get nothing from the efforts of their slaves. We will starve them of stone, wood and slate, of everything they are stealing from your lands. All roads will be closed to them," he said.

"But Drapisces is condemned to the mine. We think we know the exact one. We must attack it and release him," the senior of the messengers implored.

He sat forward.

"Listen to me Carveti. The Brigantes are your overlords, and you will do as I command. My men are assembling to join with you. Drapisces will be released if Borwenna permits, but mark me well, this is not just about Drapisces. There are bigger wolves that need killing in the forests than Drapisces."

"If we close the roads, the soldiers will come from the great forts. There will be war," the Carveti replied.

The priest smirked a little at his side.

"War is inevitable. The oak grows, the leaves fall, the snows come and go, and the oak grows. Not to fight is worse than fighting. Only a blood sacrifice can tame this evil. It's time we remembered whose lands these are. Borwenna calls out to us for vengeance. She demands it. Our little gatherings of her stone are like nothing more than picking the flowers around her skirts. We give her offerings. We never rob her. What earth mother would complain at that? But, the wolf-soldiers, they want to take everything without payment and show no gratitude," the priest said.

Losatas nodded. His counsellor did too. The two Carvetii bowed, conceding the argument. Besides, fighting in the open air was infinitely preferable to trying to storm the entrances to mines in search of Drapisces.

"When my lord?" one asked.

"I will send word out again today. The men will gather, and we will decide how to begin. We will not lay siege to all the roads and invite the legions out of the forts. We will begin by pricking their skin. A waggon of logs here, stone there, ore whenever, nip, nip, nip, like wasps. We will squeeze them slowly at first," he said, "then they will realise our fingers are round their throats. We will choke the life out of them. Then Borwenna will appeased," he vowed.

"And Drapisces lord?" the other messenger joined in.

"Drapisces will have to take his chances until we find out where he is. It is his punishment for surrendering to the Romans," his priest snarled.

He let the judgement lie. The priest had an uncomfortable habit of hearing the words in his head.

*

The first ambush happened three days later, far to the north of Cantiventi, but word came trickling back to the Twentieth. Velio was in full flow, dictating the revised report for Servius Albinius and the details of his promise to the Delmatarum garrison. Liscus tapped on the tent pole and ducked his head through the entrance.

"Salve Liscus," he smiled.

Marcellus looked up and smiled too.

"Salve, centurion I have news, your traps are beginning to draw out rats," Liscus reported.

He sat down on the spare stool. Marcellus finished scribing the last few words Velio had dictated.

"So soon, that is gratifying. Anything tangible I can add to this report?" Velio enquired.

"The mines are quiet. No attempt to rescue Drapisces so far. But reports are coming in that war bands have attacked convoys," Liscus intoned, "it's not confirmed, but Brigantes woad markings have been reported. It rather changes things," he summed up.

Velio sucked through his teeth, "you are sure they were Brigantes? They have come to the feast faster than I expected. What about casualties?" he said.

Liscus half opened his hand and put his other fist on his knee. Velio knew his second in command well enough to see diplomacy in action.

"Silly question Liscus, I was being optimistic. Of course, there have been casualties. Send word to the three mines, particularly Plautius, to stand to guard. I'm taking half the century up to the hill fort. I promised Civius our support. That road needs securing, the others don't matter so much. The garrison up there are windy, I sense it, and the marine garrison at Uiliocenon must be warned too. You will remain here with the other half and support Plautius, as he requires. I want Drapisces returned in one piece," he commanded.

He rapped one of Marcellus' spare stylus against his teeth.

"If you have to move to support Plautius or either of the other two detachments, leave our wounded here to hold our camp, we will alert the Cantiventi praefectus of our intentions. He will give support if needed. We will leave tomorrow, organise it will you Liscus? Marcellus, I want you here to liaise with the praefectus and relay messages to Deva Victrix."

"Half a century is not a lot of men, sir," Marcellus replied, eyeing Liscus for his reaction to the plan.

Velio smiled at their concern and tapped the site of the arrow wound.

"My gratitude Marcellus, but this is feeling better. I do not intend to dawdle. We will be up and over the pass faster than wine going down the legate's throat," he promised, "the signum will come with me. I will leave you the cornicen. I don't want the men here to feel abandoned," he said.

He let Liscus sort the century out for himself. Picking out men when all were willing to go was never popular. They would take two hand carts for tents as a precaution. He had no intention of getting caught out in the wilds tonight with such a small force. He toyed with the notion of asking for auxiliary cavalry support from the Morinorum praefectus. But Cantiventi and Uiliocenon had to remain fully manned and defended. Cantiventi especially was the key to the Iter X. If anything was to be lost, far better it was the midway post in the hills. All things considered it was better to march in a compact column with men he knew and trusted. Orann could scout for him when he was not leading his spare mount.

The next morning, he mounted up and watched the parading of the company standard before the men. The century cornicen blew Farewell Brother. Orann held back before tagging on at the end of the small column. Liscus raised a fist to him in salute.

"Don't lose this one," he said pointing to Velio's spare mount, only half joking.

Orann lifted his spear in reply. Velio saluted the standard. Liscus had selected sixty-five of the very best men for him, very nearly the strength of a regular cohort century, leaving nearly an equal number behind. It had led to raised voices yesterday which he pretended not to hear. No one wanted to be left behind. He was delighted in the show of loyalty. Rather than put the tesserarii in the firing line for the men's discontent Liscus selected the bulk of them in whole eight-man squads. An astute piece of leadership.

"Poor luck at Fortuna's altar lads, the rest of you are with me," he cried out.

Marcellus saluted from the door flap of the headquarters tent and went back to his inevitable reports. The weather was settled. The lake at their back was flat calm. Velio sniffed the air and expected good progress up to the hill pass, they should make it easily today. A hard old slog but good for the men. The affair with Drapisces had whetted their appetites for enforcing Pax Romana. The Iter X would make moving the baggage carts a speedy affair.

He led them over the bridge at the head of the lake where the pretty stream aspired every day to be a river. Striking west on the right-hand side, it was soft going, in a soft gentle landscape. As the birds flew, it was about a ten-mile march, but it was farther than that on foot as the road twisted its course. Praise the gods for a good, paved road. Coming back to Cantiventi on the downhill had been a much easier ride than this was going to be. Still, the lads had all done it before, and this should be the last time he required it under his command. A ground devouring chant started up behind him and he smiled and murmured the words along with them, a roll call of the emperors who had ruled Britannia since Julius Caesar first scrunched his galley keels into the beaches of the south coast. His horse pricked its ears up to the thud of boots on the road and tossed its head.

*

Losatas set up temporary camp in one of the long passes the Carveti lands were renowned for and sent men out to spread word of his arrival. Bands of local warriors began flocking in to greet him. His own scouts returned bringing movement reports from all around. The Roman convoys were responding with heavier escorts. The Carveti and parties of his own men were assaulting the forest sites, bring new felling to a halt. He stayed for a week before feeling he was straining the local hospitality and shifted camp. With timber felling effectively ceased, it was time to go after the ore convoys, perhaps locate Drapisces and liberate him. The legions should be responding to the provocation by now and the lack of mounted wolf-soldier patrols was not like them. Not at all. They were usually fast to draw the sword when resistance flared up.

The next camp had good water and a splendid view of the stone pathway through the hills. Convoys moving in either direction would be ripe for picking. And he had the bonus of escape routes and good lines of sight for his scouts to warn him of danger. His men brought deer to the fires and the Carveti brought ale. He ate and drank and pondered what his late cousin's next step would have been. There were two forts within easy reach. Would Orgidor have considered an outright attack on either of them? He wrestled with it. A declaration of outright war would commit the whole Brigantes federation to months perhaps years of strife. The casualties amongst women and children would be enormous.

Losses of animals, halls and homesteads burned. And his only provocation for it was the mining in the Carveti lands? There was mining in his own lands too. It was not only a Carveti problem but without a Roman atrocity to fire up the warriors, a call for war was unlikely to be well received by the elders. And without their support his position was tender at best. He snorted at that. The sons of the wolf had never been convincingly beaten by any tribe since the weak legion in grandfather's time. The only time they had a complete victory. Even that had not dampened the Roman determination. They replaced the losses and cracked down harder. It was not so easy to replace lost sons and brothers. On the other hand, the Carveti would follow his wishes. If he chose to attack the forts they would comply. He was their overlord. And if he failed, he would be weakened by a loss in dignity.

He sat apart from his men as they ate and decided the answer would be clearer in the morning. He heard the mood around the fires and did his best to join in. His men dragged him with wry humour and jokes into singing and drinking until one by one they all began nodding by the fire. Sleep came with dreams of screaming down from the hillsides in great numbers and making a mighty slaughter of the sons of the wolf. A slaughter to avenge Borwenna and pacify his ancestors, a slaughter to silence Origidor, a victory worthy of a war leader of the Brigantes.

The next morning, he sent men out to the west, shadowing the road for traffic coming in from the sea. He had forty or fifty of his best warriors close at hand and many more spread out over the hills. His strength was improving with the Carveti near at hand and Brigantes coming in by the hour. The Carveti liked the idea of harassing a fort up in the hills to keep those Romans fixed in place and isolated. He mulled it over as the day wore on. Disruption without loss of warriors was very appealing while his men kept pressure the convoys. It was clear many of the Carveti wanted Drapisces back, even although those under his direct protection were lost and unsaveable. He sat by his fire and talked to his priest. In the distance a warrior came hurrying up the long valley. The stone road leading down to the bottom lands and the lakes in the east was empty save for this one warrior, a Carveti by his garb. He was a long way off. A stiff wind was rising in their faces, bending the grasses, making the ravens dance in the air. High in the sky clouds were drifting inland, oblivious to this contrary little breeze. The priest continued expressing his opinion as they both watched the messenger. It felt like the man was not getting any closer. He got to his feet and picked up his spear and shield. His priest followed and together they headed down the hill to meet the warrior.

"Romans, my lord. A big patrol is coming this way," the Carveti blurted out.

"How big?" he queried.

The Carveti looked past him at the men arrayed in groups and clumps around the campfires.

"You have enough," the warrior replied with a single sweep of his eyes at the resting warriors, "they are behind me, but they will be here soon lord."

"You are going to attack?" his priest interjected.

"Yes," he replied.

What other option did he have, having brought these men here?

"How?" the priest asked.

He turned and inspected the hill rising towards the final summit stages of the pass, cowed and dominated by the peaks themselves. His men started getting to their feet, sensing that something was happening down below. He assessed the ground and the road trailing off to the valley floor below. They were in a good position to stand as they were and block the road. No Roman patrol could pass without a fight. He could save his men's strength and wait for the sons of the wolf to come to him.

"Here," he said, pointing, "the men are already in place. The gods might have placed me here for this very purpose."

"And the hill fort? We leave it for now?" his priest confirmed.

He nodded.

"The hill fort will not even know we are killing their men," he replied, "they will see none of it, it's perfect," he said.

He scratched his chin.

"Although it would be wise to send the Carveti over the top and keep the fort occupied while we deal with these dogs."

The messenger smiled.

"We can do that, just be sure you kill all of them," he growled.

Losatas nodded and went to rally his kinsmen. Smoke from the fires was drifting in the air. When the Romans entered the bottom of the pass and looked up at the depressingly long incline ahead of them, the first thing they would see would be the fire smoke and then his warriors. They would accept the challenge, order their formation, and tire themselves ascending the pass. Every step bringing them closer to his welcome of arrows and spears. His advantage of height would wreak havoc and then they would swarm down and finish it. He licked his lips and tasted victory.

*

The minutes passed. On either side of him his men settled into positions to fight. There would be plenty of time to make the fighting speech to goad them and beseech Belatucadrus. He stepped onto a rock and stared at the distant end of the valley where the road took a swing to the left. Somewhere beyond that bend his enemies were marching in this direction. His priest said nothing, for once. He noticed a bloody hand and a smeared thumb; the holy man had made his oath already.

"Drapisces did not fight hard enough," the priest said.

He agreed but did not take his eyes from the long road. He sniffed as a solitary figure on horseback moved into view.

"They have scouts," he murmured.

"No matter," the priest replied, "their formations will not work on this ground. They will stick to the road like flies to a horse. You have them my lord. They will march up this road and you can eat them up. It will be a great coup for the Brigantes," the priest crowed.

He searched the hillsides for signs of more enemy horsemen. Did they really only have the single solitary scout? The gods must be smiling on the house of Losatas.

## Chapter Thirty-nine.

## The hill pass.

Velio called Orann to the head of the column, leading the spare horse.

"Hand those reins over," he said.

Orann thought the Master was sounding a little nervous. Had his encounter with the Carvetii shaken his nerve? No, it was not possible. He did as he was told. One of the tesserarii took possession of the spare horse and led it to the back of the formation. He eased his spear across his own animal's mane, the point jutting out over its ears like a thin, dangerous horn. Velio grimaced.

"Go ahead of us Orann, see what is out there, stay on the road. No pursuits, understand? I want you to come back often and tell me what you see," he warned.

Orann gave him his army-salute, the one he had been practising. The legionaries cheered.

Velio looked at Voccia's servant, without Orann he might not have made good his escape from Drapisces' men.

*'And he has no idea,'* he fancied.

He returned the salute and sent Orann off to patrol. The Votadini set his heels to the horse and went cantering ahead, looking more and more like a true warrior of his tribe at every stride.

Orann spurred on, taking in the deceiving nature of the ground. The bumps and hollows, the wending streams with deep cut banks where men could lie in wait and ambush the road, all worth his attention but none of it merited a second look. What the Master undoubtedly wanted was reassurance that no major tribal war party was waiting to threaten their journey to the hill fort. He eased the reins and let the horse slow to a walk. With a quick check back, he saw the column was temporarily out of sight. He kept moving. His pride at being trusted with this task made him determined to cement his status among the centurion's men. Daily they were growing friendlier toward him. The road descended down to a river and began a wide skirting of a bog, thick with green bullrushes and still, dark, pools. Noisy waterbirds scuttled into the reeds at his approach. The road stayed up on a slender ledge of dry ground and needed a bedding of rock to cross the narrowest part before it got clear. He paused and surveyed the trees and woodland. This was most definitely a dangerous place for the centurion and his men. If they got themselves pushed off the road, with the bog at their backs, they would struggle in their heavy armour to get out of here alive. He sat waiting, hoping to draw out a challenge if any Carvetii were hiding and watching. The branches of the trees swayed a little as if they waited too, but there was nothing more. He had another check on all sides and dug his heels into the horse's ribs. Now the road began rising away from the river to dryer ground. Towering and dominating everything a great rugged corner of rock was standing up as if it had broken off from the surrounding hills and tumbled down to this spot. He stared up at it, amazed, then suddenly realised it must be the home of a Carvetii god and dropped his gaze in respect. He had never seen anything like it. It might have made a magnificent stronghold, but the plain fact Carvetii were not living up there decided the question. It would have made an impregnable citadel for Drapisces. A far better one than the hill he had chosen. Drapisces' respect and discretion explained everything.

Orann raised his spear to god on the rock, then nudged his horse, trusting he had caused no offence. The Romans had built their road below it. He would ask the Master if he realised what this place was and whether they had left gifts when the road was completed. Part of him knew they had not considered it holy. More likely they had heaped curses at it for causing them more work.

The ground opened out to his right as he entered the tail of a great valley. He wished the Master had taken him with his century when he first left the fortress at Deva Victrix: this would be more familiar ground. He would know where the road led and how it got there. He felt his skin crawl. There was danger here. His horse neighed and pranced sensing his disquiet. She danced and sidestepped across the road, and he tugged hard to drag her head back to face the front. Was the god on the high rock telling her to go no further? Up ahead in the distance he could see the headwall of the valley. That must be the start of the pass to the fort. He doubted he was seeing all of it. There would be shoulders on the hillsides, hiding other steep slopes beyond, to tire the legs and sap the spirit. The road led his eyes to an array of warriors, spread like a necklace at a woman's throat across both sides of the road, barring it. He did not need the eyes of a hawk or eagle to know the distant glitter of spears was the union of Brigantes and Carvetii. The centurion had his answer.

The mare was still playing up and he bunched her reins in his fist, tugging even harder than before to make her obey. She fought back and he slapped his spear hand against her neck and shouted a short bark at her. Her ears pricked to listen, and he lowered his head close to them, whispering, calming, settling her, praising her. She tossed her head: defeated. He kept soothing her, scanning the lower parts of the valley for danger, gripping the reins ever tighter in his fist, poised to turn and flee. The rough grasslands were empty. The threat was up ahead, the challenge unmistakable. He began pushing the mare on further. The Master would want to know the number of warriors opposing him. He could afford to get closer but the unknown nature of the Carvetii od on the hill behind him, now that it was watching him, was unsettling. Going further would be folly and the longer it would be before the centurion got the news. Surely, that was the most important thing? He wheeled about and galloped for the column, keeping his head low over the mare's neck as he passed the high rock.

Velio saw Orann come pelting back down the road, his shield bouncing on his horse's withers, and raised his vine stick to halt the column.

*'Slowly Orann, slowly, whatever it is, good soldiers stay calm,'* he rebuked him in his head.

Orann skidded to a halt on the road, whirled the horse alongside Velio's making the standard bearer and the trumpeter step back from the hooves and the spear tip in front of their faces.

"Speak,' he said and tried to dampen down the effect of Orann's pell-mell return.

The mare settled like a swan beside his horse.

"Many enemy warriors are blocking the upper section of the next pass master, they have a good position and there are many of them," Orann said.

Velio looked Orann straight in the eye.

"How many Orann?" he probed.

Orann leaned close and lowered his voice.

"I fear there are too many of them for your men," he replied, "they have the high ground. This is a bad place to fight Master. There are Carvetii gods nearby, perhaps Belatucadrus himself. You should not fight here," he implored.

"Belatucadrus? You are certain?" Velio said.

Orann shook his head.

"No Master, but it feels bad. I would not fight here," he answered.

"Show me," Velio kept his voice down.

He could not let the men at his back get spooked by Orann's fears. His unhappy expression was speaking volumes. Orann should be relishing the chance to take more heads.

"Tesserarius, bring the column on at the Alert. Enemy warriors have been sighted," he ordered.

Nodding to Orann he went to look for himself.

*

Titus Vindex shared a feeling in common with Liscus Aulus Manlio. Across the river gorge from the fort was a stand of trees neither of them liked. Neither the look of them, their position as a place for hostile scouts to watch the fort, nor the louring atmosphere they managed to impart. It was bad enough that Junius Cita's corpse was still tied to the execution post on the parade ground awaiting Civius to order its removal, but having the trees watching the fort was unlucky, somehow.

*'I'm going to cut you down,'* he decided, *'like you should have been when the fort was built.'*

He leaned on the stone rampart and clenched his fingers together. It would be his watch soon. It was surely time the body was removed from the parade ground.

*'For the love of the Holy Mothers of the Parade Ground, what good is it doing Civius? What insults do you lay at their feet? They will turn their faces from all of us and leave us to the mercy of the savages. And if they do, I pray to Mithras you take the first arrow,'* he fumed.

Uncut trees and corpses left on the parade ground: whatever great scheme Civius was playing was a mystery.

*'Perhaps high command does that?'* he speculated.

He saw Acro heading over the compound towards his billet to put on his full uniform for guard duty.

'Why am I cursed with you, Arco?' he scowled.

The soldier saw him and saluted. He returned it. But Arco's eyes were not looking at him, they were fixed on something in the distance. He turned around wondering what Arco had seen. From behind the stand of trees and on the high ground leering down on the parade ground, the Carvetii had brought their spears.

"Hostiles, Carvetii," Arco shouted the alarm.

Across the fort heads turned.

"Hostiles," Titus repeated.

The numbers were large, larger than he had ever seen in front of the fort. There were more Carvetii warriors than he thought existed. Hundreds of them, maybe more than hundreds. There was no sign of a delegation riding toward the gates to parley. Centurion Pinneius' lucky escape had left no doubt the Carvetii were on the boil. He doubted Civius would have bothered to relay this intelligence down to the port commander at Uiliocenon. Titus drew a rapid deep breath.

"Sound 'Stand to the Eagle',"he bawled from the pit of his stomach.

The duty trumpeter at the headquarters entrance turned his head at the order, met his eyes and came running forward with his instrument. He glared at the trumpeter.

"Blow 'Stand to the Eagle', damn you, or I'll have the skin off you before nightfall," he snarled.

The trumpeter paled and put the horn to his lips. Within seconds the fort went into foment. The second centurion strode to his side.

"Report," he said, favouring discipline over the obvious.

Titus saluted.

"There are Carvetii hostiles, sir, on the praetorian and sinistra quarters of the fort in significant numbers, sir," he replied, "they have also taken the parade ground heights."

"So, I see optio," the centurion nodded, weighing the situation for a moment.

"Sir? Movement on the parade ground," a sentry called.

Together the centurion and Titus marched further along the ramparts to see the cause. A small group of warriors were inspecting Junius Cita's body. Civius joined them in his armour.

"What are they doing centurion?" he demanded.

"Removing the body before they attack, I believe sir. Superstitious lot. They probably don't want him there in front of the fort. Mithras knows why, can't see what earthly difference it makes," the centurion said.

"Happy to put our heads on trees when we fall into their hands but not leave a man we have executed on display. What perversions they hold," Civius replied.

The centurion bit his lip. Junius Cita was performing his last duty in death, however macabre: spooking the Carvetii.

"We could send a squad out and chase them off," Titus said.

The centurion frowned, “too dangerous Titus, and for no purpose, we should wait and see whether they attack, Civius,” he advised.

Civius tapped the pommel of his sword with his fingertips.

“I agree. Let’s wait and see what they do. We have no convoys scheduled for today so they can stand there all day for all I care, as long as they do not attack. Keep the men on the walls and keep me informed if anything changes,” he said and strode off to the principia.

“I think we should chase them off,” Titus repeated.

“Two centuries aren’t enough to go out there on two fronts and defend the fort too. We hold tight optio and see what develops. We are not getting lured out into a fight on this kind of ground. It would be madness to fight here, the odds are all in their favour,” the centurion adjudged.

He rapped his vine stick on the stone parapet in sudden fury.

“You know something, optio? This is what comes of putting a half garrison into a fort. This is what comes of it. Fucking madness, we have more wall than men, and those bastards can see it for themselves. Plain as day, they just have to pick their spot and we’ll be hard pushed to keep them out,” he raged.

“Could we send a rider to Uiliocenon sir?” Titus offered.

The centurion assessed the road below.

“That we can, provided they have not set a trap. Organise it and I will alert the commander. And get that alarm beacon lit. It may be all we can do. Get the infirmary cleared. I want every man on the rampart in full armour. I don’t care what the medicus says.”

Titus saluted and hurried off.

Arco took the jeers as he helped align three of the fort’s scorpions into position facing the warriors holding the ground overlooking the parade ground. He hoped he got a chance to fire one of them. Barrels of iron bolts were already in place for the three other machines facing the Carvetii opposite the front gates. But firing the bolts might just as easily be sufficient provocation to the Carvetii to attack.

"You could go out there and tell them all to fuck off, couldn't you Arco? I mean they're your pals, ain't they?" a voice barracked.

"This'll teach you to play silly buggers with these savages," another taunted.

"Bet old Junius whatshisface is laughing now. Our turn to face the shit."

*'Come on,'* he fizzed, *'we'll trade you iron for iron.'*

*

Losatas watched the small column of Roman infantry change formation into six abreast, taking up every last bit of the paved space, maintaining a secure footing. That made them a compact rectangle with the centurion in front on his horse and the emblem pole directly at his back. The formation made it clear they were not going to try and manoeuvre around his men. He half admired the astuteness of the Roman officer's decision. The road was a platform, almost a parapet in the rough ground. It was not going to stop him sending in a flanking attack, but it conferred an advantage to them. He felt anticipation rising in his men. Undoubtedly their lone native scout, the one now riding to the rear of the column, had alerted them. Nevertheless, the Romans were coming to fight, taking his challenge head on. There would be blood and heads taken and glory. The formation halted. The officer dismounted, the scout came forward and took control of the officer's horse. He must be a skilled scout. They were protecting him. He could see them conversing. The officer took the shield hanging from his saddle and joined the front rank. The scout retired with the officer's horse to a position behind the formation, giving himself ample room to turn and flee if attacked. The formation was within bow range. The first few arrows went winging up and away towards them. He watched the flight on the wind. A command was barked, the words faint on the breeze, and the Romans raised their shields above their heads in one single practised movement. The lone scout remained stationary on the road as the legionaries advanced to fight. They came on in silence, crunching the stone with their iron shod boots. He half expected to hear them begin a chant or song to keep their courage up and spur them on, but this was not simply a discipline to save their breath. The scrape of their boots on stone: eyed fixed, weapons raised, silent intent; the wolf skinned pole bearer marching with his head held high, unprotected by shield or spear. Neither was the officer pushing the pace of his men. This slow confident approach was mute intimidation. He snickered: it probably scared other lesser tribes in the south but was not going to work on his seasoned Brigantes. The arrow flights increased and his knots of his men broke ranks around him, leaping over the springy, tussocky ground. Others, already in position higher up on the road, were sprinting into the fight. The Roman formation adjusted itself to the new threat. The Romans heaved out one volley of javelins.

Velio blew his bone whistle in a shriek that rent the air.

*'Even the best soldiers like to be reminded they're in a testudo, it's the safest formation in the army,'*

Gallus' favoured mantra had never sounded truer than it did today. The gravel surface scrunched as the men took stance. The charging warriors would bring relief from the arrow rain. A low murmur of "Swords, Swords, Swords," broke out around him: his nickname from his days as an instructor. They never usually dared to say it in his presence. Today was clearly different. The standard bearer was grinning, as he drew his own pugio-dagger. Very well, so be it: Velio took a deep breath.

**"Testudo.**

**Testudo, halt.**

**Testudo, front and outside ranks, shields to the front.**

**Testudo, at the ready.**

**Outside ranks fire pila.**

**Now.**

**Testudo, stay in formation.**

**Testudo, draw gladii.**

**Testudo, prepare to engage.**

**Testudo, Mars Ultor is with us.**

**Testudo, you are the First cohort. We fight for each other and The Boar. These heathen dogs are in our way,"**

He barked the command sequence. The left-hand front corner of the testudo took the first impact of the onslaught. The crush of muscle and bone into shields and armour shook the formation.

"Eyes front," he yelled, "watch to your front."

The murmur ceased. He felt a rippling movement like a muscling snake as the left rank absorbed the blows and regained balance. A chorus of grunts and screams of agony broke out. The Brigantes sweeping down the road hit them next. Velio butted his shield into the first man's face and swept his gladius low taking him above the knee. A push and the man fell down. He jabbed down, ending it and fended off the next sword. The men on either side of him were his best and the six of them chopped and slashed and stabbed out, quickly raising a useful impeding barrier of dying Brigantes in front of them. Down the right-hand side, where the hillside came close to the road, enemy warriors began flinging themselves onto the testudo shields, hammering away, trying to open up the roof of the formation. The noise was getting louder. His men were fighting in silence except for the harsh hiss of their breathing and the victory snarls as another warrior fell. He risked a backward glance to assess the situation.It was getting time to refresh the outside ranks. The rear facing rank was coming under pressure. He could not see what was happening. This would not do and there seemed to be no end of surging Brigantes. He blew his whistle. The switchover was so fast the Brigantes seemed stunned. He took the opportunity to push into the centre and assess the condition of his men.

**"Pila,"** he ordered.

Every man within the inner ranks still had two javelins available.

**"Inner ranks will fire pila.**

**Outer rank will lower shields on my command. Make it fast, men.**

**Lower shields."**

The testudo became temporarily naked.

**"Fire pila. Fire."**

More warriors tumbled backwards under the violent impetus of the javelins.

**"Raise shields,"** he called.

The testudo was restored. There was an answering roar and the Brigantes flooded forwards. Velio let them crash into the shield wall and bleed on the short swords of his men. So far, virtually all his men were all standing, some more bloodied than others. A couple of crumpled bodies had fought their last action for the emperor. Far fewer than he feared but he knew it could not last. The Brigantes launched their own spears from the high ground on his right, over the heads of their own warriors and his new front rank crumbled as the spears whistled in without warning. His men replaced the front rank and hauled the wounded back into the centre of the testudo. He called for the second pilum strike. It had the same deadly effect. How long were the Brigantes going to stick at this? Their fallen warriors were making obstacles for closing with the testudo. They eased back, even as he had the thought in his head, gathering their breath. He blew his whistle and got the last of his fresh men into the front lines. A sudden hailstorm of arrows struck the raised shields of the testudo and three more men fell with arrows finding the tiny gap at the front of the throat, horrible wounds, made worse by sounds of incoherent, gurgling agony. The only part the helmets and shields did not protect. Their distress created fear in their comrades. More arrows came flighting in horizontally, more men went down.

"Centurion," the signifer called out, his face defiant but questioning.

"We need to get moving, men, can you wounded lads all walk?" he barked

"Not all, sir," the signifer answered, "we have lost ten or more, if we move we will have to leave some wounded behind, we can't protect ourselves otherwise," he said.

Velio calculated the appalling odds between holding fast here and keeping his wounded protected and pushing forward with the fit men. He could not bring himself to order the despatch of his own critically wounded. They were not loyal simply to be betrayed by their own commander.

"Don't worry sir. It's best that I take care of it. Wouldn't be right for you to do it," the signifer said, "and I won't let them be taken by these bastards."

"Then do it quickly," he muttered.

He felt aghast that he could give such an order and feel nothing but concern they were holding him back. It felt like a matter of moments until the signifer stood back before him, his eyes blank as a fish.

"Men we have to push forward up this slope to the hill fort. It's just over the top. It's a hard push, but once we get moving, we do not halt. Do you understand. Any man who falls and cannot get up must be left. We are going to get over these bodies and stay in formation. Don't give the dogs a chance to get in," he called.

The signifer nodded back.

"C'mon, lads," he roared.

**"Testudo.**

**Testudo. March,"** Velio ordered.

He pushed his way back into the front rank, thrusting his gladius up like his own banner. The men cheered and in one concerted step the whole unit went with him, the rear facing rank most in danger from tripping over the men felled by the front rank as they sealed the rear of the formation. He moved at half pace for thirty steps reckoning that would be sufficient for the back men to get onto the clear road.

"All clear sir," called out his signifer.

He lengthened his stride and led them toward the regathering Brigantes. At a critical point the road bent back and up in a sharp angle as it contoured a precipitous section. It was the most hated section of the road for the waggon convoys. The place where badly laden vehicles tipped over, dragging men and animals in a bloody skelter if not properly braced with men back-hauling on guide ropes from the opposite side of the road. Velio road raised his head and took stock, remembering the corner from before. On a horse it was not too much of a problem. For legionaries it was tiring to slow down from marching step to an orderly crawl that got worse from here on up. Everything west of Cantiventi up until this point had been a preamble. This was where the real fight was going to happen. The men were tiring, their labouring breathing sounded loud in his ears. If he could march them up past this trap point, they could dig in and rest for a short time. The Brigantes were gathering numbers but they must be tiring too. The road ahead looked vertical and there were enemy warriors standing above them in ideal positions to send rocks crashing down on his men. More rocks were coming at them from the right-hand side of the road. The hill streams were cascading beautiful cold water almost within reach. The mountains were torturing them. The men were still riding the storm as warriors darted in to stab and slash, though the first great waves had ceased, they were coming in repeated, violent surges. The reduced testudo was holding, so far. He felt parched.

*'You fool, the men must be thirsty too. A quick drink from the water skins. Two gulps and keep moving. We have to get past this bend,'* he calculated.

**"On my command, inside ranks may drink two mouthfuls. On my next command, outside ranks will rotate and drink**

**two gulps. That is all you may take. This is the tough bit lads,"** he barked.

He shouted the order and the flurry of passing water skins proved him right. He sipped from his own. When they had all drunk, he made the bone whistle shriek like an angry hawk.

Losatas was horrified as his men allowed the Romans to start moving. Stationary, they were an easy target, ready to be worn down to the final soldier. On the move they assumed a defiant spirit that would need breaking. Now, he had to make them panic and run, split them up, each one for himself. The steep slope was still in his favour. The Roman dead were being torn to pieces by men seeking trophies and revenge. The bodies stripped and naked within seconds, headless and mutilated soon after. Triumphant warriors began retreating back with their spoils to the camp, no longer interested in the fight. He had lost them. The toll so far had been heavy. There must be more than twenty, perhaps thirty of his men lying in forlorn clumps, bleeding onto the stone road. Others were retiring with slashed limbs, punctured arms, legs, even chests. These Romans were not the usual bread of the legions he had met. Down below, his priest had lost control, and was stamping and screaming just out of reach of the advancing soldiers, waving his spear and smacking his fist on his bare, painted chest. A knot of young men went rallying to his taunts. The soldiers' eyes and the rims of their helmets were the only parts visible above the tops of their shields. They appeared intent on pushing up to the summit of the pass. Hefting his own buckler and spear he signed to his immediate loyal guard and threw himself into the attack. After twenty minutes he called them back to regather. His cavorting mad priest was pulled back by a brave man risking his arm to the holy man's swinging sword. The Romans had come to the crook in the road. Though they were trying to ascend, they had lost momentum and the hillside, perhaps Belatucadrus and Borwenna herself, had come out to fight them back. The Romans were struggling to get up and forwards because they had lost half their men and the shelter provided by their shields dwindled after every assault. The road itself was a bloody, trailing swathe of carnage.

He had seen the Romans stab down as they passed over the bodies of Brigantes men struck down by the leading rank. The rear rank spewing out a harvest of corpses as they passed by. It was time the Carvetii shed some of their blood instead of lingering up on the high pass holding the fort at bay. He looked up at the sun. The day was moving towards early evening. The fight had been going for longer than he imagined. He had them pinned on the road. It was a standoff. The Romans were for the time being unwilling to move and his men content to fix them in place.

*'They won't rest for long,'* he decided, *'only enough time to gather their strength. They will want to fight in daylight. It has to be now.'*

"Go to the Carvetii and tell them the fight is here. We can finish this before the soldiers in the fort know what is happening. Go now. Be quick," he shouted at a counsellor.

*

Orann saw the centurion lead his men up the pass. Incredibly, none of the circling Brigantes were paying him the slightest bit of attention as they milled around the bodies. As the fight moved higher, leaving a smear of bodies in its wake, the first distracted warriors began kneeling and tending to the bodies of their sons, brothers, fathers. He could see wounded men limping against their spears, all interest in the fighting over. In the distance the small command disappeared behind a curtain of Brigantes, but he was confident the Master was still fighting and leading his men. The glimpse of the signifer's standard was enough to tell him the fight was not over. He saw the testudo climbing the road at the base of what looked like a vertical section. Suddenly it was clear. He turned his horse and galloped.

## Chapter Forty.

## The hill pass.

Titus was thinking about permission to stand the men in his century down to eat in rotation. Nothing appeared to be happening outside the walls. The Carvetii were just standing there like pillars. They were going to need shifting soon. It was insufferable they should be allowed to send the garrison into cover and not attack, as if this was their land and they had full control of it.

"I think they are leaving, sir," a voice called.

He rushed out the door to the rampart from the room where he had been snatching a bite to eat himself. He brushed the guilty breadcrumbs off his armour and pretended the lapse had not happened. Sure enough, the Carvetii posted above the parade ground were moving off: pulling back. Within minutes they had gone. The mountain side was bare once more.

"Tell the centurion and the commander," he instructed.

"They're moving on this side too sir. Looks like they've had enough," another happier voice called out.

'*Aye, but enough of what?*' he wondered.

He turned his gaze to the front of the fort and the trees on the far side of the river gully. The main Carvetii force was pulling back and slipping out of sight under a fold in the land as easily as it had first presented itself.

'*What do we do now?*' he fretted, '*what has all this been for?*'

Movement in the distance caught his eye. A section of cavalry was coming up the Uiliocenon road. That must be it. The Carvetii had spotted the reinforcements from the port and decided not to make a stand. Iuliocenon had three hundred and fifty legionaries and one hundred and twenty cavalry. It looked like the whole cavalry arm pounding up the road. Even if the mounted messenger had not made it through, the signal fire must have been correctly interpreted. The decurion at the head of the cavalry halted his men on the road beneath the Praetoria gate and rode up the incline to the gate. Civius reached the ramparts and leaned out.

"Salve, decurion. You have chased them off. Check the road to the east is clear and report back," he ordered.

The decurion saluted and returned to his command. There was a short pause. Civius fidgeted as he watched, waiting for his order to be hastened. The Carvetii had now vanished entirely from the hillsides. What was the decurion waiting for? At length, the decurion kicked his heels into his horse and led them at a walk up the shoulder of the pass, snaking up the gradient to the summit and disappearing beyond. The final sight of the men crossing the skyline made Arco shiver.

*

Velio drew in his breath and snatched a drink of water. The signifer had disobeyed him but it did not matter now. The standard was jutting up from a crevice in the rock. The signifer standing beside it, armed now with the shield and gladius of one of his fallen comrades. 'Rugio's' if he was correct. How strange that after all the campaigns and miles marched it was all going to end here, surrounded by a dozen men still capable of fighting and a signifer. A signifer wielding the weapons of a man with the same name as one who tried to bully him when he first joined up. The signifer should be gripping the standard in his left hand and fighting with the right. It did not matter. He had left the century trumpeter under Liscus back in Cantiventi: it had been a bad mistake to make.

Now he was unable to summon help or even give pause to the Brigantes with the sound. The Delmatarum would probably not hear him anyway. The Brigantes had him bottled up and there was nowhere to run. Voccia would hear eventually that he had fallen with his command. Her child would be fatherless. His name would be a stranger's for the nights when the boy asked questions about him.

"They're coming again sir," a wounded legionary called out.

"Shields up," he called, "one more push brothers and they will call it quits. We've stolen their dice."

It was true. The ground around them was thick with dead warriors. The Boar were making the Brigantes pay a tough price.

"Balls of Dis, Carvetii," another voice spoke.

"The Carvetii are joining them, sir," the signifer repeated.

"Look around you. Count the bodies. The Carvetii have eyes. They'll soon see we're a tougher nut to crack than they expect. One last push and they'll fall back. Trust me lads. Trust in the gods.

**Mars Ultra, we fight to honour you.**

**Jupiter, Thou Best and Greatest, I ask you to stand with these brave men today.**

**Fortuna, hear us and love us.**

**Holy Mothers of the Parade Ground do not forsake us.**"

Velio bayed for the men at the top of his voice. He stepped forward to the front of the small group and pulled his sweaty helmet back on. He swirled his gladius the way he did when he liked to intimidate a fresh pupil seeking a sword lesson, or an opponent. The low barricade of native bodies was spiked like a thorn bush with discarded weapons poking up like fangs seeking flesh.

"One last push lads. One last push. They've got to get over that," he pointed, "ones and twos, we'll have them all until they're gut sick of it."

*

From his vantage point Scribono saw it could not last much longer. Velio Pinneius was going to die, fair enough, but it would not be at his hands: not fair enough. It was not right. Cousin Brutus was not going to be avenged. And what would Brutus say about that when they met in Elysium? Nothing polite or grateful, that was as certain as winter fog. He could either sit up here in this eyrie, like the emperor in his box at the 'Games' watching as it all happened. The best seat in the Colosseum. Or he could go down there and fix the odds for Brutus. Those bastards at the fort had stoned Junius to death and taken their time over it, until his old comrade was nothing more than bloody meat and rags. He could not save Junius. But he would be damned if he was to be cheated out of revenge for Brutus. The bloody fools should not have tried to force a way through to the hill fort. Retreat would have been the obvious decision. With the head start they had between them and the Brigantes, Pinneius could have got them back to Cantiventi. He must have seen he was heavily outnumbered and still he took it to them.

He tried to douse the tiny morsel of respect in his chest. Pinneius must have looked up the valley at the reception laid out before him and known he had two choices, to press on or to retreat. The Iter X was a Roman road and a key part of the pacification of the north. And a legion centurion would never have entertained the notion that a tribe could dictate who or what could travel on it. Every step up that road would have had his men thinking and fighting to hold their nerve. No First cohort legionary was more immune from fear than the lowest recruit in the training cohort.

"So be it Pinneius, you bastard, this is what you get," he jeered.

There were weapons aplenty down there for picking when this was over. The Brigantes would take the heads and the best of the weapons but if he got in amongst them now, he had a good chance of picking up spoils and getting back into favour. They would not know that he and Junius had deserted Drapisces to his fate. Something must have changed at the fort. The Carvetii were pouring over the lip of the pass as he spied the final acts playing out on the road below. They flooded down the road towards the bloodbath. It was now or never. He cursed his own stupidity and stashed the army cloak given to him by one of Liscus' men behind a rock. He made the sign against evil and slithered down the hillside directly above the spot where the remnants of the Roman testudo were making a last, desperate, stand.

*'I hope you fuckin' appreciate what I do for family honour, Brutus,'* he brooded.

The Carvetii pulsed against the slender Roman shield wall, making it bend and buckle. But somehow it held. They traded blow for blow but the body encompassing scutum shields with their proud red running Boar emblem gave more protection than the narrow, native ones. He saw droplets of blood flying the air as the last legionaries fought it out. They were down to seven now. The signifer had gone down but the standard was still there, standing defiant in its stone clasp. He was lying with his hand stretched toward it, jerking from a fatal thrust. The Carvetii pulled back gathering themselves for the last dash. The feather helmet of the centurion was at the centre of it all. Any moment now and it would all be over. He was going to have to hurry. The Carvetii surged and the sheer weight of numbers foamed over the top of the Romans. He scrambled down the last few feet, grabbed a sword off the ground and took the head off a dead legionary for protection. The centurion took a fierce spear jab to his shoulder from a huge warrior and went down. He had to hurry before the warrior ruined everything. Beside him the final two of his men fell and their last ditch, distracting defiance bought their commander a reprieve. The huge warrior hesitated, distracted by them. He barrelled through two exulting Carvetii, pushed the warrior aside and straddled the centurion. The furious warrior roared in his ear, but he refused to turn his head. The centurion's eyes were open. He was alive. The spear had sneaked through an opening in his guard and taken him on the shoulder. The force of it had knocked him off his feet. The shining mail coat bore an ugly dent and twisted links. A smear of blood was seeping out. But he was very much alive.

"Lie still," he barked.

Velio recognised him.

"Should have killed me before, Scribono," he snarled, "you can do it now, you've got a second chance, you coward. Better you than these dogs."

"Shut up," he snapped.

He swooped the blade of his sword down and raised the dead Roman head at once, praying the inept deception might work. He reached and wrenched Velio's helmet until the chin strap tore apart. Velio thought Scribono had changed his mind and was trying to break his neck. Scribono held up the head and the helmet and flicked the hem of Velio's cloak over him with the tip of his sword, betting no one would notice the illogic of the dead centurion's head being separated from his helmet. The huge warrior looked puzzled for a long moment and began looting another body. Scribono ignored him.

"Lie quiet, you fool," he hissed at Velio, displaying the head and helmet in his fist.

"I claim the centurion's head in revenge for Drapisces," he crowed, "I claim sanctuary in your halls tonight as a friend of the Carvetii people."

A trumpet blared. He did not have to think.

"Roman cavalry. Take the spirit pole," he shouted.

No one questioned his command. The standard was ripped out of its rock. The sound of horse hooves came rattling down the pass. The noise echoed. He knew it was impossible to estimate from the sounds how big a rescue force was coming. The Carvetii snatched last prizes and began breaking away, following the Brigantes, leaving a toll of dead warriors far in excess of the dead Roman forces. It was time to run. He flicked the cloak back off Velio's ashen face. He had his hand clamped against his pierced shoulder, the opposite side from the arrow wound if Scribono was not mistaken.

"Stay alive centurion. You, me, and Brutus Carruso have unfinished business," he vowed.

He dropped the dead legionary's head next to him. Velio looked up, stunned. Scribono could see the cavalry despatching a turma to pursue the stolen standard. The rest came thundering on. He swapped the native sword for a better legion one and started clawing his way back up the slope to where he had left the cloak. He was out of reach within moments and dumped the bright, attention drawing, helmet behind a rock. The shouts of the cavalry as they found the massacred ruins of Velio's command reached up to him. No one down there was paying any attention to his side of the hill. The mass of Carvetii and Brigantes were taking centre stage, taunting the Roman force to come off the road and fight them. He stopped to get his breath back, wondering if he had been a fool to dump the helmet. It would open doors on both sides of the divide. Too late, it was done. He would never have a better opportunity to kill Velio Pinneius but somehow finishing off the wounded man lying on his back would have been a cheat to Brutus' memory. When centurion Pinneius died it would be his doing entirely. Quite how it was to be engineered now was admittedly a bit of a poser. And Junius was no longer around to help. On the upside, Swords Pinneius had been twice wounded and lucky to escape death. Their confrontation, when it came, would be an easy affair. A late-night stabbing in the tent lines: that was do-able. He could act the part in Cantiventi or wherever. All the kit he needed was right there on the road for the taking.

*'Not so invincible now Centurion Pinneius, are you?'* he sneered.

## Chapter Forty-one.

### The Hill fort. Two weeks later.

"First cohort commander Morenus is on his way with his cohort. Be warned. He is less than two miles from here," the courier announced.

He was one of Servius Albinius' 'exploratores,' a regular legion scout, part of the cavalry ala of the Twentieth; elite and proud. He wore his armour with pride and displayed his courage and loyalty awards without any attempt at modesty or to mask their intimidating and patronising message. His helmet was plain and featherless to make him marginally less visible whilst on patrol but everything else about him seemed to glint. Civius bit back the temptation to put the aloof courier in his place. Besides, the Morinorum commander had relayed the news of Morenus' march the previous day. And he had told Uiliocenon. So now everyone was safe in their billet. The First cohort was here to take charge and was only two miles away and was most likely to take great delight in his discomfiture, no doubt.

He snorted at the courier without replying and dismissed him. He was certain he was going to be relieved of his small command. The incarceration of Drapisces in one of the mines had failed to spark the anticipated attack to release him. The fact such a simplistic tactic had failed, gave him no joy. Centurion Pinneius' plan had been reasonable, but it had not worked. The tribes had thwarted him. The road was still in a state of flux; the safety of the convoys unpredictable. The Uiliocenon cavalry were working hard but they had a limited number of horses. A full half century of Velio's men were dead, their standard missing, weapons pillaged and the man himself was only now beginning to recover in the infirmary from his shoulder wound. The reports of the Uiliocenon cavalry had been unequivocal. They had reached the skirmish in the fraction of time necessary to prevent the centurion following the last of his men into the afterlife. He was the sole survivor. The cavalry, being a superstitious lot, naturally put it down to the intervention of the gods and not their own precipitate arrival.

*'You lost all your men, my dear chap. Led them into a trap from which only you have been fortunate enough to survive. Not a good legacy at all. They won't speak well of you in Deva,'* Civius jeered.

He could not help a chuckle of amusement for the reversal of fortunes. Such a delicious irony that the officer sent here to make his life a misery was languishing with his reputation in tatters and a damaged shoulder; his second wound. One might almost think he had been deserted by his gods. One could only hope. He smirked, wiped his mouth and drank a little watered-down wine, taking the silver cup over to the main door of the principia to gaze out on his domain.

The loss of the signum-standard gave him no pleasure. He felt nothing for the dead legionaries, but the signum grieved him. There were things higher than personal ambition. Retrieval of it might help his chances of retaining command. It was a pity that little weasel Arco could not buy the information, but Drapisces and his enclave had been slaughtered or imprisoned. There was no one left Arco could possibly bribe to find its location. The optio Liscus remained at Cantiventi with the other half of Pinneius' century, sticking to the plan to support the three 'bait' mines, which was just as well. The fort was going to be crowded once Morenus and his men arrived. And it was not impossible Liscus would be pulled up here to provide some first-hand local knowledge.

The value of his own personal coin was diminished. Morenus would hardly care what he thought, probably not even deign to ask. He would march in and take command, as was his indisputable right. He swirled the last of the wine around in the cup and suddenly tired of the taste, threw it onto the gravel path. The wet stain spread and glistened. If he could get hold of Velio Pinneius' lost standard, he might yet retrieve his position.

*

Morenus found Velio as he expected, alone and moody, brooding and filled with self-recrimination.

"How is the shoulder?" he asked.

They shook arms. He was relieved Velio had any strength left in that arm after what he had been told.

"Buggered," Velio replied, "I'll never carry a shield again. That spear did not go deep but it's done a bit of damage. And the squamata needs a skilled hand to repair it, but the brother who lent it to me says it did its job. Still, it's a nice piece of armour ruined. I think I should offer to buy it from him instead and get it repaired properly. What do you think?" he asked.

Morenus shrugged. He was not here to discuss damaged armour. Velio sensed Morenus' mood.

"Come, let's get out of here and find peace to speak," he said.

Out on the north facing rampart he took stock of the view over the deep gorge where Junius Cita had been captured and Scribono had escaped. Morenus sniffed the sharp air and decided to skip all the obvious questions and get straight to it.

"I bring greetings to you from our legate Servius Albinius. He is happy to learn you are alive, but he orders me to tell you, your time in the legion is over. I am to stay here, and you are to return to Deva, and sign your papers. I'm sorry Velio, it's over. I'm sorry it has to end this way," Morenus confided.

"You are to stay and sort out my mess. Wipe my arse. Is that it?" Velio growled.

Morenus faced him. Velio had joined the cohort when Hanno Glaccus held temporary command. Since Hanno's retiral, he and Velio had struck up an easy and respectful friendship. They both had the emperor's scars: inside and out. He poked his finger at the stark wilderness in front of them.

"Velio you've just told me you can no longer bear a shield. You are due to muster out. Go and make wine with Gallus and that chancer Hanno Glaccus, like you have talked about. You deserve it. You have put in the years my friend," he said, "take the pension and the gratitude of the emperor and go. You've shed enough blood for The Boar and saved your fair share of it too. There's no disgrace Velio. But Servius is ordering you to return to Deva," he finished.

Morenus curled his finger back into his fist. Velio dragged his fingernails over the rough stone of the parapet. Hanno Glaccus had gained temporary command of the First cohort as a favour from Servius Albinius for all his service up on the turf wall of Antoninus Pius. Now that he and Gallus had 'taken the pension" Morenus was restored to his command, bearing little animosity so far as Velio could deduce. He was a good officer. Was he better than Hanno? Well, he was different in nature and younger, less beaten down by the province. A sunnier person? May be that was the description that suited him best? Hanno had a political mind, a schemer's soul, a hardness at times that kept you at bay. Fighting alongside Morenus would have been a pleasure. And now, as his commander, he was telling him it was finished.

"I lost them all, Morenus. Every man I took into the pass. All of them," he confessed.

He pounded his hand on the parapet. It did not hurt in the slightest. Morenus held his tongue and waited. Velio dragged his nails over the stone, in self-punishment, taking the skin and drawing blood. Morenus laid his hand on his arm.

"Velio, there is a reason. Though I'll be honest, I can't fathom what it is. You are no coward. No one has ever had cause to accuse you of that. Jupiter has spared you. Though a gift to the decurion of cavalry at Uiliocenon might not go amiss. But for them, your worries would be over," Morenus retorted.

"I wish he had not," he replied.

Morenus' face hardened, "who, Jupiter? Then take your pugio Velio and finish it, but don't give me sacrilege or self-pity. Not you. We are soldiers of our emperor. If it's any consolation, with the whole century at your back you would have made it through, I'm certain. I've inspected the spot where you were trapped. It was down to lack of numbers Velio. That's all it was. Your instincts were right. You had to support this garrison. From what I can see they need all the support they can get. Now, we will eat together tonight, and you will address the cohort. They need to hear first-hand from you what they are up against," Morenus demanded.

"As you command me sir," Velio replied.

He paused and inspected his blood smeared, raw skinned, fingers.

"And tomorrow I leave for Deva, marked a failure," he said.

"Nonsense. Velio I'll hear no more of this. You will be remembered as the man who found the Ninth legion and helped lay their spirits to rest. You did more for the emperor than thousands who have fought and died. There are young soldiers in The Boar who are afraid to even speak to you, because you are so famous. There are others too timid to ask for a sword lesson even though it's been years since you were an instructor. Velio, this last setback is unfortunate. But it does not change who you are. Ask Liscus, ask Plautius if you don't believe me, I've no doubt he'll give you a straight answer," Morenus snapped.

Velio felt embarrassed and foolish.

"I only found some of the Ninth," he said.

Morenus eased back, "well, it's more than the rest of the army of Britannia managed to do, so buck yourself up," he cajoled.

A wry, deprecating grin flitted across his lips for a moment and then he sobered.

"I've never heard you talk about it."

Velio pushed his palms down on the parapet. His right shoulder was nipping. The story had followed him like a bad smell. Sometimes he regretted ever stepping foot in that high valley. He should have taken a quick look and scarpered out of there and kept his mouth shut. Perhaps Marcus Hirtius would still be alive today if he had followed that instinct?

"Because it was a terrible place, Morenus and I wish I had never found it," he whispered, and made the sign.

Morenus had no answer. He gave Velio a sombre nod. No point on dwelling on the past.

"Morenus, I need to find my standard," Velio pleaded for more time.

"Too late Velio, it's my problem now. Servius was explicit. You are to return to Deva Victrix with or without your secretary Marcellus, it's up to you whether you leave him here, and your tame Votadini servant. Liscus will remain with the rest of your century. Servius wants a full written report for the legion records before he lets you retire. Don't worry about your standard. I'll get it back. These heathen bastards are not keeping a First cohort standard. Not if I have anything to say on the matter. This is not the Ninth legion, you know. If it's damaged, I'll will slaughter the whole damn tribe. If it makes you feel better, leave an address with Servius' clerk and I will send word when we have it back, eh?" Morenus promised.

"Orann is still alive?" Velio said.

Guilty relief that he had not got him killed with the other men was like a rope to cling to.

"That he is. He brought word to Deva of your predicament. It's why we are here," Morenus affirmed, "frankly, from what he reported I thought you were dead, so did Servius. That's why he sent the whole cohort up here. He wanted retribution. He had the other cohorts begging to be sent too," Morenus vouched, "as a matter of fact he also wanted to know why Civius had not supported you. But that is a matter for another day, I fear," he added.

"Voccia's going to get a nice surprise then, isn't she?" Velio mused

Morenus nodded.

"I am keeping the First cohort here until all this these attacks on the mines and the waggon convoys are mopped up. One century could never have managed it Velio. Don't feel too bad. Marcellus briefed me on your use of the man Drapisces as bait. It's a good plan, it may yet work," he allowed, matter of fact.

"Who will command my century"Velio asked, "Liscus? Can I make a recommendation or have you already decided?"

"I'm not sure Liscus is ready, but he is your optio and your recommendation will not be overturned without serious good reason. So, it will look like a reprimand if you want him, and I do not promote him. Once we are back in Deva your century will be brought back to strength from the best volunteers in the legion. I have a list in my office. I'm always being asked about it. There is no shortage of young men wanting a billet in the First cohort, the privilege of carrying The Boar shield. And your old company will be a popular one," Morenus said.

Velio thought it sounded like a eulogy.

'*Without me in it,*' he thought.

The firsts pangs of grief struck home.

"I'm not dead yet," he muttered to Morenus.

"It's how it has to be my friend. The legion never stands still. You know this. Men move on, one way or the other, and new men take their places. The Boar is the important thing, the legion must go on, with us or without us. Besides the word is you and that reprobate Gallus Tiomaris plan to poison us with your new wine. I'm looking forward to tasting it. You should do the decent thing and mark it 'caveat emptor -buyer beware,' eh Velio?"

"Very funny, Morenus," he growled.

But the joke made him feel better.

It went better than he expected. The First cohort assembled in the open spaces of the fort, filling it out and pushing the Delmatarum to the edges to hear him speak as best they could. Civius stood at his raised stone plinth in front of them, saying nothing but judging everything. Leaving tomorrow with Civius left unpunished left a sour taste but Morenus had been adamant, his time had run out. Titus Vindex was looking fervent and struck by the atmosphere. The First cohort brought a strange stillness to the evening light. The sun was dying in beauty over the western horizon. The day's last warmth beginning to seep down into the grass. He suspected by the rapture that Titus had not seen a First cohort being briefed before up close. The mystique of the elite. It seldom failed to impress those excluded from membership. Burnished armour, spotless shields with that impressive emblem; feather crested helmets adjusting to the westing air. He stepped forward, greeted them and told them all he knew of the situation. He stepped back when he was finished. That was it. Pretty much his last operational act. Morenus took his place beside him.

"Some of you know Centurion Pinneius leaves tomorrow for Deva Victrix. There he will drink the well-deserved pension cup and leave The Boar forever. But we cannot let a good man go out into that dangerous world without protection," Morenus brogued.

He heard ripples of laughter. Morenus had a nice way with his humour.

"Centurion Pinneius, I ask you to accept this gift from the First cohort. We hope it meets your standards and that you never have cause to use it," Morenus announced.

A square faced legionary standing right in front of him grinned and brought a scabbarded sword out from behind his back and passed it to Morenus. Morenus offered it in both hands up to the sky and the cohort to see, then handed it to him before shaking his arm. Velio took the gladius from Morenus and pulled the sword from its sheath. A shining weapon of sweet balance and workmanship sparkled in his hand and charmed his eyes. He wafted it a couple of times and felt a hard knot tightening up in his throat. He thrust it back into the scabbard. They had wrong footed him, everybody seemed to be wrong footing him these days. It was time to go. He drew himself up and crashed out a soldier's salute that rattled off his armour. The entire cohort saluted him back in a single unified movement. Titus felt himself trembling.

Velio scrabbled to find further words and knew it would not work. Raising the gladius aloft, he nodded to them all and turned, striding back to the barrack block and the room he had been living in for the last two weeks.

*

The next day the medicus finished his morning rounds by checking Velio's healing shoulder and deciding it had been prodded enough and no longer needed a bandage. Velio had been obedient to his instructions. It had sealed up without red swelling infection and the arm function was reasonably unimpaired, if you were a civilian. But the very actions of bearing a shield and taking close-contact combat were well beyond the power left in that shoulder. Not a mortal wound but a career ending one. Time might make it better but then, it might not.

"I hope I don't see you again, centurion" he remarked.

Toying with a quip about sword lessons he decided to offer his arm instead. Velio's grip was reasonable. He left it at that and packed away his probes and implements.

A few hours later Velio heard the hinges of the Porta Praetoria gates began their daily protest as he left the barrack block. Farewell Brother, began blowing as he mounted up. A rendition of spine tingling intensity, like no other he could remember ever hearing in all his years. The bastards seemed determined to unman him. He could have cheerfully about turned his horse and slaughtered the lot of them. Orann plodded on his horse taking a position just to the right-hand side of him and kept his head down. This time he had a full century and two turmae of troopers from Uiliocenon as escort to see him down the road to Cantiventi. Morenus was taking no chances.

<u>Chapter Forty-two.</u>

<u>Cantiventi.</u>

Scribono heard the faintest sound of army trumpets in the distance. He slipped out of the Brigantes camp. Assuming the air of a man stretching his legs, he wandered away, back in the general direction of the road. Anyone watching might think he was going to gloat at the site of yesterday's victory. He ducked down under a shelf of rock and pulled out his bulky sack of looted legion equipment and followed the call. It was harder to carry than to wear. The shield was bulky but wholly necessary for his deception. He needed to get closer to Cantiventi before daring to don the uniform. Out here he could not dress like a solitary legionary and expect to live. It was nightfall by the time he reached the environs of Cantiventi.

He reckoned the Boar encampment would most likely be sitting very close to the walls of the fort. He hid in a stand of trees by the water's edge and shed his mix of old tunic and barbarian clothes. He dug into the sack and pulled out the armour and tunic of a dead First cohort legionary. Tying off the lorica behind his back was a frustrating business but he persevered until it was done, and the armour felt snug. The single problem dogging him was the watchword for the gateway. Today's word, set by yesterday's duty tesserarius, would have to be a complete guess. There were a few familiar favourites that the officers tended to rotate. It saved the lazy bastards the mental effort of devising new ones.

'*Just have to try one and bluff it from there?'* he reasoned.

He moved closer and saw the high flicker of torches on the Cantiventi gateways. Over to its left-hand side were the smaller lights of the Boar camp. He stood and took stock of the layout for a while, steeling himself for what was going to be the boldest move of his life or the shortest walk to death. He hefted the shield and circled around to the lake and the quayside, using the gloom as cover. The Decumana opening might be fractionally easier to slip through than either of the others as it faced the lakeside; the safest aspect of the camp. Over the low, thigh high, earth rampart he could make out the dim shapes of men and scattered low fires burning; the scent of baking bread. The memory of legion loaf brought saliva to his mouth. They were still eating and settling down for the night. The cavalry troopers were busy currycombing their animals. There were far more men than he expected and a low hum of noise like a purposeful beehive. Where normally they would have already settled into the tents by this hour, there was enough activity still going on to provide a distraction, make him inconspicuous, just another soldier.

"Password?" the guard demanded.

He made a play out of it.

"Is it emperors or famous generals today, buggered if I can remember," he feigned.

"You tell me," the guard scowled.

"Agricola," he stabbed.

"No, it fuckin' ain't. He was yesterday," the guard retorted.

"I can't keep up," he babbled, "funny though, so Agricola is yesterday's man."

"Ha bloody ha, get through, and it's Tiberius, in case you're interested mate," the guard snapped.

"Thank you, Tiberius," he mocked.

He gave a half salute and stepped across the invisible boundary separating the Cantiventi vicus from the bounds of Rome. It was clear the camp had been very recently expanded into a larger defence. Enough for two normal cohorts. Except the First cohort was a double strength unit. Hence the space needed. Housing sixty cavalry in addition certainly helped fill things up. The smell of food was a torment but getting close enough to get some would reveal his face to the men at whatever campfire he picked. The armour and shield would only let him pass without challenge around the camp. It would not buy food. He tightened his belt and spat. There would be time for eating once Pinneius was dead. Whole haunches of deer, an entire goose even. Buckets of local ale or flagons of wine. Once it was done.

The torches outside the principia tent gave him a bearing. It was time to hide for a while by a fire. He found a space by the dextra side and struck a flint on a burned out set of sticks that looked promising. The sparks took on the handful of dry grass he fed them. He knelt down and hid the shield as best he could in the grass and took the helmet off for good measure. The leather chin strap was chafing like it used to do. There were things he did not miss. Hunching over the tiny fire he turned his back and tried to be invisible. He nodded off.

"Fallen out with our mates, have we chum?" an amicable sort of voice asked.

He started and rubbed the haze of sleep away as fast as he could.

"Something like that," he answered, "I'm in a contubernium led by a right sod of a decanus."

He could have bitten his tongue off in full flow, swallowed his own blood and been grateful for the punishment. The night guard would have to be a dullard not to ask the obvious next question.

"Calenus, you know him?" he went for it.

"A decanus, called Calenus, there's plenty of sods and worse in this army so, you got me there, brother. I can get any two out of the those three. Sleep well," the guard replied.

He lifted a hand to cut short the wordplay, gesturing a wave and turned on his side to make good his lie. The camp was quiet. A little bit longer and he could go hunting through the officers' tent lines. 'Tiberius' was going to get him safely out of this. It grew quieter as the sentries settled into their watches. High clouds moved across the stars and the moon came and went in intermittent flashes of white. He got up and looked around. He appeared to be the sole nocturnal vagrant. The goat skin tents had swallowed up the garrison; the late-night fires were either out or burning down to embers. The torches burning at the principia picked out the shapes of the two men on duty, playing across their armour in warm yellow swathes of light. The night was still, no air moved. The lake lying out in the greater gloom was silent and noiseless. He stole a pilum from a stand outside the nearest tent. The javelin would mark him out as a duty sentry to the casual eye. The stone walls of the permanent garrison had gleaming pools of light from high set torches and the passing shadows of other guards, more secure behind their sturdy walls. There was a flitting, flicker of movement in the night.

*'Bats,'* he reasoned.

He ducked his head at one that came swooping close to him, glad of his helmet: horrid, vile things. The officers' tents would lie in a broad line at the head of each century, matching the arrangement used in permanent barracks. The tent size would be the same, but its position would signal the rank of its occupant. The century of Pinneius had been severely diminished thanks to the Brigantes and Carvetii attack. It was easy to distinguish the lesser row of tents as the one belonging to his shattered command.

'Time to go hunting for Brutus,' he told himself.

Now that the moment had finally arrived it was odd to think Brutus had died more than fifteen years ago. It had taken fifteen years, all that time, for him to engineer the opportunity to avenge his cousin. Ironic really that two cohorts of the same legion, the Fourth and the Eighth, had in all those years not been posted sufficiently close enough, and for long enough, for him to have acted before now. Forced to watch Velio Pinneius' start his cocky rise from tesserarius, one of Gallus Tiomarus' select little band of instructor-know-it-alls. The soldier with a fast, sinistra, sword hand. Just that alone made him awkward to bout against, if everything they said about him was true. Waiting for the right moment had not been so hard, in the circumstances. Delaying only meant a sweeter outcome. But sometimes deserting is better than enduring.

He had slipped out of a camp not too different to this one on a similar dark night and taken his chances, consigning family revenge to the list of things he would never fulfil. Over the weeks he avoided patrols and worked his way north on foot from Deva Victrix, buying food until his money ran out, then stealing as he went. The Carvetii guessed what he was; and what they thought of him remained unspoken. Had they reviled him as a coward from his own kind, or rejoiced at the evidence the invaders were losing soldiers? Who could tell what these taciturn people thought? But he suspected they were indifferent as long as he could pay for the vittles in kind. He tarried in small halls of farmers, working and sweating, moving on when he sensed his welcome was on the wane

Meeting Junius Cita had been fortuitous. His legion was the mighty Sixth, the Eburacum garrison. Junius had not run because he had taken a flogging, he had run simply because he had had enough of his lot in the army, stuck in this cold province far from home. He brought Scribono to a strange welcome at an isolated hilltop stronghold of a Carvetii warlord: Drapisces. Drapisces valued fighting men and so long as he was prepared to pledge his sword, they had a refuge until something better came along. Quite how Junius had made that connection he never explained. There were things Junius chose to keep to himself, like how long he had been in these hills, and how and when he began to develop an occasional trade with an auxiliary soldier posted to a minor outpost. Junius never really squared the facts off properly. He got a bit uppity whenever pushed for details of how he knew Arco. A sure sign he was not used to being questioned by ordinary soldiers. So, who was he? Perhaps, it was not Arco that he had actually known? Now there was a thought. It made more sense now that it dawned on him. Junius must have been dealing with one of the regular legion soldiers detached to the Delmatarum. Someone he had known or met during his time in the Sixth. Arco was just the 'bag-man.'

The trade had grown exponentially from the odd weapon in exchange for a well-made silver brooch, to loot from the waggon convoys, paid for in various ways. Now Drapisces was captured and Junius, the only real pal he had left, the one who always seemed to know what to do, was dead, their partnership destroyed, leaving him adrift once more with his life in ruins.

He pulled himself back to the task in hand. Once this centurion was dead, he would strike south for the ports and hideaway amongst the scores of retired veterans living in Gaul. He would be just one more Roman face speaking soldier's Latin.

This piece of revenge tonight was not going to bring Brutus back, the poor, dumb bear, but it was justice for him.

Snores were coming from the nearest tents. He waited and listened for voices, late-night murmurings of men still awake. There were only snores. He stalked along the shorter of the two lines of tents arriving outside the final goatskin shelter. He hid at the rear most side. Nerves fluttered in his stomach. He put down the pilum and shield on the grass and drew his gladius. It scraped.

*'Too loud, too loud, you're going to wake the whole fucking camp,'* he berated himself.

Slipping his pugio from its sheath he stepped around the tent to the front and slit the leather ties that closed the flaps. One more step and he would be inside, one quick stab and Velio Pinneius would be dead in his sleep. His heart stopped. There was someone standing behind him.

*

Orann felt his inside roiling with the full weight of food he had stuffed down his throat. Whatever side he lay on was equally uncomfortable. His master was fast asleep on his camp bed. The surrounding tents were silent. He tried lying on his back and did not like the sensation. On his front was too painful. He was sweating. He threw off his cloak and tried to breathe the discomfort away. It made no difference. There was only one thing left to do. He threw the cloak off, got to his feet, slipped open two of the thongs securing the tent flaps and walked away. After a few steps he knelt down on the grass and vomited it all out, like a dog. He wiped the spittle dribbling from his lips and spat out the sour, familiar taste until it was only the smell up his nose that offended him. There was water in the tent, but he did not want to disturb the Master. He lay in the damp grass and let cooling night air wash over him. His hot forehead turned to icy sweat. He rolled up onto his knees and wiped his face and hair. By the outline of the tent a shape moved, stooped and stood upright once more. He blinked his eyes and stared, wondering if it was just his tiredness tricking him. The shape halted at the door of the Master's tent. The rising hairs on his arms and neck brought the old wariness of danger. He kept low and circled around the nearest of the tents, Liscus and Marcellus'.

His bare feet touched a cold metal in the grass. He slid his hand over it exploring the shape of the pilum. Curling his fingers around the haft he lifted it up from its lair in the damp grass. It was much heavier than his own hunting spear. It had more weight to stop a man in his tracks. He padded past the rear of Liscus' tent and approached the man loitering at the Master's tent. The glint of a dagger flitted at the tent flaps. In the other hand was a gladius. It was a legionary. The tent flap parted as the leather ties severed. The point of the sword rose from the ground into a low striking position. He stepped in close and saw a gap below the soldier's lorica and the back strap of his waist belt. He gripped the pilum in both hands and buried it into the assassin's back, pushing until he sensed it bursting out of the front. The man sank with a loud exclamation of exhaling breath, surprise, shock and horror. He hauled on the spear and the man tumbled backwards. The hand with the sword flailed, the pugio already lost to the ground.

Orann stood on the sword arm, trapping it and let go of the pilum. Blood was pumping out of the soldier's mouth. Suddenly the Master was there with his new sword in hand.

Scribono blinked up at Velio. Velio laid the point of his gladius on Scribono's throat. In the distance the night watch was running to sound of the noise. Marcellus was up too, his own sword at the ready. Then Liscus' and the nearest tents emptied. Scribono was on his side like a fish, the pilum sticking out of his back and the evil, square headed, point poking through his belly armour. Orann picked up the assassin's sword and stood back clutching it. Velio stared at him then down at Scribono.

"My gratitude Orann, it seems you are determined to keep me alive," he said.

Scribono wheezed blood from his mouth, clutching the brutal point of the spear.

"You should have killed me back at the pass when you had the chance Scribono. You and Brutus are the same. I see it now. Cowards who attack men when they are unprepared. For the record Scribono, it was not me who killed your cousin, it was my good friend Gallus Tiomaris. We were sent to slap down some Votadini up on some shitty hill south of the turf wall, we were right in the middle of it, and your cousin tried to kill me. Mithras, curse me if I lie. Gallus put a pugio to his neck, one quick push, and that was that. And now a Votadini stable lad has been too smart for a useless deserter like you. Farewell Scribono, you can lie there and bleed all night for all I care, I'm going back to my bed, and if you are still alive in the morning, I'll drag you down to the lake on that spear and drown you like a worthless rat," he promised.

"Oh, he won't be alive in the morning centurion, you won't have to trouble yourself on that," Liscus replied to him.

He nodded. Scribono lay aghast, his eyes flickered to Velio's granite face. There was only once final chance left to end the confusion.

"Why Scribono? Why you and Brutus? I did no offence to either of you," he said.

Scribono's jaws opened and closed as if he was trying to coax the words from his throat like poison vomit.

"Ask Centurion Hanno Glaccus. I told you. We did not start this. He did," Scribono wheezed.

Under the yellow light of a torch the sheen of sweat on his face looked fatal. He would not trouble the dawn.

"You lie Scribono. What cause did Hanno Glaccus ever have to see me dead?" he snapped.

"Why don't you ask him?" Scribono managed a last defiance.

Velio's patience snapped, "take the spear Orann," he said.

Orann tugged the shaft of the pilum and ripped it out of Scribono. A flood of blood swamped the strips of lorica armour on his back, matching the agonising groan of pain from his mouth. His head lolled sideways on the grass.

"I told you he would not be alive in the morning, sir," Liscus chirped.

A chitter of amusement applauded the quip. He grimaced at the body staining the grass at his doorway. Every commanding instinct told him not to join in their humour.

“Get rid of it,” he said, “I’m going back to my bed, I suggest you all do the same.”

Inside his tent, he looked up at the dark ceiling and the ridge pole.

*‘Why don't you ask him, why don’t you ask him?’* Scribono’s taunt rattled around in his brain.

He scowled in the gloom. He was not going to get any sleep now. Could it be true? Could Hanno have ordered his death? They had served together building the wall for Antoninus Pius and evacuating it. And in between times too. There was no slight between them. He was certain of it. They were partners in Gallus’ wine enterprise. But Julius Caesar had once been part of a triumvirate pledged to take Rome to a better destiny and those far greater men ended up destroying each other. Outside the last voices ceased murmuring. The tent lines quietened down. The tent flap opened, and Orann lay down on the floor under his cloak, more guard dog than warrior.

“Thank you Orann. I shall not forget this,” he said.

## Chapter Forty-three.

## The vineyard, Argentomagus.

Nahan laid Gallus back down on his bed, calling for Hanno to come. The arrow sticking out of Gallus was dangerously close to the groin. Gallus moaned at the movement and opened his eyes in a flutter of pain. Hanno was there in seconds pushing past him. Nahan stepped back and went to fetch water and bandages.

"Balls of Dis, Gallus, this is a bad one," Hanno muttered examining the wound.

Gallus hissed air in gasps.

"Did they hurt the dog?" he gasped.

"No, sir," Bodusio answered, "I have him here."

Gallus relaxed a fraction.

"Why Gallus, what is going on?"

Hanno stared in his eyes, reeling with anger and confusion.

"This is not the north wall of Britannia, what is going on?" he repeated.

Nahan returned with a bowl of steaming hot water and bandages.

"Bring more light," Hanno ordered, "see if any of the kitchen women have knowledge of wounds."

He turned to the room which was now crowded with the small number of slaves who slept in the villa.

"I doubt they have dealt with arrow wounds, sir," Bodusio argued, "we can help him. We have done this before," he said.

"Clear the room. You two can stay," Hanno ordered.

He stabbed his forefinger at Nahan and Bodusio.

"Eudo was always good with wounds sir," Nahan replied.

"Eudo, you stay here too," Hanno barked.

"Let them stay," Gallus said, misunderstanding, "I need good hands and Aesculapius covering my back."

Eudo knelt at his side and washed the worst of the blood away. The arrow was a new one, the wood still clean and unmarked.

"What are you waiting for, get it out," Hanno bullied.

"It's in deep, sir, so it's either from a short range or a powerful bow," Eudo rebuffed him.

He risked a barb of his own.

"The shape of the arrowhead will tell us how much damage it has done."

"Hanno, shut up and let him try," Gallus hissed through his gritted teeth.

Hanno bit his tongue and marked Eudo for a reckoning if this went badly for Gallus. Eudo placed his fingertips on the arrow shaft. Gallus stared at the plain timbers of the ceiling and fought to choke back a moan as Eudo's gentle touch sent fire through his loins. The wound was inches from the hip bone where a firm pull would be agonising but relatively safe. The closer to the groin, the softer the flesh and the greater likelihood of massive blood loss after extraction. The room was pregnant with the sound of Eudo thinking how best to do this operation. Nahan held a torcher closer at Eudo's slight gesture.

"Tell me about Britannia, sir, I never served there," Eudo coaxed, probing the wound, trying to sense what kind of arrow barb he was having to remove.

Gallus writhed under the examination and opened his eyes, panting in pain.

“It’s alright lad, I’ve made my promise to Aesculapius. At least it’s not a spear in the spine like old Pomponius got, remember that one, eh Hanno?” he croaked.

“I remember, my friend, and Eudo will have you up dancing before the cook starts preparing your jentaculum,” Hanno whispered a half prayer.

“Do it lad, I’m ready,” Gallus said.

Eudo smiled, “ah, I know what this is, sir, it’s a slim headed hunting arrow, probably feels much worse than it is,” he lied.

Gallus felt relieved and tried to relax as he breathed out at the good news. Slim headed or otherwise the news was not lessening the pain. Eudo twisted before he tightened again. He screamed as he felt ripped apart, filling the room with pain, Nahan held him by the shoulders. Eudo held the arrow out with his hand for someone to relieve him of it and pressed bandages into the wound with his other fist. Hanno took the bloody, broad headed military arrow and felt sick.

“That the worst of it sir,” Eudo soothed, “and you're still a whole man.”

Gallus tried to smile.

“Good, I must get this bleeding to stop. This will need mosses to prevent infection. I will l go to the forum tomorrow, with your permission sir. Meanwhile I will wash it in posca,” Eudo said to Hanno.

Gallus was lost behind his eyelids. Hanno stared at the arrow. Eudo had talked Gallus into relaxing as much as he could, easing the operation.

“Easy now sir, easy,” Ludo coaxed, reaching for more bandage.

“That’s the worst of it,” Nahan added.

Bodusio watched on, keeping his counsel. He exchanged a worried look with Hanno.

"If he makes it to sunrise, the three of you will eat with me," Hanno replied, "and if he does not, you did your best and I am grateful."

*

Eudo returned from the forum with the necessary medicines before the day had begun to warm up. Hanno sent a messenger to the Eighth garrison to ask whether their medicus was willing to attend. It was a long shot favour, but he trusted their reputation would swing the decision. The doctor arrived with the friendly decurion and the usual escort, inspected how Eudo was treating the wound, pronounced it correct, and left. Hanno saw him leave and wished he was still in the legion with the power to command. The man could not have delivered a more perfunctory examination if he had tried. So much for the local ties with pensioned soldiers. The decurion had the grace to look embarrassed. Eudo spoke something in German at departing man's back.

"What did you say?" Hanno asked.

Eudo wiped his hands. There was still a remnant on dried blood under his fingernails: Hanno reminded himself it was Gallus' blood.

"It was because of men like that we were condemned. We had not mutinied, we did not want to mutiny, disobeyed no orders, plotted no deaths, stood our watches, took no bribes at the gates. We only wanted better food and to be paid on time. Like any soldier does. And for complaining too loudly they picked some of us out, branded us traitors to the legion, said it was 'se, se, - some word I cannot remember, and that we were lucky not to be executed," Eudo said.

"Sedition," Hanno said.

A pang of sympathy rose in him for the auxiliary. But moaning soldiers was hardly a cause for such heavy-handed discipline. There had to be more to it than that, besides, he reckoned if soldiers were not moaning about their pay and conditions then something was seriously wrong. They were ringleaders of something more serious? Maybe sedition was on the horizon and the centurions acted to nip the bud? Mutiny on the Germania frontier was a threat to Rome herself.

"Men like that one, who thought we are no better than the tribes we are prepared to fight," Eudo spat the words out like bile.

*'Men like me, you mean,'* Hanno guessed.

Eudo might have heard the thought because he shook his head in denial.

"We served Rome, we accepted Rome. We had turned our backs on the old ways," he complained.

"Well, thanks to you and Nahan, my old friend still lives, and the bleeding has stopped for now. He has seen the sunrise and I promised you three could eat with me. Meet me in the atrium I want to speak to all of you," Hanno answered.

Nahan insisted on checking on Gallus first and feeding him a large bowl of porridge enriched with copious amounts of honey. He turned him and helped him void his bowels with dignity before settling him back down. Gallus was white faced with the pain. Sweat broke out on his forehead. He nodded his gratitude to Nahan. The Mattiaci gave him a half salute.

"What did you do in the legion sir?" he asked.

Gallus assessed him.

"I was a cohort hastiliarius, since you ask," he replied, keeping it matter of fact.

Was there an unknown grievance the slave had in his pouch? He was defenceless. But Nahan's expression only widened. The wounded man on the bed was more important to men like him than the bravest of centurions.

"And the other master?" he asked, whisking Gallus' bucket of mess aside.

"He was the senior centurion commanding the First cohort of our legion," he answered.

Nahan's eyes widened even more as the implications of Fortuna's benevolence hit him.

"Close the door," Gallus said.

Hanno let them eat the same food that he was eating, debating in his mind how much to tell them. Imprisonment and transport from the Germania front had done nothing to diminish their strength, or their willingness to help, which surprised him. Gramalcus had not managed to stamp that out of them, Fortuna be praised. A visit to the bathhouse was required for each of them, but other than that, with clean tunics on their backs and fresh caligae they would pass for soldiers. The bathhouse stuck in his head. Out of the miasma of possible ways he could explain the situation he found himself in, the bathhouse image decided his strategy. Priscus had built no such luxury but he had a cold pool. Letting them use that was a step too far.

"Once you have eaten ask the cook to boil up sufficient kettles of hot water so you can bathe. We have spare tunics you may have. This is your reward for helping Gallus. If you decide to do more to help on the estate I will either write to your cohort commander on your behalf and ask for you to be reinstated, or I will give you freedom at the right time. If you choose not to help you can remain slaves like the others," he said.

"What more do you want, you know we are not wine makers?" asked Bodusio.

Hanno's heart pumped a bit faster. They were still soldiers at heart.

"Last night's attack was the work of men who want to drive us out and steal our wine. We are not going to be driven out. The soldiers of The Boar have never run and we are not about to run now," he replied.

Their eyes gleamed in the sunlight. Gallus had been right in his opinion of them. One mention of The Boar and they were poised like litter-mates of Trajan. He folded his arms, flexing his biceps and surveyed the three of them.

"We are going to defend this estate at all costs until our wine is ready for selling, and we are going to avenge the dead wife of a brother. It will require a bit of killing," he said.

Bodusio scraped the edge of his mouth with a finger.

"What if the hastiliarius dies, what if everything Eudo does fails to save him?" he asked.

"Gallus has to fight his own battle now. But you have given him a chance. He wants the vineyard to be protected like I do. What do you say? Will your people speak of you as slaves or soldiers?" Hanno invoked.

"Soldiers," they replied.

"Splendid. Once the cook has water on the boil you will find there is an old sack in the barn with something you will recognise. It might be past repairing, but Gallus thought it worth having. See what you can do with it. We may need it," he said.

He got to his feet. Breakfast was over. They got up. There was a tiny delay before Nahan threw him a legionary salute. Bodusio and Eudo followed suit. He surprised himself by returning it.

"I will tell my overseer you are on new duties," he said, "and don't make a habit of saluting. It's best we keep this as much of a secret as possible," he said.

"They are not ready to be given swords, Hanno," Gallus tried to keep his voice down low.

Eudo was in and out the room checking on his condition. So long as he did not try to move off the bed the wound was staying sealed. He had no intention of giving it a second chance to bleed him dry.

"I was not planning on going that far quite yet Gallus, but they are too useful to be kept down as slaves. We need to offer them hope of reprieve if we want them to fight for us," Hanno raised his palm to pacify his fears, "I've set them to rebuild the broken scorpion you pinched from Deva."

"I paid for that scorpion," Gallus snorted, "there was no pinching needed."

"Gallus, you had it pinched from the day it landed back in the weapons store for repair," Hanno mocked.

"Don't Hanno, it bloody hurts," he complained, "besides it is an old one, fit for the rubbish pit."

*'Which is why you tucked it away out of sight, isn't it Gallus,'* Hanno laughed inside.

"Can you still piss? Do you piss blood?" he said.

"I can and I don't," Gallus replied, "if there's any wine, I'd like some. It's hurting like buggery."

"Stay put Gallus, I'll get you some wine. A few days rest and you'll be out of that bed chasing the pretty ones," Hanno chirped, hoping his false confidence would settle Gallus down.

Gallus laid his head back and looked up at the timbers in the roof. Outside the open window sounds of voices and birds drifted in the warm morning air. The room was heating up as the sun struck down on the tiles. He hoped Hanno's optimism was right. What was it the man Eudo had said, 'either a short range shot or a powerful bow'? He let the cogs turn in his head: a Parthian perhaps? The Parthians made good bows. The thought of an archer firing such a weapon from short-range made him go cold. The double curve Scythian was favoured by the cavalry, the single curve by the infantry. Either way, no peaceful civilian in Gaul would own, let alone use, such a weapon. Retired soldiers or auxiliary might have such a weapon. So, who had shot at him? And it got him thinking.

Three days was as long as he could be restrained from putting his feet on the floor to test his strength.

"I need to sacrifice to Aesculapius, Hanno, and then I want to sit outside in the sun and drink some wine," he announced.

Bodusio and Nahan had him in a vice grip on either side, Eudo put a staff in his hand. Step by step they shuffled out of the room like a blind man's dance through the atrium of the villa to his usual spot on the dicing table where a jug and cup were waiting, strategically placed by Hanno. He was sweating a lather by the time they got him there, more carried than marching. Eudo insisted on checking the wound once more. It was still holding shut. Under the pad of pain reducing moss, Aesculapius had closed the skin in a dark red crust amid blue bruising that spread up past his navel. They brought a goat on a leash for him to consider. He dismissed it, shaking his head. Hanno stood behind him with his arms folded in his usual fashion. The slaves raised questioning looks toward him. He did not reply with any sort of acknowledgement. Stepping forwards he leaned over Gallus with his arms still folded.

"A bull, Gallus?" he said.

"Can't be anything less than that," Gallus replied.

He did not argue. He turned to the estate overseer.

"We need another bull, get one from the cattle mart. Get a good one."

"With respect sir, I can't just get another bull for sacrifice this morning without putting the word out among the local farmers," the overseer replied, "they get huffy when they find out their animals are for execution rather than stud. It's not the price, it's the good bloodlines wasted they don't like," he finished up.

Gallus eyed him, seeking signs of impudence. Overseers could be replaced.

"Do you want to be shaved while we wait, Master?" one of the house servants stepped in. Gallus nodded.

"Try," he said to the overseer, not ready to concede the point, "hold the goat in case we need it."

The overseer saw the baleful light in his eyes and backed down. Gallus let them fuss over him with hot water and the sharp razor while the sun beat down. The winemaker requested words with him, but he saw it was more akin to reassurance he was still in the land on this side of Elysium's walls.

"I have things to be getting on with while you loll around injured. Drink some wine and don't frighten any more of the servants," Hanno grinned.

"Go on, sod off and leave me in peace. You frighten them more than me. Nahan, you stay here, I might need protecting," he jeered back.

## Chapter Forty-four.

## Cantiventi.

Velio raised the sword Morenus had presented to him. His century sat before him, as ordered, in a semi-circle on the grass, not the normal way he briefed them. Just eighty-one of them left, included four still recovering from wounds inflicted taking Drapisces' hall. More than seventy men lost since arriving to inspect the hill fort's dubious toll practices. Seventy-six men to be precise. Marcellus was nothing if not precise in detailing the muster roll. An act that pricked his conscience each time he saw it lying in the headquarters tent. Seventy-six recovered bodies, to extend the bounds of Cantiventi's graveyard in a flowering of mounds, causing him remorse every time he caught sight of them.

Not all his lads were whole under their mounds. It did not do to dwell on heathen head hunting. Morale was no stronger than thread at times like these. And his own felt sore and tight after Scribono's attempt to kill him. He pushed Scribono's face out of his head and concentrated. Seventy seven effective legionaries: that was it, all he had to command.

His cavalry escort from Delmatarum and Morenus' accompanying legionaries were on their way back up there. Both decurion and centurion officers giving him grave salutes before leaving. What was he to read into those final cold salutes? Morenus had passed no final comment at their last meeting. What was there to say? What point in rebukes? He had attempted to punch his way through to the hill fort in support of Civius, who was safely tucked up inside his walls, and led his men to annihilation. His reputation was tarnished if not annihilated as well, in the process. Morenus had obviously chosen not to rebuke him because the First cohort did not run from a fight and were not dictated to by the intransigence of minor, local tribes. He would have done the same if their positions were reversed. Worse, he could imagine Morenus uttering that same phrase, 'minor, local tribes,' and felt his face getting hot at what was implied. He had never lost an entire command before in a single skirmish.

*'What is it Servius says to the new recruits? Don't ever come back alive without your commander, or his body?* he tortured himself.

The legate of the legion would not be complimentary. He would get roasted.

*'Ride off into retirement with the ghosts of half your century at your heels for company,'* the idea was beyond bearing.

He hauled himself out of the bleak pit in his head and looked at his men. Marcellus and Liscus were sitting along with them. The top of Plautius' head was visible behind the brute bulk of the century blacksmith. He was the only one standing: the orator. They sat stock still, like statues of soldiers. Some chewed a blade of grass between their teeth, others waiting, poised, unused to being ordered to sit for a commander's address. None of them cocky enough to lean back on their elbows with legs outstretched. He was still the centurion here. He dismissed all doubts in his head as a plague on his spirit. He cleared his throat. It was time for a change of tactics.

"This sword was presented to me as a parting gift from the cohort, from you, even though you were not there to see it. A gift for my years of service to The Boar and the emperor. You have my gratitude. It is a fine weapon. Shame I won't get the chance to use it much."

He swirled it for effect and because it felt the most natural thing in the world to do. The joy of holding a balanced sword was healing balm to his shattered self-belief. They laughed and gave him hope. Their faces were loyal and open. His legendary indestructibility was alive and well in their minds.

"I am supposed to march from here to Deva Victrix, sign the papers, drink the 'pension cup' and leave the legion. Morenus and the cohort will find the standard and return it to you. Morenus will even write to me and tell me when it has been recovered. Which is kind."

He did not mean to mock but the way it came out made it a jibe. A snicker of derision broke out. Liscus craned around to put names on them. The mood settled.

"But I can't do that. I will not do that," he could hear his voice clear and firm, the way he liked to hear it in his ears.

No doubts, no quavering words or 'uhhmms' and 'aaahs.' He hoped Liscus was paying attention to the demonstration, it was something he could improve upon. He pointed the shining gladius at the hills behind, darkening under the shadows of onsetting rain clouds. If heavy rain was coming, the river and streams would become torrents and the floors of the valleys marshes. It felt like an omen of fortune. Jupiter, Best and Greatest, was listening.

"Our standard is out there and I'm not leaving you or this place without it," he snarled.

An immediate rumble of approval broke out in the semicircle. He let it run its course. Marcellus had a hazy smile on his lips and Liscus was hanging on every word.

"I made a mistake, men, I tried to use the Carvetii chieftain Drapisces as bait to get the tribes to attack the mines. That was the 'mule's balls.' A complete waste of time," he admitted.

Marcellus snatched a glance around the semi-circle. Velio's magic was working because they were starting to laugh with him once again. If Centurion Velio Pinneius had made a mule's balls of it there was hope for them all. He could not help admiring Velio's blatant working of the mens' taut feelings.

"You will all know by now I have decided we should stop wasting time and the squads from the mines have been recalled. Now that Plautius has brought Drapisces back, I'm going to get on my horse with my shiny new gladius and I'm taking Drapisces in search of the standard. And if the Carvetii do not return it, I'm going to slaughter him in front of their eyes. And I'm going to burn every stick of every stinking mud hut they call home until I get it back," he barked.

"When do we leave, sir?" Plautius called out.

He got cheers, others nodded, a few scowled, ready to get out and fight without further orders. He re-scabbarded the sword and folded his arms, masking the weakness in his right shoulder that felt like it would be there for the rest of his days.

"As soon as we have told the fox where the goose is going to be," he said, "our local mine owner Auvericus is unhappy we have taken Drapisces away from him. I hope Auvericus is bitching in the tavern about that right now. We leave tomorrow with tents, full kit and ration bread," he paused and licked his lips.

His mouth was dry.

"Let me be clear. I am not coming back without my standard," he snapped, "I have brothers to avenge. We all have brothers to avenge."

*

Velio stood where Liscus had stood, at the bottom of the path below Drapisces' hall. This time the hilltop was quiet. No worried or curious faces peering at them. No skeins of smoke from cooking fires. No distant shouts of children, no animals grazing down here below. The pre-eminent sound was the steady grey rain.

"What is the plan sir?" Liscus asked.

Velio handed his horse's reins to Orann. He hoped the stronghold was as unoccupied as it looked. Drapisces and all his immediate retinue and families had been cleared out by Liscus.

"We are going to reoccupy Drapisces' hill, get cooking fires burning, and invite the Carvetii to come and get him," he said, "it gives us a strong defensive position, our numbers are sufficient to hold it and I am hoping, this time, it will be much too much of an insult for them to ignore," he replied.

"Doesn't get the standard back though sir," Liscus ventured.

He fastened his borrowed helmet and tied the chin straps. The feather crest was not a patch on his proper one, but as Morenus had pointed out, beggars cannot choose. It matched his mood.

"Liscus, I am counting on the fact the Carvetii and the Brigantes will be so cock a whoop at their victory against us that they will not only attack us but parade our own standard in front of us as an insult, and perhaps even as a taunt to draw us out of the walls," he explained.

"What if they don't come, sir," Liscus persisted.

Velio leaned closer, "I am not a fool optio. Morenus will support us. He will bring the cohort. Together we will pin the Carvetii and Brigantes here and smash them. At the very least we will extract the information of the standard's location before the last of them dies," he snapped.

"You did not tell me, sir," Liscus whined.

Velio flexed his right arm, it felt better today, better than he expected. He might be able to carry a shield after all, or at least for a while, as an example to the men.

"My dear Liscus, I wanted the word of Drapisces to get out. Nothing else. They won't attack us if they know the First cohort are coming to support us, will they?" he softened.

"So, it's not just about the standard is it sir?" Liscus answered, "and how will they know when to support us if they are at the Delmatarum fort" he asked, confused.

His voice sounded thin even to his own ears. The men close by were listening. Why did the centurion have to make him feel like such a novice at times like this?

Velio gave him a wolfish smile and strode ahead to the rising path already running with its own rivulets of water. Plautius following at his heels like a hound.

"We've already taken this hill searching for you the first time," he felt like reminding Velio.

He about turned to order the men. Their faces said everything.

"Wipe the smirks off your faces or I'll wipe them for you," he growled.

Velio reached the charred remains of the open gateway. Inside a scene of blackened desolation greeted him. The lingering smell of destruction. The rain was making puddles of the grime. Even this small step up in altitude brought the clouds lurking closer.

"The optio's orders, sir. We burned it all," Plautius remarked holding the pommel of his sword at the ready.

Velio's skin crawled with the same anticipation. He could sense the presence of Drapisces and his people amongst the carnage.

"A good decision I'd say. Nothing better than the sight and smell of homes burning to keep the natives worried. Gives them else something to think about," he quipped.

"We will have to rebuild the gate sir, and there's a small water gate on the far side that will need constructing," Plautius advised.

He kicked a burned timber with his boot. Velio took it all in. The hut where he had been imprisoned, the one where he had killed the old woman, was gone along with Draspices' hall and those of his kinsmen. There was not a barn left standing. He put his hands on his hips and sucked through his teeth.

"If you were setting a trap, Plautius, would you make it difficult or easy for your quarry to bite the bait? Put unnecessary obstacles in the way, I mean?" he posed.

Plautius was quick on the uptake.

"Clear away the rubble so we can keep our feet and invite them in, to our very own little arena. No need to pay at the gate because entrance to the games is free. It's a killing ground, no mistake sir. Gives us no margin for error sir," he went on, "this could become a trap for us too. If they get up on these ramparts with their bows, it could get sticky for us in here, sir."

"It could indeed tesserarius. What I want to know from you is whether you think a half century can hold this place?" he asked.

"Depends for how long sir. Gates would give us protection. We can lock them in as well as lock them out," Plautius answered, "if they don't attack, we will have to post a sizeable guard on the gate at all times. Day and night. The Carvetii won't throw their lives away for Drapisces. For all we know they may have chosen a new chieftain by now," he said.

"Gates then," Velio decided.

The possibility that a new chieftain might not come to the rescue of Drapisces was discomforting.

"No point in tempting the gods. Send a squad out for suitable timber and get started. It's all about the standard Plautius, that's all that matters here. Drapisces will get a sword in his gut whatever happens. Set the tents up in the middle so we have room to fight around the perimeter. Ten men to each tent. I don't think we will be getting much sleep up here and I don't want tents cluttering up the space. Just the minimum number for shelter. I'm going to inspect the walls. That's all, carry on tesserarius," he ordered.

# Part Three.

## Chapter Forty-five.

### Losatas' hall, Brigantes territory. Shortly after the skirmish.

The Carvetii were crowing the victory was theirs, not openly to his face, because that would have needed more courage, but behind his back, from the safety of their own halls. Losatas ground his teeth, furious, and pounded his fist into the arm of his oak chair.

*'Ungrateful dogs,'* he raged.

It was his warriors that had begun the attack, borne the brunt, slowed the Roman formation down, fixed them in place for the Carvetii to finish off. And now the dogs were refusing to hand over the captured spirit pole. It was his to claim and theirs to surrender. Of all the spoils, the pole had the greatest value. They were saying they had lost track of which warrior carried it from the battlefield and thus its true location was a mystery. The last emissaries Drapisces had despatched before his capture were still in court. Had it been Drapisces leading the Carvetii there would not have even been a need to ask for the pole. Such was Drapisces' sense of honour between them. They stood before him to answer for it.

"I hear your chieftain still walks under the sun. The sons of the wolf did not kill him after they stormed his home and enslaved his village. Neither has he died in their mines."

He flicked the arm of the chair with his fingernails. They waited.

"Had Drapisces fought with us, he would not have denied me the pole. He would not have insulted me. He never insulted me or my people. Drapisces knows the value of honour among warriors, courage in battle, faithfulness to the gods," he persisted, tapping away at the arm of his chair with his nails.

"I came to your aid, because you asked it of me, because your chief was defending Borwenna's sacred earth, because Belatucadrus demanded it. I was happy to lead my warriors. Happy to share the victory over the Roman pigs with my brothers the Carvetii. But I want the spirit pole as my payment. Go and bring it to me or I will bring my warriors again to your lands and I will take it with my own hands."

He kept his welling rage down low. The elder of the two Carvetii cleared his throat.

"Speak," he said.

"Great chief," the messenger began.

*'Flatterer, you know I am not a Great Chief yet, but you choose to call me that to please me. It will not work, I want the spirit pole, nothing else,'*

Losatas kept silent.

"Not all of our leaders are as wise as broken faced Drapisces who earned his scars fighting with your people. It is well known he calls you brothers and kin. Now that he is captured there are others snapping like dogs to take his position. Our own high chief allows it. He does not step in and plant his spear in the earth and say, 'enough of this,'" the messenger professed.

"He should," Losatas replied, "your high chief has the Brigantes to thank for his position. We put him there. My grandfather did that. My father kept faith with him and so have I, until now. Tell me, have I reason to doubt him?" he purred.

"Our high chief is not as young and strong as you lord Losatas. I am certain he intends no offence. Perhaps he only wishes to enjoy the sight of a captured spirit pole among the many trophies in his hall. He was a mighty warrior once and to have such a prize, well, he wants his people and his bards to see what he has achieved. He is only savouring the glory, my lord. Would you hasten its return from an old chief's hall?" asked the emissary.

His fellow Carvetii blanched at the implied criticism. Losatas wondered if they were going to start arguing in front of him. He leaned forward spreading his hands apart, pretending a gesture of peace, hiding his real feelings of disgust at their duplicity.

"You show your chief no respect. You do not dare pose questions to me. I am Losatas and I can send your flayed hide back with your tongue. Your words are like the whisperings of a stoat. Be that as it may, you will go back to him and your people, little stoat, and tell them I want the spirit pole. And then I want you two to bring it back to me. Or, find Drapisces, set him free and he and I will resolve this insult," he ruled.

They dropped their gaze, nodded and backed away, glad to be dismissed. The sounds of their horses' hooves on the grass told him they were gone within minutes. He got up from his chair, folded his arms and walked around his fire, thinking over the next steps. His senior counsellor came to his side.

"Tell the men to ready their spears and prepare for battle, I fear the Carvetii are no longer to be trusted. Now that Drapisces has been captured our alliance with them may be at an end. They are defying me,"he growled, incredulous.

"So soon, my lord?" the counsellor quizzed.

Losatas scowled.

"When those Roman horsemen came over the pass and chased the Carvetii I was pleased the spirit pole was not recaptured by them. I did not expect them to withhold it from me afterwards," he tutted at his own mistake.

"The next time I will take more of our warriors with me. I will take it by force if I have to," he promised.

"It would be better if they concentrated on setting Drapisces free," the counsellor chimed.

He turned to him.

"Send our best men back into their lands. Find out where the Romans have taken him. Find out if Drapisces still lives. I will go and rescue him myself if it gets me the pole," he said.

"And then you will make him high chief of the Carvetii? A man you know you can trust?" the counsellor suggested.

"You grow more fox-like each day my friend and you read my thoughts too easily."

Losatas gripped the counsellor by both his shoulders. He could feel his mood shifting.

"It would serve a lesson to them," his counsellor pointed out.

He chewed his lip at the very idea and let go of the man's shoulders.

"We should be fighting Romans not each other. Orgidor would be screaming for their heads to be stuck in the oaks for their stupidity if he was alive right now. He would have their high chief bound and thrown into the nearest bog for insulting us," he replied.

"But you are wiser than Orgidor, my lord. Great fighter and leader though he was, he died needlessly. He threw his life at the Romans, and they ate it up. To outlast them we must never surrender. That is all we have to do my lord. Keep the resistance alive. I believe one day when they have taken all the lead and silver, and wood from the forests and slaves they want, they will sail back to Gaul where they came from. The spirit pole should be given as an offering to that day. It would be well received, so I am told."

"Have you my druid been plotting?" Losatas asked.

The counsellor tilted his head, acknowledging the possibility.

"So, even though the pole is mine by right of battle, I must give it to the gods as an offering?"

Losatas felt the happy mood evaporating.

"Do you want to speak to the druid?" the counsellor offered.

His stomach started tightening at the idea. The old druid was being sly again, intervening without being asked for his opinion, yet giving it all the same by this oblique route.

*'Speak to the scary old crow?'* he fumed in his head.

He had been terrified of the priest all his life, the man knew it and played on it.

"And he is certain?" he asked aloud.

"He says nothing concerning the gods is certain, my lord," the counsellor countered.

"Send out the scouts. I want Drapisces found," he answered.

Orgidor must be laughing at him, for sure. He raised a finger as a thought struck him.

"Tell the druid the pole will go to the gods as an offering with my blessing, but only after I have driven the sons of the wolf away from our lands."

The counsellor frowned. Would Losatas be the one, of all the Brigantes chiefs who had ever lived, to succeed in driving the Romans out of their lands? Discretion told him not to question it. It appeared the spirit pole had not finished spilling the blood of warriors. The sooner this Roman talisman was drowned in a bog, the better.

## Chapter Forty-six.

## The hill fort.

The despatch rider from the Cantiventi commander brought Morenus and Civius the same news in separate, damp scrolls; they read them in different rooms. The scrolls said Centurion Pinneius had taken the rest of his command and the Carvetii prisoner Drapisces out of camp to provoke the location of his lost standard. None of the Morinorum garrison had been requested as support. Centurion Pinneius was now heading to the stronghold once held by Drapisces. He would send a native messenger with a credential if he needed military support. His only intention was to preserve the honour of his century, cohort and legion by smashing the Carvetii and rooting out the standard before he returned to Deva Victrix.

'*Hail to the emperor Antoninus Pius, Father of the Country,*' it closed.

"Damn you Velio Pinneius," Morenus snapped, aghast at the defiance of the legate's order, "I told you to go home and leave this to me."

In the room next door Civius grinned, guessing the muffled comments he was hearing were not of delight. He got off his chair and went through and leaned in the doorway, dangling his copy of the message. Morenus was sitting back in the chair clawing the back of his head as if he was lousy with fleas. His copy was on the table in front of him.

"What do you think? Audacious, foolhardy, which?" he intrigued.

Morenus turned his head and glared with all the intensity of Medusa. Civius' blood ran cold. Perhaps light bantering was not Morenus' style? But then the First did take themselves as paragons of all things military.

"I think our colleague's sense of honour overwhelms his common sense. The bastard is either going to get himself and the rest of his men killed, or he will retrieve the standard and make the rest of us look as if we are sitting around with our thumbs up our arses. Either way, not a good outcome for those left to pick up the pieces. I could murder him with my bare hands, I really could," Morenus spat.

Civius nodded, "then I'd best leave you to it, shall I?" he replied, "just ask if we can help in any way."

Morenus regarded him for a second.

"Send word to Uiliocenon. Tell them I may need all their cavalry transferred to my command. I will make it an order if their centurion needs it in writing. You know where this stronghold of Drapisces is, I presume?"

Civius pulled himself together.

"I will get you a map. Do you want it placed under surveillance?" he asked.

Morenus considered the idea and softened his temper a little.

"Just the map for now and an estimate of the marching time."

"You won't be able to approach without being spotted, and in this weather the valley bottoms will be awash," Civius said.

"You are forgetting Civius. It is Velio Pinneius who is holding the fort. I am not trying to hide," Morenus replied.

Civius digested this and nodded.

*

Velio inspected his reinforced hill top. The resurrected main gate was passably robust. The tent area, neat and tidy, the remnants of burned-out timbers had been tossed onto the tops of the ramparts to add to the general obstruction. What had been the inner open area of the small village had been completely cleared for the men to form formation and fight. It was a killing space. Archers would have been helpful in securing it. He cursed his own stupidity for not checking whether the Morinorum carried a detachment of bowmen in their ranks. He turned to Orann.

"You have questions?" he posed.

"I will try and find the Carvetii chieftains master. I think they will know you have brought Drapisces here. These hills have ears and eyes. I think they will also know you want the standard back. But I do not know if they will trade for it, master," Orann replied.

"They will let Drapisces die?" Velio asked.

"Drapisces is a warrior. He fought and lost. His people have been taken by your men and sent south to be sold. He has lost his place among the Carvetii. His power is over. To them he is already dead," Orann shrugged.

Horror flooded Velio.

"Why did you not tell me this before?" he gestured at the defences.

Master, you are the centurion. And you did not ask," Orann answered.

"Then they will not attack? And all this is a waste of time? I would be as well giving Drapisces back to Auvericus and marching back to Deva," Velio said.

Orann tugged his youthful moustaches. A new silver torc was glinting around his throat. Twisted silver bracelets decorated both his wrists. The head of his hunting spear had ties of woven dark brown human hair. The two Carvetii heads had not been discarded as wholly as he imagined. No wonder Orann had not put up much of a fuss at his demands.

*'Master, you did not ask, spoken like a soldier or warrior. You fool Velio, you are walking round with your eyes shut,'* he berated himself.

"I did not say they will not attack, Master. They know you escaped from Drapisces before the optio led his attack and they thought they had killed you with your men at the fight on the road. The Carvetii at Cantiventi are saying you cannot be killed. I told you. They will know you want the standard. I think they will come to finish off your men and take your head. Master, I think they will attack for the glory of killing you." Orann replied.

A cold jitter raced down Velio's back. He clamped his hand on the pommel of his gladius and nodded to cover his unease. Being attacked by the enemy had never felt personal before now. It was always the century, the cohort, the legion that was at risk; the red cloaks, the shields, the wolf-skin capes of the signifers, cornicens and buccina trumpeters; it was the emblems of Rome that drew attention, not the faces in the helmets. The rank feathers marked him out, but he was always only one of many officers. They never came for Velio Pinneius. They never wanted to nail his particular head up in an oak.

*'No, that's not true. The Caledonii wanted your head and Gallus' too. It's just Orann saying it out loud that makes it true,'* he realised.

"Go out on your horse and see what can find Orann. They will talk to you, won't they?" he asked.

Orann gave him the salute he had been working on. Velio returned it. Orann's was getting better.

"Don't do that out there," he cautioned.

Orann did not smile back and Velio felt a tickle of unease that even this soft joke fell flat.

*

Orann cantered along the valley towards the place where he had killed the boy farmer. By now the body would be covered by tall grass, picked clean, and unlamented. He felt no remorse for a fair fight. It had been unnecessary but fair. The farm boy should have listened to his warning and retreated. But he chose to fight. Brave and foolish, he was lying out here, somewhere in the tall grass. He focussed on what the Master wanted. Finding the Carvetii and getting them to talk about the standard were different problems. He halted and let his horse drink, decided to join her and slipped from her back. To succeed, he would need to convince them he was not a spy for the legions and trustworthy. There was not the time for that trick. It could take a lifetime to earn that amount of trust. If he could find the Carvetii he would have to explain how he knew about the standard at all. There was simply no chance they would divulge information to a passing Votadini stranger, far from his own lands. Just asking about it would be enough to put them on their guard. The Master was sending him on a useless errand. He stopped drinking and wiped his mouth on the cuff of his woollen sleeve. This was a good spot to rest for the night even although it was too early in the day. He spied trout in the stream. There were handy rocks for shelter. He would try letting the Carveti find him. It would be one less thing to pretend. And if it did not work he would ride on tomorrow.

He woke to an audience and a spear point. The sun was setting, sending gloom and shadows into the valley. The air by the stream had grown chilly. Four burly Carveti wrapped in their cloaks were sitting on their haunches at the far side of his little fire, feeding it with the sticks he had gathered to last the night. A fire burning in the evening darkness had been his plan to draw them out. It had not taken long to spot it. They had probably been watching him fish in the stream with his hands under the banks. Had they approved his success? An idiotic voice in his head was glad he had cooked and eaten them as soon as he caught them. Three sat in front of him and one off to the side, no doubt in case he tried to resist. Their leader toyed with a forked stick.

"What tribe are you?" he asked without any rancour.

*

Orann faced the assembled Carvetii warriors and, worse still, by the dour, uncompromising look of them, a contingent from the mighty Brigantes. Falling asleep by the waterside had brought him to the right place. The goddess of the water must have smiled on his travail. She must have been there while he fished for her children and granted him two small victories. If he survived this ordeal, he would go back and throw one of his new bracelets into her pools as thanks.

There was a long fire pit with only a small, token stack of wood burning. The large hall was half filled but he could see these were powerful men. Rows of mature, bearded warriors, counsellors as well, no doubt, and in amongst them there would be a druid shaman or two. If anyone in these hills had the standard, it would be these men. The Brigantes' blue marked arms bore familiar symbols.

He had ceased using his Votadini markings. The Romans did not like painted people in their midst. Mistress Voccia said to stop provoking them. The earlier Carvetii confusion was understandable. He must appear to them like a man with no tribe. An outcast or an outlaw with his horse and a hunting spear. He was no threat to these men; they knew it and so did he, but they were curious. The human hair on the spear head would earn him the benefit of the doubt. But for so many of them to assemble to hear what he had to say could only mean something else was afoot, or were they going to torture him and send him to his ancestors as an offering? He pulled himself together. He had committed no crime. In their eyes he would be innocent. In ordinary circumstances sacrificing an innocent stranger who had not been taken in battle was fraught with ill omen.

The chief in the centre gave him the sign. He decided there was little point in bluffing. The centurion and his men might be willing to die for the spirit pole, but its reverence was lost on him. It was a dead thing, not like a tree or a river, a rock or a waterfall. The way they fawned over it was ridiculous.

"They want the signum back," he began.

Puzzled looks spread on their faces. The hall was very quiet.

"The spirit pole," he explained.

He sounded to himself like he was shouting. The looks altered to comprehension but defiant rejection as well. Words passed among them. The chief raised his hand a mere fraction and the hall fell silent. Orann swallowed.

"They will trade Drapisces for the spirit pole, this is their message, this is what they want you to hear," he continued.

There was no need to explain how he knew Drapisces.

"Why would they do that? The wolf soldiers do not trade until they have won their victories," the chief queried.

He was perplexed. This young stranger had rocked his hall. This was no passing outcast, even if he did look like one. Orann guessed the next part was going to be difficult to explain, let alone for them to understand. It might even make them laugh. He looked around. None of them looked like they found him a fool.

"Their war chief is leaving. He wants the spirit pole back or his gods will be angry. He says he cannot leave until it is returned," he hazarded the closest thing imaginable.

A ripple of delight and incredulity rang out.

"Tell him to come and get it," a warrior catcalled.

"Does he take all his men too?" a voice barracked.

"No, no they are staying," he admitted.

A ruffle of derision sounded on all sides. The Brigantes looked to the one who must be their own chief. This other chief was staring at him. His Carvetii counterpart replied for the room.

"Then they cannot have the spirit pole. We won it in battle. It is ours. Drapisces is a great warrior. He deserves to die a warrior's death. He is not a bull to be bargained. What Roman nonsense is this?" he said.

Orann saw the Brigantes chief incline his head listening to a piece of advice from one of his men.

"Then, if you permit me, I will take your wisdom back to them," he said.

"You are their messenger? What tribe are you?" the Brigantes spoke.

The room hushed.

*'You are more powerful than the Carveti, you are the one I need to convince,'* he sensed and straightened up.

"I am Orann of the Votadini, from the lands to the north of yours, by the sweeping river that runs past the fort of Trimontium. You know this land I think, my lord? It is good horse land. Cattle grow fat. The barley never fails. The rivers run fast and cold. But you will not have heard of my home. I served a man called Eidumnos and his family. Now I serve his daughter Voccia. Eidumnos and his wife were murdered by the Selgovae prince Segontio after the tribes destroyed Blatobulgium and shed much blood on the ground. It was then that the sons of the wolf abandoned the earth wall and fled south to the great stone wall," he explained.

The Brigantes were nodding, the Carvetii attentive; soaking up his testimony. They had been at peace during the evacuation of the northern defences. This young stranger had seen it at first hand. Orann felt they were warming to him.

"The Romans killed him, Segontio I mean. Segontio was lost to reason, his head was filled with anger at the sons of the wolf, but I think he feared his allies more. He had to attack Trimontium to prove he was worthy of leading his tribe. My master Eidumnos' farm passed to his eldest son who had sided and fought bravely with Segontio but was wise enough not to attack Trimontium. And Voccia has come south, I brought her. She has no place in her brother's hall. He did not make her welcome. She follows the Roman who wants the standard. She carries his child, she is his woman," he said.

"That is quite a tale. So this Roman, he is your new master, is he not? You serve the Romans. I am Losatas of the Brigantes. Tell me,

Orann of the Votadini, what will the soldier, your master, do when he hears his standard will not be returned?" he posed.

"I serve my mistress Voccia," Orann refuted.

The Brigantes stared at him. Orann stiffened himself for the likely reaction.

"He is going to come and get it," he predicted.

Losatas bared his yellowing teeth. This young Votadini had guts, and sand in his craw.

"Is he, indeed?" he growled.

The Carvetii chieftain lifted his hand. Losatas sat back.

"Take back our message, we will not trade. We honour Drapisces too much to do that." the Carvetii said.

Orann nodded, unsurprised.

"My master and all his men honour the holy standard too much to let it go. You will have to fight to keep it," he said.

He stepped back and looked at the ranked warriors and counsellors. Two tribes in a single room. Lords of the sky and hills. Part of him wanted to raise his fist in salute and shriek the war cry of the Votadini. A white moustached man came toward him. He wore a tattered robe of plain spun wool.

*'It must itch all day long, like floundering into a bed of nettles,'* Orann surmised.

The druid smiled the faintest of wan, cold, smiles.

"Run, little Votadini, run. Your spear is waiting, and your horse has been fed. Tell your master, we have his death here if he desires it. Run."

Challenging those thick browed eyes was the hardest thing but he refused to back down to the druid.

"It's here, in this hall, isn't it?" he whispered back.

The druid's eyes bored into his.

"Your death is looking at you, if you wish Votadini," he replied.

*

"Are you telling me they will not attack?" Velio said.

He could feel his anger rising, not at the message but the time he had wasted in refortifying the hill top. Orann leaned on his spear.

"Master, they do not want to trade," he said, looking at Drapisces chained to a fresh timber post in the centre of the compound.

Velio recalculated his plans.

"What did you say to that?" he countered.

"Master, I told them you are coming to get it."

Velio chewed that over for a moment.

"Good lad. Spoken like a soldier of the Twentieth legion. Are you ready to make the oath to the emperor and wear the lorica, follow every order, die for the emperor if you have to?"

Orann leaned harder on his spear.

"I serve the Mistress, your woman, Master. I serve you and the children she will bear you. I will scout for you and your men, defend you from murderers in the night, but," he paused.

Velio sensed what was coming.

"I have decided I do not want to serve this emperor. Where was he when Eidumnos and Bractia were murdered by Segontio?" he said.

Velio shrugged. There was no answer to that one.

"It was you and Gallus that saved my mistress, not your emperor. It is because of him that I am here. My people are gone except your wife. I do not make this oath. You ask too much," Orann blurted.

Velio patted his arm.

"I understand. Forgive me. I thought it was what you wanted."

He spent the rest of the day pondering his next move. If the Carvetii refused to attack, Orann's instinct that he would go after the standard was correct but seventy-plus men was not going to be enough. He had no intention of sacrificing them in a repeat of the débâcle on the road. Fighting outside of Drapisces' stronghold for the next few days would be folly. The rain had set in from the west in a continual downpour. The rivers were beginning to spate. The low ground would be treacherous. It had always been about luring them here and sending Orann to summon Morenus from the hill fort. Now it was up in the air. But there could be no repetition of the last time, the débâcle on the road.

## Chapter Forty-seven.

## The hill fort.

Once his irritation drained away Morenus pondered his next move. Clearly Velio was not to retire gracefully. Had he been playing games or was it a sudden impulse that he could not let this go? An affront too unbearable to accept?

*'Typical of you, Velio, you stubborn old mule,'* he mused in sympathy, '*setting an example to the very end.'*

The map Civius provided was marked up for him with the location of Drapisces' hall and the last known holdouts of the major Carvetii sub chieftains. The map extended across to the lands of the Brigantes becoming cluttered with so many ink markers for forts, signalling towers and suchlike to be useless.

Where was the standard? Was it hiding in plain sight nearby, or buried deep in a bog where no man was ever going retrieve it? Civius was being coy with his advice. His comrade centurion was making the right noises, but it was clear neither of them had the appetite to go out and lay down the law. Putting a cavalry station here would have served the emperor better. Footsloggers were hard up against it. All in all, from what he had seen of the officers, he much preferred the look of young Titus Vindex. At least he had a bit of spark and energy about him. Small surprise the local tribes had felt able to launch a series of attacks on the mines. There was nothing here to stop them. It was as though the regular traffic of the road had somehow dulled Civius into thinking that because it was busy, all was well.

That misconception was about to be remedied. His four centuries amounted to six hundred and fifty men. Velio must have the better part of a hundred men left, added to the one hundred and twenty mounted troopers from Uiliocenon. He could demand Civius give him support but would have to leave one of his own precious centuries behind to compensate. The Delmatarum maniple was adequate and suitable fodder for arrows and spears. Close to a thousand men in total. He checked the map once again, wrestling with the distances and the times involved. In these narrow valleys and passes a thousand well placed, trained men would be a considerable force. But the heavy weather slowed everything down, even the cavalry. He summonsed Titus Vindex.

"How well do you really know these hills optio?" he asked.

"Well enough sir, though they can deceive you in poor weather like this. It's easy to get lost when it closes in. One valley looks much like another around here. Sometimes it is wiser to wait it out and move when it lifts. It can change quickly. That is part of the problem up here," he admitted.

"Yes, yes. Apart from that, can you read this map and show me a place where I can set a trap, a closed valley perhaps, where we could stopper up the Carvetii long enough to give them a good hammering?' Morenus said.

Titus ran his finger over the map. Morenus waited for him to answer. The optio was hesitating.

"You don't know, do you?" he accused.

Titus flushed and stabbed a finger onto the map.

"This spot will do the job perfectly, sir. It's just that I do not see where the standard fits in," he replied.

Morenus looked at the spot and circled it with a pen.

"You are sure? You will take me there, I want to see the ground for myself," he said.

Titus nodded. Morenus could see the unanswered question in Titus' eyes. It was time for a bit of hard reality, a slice of Pax Romana, dished up cold.

"Forget the standard, lad. It has gone. Centurion Pinneius believes he can fight the Carvetii and get them to hand it over. He is a fool. We will never get it back. This is no longer about retrieving the standard, this is now about punishment for daring to take it, and daring to attack the convoys. We are going to hit them so hard they will wish they had sneaked up and left it up against the Praetoria gate for us to find in the morning. I am going to slaughter the Carvetii to the last child and goat. And if the Brigantes want to stand with them we will slaughter them too. I will nail their bodies up along the Iter X like Crassus did to Spartacus on the Via Appia. This is the First cohort of the Twentieth legion of Rome. We are The Boar. Our standards will not be taken with impunity. I am the Primus Pilus, and I will not stand for it. Do you understand?" he blared.

*'That does simplify things,'* Titus thought.

He swallowed down the cheeky riposte he might have offered to a lesser rank. Morenus did not look like a man who took humour from junior officers.

"Now get me two good horses optio, bring a warm cloak, you are going to lead me to this place. Nice and quietly, no fuss, no escort, no trumpets. Quietly, got it?" Morenus coached.

*

Morenus picked his way through the rocks along the valley floor to the end where its steep sides met in a kind of headwall blocking further movement in that direction. Titus kept a respectful horse length gap behind and his lip buttoned. This might be the way of getting out of the Delmatarum posting and back into the legion. He steeled himself to answer the centurion's questions and resist voluntary opinions. After thirty minutes or so Morenus ceased riding up and down and dismounted. The centurion seemed indifferent or immune to the cold rain.

"How far is this hall of Drapisces where Centurion Pinneius and his men are billeted?" he asked.

Titus twisted around in his saddle pointing to the west.

"Roughly two to three miles in that direction," he replied.

Morenus lifted the hem of his cloak and signalled Titus to come over. Together they tried to shelter the map from the rain.

"So, as far as our intelligence goes, the remaining Carvetii strongholds in this area are more to the north. Is that correct?" he asked.

"We believe that to be so, sir," Titus answered, trying to be helpful.

"Hummph," Morenus snorted.

He gazed back and forth from the rapidly disintegrating map to the hillsides.

"If Centurion Pinneius decided not to stay in the stronghold and wait, but came out intending to attack one of the Carvetii chiefs, to get his standard back, which way would he go from the stronghold. I mean, would he march past this valley?" he queried.

"Excuse me sir, but why would he abandon a defensive position and come out onto the low ground in these conditions when he does not know which Carvetii chief has his standard? Is he not trying to get them to throw themselves at his defences?"

Morenus gave him a freezing glance.

"Because maybe he has orders to do so, optio?"

Titus rallied and frowned.

"I would not march men this way, but unless he has a local guide, I doubt he will have enough local knowledge to use the better route," he surmised.

"Then we need to tell him to do exactly that, and we will spring a trap, right here, in this dead end," Morenus plotted aloud.

He rolled up the sopping, water ruined map and sprang on his horse.

"Time to get moving before we are spotted by the natives. Let's go on to Drapisces' hall. I want to see how long a march it is."

*

"Riders, sir," one of the guards called out to Plautius, "two men, ours sir."

They drew closer, and began the ascent of the main path, passing the eight man guard at the foot of the hill. Plautius saw them saluting and hurried to find Liscus or Velio.

Later, once they had eaten and inspected Drapisces, he saw Velio walk with them to the main gate. Velio shook Morenus by the arm. Titus Vindex saluted Velio. Velio stood at the top of the path and watched them descend all the way to the bottom of the hill. A cold dread filled Plautius. Morenus outranked Velio and from his face, he did not much like the order he had just received.

## Chapter Forty-eight.

Velio brought Liscus, Marcellus, Plautius and the other remaining tesserarius, Metius, to his tent.

"We are ordered to lure the Carvetii into attacking us in a valley near here. A closed place with only one way out. Centurion Morenus and the rest of our cohort will close the door behind them. Together we will smash them and, Jupiter and Mars willing, we will get our standard back," he said.

"You think they will parade it in front of us?" Liscus asked.

Velio opened his hands up.

"If it's not already been destroyed, then I think they will delight in humiliating us with it. But mark my words, if they bring it, it will be kept back, so far out of our reach we will struggle to reach it. But if we kill every last one of them, there is a chance we can get it back," he replied.

"When do we leave sir?" asked Metius.

Velio hesitated. The plan was chancy at best. So unlikely to succeed he would never have made it an order to his own men except under duress. The duress Morenus had placed on his shoulders. It was testing loyalty to its limits. Asking his men to forget what happened to their comrades on the road and march out in the happy dream this was an ordinary, punitive, patrol.

"Tomorrow, we are going to march three miles with Drapisces in tow and set up camp. There we are going to sit and wait to be attacked. Drapisces is still our best piece of bait but now we are ordered to stop hiding him up here and go out there for the glory of the Twentieth," he summed up.

There was a hush in the tent. It was hard to tell what thoughts were whirling in their soldier brains.

"For how long? How long do we wait in camp out there, three miles from a much more defendable hilltop," Marcellus chipped in.

Velio raised his eyebrows at him, and his privileged position, and chose not to reply.

"For as long as it takes," Liscus answered Marcellus.

It was a good answer. Velio thanked him with a fraction of a nod.

"Won't they smell a rat, sir?" Plautius said.

"Centurion Morenus is confident their desire to free Drapisces will overcome their wisdom and we, are being given the chance to atone for losing the standard," Velio replied

"Servius himself would not ask a mere half century to do this," Marcellus said from the side.

The two tesserarii bit their lips. Liscus tilted his head in anticipation of the fight to come but his face was taut and grim.

"Legate Servius Albinius is not here, and neither is the rest of the legion. Gentlemen, we are the First cohort, and we will follow these orders," Velio clamped down.

He realised it was a bitter message. Not quite suicide but wholly reliant on the timing of Morenus to support them, as they had surely worked out for themselves.

"A prayer to the gods you hold dear to you will not go amiss tonight,"he suggested.

"A battle lustratio for the men, sir?" Liscus asked.

"I will do it tomorrow at dawn. Assemble them and get me something for a sacrifice," he nodded.

*

Losatas had his men rise early. They moved before the Carvetii dogs and geese twitched and scented the dawn. The temptation to storm the hall and seize the spirit pole by force made his head pound but the little Votadini messenger had inadvertently given him an idea. Holding his hands to his mouth he signalled for silence and took the Brigantes away from the slumberers who still thought it safe to withhold the tribute he wanted from them. When they were well clear of their hosts' village, he rested his men in a pleasing meadow to wait out the day until his scouts returned. An amicable Carveti farmer with a round, guileless face, traded a cow for silver and the animal was quartered up and roasted in pieces on fires. The smell of hot beef filled the air.

The scouts returned in the early evening. Drapisces' hall was within easy reach. Nothing they said changed his determination to fight the enemy, attack them before dawn tomorrow while they slept, scale the earth walls and kill them all, including their cocky warrior chief. Once Drapisces was secured and installed as the new Carvetii chief over that aging fool, he would ensure the standard was given to him. As it should have been in the first place. And if the Carveti thought he was going to sit about waiting for Orann the Votadini's master to pick and choose the time they were mistaken. The gutsy little Votadini could go free if he survived.

He told the scouts to go back and keep watch and report movements. He ate his portion of meat and lay back on his elbow to rest. He fell asleep, sated with beef, while his men conversed around him. One of them laid a cloak over him. He awoke to the sound of urgent voices.

"What is happening?" he asked.

"Lord, they are out. The Votadini spoke the truth. They really are coming to get the standard," his scout reported.

"How many?" he probed.

"About the same number we fought on the road, no more, my lord," the scout vouched.

"Where are they?" he asked.

"They are in the bottom lands. We waited to be certain. They are coming this way," the scout replied.

"They cannot know we are here. It is impossible. Go back and track them. They cannot reach any of their forts tonight in these rains. I do not understand what they are doing. Bring me word of what they do and where they are going," he said.

The scout nodded and turned to go.

"Wait, show me," he commanded.

The warrior led him out of the meadow and over up a crest and pointed.

"This valley leads to another that leads to Drapisces' hall. I saw them come down from the hilltop. Lord, it is if they are blind, they are coming to you."

"Did you see Drapisces? Were you close enough to see him? Is he with them?" he asked.

His old ally was coming to be rescued.

The scout dropped his arm.

"They have a prisoner. It was too far to tell if it was Drapisces, but who else could it be, lord? There are paths that cross below us here. Perhaps they are going to their fort in the hills?" he suggested.

Losatas pondered that.

"But why start out in such rain? The rivers are flooding. It makes no sense. We will move across and wait here. Perhaps we can ambush them, hit them from these heights where there is no cover for them to hide behind. No walls for us to climb," he said.

The evening light was failing by the time he returned with his men.

"What are they doing now?" he demanded.

The row of scouts he had set pointed as one to the Roman column now in plain sight and turning off the path. The column slowed to a halt. He watched, not understanding what they were doing. A steadier, less violent rain was beginning to fall. From the heights they could just make out the ground pooling with water rising through the grass. The Romans began moving into a nearby side valley. He looked at his scouts. They shrugged back.

"Shadow them," he said, "I want to know what they are doing."

He climbed up the slope back to where his warriors waited in the soaking grass. They listened to his news and wrapped their cloaks tighter. Water dripped off iron helmets, ran down shields and odd pieces of stolen armour. Standing about was wearying. He reached a decision and led them over the crest to where the scouts were hiding. One of them looked up. In the distance one of them was hastening across the contours. The Romans had now disappeared from sight. The man struggled through the wet heathery hillside.

"They are making camp," he cried up to Losatas, "they have trapped themselves. There is only one way out, past us," he exulted.

A cheer rose from his men. Losatas heard them celebrating all around. Why not, it sounded like they had boxed themselves in? But why so late in the day when the rain gods were feasting?

*

Velio inspected the ground Liscus was suggesting. Down in the depths between the hills it was very gloomy. There was just about enough light to see and make choices. Pools of water were lying on the gravel beds where a stream was running dark brown. Blackening clouds seemed to press their fingers down to the tops of the hills. The whole area was dull and unwelcoming. He sniffed and declined Liscus' plan.

"We need to go further in, find a decent piece of elevated ground to pitch the tents and dig our defence lines," he demurred.

Liscus did what he was paid to do, he pointed out the repercussions of what might be a bad decision on Velio's part.

"Any further in and we risk being trapped like fish in a barrel. We could drown before Morenus gets here."

"Then we must do our best not to. I don't expect anyone will try to attack us in this," Velio replied and flicked his hand upwards.

"Is that why you brought us out, sir?" Liscus' expression lightened.

He splashed away while the men rested under their raised shields, the rain tipping on either side of them. Liscus shouted and the century moved forwards. This was the worst place to set a camp but if it did not bring the Carvetii tumbling out of the hills to attack in the morning he would walk home to Deva in his bare feet.

Twenty minutes later Velio approved Liscus' next proposal. The baggage carts along with the dolabra and the turf cutting tools were pulled to the centre of a flat shelf of lush grass. A low ledge ran roughly knee high across the rear, decumana part, of the nascent camp. A ditch of any depth at all would secure that side to good effect. The hillside to their rear was a bit too close for comfort. If the enemy took control of the heights they could be in a sticky position. Other than that, it was the best they could do. The light was fading with wicked speed. The men stacked weapons ready for the command to set to, glad of new activity to keep them warm. They surveyed the small site and calculated the time before they could take shelter in the tents. The soft ground surrendered to the dolabra. The ditch lines were an irregular oval. The men worked with a fury and with the spoil heaped up on the outward face the barrier was hip high in short order.

Velio paced along its edge with Metius and Plautius. The men could dig it deeper, but it was a judgement to call a halt and settle for the obstacle they had created. If the enemy got this far the soft dug earth would give difficult footing. He nodded.

"The final touch. Make a hedge of spikes along the mound with the dolabra. Leave gaps to act like funnels," he said.

"What about him sir?"

Plautius flicked a glance at Drapisces who was grinning for the first time since he had been captured.

The eyes in that ruined face were bright, sparkling in the rain that ran down his hair plastered forehead.

"Take his clothes off, tie him like a hog and put him by that rock. If he so much as twitches or calls out in the night, slit his throat. Post a man to guard him, rotate through the watches. I want full camp discipline. Plautius and Metius will lead the night watches. I will be with them. You had best get some rest Liscus. I need you to be fresh for tomorrow," he said.

Drapisces stood aloof as Plautius ordered a soldier to cut away his clothing.

*'Let's see how warm you are in this without your cloak and breeches,'* Liscus sneered.

"No food or water. He is only to live until we get the standard back," Velio commanded.

"He could freeze tonight if it does not let up," Plautius replied, matter of fact.

Velio scoured the flat bottom of the valley floor, the grey wet rocks, the gushing stream and the increasing, persistent rain. Plautius was correct. A man without shelter could die in this kind of weather. It reminded him of another valley where he and Marcus had stumbled on the greatest discovery of their lives. This one was different, and Marcus Hirtius was long dead, but the atmosphere was not so very far apart. That same gloomy foreboding emanating from the rocks. He shivered at the memory.

"Secure the horses," he snapped.

The first guard, Metius' men, stepped out with their javelins and shields. Behind them the tents rose, and the light finally died. The rain lessened, as if its work was done but the stream rattled and roistered. Velio flicked a glance to the tents and Liscus sent the rest to shelter. He caught Plautius looking at him, drenched, hungry and ill at ease. No one would sleep tonight, rubbed by wool and armour. Part of him took solace. Tired, angry men would fight like twice their number. He watched them slipping into the tents.

"The Tempestates have decided lads, they will stand the watch for you tonight," he called.

Anything to hold morale: anything.

Velio woke to a silent, sodden world. The rain had ceased beating the goatskins. He eased open the tent flap. The valley was wreathed in low mist, the air was soft and wet. It was early. He rubbed his arms to generate warmth. If his best fire makers could coax flames out of this watery wilderness, porridge would hearten the men. The stream in front of the position was now the best rampart he could have wished for, swollen and running wide and deep, swirling closer to the tents than last night, tugging the rough grass to go with it as it passed. Crossing it would be a hurdle instead of easy quick steps. The Tempestates had indeed favoured them. Today he would make it red with enemy blood. Plautius joined him and saluted. He looked weary; his eyes dark rimmed and lined.

"The prisoner?" Velio asked his tesserarius.

"Alive, sir. Not quite drowned, yet," Plautius replied.

"Get men working on a fire. We need porridge Plautius, and check the dolabra are still in place. This rain," he waved, lost for words.

"You still want to fight here, sir?" Liscus joined them.

Velio watched the stream running across the front of the position. "You chose well Liscus. Have you ever seen anything so beautiful as that, better than a double ditch, there's hope for you yet," he replied.

It was time to praise Liscus in front of his other officers. Liscus purred in gratitude, his eyes shining.

"Hostiles. Looks like hostiles,"

A sentry voice called out from the hillside at their backs. Velio and Plautius looked up.

"Get every man out and in position. Sound Stand to the Eagle. '*And may Hades have your bones if you do not come, Morenus,'*" he cursed inside.

"This will have to do, Plautius. Form the men. It's too late to worry about porridge now."

"I can't see anything. This damned mist. They must have been watching us all the time," Liscus panted.

"Brigantes," the same voice on the hillside called out.

"Well, it appears they are out there, Liscus. Are you certain they are not Carvetii?" Velio called back up to the sentry on the hillside behind them.

"Definitely Brigantes sir. Coming on fast," the sentry shouted back.

Velio looked further along the hillside from the sentry, searching through the clammy mist for the spot Orann had taken last night. He drew his gladius and raised it above his head praying the Votadini was seeing him. Off to left, much further than he expected, he spied the grey fuzzy movement of a spear waving in return. The spear was waving frantically. Orann must have had the Brigantes in sight before the army scouts detected them.

"Run Orann," he breathed, "The Boar needs you again."

The spear ceased moving. Orann was up and away.

*

Losatas brought the warriors to a point out of range for any bowmen the Romans might have in their ranks and took stock of the enemy camp. The stream divided him from the small slight platform of grass where the Romans had dug their usual defences. He could see the shields were up and the lines formed. They were a red clump of hatefulness. What had begun on the road was going to be finished off here. There was just one last thing to know before he unleashed his warriors. He signalled them to wait and strode forwards over the gravel and tussocks of bullrushes with his favoured spear in one hand and his decorated shield of curlicues and spirals. The Roman shield line was completely silent as he came close.

"Drapisces. Are you there?"

He called out through the rain. There was no reply.

“Drapisces of the Carveti, this is Losatas of the Brigantes. Are you there?” he repeated.

A voice replied in rough Brigantes, “if you want him come and get him.”

“Speak to me Drapisces,” he refuted.

“I am here Losatas.”

It did not sound much like his warrior friend. It might be him, but it might also be a trick. He waited for them to say more but all went quiet.

“Roman, we want Drapisces. And you want the spirit pole. Do we eat from the same bowl?” he called out.

The Roman lines stayed silent. Then the line parted and a soldier led a naked man through the gap with an iron chain at his neck.

“I am Drapisces,” the naked man proclaimed.

He looked a sorry mess. Losatas stared at him but was not sure it really was the Carvetii.

A legionary jabbed the bottom edge of his shield into the back of Drapisces’ knees. He fell forward. The same soldier stepped in close, tugged back his head and slit his throat wide open with a sword. Drapisces pitched into the grass with scarce a twitch. Losatas watched the clinical execution with horror. The shield wall sealed itself up again like a curtain closing on draughty night. Drapisces was a white shape on the grass. He turned and lifting his spear. There was no more bargaining now. Behind him the first wave of his warriors came rushing through the grass. Rain began falling.

“**Ready lads. Pila, now,**” Plautius and Metius commanded.

The javelins flew into the Brigantes as they struggled in the stream. Bodies splashed backwards and began floating in the tug of the current.

"**Second pila. Now,**" Metius and Plautius barked.

The second volley creased the line of Brigantes into piles of wounded and dying men.

The surviving wave swept on and struggled past the underwater barrier of the stream's submerged bank. They barged up against the outcast mound. The dolabra funnelled them to the gaps where Plautius and Metius had set their best men. Others began wresting the dolabra out of the earth, but they were within touching distance of the legionaries who began stepping forward and cutting down the defence wreckers.

"**Hold your place. Close shields. Wait for the whistle.**"

Velio bellowed phrases they had trained and practised to on hot sunny days at Deva Victrix. He paced along the interior line of his defence. The Brigantes attack bent past the front of his line and met a prickle of withheld pila jutting out from the shields. They found their way to what would have been the decumana side and stepped up over the little obstacle, proving it was not the deterrent he had hoped. He saw his men falling and blew the whistle to rotate the rank. The neat and tidy 'step-aside and reset' was like a little dance that brought joy to his heart. He hauled a wounded man back out of way of his comrades. He had taken a dagger wound through the join of his armour strips. Blood was flowing and spreading down the wet metal. The man grunted his thanks and dug his shield into the grass levering himself to his feet. The solitary capsarius was at his side with a bandage, stuffing it into place. Velio nodded and left him. There was a coordinated grunt, and the front line butted a step forward throwing the Brigantes off balance, then stepped straight back. It seemed to catch the warriors by surprise. Cries of pain cut through the shouting and clanging of weapons. It lasted for a bit longer and then the Brigantes pulled back, dragging Drapisces' body away by his arms. The stream washed his throat and chest clean.

"No standard," Velio he called over to Liscus, "they do not have my standard. They would be waving it at us to break formation if they had it," he cried.

"If they keep this up, we cannot repair the damage to the ditch, sir. It's not holding in the rain. We will have nothing to rest behind tonight, Liscus panted,

"Quietly lad. We will break them long before night comes," he promised.

A flurry of light throwing spears came flighting out of the gloom.

"Testudo. Get those shields up. Or I'll have to go out there and get my new gladius dirty with heathen blood," he jeered.

The legionaries around him laughed.

"How many do you say?" he asked Metius.

The Brigantes forces were congregating as their war chief fell back.

"Perhaps three or four hundred. It's hard to be sure in this murk sir," he replied, "they could be hiding their forces from us. Bit of a surprise though sir. The Brigantes. Where are the Carvetii? I thought this was their land?" Metius queried.

Velio stared at Metius.

"Good question. If it's three or four hundred, then this is only a raiding band. It can't be the whole tribe. Tell that to the men," he said.

Four hundred lightly armed warriors against eighty heavily armoured and trained legionaries were a far more palatable prospect, if Metius' assessment of their numbers was correct. But these ones were proving more aggressive than normal.

"Seventeen wounded, four dead," Plautius reported.

"How bad are the wounded?" he retorted.

He withheld his surprise at the high count. The men had appeared to hold the upper hand.

"A mixture, as always, sir," Plautius replied.

"Get them patched up and swords at the ready if they want to march out of here," he snapped.

The first two or three charges were going to be the fiercest.

Losatas went forward and drank from the stream while his men recouped their strength. Rain stippled the surface and grew heavier. There were bodies of his men in the water and all around it. The Romans watched him drink and saved their spears. They were plucky. Their heads would make fine trophies to take back to the halls. One of his warriors pointed to the valley mouth.

"The Carvetii are coming, my lord" he grunted.

## Chapter Forty-nine.

## Argentomagus.

Hanno got off his horse and took a drink from the fountain, soaked his neckerchief in the stone basin and washed the unpleasant sheen of sweat from his face and neck. He swirled the cloth in the sun warmed water and retied it, enjoying the cooling wetness dripping down his back. His horse put her muzzle to the basin and together they relaxed in what was feeling like the hottest day of the year so far. The forum was emptying as the townsfolk headed for the nearest shade, leaving the vendors temporarily abandoned.

The garrison commander had just shaken his arm to take goodly quantities of the forthcoming posca and lora for his men. They had a rueful discussion over the lack of available Falernian for the officers, but he was confident that once they had some, in fit state to supply, it would take little promoting to sell. Gallus' wounding was the talk of the visit.

The Eighth was not a legion he really knew too much about, but this vexillation were a decent enough bunch. He erred away from mentioned the plain, ineluctable fact that when Priscus' estate was raided there must have been a sizeable and valuable stock of accumulated Falernian in his warehouse. The commander of the Eighth sidestepped the subject as well.

A flurry of activity broke out in the slave pens of Gramalcus, interrupting his thoughts. The man himself had taken time to send Gallus a jar of honey to aid his recovery. It was a decent gesture he reckoned. The sibilant venom of a whip was followed by a gasp of pain. It was much too hot to be waving a whip around. He could see men moving inside the cages. The whip cracked once more and then it went quiet. The nature of the disobedience stayed unclear as Gramalcus crossed over from the civic building to find out what was going on. He raised his palm in salutation as he passed. Hanno returned the greeting. Gramalcus was playing fair with them. The replacement slaves he supplied were strong and able: their prices reasonable. The three German auxiliary were proving to be an asset.

The procurator made an appearance at the door of the administration building. He watched Durus scanning his little empire within the forum, accepting the instant sycophantic greetings from the silver merchants and food sellers resisting the heat. The auxiliary on duty at the door had a relaxed posture. Procurator and guard seemed to be sharing a joke about the slave pens.

Hanno sat on the stone lip of the fountain and patted his horse. She shook her head and bobbed her mouth down to the water, snorting and waiting. This was a long way from Velunia on the turf wall where he had frozen his balls off for the emperor for more than ten years. He felt the neckerchief drying on his skin. Up there a wet bit of cloth might have turned to ice. He had wanted retirement in a warm climate. His creaky old joints demanded it. And here it was, all he could have wished for; a good comrade for company and a business to keep the mind occupied. So why was he so ill at ease, he wondered?

"Snakes," he said aloud.

His horse turned and looked at him.

"Those two know far more about Priscus' wine than honest men should. I'm going for a walk. You be good," he told her.

He tied her to the watering post, gave her a pat and meandered his way past the bread and cheese sellers, the herbalists, the beekeepers, his wine competitors who nodded to him in perfectly amicable terms. Whoever had taken the wine, his gut instinct said it was not one of them. Chewing on a gifted piece of cheese he arrived at the viewing area where Gramalcus chained his stock for inspection. Twelve thick posts were set in a row in front of the iron cages. Water buckets were spaced between the posts. One had been overturned and the puddle stained the earth. A solitary man sat hunched in irons with his head buried in his knees. Two red weals running over his head and shoulders marked the strikes of the lash. The man was babbling to himself. Hanno did not understand what he was saying. Gramalcus appeared at his side faster than a bolt from a scorpion.

"Buying today, are we? Not this one I would suggest. Unreliable for your purposes. Speaks no Latin. Understands the whip better," he commented.

Hanno screwed his face up at the split water. To be allowed to drink clean water without asking was not something a slave would reject: not in this heat.

"He's too surly. My man took his water away."

Gramalcus performed a sweep with his boot against an invisible bucket.

"Needs to learn before I can sell him. I probably shouldn't have bought him in the first place, but you know how it is? Sometimes in amongst a batch there is a bad one. We'll get him broken and then he'll go," he snapped his fingers.

Hanno nodded.

"Gallus has asked me to thank you for the honey," he said.

Gramalcus brightened.

"Good. A terrible thing that was. Taking an injury from thieves like that."

Gramalcus scowled then posed a finger to his lips clearly considering his next words.

"Hanno Glaccus, would you care to eat with me? I was about to go inside. I would be honoured if you would join me," he offered.

"That is kind. I would be happy to," Hanno replied.

He wondered why Gramalcus did not bother enquiring about Gallus' progress. It felt like the natural follow up, especially for a soldier.

"Excellent, let me give you the tour while my cook sets something up for us. Something cold, I have ice from the Alps. Still got two barrels in the cellar left from last winter. It won't last much longer in this, even storing it underground," Gramalcus buzzed with hospitality.

Gramalcus' villa was set back from the forum on the next parallel street. As soon as he entered the fountained atrium, Hanno felt the heat fall off his face like a sickness leaving after a hot night of fevered sweating. He lingered by the pool absorbing the cool air, feeling the sweat on his skin drying. He resisted the temptation to wash his neckerchief once more in Gramalcus' fountain. The villa had a cheerful bustle about it that was altogether unlike the estate. He questioned the thought, found he was getting irritated by the comparison and pushed it away. Gramalcus waited, oblivious to his inner envy. The layout was like a trip to Rome herself. Painted plaster on the walls, good furniture, decorous statues. Gramalcus paused at the door of a side room.

“My souvenirs, a modest collection,” he brightened, sweeping his hand for Hanno to enter.

It was Gramalcus’ private den with a writing table and all the comforts. One wall was dedicated to his time in the legions. There was a Parthian bow on the wall. The slave trader caught his interested look.

“Did you ever get the chance to use one of these, Gramalcus?” Hanno feigned.

Gramalcus followed his eyes, took it from the wall and handed it to him.

“Well that you ask, it’s lovely weapon, I take it down and fire shots at a target every now and again. Keeps me in shape. No, I never used one in the legion. I was strictly a pilum, gladius and scutum man. Gallus knows all about it. You should ask him. That was before he ascended to greatness,” Gramalcus teased.

“No, I never fired one either. Always left it to my auxiliaries. It’s not like a legion bow,” Hanno fenced.

Gramalcus was a little too self-deprecating. Nothing pissed Gallus off more than a soldier who could not deliver the bread and olives.

“No indeed. This a much more powerful beast, harder to make, but what results,” Gramalcus enthused.

“Heavier string too, I should imagine?” Hanno played.

“Here, let me show you. I have one here abouts,” Gramalcus fussed around in the drawer of a cabinet, “ah yes, one like this.”

He put a coiled bowstring into Hanno’s palm. It was pristine, untouched by weather or grubbed by sweated fingers. It lay in his palm like a snake. The snake that stuck a fang into Gallus?

“I have a nice sword from the Egypt queen’s army. Dates from Marcus Antonius and Cleopatra’s desert campaign in the last days after Actium, if you can believe it. That's what they told me and by the price they charged me for it, it must be true, let me tell you. It's supposed to be from one of her Royal Guard."

Gramalcus pulled a curved sword off the wall for him to inspect. He exchanged bowstring for sword, holding it hilt up and blade down in his fingers, examining it while his mind raced. There was a discreet cough at the door.

"The food is ready master," a servant announced.

"I have some Falernian I bought from Priscus while he was still with us. Shall we have it to venerate Bacchus and dear old Priscus? I think it would be proper. A salute. It'll give you an idea of the quality you are trying to follow."

It was the first direct barb the slave dealer had fired. Hanno felt a sudden relaxing of all his tension. He had found the enemy. He knew how it was armed. It now required defeating. It was a purely military problem.

*

"You think it's possible Gramalcus had a hand in stealing the wine Hanno? You think he had a hand in this?" Gallus said.

He touched the wound in his groin. Hanno lifted his brows and did not reply. Gallus considered the unpalatable idea that a man he marked down for a friend could have, would have, conspired to murder him. He spat his distaste onto the grass.

"You think he still has some of our wine?"

Hanno rubbed his face and the callus under his chin.

"Think about it, Gallus. He has waggons going all over the country dealing in slaves. He is close with the procurator who has sat here and told us to our faces how much he wanted to buy this place from Priscus' wife. They have enough money and resources to hire mercenaries to do the dirty work, though Durus Decimus has enough of his own men, come to that. They hear you are on your way, the bent wine master tells them that bit of information. They ride up here, destroy what they cannot carry off and silence the old girl to put an end to that. Somewhere in Argentomagus I bet there is an underground vault full of Falernian belonging to us, and as for the arrow. I have no idea whether he was involved or not," he said.

"If it is as you say, Hanno, then the Falernian is long gone, drunk, sold or distributed across the province. Balls of Dis, it could be selling right this moment in Rome itself. There will be none of it left to get back. What can we do? Challenge every citizen in Argentomagus who happens to have a few full flasks and amphorae in their cellars? Let it go Hanno. Priscus' wine is lost. We must begin again," Gallus counselled.

"And the arrow in your groin, Gallus, do we let that go too?" Hanno spat back.

He was angry and overtaken by Gallus' apparent surrender to the Fates that nothing could be done.

"Some bastard creeps up in the night and just because you and the dog hear him, fires off arrows at you. Tries to murder you, Gallus," he snapped.

Gallus shook his head.

"I don't know much about making the stuff, Gallus, but I know it takes years to get Falernian aged up to standard," Hanno continued.

"My friend, look at us. You and I do not have the luxury of time. Velio might have, but you and me? We have marched down too many roads. The gates of Elysium are always closer than we think," he spat.

He made the sign and shrugged off his uncomfortable truths.

Gallus grinned at him from across the table.

"Speak for yourself, centurion. I intend to go on forever," he grinned, and hefted his staff like a pilum.

"Hanno, we just have to make a decent posca to see us through the first year. With a bit of goodwill, we can sell enough to cover our costs. We keep Durus Decimus at bay for a couple of harvests and we will be home and dry. Besides Velio should be on his way by now with Voccia. His time must be up by now. He is not going to take defeat lightly," he soothed.

"So, we do nothing?" Hanno brogued.

Gallus turned his face to the hot sun and closed his eyes.

"I don't think we should tell him about my arrow. It will only get him stirred up. The lads have got that old scorpion working again. I told you it was repairable," he said.

Hanno waited.

"The first forum-dancer that tries to steal any more wine is going to get nailed with a scorpion bolt. Let's see how Durus Decimus fancies that,"Gallus said.

He turned his face back and stared hard at Hanno.

"You really think it was Gramalcus who fired this arrow?"

He touched his groin again.

"How you ever managed to pinch a scorpion beats me," Hanno sidestepped the question and marvelled.

"Old tradition amongst those in the know. The outgoing hastiliarius gets to wander through the weapons store on the day he leaves and provided he does not take the piss, may take few mementos, if he wants to," Gallus explained.

He let the unanswered question pass.

"Well, money can make enemies out of friends. I would bet that you turning up here after all these years made Gramalcus; bathwater go cold," Hanno said.

"Then, how are we going to finish this, Hanno? We've sacrificed the bull. We've given Priscus' wife a proper burial. I mean this cannot go on. One way or another we must deal with Durus and Gramalcus and put an end to it. This is Gaul, not Britannia. We are supposed to be at peace here. We can't be watching our backs every minute of the day," Gallus complained.

Hanno nodded and a cold question came to mind. He lifted a finger to catch Gallus' attention.

"How did Priscus manage to keep the wolves from his door. I mean did he have armed guards permanently on watch every night? His barns and warehouse look no sturdier than any other I've seen in Argentomagus," he posited.

"I don't know Hanno. I really don't know," Gallus sighed, frustrated.

"One more thing, Gallus. You, Priscus and Gramalcus all served in the Second legion at the same time. You knew Priscus and Gramalcus, so they must have known each other as well, yes?"

Gallus sent him a wary nod. He leaned across the table.

"Have you considered Gramalcus might have been settling old scores.?That he was jealous? I mean, look around you Gallus."

He opened his arms reinforcing the point.

"His wife said Priscus died in his bed, Hanno. Gramalcus did not kill Priscus," Gallus said.

Hanno sat back, "perhaps not but that does not mean he did not try to kill you."

"Gramalcus and I have no scores to settle. He's sold us good slaves. He sold us the three auxiliaries if it comes to that. Why would he make us stronger if he wanted revenge? It makes no sense to me. Let it lie Hanno. No good will come of it and I'm in no fit state to do much about it, even if I wanted to," Gallus replied.

*

Gallus' calm acceptance that the precious hoard of old wines was lost rankled Hanno's sense of justice. The Parthian bow so brazenly displayed on Gramalcus' wall troubled him. The more he thought about it, the more it felt like it was put there to be seen by him. A deliberate taunt? There was no way of proving it had been used in the attack on Gallus, and there were plenty of retired soldiers in the area and likely plenty of old army bows kicking about to boot. He decided to go and beard Durus in his office. It had been months since they reported the pillage of the estate and Durus had hardly come near them since.

It was late afternoon. Gallus limped off to rest inside, waving away Nahan's dutiful offer of support. The estate was in one of its quiet hours, the overseers had a little time to themselves. Hanno told them where he was going and let a slave saddle his horse for him. He waved goodbye and walked the mare down the estate road. He decided to take a stand with Durus. He mounted up when he reached the road into town.

Jasmine was flowering on the roadside and the scent was sweet. He savoured it. The pretty river running to the south of

Argentomagus came into sight. A part of the town's natural defences. The road went down into the western valley outside the town, through the defensive walls and climbed up the hill to the plateau. He reached the forum, dismounted and secured his horse outside the civic building. The sentry had not been dismissed for the day so Durus must still be working. He walked up the steps to the door. Today it was an auxiliary on duty not a legion regular.

*'Durus must rotate his guards,'* he mused.

The sentry managed a slovenly stiffening of his spine. Hanno gave him his old stare. The man stiffened up a bit more. Hanno waited. The soldier's face began turning red. He saluted Hanno.

"Good. I was beginning to wonder if you had forgotten how to do it. I can put in a word for you if you fancy a spell on one of the walls in Britannia. I still have contacts in the Twentieth legion you know. You'll soon get the hang of saluting again up there, my lad," he hissed.

"Sorry, sir," the sentry replied, the redness fading to ashen.

Inside the Bituriges clerk intercepted him from behind his desk, like an advance guard.

"Is the procurator in?" he asked.

The Bituriges shook his head.

"Has he left for the day?"

The clerk gave him a 'hmmmff', exhaling through his nose which might have meant anything.

"I'll wait in his office then, shall I?" Hanno breezed.

He pushed open the procurator's door and sat down in the visitor's chair in front of the main desk. The clerk followed him.

"Perhaps I can help you sir?" he said.

*'Enough of this,'* Hanno fumed.

"Well, I really came to find out where the old wines that Priscus must have had in his warehouse went to. Who took them, that kind of thing? Where they are now? Who has them? How much silver they want to return them to my partner and I."

Hanno tried to keep his voice conversational, denying his instinct to bark orders at the clerk and send him chasing round the cupboards to find where Durus was hiding.

The auxiliary sentry came to the door. The haphazard, gormless look was now a memory. Instead, he looked transformed: every inch a killer. Hanno realised he might have underestimated the man and he was now outnumbered by two much younger and fitter men, one of whom was armoured and wearing a sword. His own pugio was worse than useless against him.

"Is everything? the guard asked.

The Bituriges took control.

"Close the door. You know what the procurator ordered if they came back poking about, looking for answers," the Bituriges said.

He pulled out a long bladed hunting knife. The soldier blocked the door. Hanno got up and backed away to the far wall, searching for a weapon other than his own pugio. The procurator's chair was too heavy to lift as a makeshift buckler. The Bituriges came close on his undefended side. The play was clear, the clerk was going to draw his attention and open him up to the soldier's sword. It came rasping out of the scabbard as he focussed on the moustached clerk. The guard was holding back, uncertain of his next move. He hoped the lad was unwilling to murder a former officer. Hanno went for the Bituriges while he had the chance. The clerk evaded his thrust and counter thrust back at him. Hanno swirled up the hem of his cloak around his forearm in a heavy wrap and tried to swat the knife hand aside. A sharp blast of pain hit him. He rolled his arm taking control of the clerk's wrist in the swaddles of his cloak and sunk his own dagger into his side. The Bituriges gasped and fell back. He stuck him again for good measure and the clerk fell. At the same instant he felt the jolt from the sword point in his side. The blade struck a rib and withdrew. The auxiliary's face wore an uncertain fear as if he was stabbing at a wild boar in the forest, terrified to get too close to the tusks. It was a light thrust, a weak attempt. Hanno knew it was uncommitted. He was striking an officer; he knew the penalty. There might be a chance to talk his way out of this. He whirled his pugio, puny in comparison, towards the soldier and retreated. The clerk moaned loudly on the floor. He was not dead yet.

"What passes here?" a voice roared.

The words were deafening in the small room. Durus Decimus had a mask of outrage painted on his fat, bearded face. The clerk hauled himself to his feet, his hands red with his own blood and looked to his master. Durus stood aghast at the carnage in his office. He put his hand on the chain mailed shoulder of the auxiliary.

"Isn't this what you wanted sir?" the clerk replied, "it's what you said you wished to happen," he said.

Durus stared at him. Words came tumbling back at him from the past. The first encounter with Gallus Tiomaris and Hanno Glaccus in this office. The bad tempered exchanges over the pillaged estate. His angry fulminations when they left. But that was before Gramalcus tried to hasten things along too much. And before he reconciled himself to waiting for time to take its inevitable toll and release the estate to him.

*'But I did not tell you about the last part. After we paid Gramalcus' two fools to keep silent. My change of plan, I never explained that further violence could not happen without raising suspicion. That Gramalcus had shot his bolt, my bolt too. And now you've done this. My mistake, mea culpa, you did this because you believed I wanted it so,'* he castigated himself.

The Bituriges could not be expected to read his mind, and the guard was not expected to think. He looked at Hanno Glaccus clutching his side. His clerk was in a worse state. The old soldier had won the first bout. The Bituriges was seething daggers of hatred at Hanno Glaccus, though he looked less than able to turn his hatred into actions. Durus Decimus recalculated the odds. It was now all or nothing. Hanno Glaccus could not be allowed to walk out of here. His men required reassurance. He gave his clerk a brief smile.

"Ah, I see. This is unexpected. Not how I imagined it at all. Well, I think you know what to do. And when it's done take him out and leave him on the road. Make it look like a robbery," he ordered.

He patted the guard's shoulder as if he was a dog.

"Gladiators, you may commence," he smirked, standing back.

The guard's façade of sloppy saluting gave way to something a good deal more concentrated. Hanno backed away from the sword and raised his cloak-wrapped arm in futile defence.

*

Torchlights were flickering on the steps to Jupiter's Temple. Hanno saw the steps to the mightiest of gods and knew he had been abandoned. The only other lights were the ones outside the procurator's office and the ones beneath the statue of the emperor. The forum was in shadows and deserted. He had lost all sense of time. Durus Decimus had left after the short and one-sided fight.

The soldier held him upright in a vice grip. He heard them speaking as if he was not there.

"Put him on his horse," the Bituriges hissed.

Hanno groaned at the pain as he was leaned against the horse and heaved up. He slumped forward. Hands thrust the reins into his own.

"Lead him back. If anyone stops you, say he's drunk. Finish him off on the road. Remember what the procurator said. Make it look like a robbery. Then go home and be here tomorrow as normal. Clean uniform, no blood. Nothing happened here. Right? And lose the horse. Don't bring it back, don't keep it for yourself," the Bituriges ordered.

"Worry about yourself. You'd best get those wounds dressed," the guard retorted.

There was a tug on the bridle and the mare began moving. The darkened forum gave way to darker streets. Argentomagus was in bed. The mare clip-clopped at the soldier's side. A fox ran across their path and was swallowed up in a conspiring alleyway. Hanno tasted blood in his mouth as he fought scalding fires of pain. He could feel himself bleeding, and getting weaker, but his assassin kept the horse moving. Every roll of its hindquarters dug into him. He clung to the reins, praying he was strong enough to make it back to the estate. The soldier hummed a little tune as he led the horse by her bridle.

"How much?" Hanno croaked, "stop the horse and let me rest. Just tell me how much you want," he asked.

The words were no sooner out of his mouth than the awful reality dawned. His gut clenched. Cold certainty put fingers on his soul. He was not going back to the estate. That was not what this man had planned for him at all. The question stayed unanswered. The soldier did not even deign to turn his head or halt his tune. They passed through the western defensive wall without a word of challenge and out into the countryside. He felt himself swooning, drifting in and out of consciousness. Fire arrows came hurtling out of north. He looked up and saw a tiny tip of flames dropping down destined only for him. The Veniconii were coming out of the mist and murk, right at the gates and walls of Velunia. This time it was different. There was something in the air itself. A feeling that this time the walls would be stormed, a dreadful certainty Mars Ultor was occupied elsewhere in the empire, hearing and answering the prayers and pleas of other soldiers. The scorpions were firing. His brave boys were falling all around. He was the last one, the last Roman on the whole wall, the barbarians had won, the fire arrow was on its way, still falling down on him, he understood it was for him alone, the horrid death he had always feared, and with a jolt he was back, sweat on his face, the fire roaring in his side, his mare walking by the soldier's side. A large area of trees made a screen from the river. The soldier looked at them and drew the horse to a standstill. He pulled Hanno from the saddle. Hanno hit the earth on his shoulder and rolled onto his back. For a moment they looked at each other in silence. He felt his breath returning after the hard fall to the ground.

"Hanno Drusus Glaccus Ticinus. Centurion of the Twentieth legion, the Valeria Victrix. Defenders of Britannia. And I commanded the First cohort, the First cohort, do you hear me?" he wheezed.

"I deserve that on my stone," he added.

The auxiliary shook his head and checked the road in both directions for witnesses. The night was black.

"Do that for me," he asked, "and you can have the money in my pouch," he bargained.

"Centurion, I'll have that when I'm ready. And besides, centurion I don't care," the soldier responded.

"You, a soldier, will leave me out here to die like a barbarian dog?" he tried to snarl, but he was getting weaker.

The words had no bite.

"I am Hanno Drusus Glaccus Ticinus, centurion of the Twentieth legion," he repeated.

"And I told you. I don't care. And you thought you could threaten me with a posting to Britannia? You should have stayed there. You are not welcome here. The bloody Twentieth legion. Too full of yourselves, I say," the soldier replied.

He drew his sword and stood over Hanno tapping the point on the palm of his hand. He spat to the side.

"But you're wrong centurion. I'm not leaving you out here to die. Who knows, perhaps one of the gods will come to your rescue: Mithras or perhaps the Holy Mothers? As you well know centurion, orders are orders," he said, preparing the single plunge to end it.

Hanno steeled himself to be calm. This was not how he wanted it.

"You are no soldier," he spat the only defiance that mattered to him.

Gallus was on his own now.

*

The overseer saw a couple of hawks circling. He stopped what he was doing and enjoyed their early morning, stiff winged pirouetting, flying together as only a mated pair could do so faultlessly: so harmoniously. He could see their heads scanning the ground, circling and circling over some poor beast lying on the ground or hiding in the grass from their terrible gaze. A voice called out his name and he took his eyes from the lovely dance in the high air over the fields towards Argentomagus. The wine was due for decanting from the dolia. It was not a day to dawdle. The wine master was revealing his tyrant side.

## Chapter Fifty.

## Argentomagus.

The wine master had the slaves at it all day. By the time the sun began descending there was a huge stack of filled amphorae in the warehouse. New wine in new clay vessels. What better sign of a fresh beginning? Gallus felt his happiness bubbling inside as his dream took a huge step forward. The strife endured to get to this point was worth it. His harvest was captured in clay. The overseer as busy with pen and ink, walking past him, around him, smiling a polite acknowledgement when he had to move out of the way. The most trustworthy of the slaves had been delegated the key task of arranging the amphorae in order of size and value. Only one vessel had been dropped. He was ready to offer a mild rebuke. The overseer's heads turned to the sound of breaking clay and the frightened gasp of the slave. The man cowered back lifting his hands up, seeking mercy.

"Be assured, that will be the only offering we make today," the winemaker broke in.

Gallus shook his head at the overseers. The slave scrabbled the broken pottery together. Everyone was nervous. They all understood the importance. His instinct to place the largest flasks of the infant Falernian furthest from the doors, met with the wine maker's approval. A new cellar would be needed. The question was, where to put it? Amphorae of posca were sitting in the middle, and the lora closest to the door. Each with the estate's new emblem emblazoned on them. Already the warehouse that had stood empty for so many months was assuming a business-like feeling. Laid into the floor were oak doors concealing the underground cavern where

Priscus had kept the Falernian as cold as he could for years to mature and develop. It seemed rather too obvious a place to keep it. He had a notion to store it under the floor in the villa. All in all, they had made a sizeable dent in the task. The winemaker had said four days to complete all the decanting from the dolia.

Hanno had not returned. He should be enjoying these fruits of the slaves' labours. The work was slowing as the sun began setting. Everyone was getting tired. He limped outside and left them to it. The head overseer watched him leave, conferred with the wine master and together they called a halt and sent the slaves to the trestles to be fed.

Gallus sat at the table in the garden and contemplated the day and all that had been achieved. Birds were settling in the trees. The vine bushes paraded in their military precision across the fields. All was well, Bacchus was generous with his mercy to old soldiers with no experience of wine making. Another sacrifice would not go amiss. He heaved a deep breath of contentment. The wound was tightening up and feeling better. He would sleep well tonight. The wine master came and sat down beside him.

"So, three more days?" he opened.

The Gaul smiled,"three careful days with as little spillage as possible and the job is done, he paused, "you can pay me and enjoy the profits."

"I would like you to stay on until we are ready to sell. A week or two. Just until it reaches condition," Gallus asked.

The wine master bowed, "I am happy to," he answered.

Together they enjoyed the warm air. The wine master made a few polite remarks, but Gallus saw his mind was elsewhere: tomorrow's task probably. He let the Gaul leave. It was all very pleasant and quite unnatural. There were no stone walls with evening guards. No trumpet calls. No rough crude laughter from off duty men heading to the vicus and the girls in the town. Soldiers, wine and girls; this was going to work, he was certain of it. Hanno must have found good company in Argentomagus. Female company perhaps: he smiled at the thought.

*'Do him good,'* he decided.

It would be good when Velio and Voccia got here too. A few wives around the estate would make it more homely: some children perhaps? If Nahan, Eudo and Bodusio wanted to become a real part of the estate, that was possible too. After a fraught start this little campaign to brew wine was making progress. He sat back and ate food brought out to him, sipping unwatered wine to help him sleep and listening to the low tired voices of the slaves as they headed to their quarters.

The next morning the winemaster ordered the slaves be given an early bowl of porridge and had them working as soon as the bowls were empty. Gallus rose at the noise of voices in the kitchen. Trajan padded out of there and came to his side, beating his villainous tail from side to side. He scratched the dog's ears with one hand while he knocked on the door of Hanno's room with the other. The bed was empty. That old dog had stayed in Argentomagus. His love life must be looking up.

Bodusio, Nahan and Eudo were busy in the warehouse. He and Trajan watched the work before the dog wandered off leaving him to return to the atrium to eat alone. His wound was feeling better this morning. He laid the crutch aside and decided to try a day without it. When Hanno returned, he would tell him the three Germans were going to be the permanent guards for the warehouse. They, and a scorpion, plus Trajan's ears, were the best possible defence against thieves. It was almost like soldiering. Once word got out that ex auxiliaries were on the payroll, no one but a fool would try their hand at night.

The sound of horses caught his attention. Horses and a cart. He screwed his eyes up. It was the decurion from the Eighth with a small escort. The horses turned in at the estate road and came toward him, changing from a travelling trot to a more relaxed walk. The sound of turning wheels changed too, from near silent to an even, regular, creak he decided would annoy the ears if left neglected: that axle needed greasing. Someone was going to get a reprimand for slacking. Trajan began barking. An overseer called out to quieten him.

"Salve citizen Gallus Tiomaris. I bring you ill news," the decurion said.

At the back of the escort Gallus saw the Hanno's mare tied to the cart. He looked at the decurion. An empty saddle and a cart. There was only one explanation. He rose from his chair as the officer dismounted. At the rear of the cart the decurion pulled a cloak aside but from the clear outline under it he already knew with horrible certainty what it meant. Hanno's body was covered in his blood. At least they had not bundled him on to it and left his feet and ankles hanging over the side.

"The centurion was murdered on the road, we think. It's been made to look like a robbery except whoever did this left his horse, so not much of a robbery," the decurion intoned.

Gallus looked at Hanno's white face. His eyes were open. Whomsoever did it had denied Hanno that small decency. He froze, dumbstruck. Hanno's face had changed. It was him, but he was wax pallored. The flesh and bone shell of the man. There was blood all over him.

"One of my men was bringing despatches in from the north this morning and spotted him first thing lying beneath some trees. He recognised the centurion from our last visit here. I did warn you that you had bought enemies when you bought the estate."

Gallus touched the bloody centre of Hanno's stained and punctured tunic.

"Two sword thrusts, and three smaller knife wounds, all of them nasty."

The decurion made it sound like a military report. Gallus supposed it was, in a way.

"They did a thorough job on him. I only hope he gave as good as he got before he went down. The horse is also covered in his blood. They must have made him ride it, or they used it to carry him," the decurion surmised.

"As good as he got?" Gallus repeated. '

*'Yes, Hanno always did that,'* he saluted inside.

"Where did you find him exactly?" he asked, struggling to believe it.

"And you said 'they,'" he queried.

"Perhaps we should sit down, sir. I don't think this was a one on one."

Gallus pulled himself together. Staring at the body of his friend and partner, he should feel guilty, he should feel angry; he stepped back from the cart, why was he feeling nothing?

*'Because he's just another dead soldier now, that's why. Hanno, Hanno, what a useless bloody way to die, my friend'* he mourned, *'I should have made you take Bodusio or Eudo with you. It's over now, brother.'*

His wound throbbed and he rubbed it. The estate yard had gone quiet. Bodusio came forward with a look of concern on his face. The Mattiaci seemed to read what had happened.

"Let us take care of the centurion, sir," he said.

Gallus looked at him. Nahan and Eudo were close at hand.

"Build a pyre, he deserves that. We'll give him a soldier's funeral," he replied.

"My men and I would like to stay and help," the decurion said.

Gallus made himself smile.

"They told me the Eighth were good soldiers. He would have appreciated the gesture, always had time for the cavalry when he was on the wall."

He started limping back to the villa and did not look back. The emotion he had been searching for found him. The yard stood silent as he passed by.

*

Durus Decimus heard the full story from his wounded Bituriges. Pain was not a good salve for injustice, and he had been unjust in not fully confiding his change of strategy. Pain was making the Bituriges impolite, which was really not like his clerk. Had he not warned Gramalcus' hired men to desist from further attacks on the estate, and had they not listened? Silver coin had helped them hear his message. More than they deserved for failing their task, but secrecy was valuable. Hanno Glaccus and Gallus Tiomaris were not in the first flush of youth. Time was his ally. He could outlive them and get the estate. Neither man had children to pass it on to. What kind of stupidity drew attention by acts of violence? The Eighth legion commander would get to hear of the death of an ex-comrade, a centurion comrade to boot, and Fortuna would turn her shoulder to him. It was clear that the arrival yesterday of Glaccus had spooked both the Bituriges and his favoured guard. He could imagine the gruff centurion-like questions, the domineering, hard-nosed expression brooking no deceit. How easy to remember he had wished the two old soldiers would meet an untimely end. His clerk finished what he had to say.

"Get Silanus in here," he said.

His clerk went to the door and called the guard. Silanus put his shield and spear against the wall at the door and saluted. He thought Silanus looked nervous. He cleared his throat and pulled two small leather bags from the drawer in his desk and held one in each hand.

"This never happened. You will never speak of it to me again, or anyone else. Do you understand?" he said.

It was more money than either of them might see in a year. A little wisdom was in order.

"And I suggest neither of you spend that money in Argentomagus. Keep it safe, that's my advice," he purred.

Their faces changed. Silanus' nervy blinking ceased.

"And when you go drinking in the taverns here, remember I have ears listening, so choose your stories carefully. If anyone asks, say you have no interest in what goes on at old man Priscus' estate, or the people who work there."

Silanus saluted, his Bituriges bowed, and they both left. Decimus picked up the day's list of routine pleadings and appointments. Food at Gramalcus' villa at midday appeared to be the highlight. Silanus was the more likely of the two to blurt it out to the wrong person. That would need mopping in due course. His Bituriges seemed to 'get it' though.

*'Is this the last of it,'* he wondered, *'it's just Gallus Tiomaris on his own. I need to be patient and let the gods take him. Patience Durus,'* he told himself.

There were amphorae cached in various cellars. They should get shifted to a safer site. It would help to tidy things up. He pursed his lips and ran his tongue over the rough edge of the tooth that regularly cut his tongue at night. The old soldier's death gave him no pleasure, but it served a purpose. Between Gramalcus' incompetent archers, Silanus and his clerk, they had successfully killed one and given the other much pause for reconsideration. It was not all bad even if he had not wanted it done in such fashion. He looked at the washed floor where the man had been struck down yesterday, and his superstition got the better of him. He was going to step over that spot every day for as long as he chose to use this room. A small prayer would do no harm. Setting aside his paperwork he closed and bolted his door, lit an offering lamp and knelt at the small altar by the window, trying to be penitent.

## Chapter Fifty-one.

### Velio's encampment.

Velio climbed a little way up the slope to the rear of his men. The Brigantes were holding back, a pause was lengthening into a hiatus. What was making them hesitate? He did not know but was grateful for the opportunity to regroup his men and tend to the ditch and the upcast mound. His officers shared that view.

"Don't just stand there you idle bastards, get out there and recover those pila," Plautius bawled below him.

A dozen legionaries broke ranks and foraged among the bodies and wounded. They brought armfuls of undamaged javelins back. Plautius send more men out. He watched his tesserarius working. If they survived this, Plautius was going to have another phalera to decorate his uniform.

"Centurion, if we advance to the edge of the water we can use it to our advantage. Stop them getting a foothold," he said.

"Carry on," Velio replied, then a thought occurred to him.

"And get setting the dolabra into the stream, like lilia, see if they will hold in the current," he shouted.

Heads turned at the idea. Grins told him he had found a plan. The digging tools had a T shaped combination spiked and a flattened spade end. If the wooden shafts held in the gravel against the current the spikes would make unpleasant surprises to a charging, barelegged warrior or two. Even set into the water flooded grass, charging men might not notice them.

"Plautius, recover all damaged pila as well. Put them in the water to the front of us," he called.

"Use the bodies in the barricade," he added.

They set to it. He turned his attention back to the Brigantes and the valley. The rain was easing but the mist and cloud thickening. It was vile stuff. The enemy had temporarily turned from the fight and a huge gathering was taking place.

"It's the final push, Velio," he said aloud and began slithering down the treacherously wet slope.

He signalled Liscus over.

"Liscus, I fear they have reinforcements. Orann has gone to Delmatarum garrison to summon Morenus. We have to hold on until they get here. When he arrives we can trap this lot and finish them. It's the way to end the attacks on the mines," he said with all the confidence he could muster.

Liscus wiped his dripping face with the hem of his cloak.

"Then let us hope Orann does not get himself lost, sir," he replied.

Velio shared his apprehension.

*

Orann struggled through the boggy ground. Curtains of grey rain came slanting right into his face. He gritted his teeth and pushed on, scrambling up the next rise. Finally, he crossed the last ridge. The Delmatarum garrison lay on its strange shelf of ground. He could see men moving within its walls. This valley was the severest. He sat down to rest. On the high parade ground men were drilling. Did they not know the centurion and his men were trapped and fighting to stay alive? He patted his pocket for the token Velio had given him. He heaved himself up and set off down the final slope, knowing that every step downwards was repaid with a step upwards on the far side. He gathered himself, dug his spear haft into the grass and pushed forward. An hour later three men guarding the Decumana gate saw him rise up from the dip in the ground, like a wraith born from the rain.

"Amicus, Romani," he called out, "amicus, amicus."

His greeting got him to the gate, but the oak timbers remained shut. The guards peered down at him from the gantry. He pulled out the seniority disc Velio had given him and waved it, trying to remember the exact words.

"Greetings to Centurion Morenus, Velio Pinneius has the Brigantes spears in front of him. He needs the boar. I am to guide you," he recited.

He held out the decorated phalera disc from Velio's armour once more. The guards looked at him.

"Wait there," one of them barked down at him.

Titus heard Arco was requesting his presence at the Decumana gate, put the two pieces of information together and decided it was not something that needed an optio's attention.

"Ask one of the tesserarii to attend," he grumbled.

His cloak was not dry from his last routine inspection of the ramparts including a loop down to the bathhouse. The fire in the barrack block was emitting precious little warmth through the damp air.

"Beggin' your permission to speak sir, but they are all busy," his orderly replied without thinking and blanched at the sight of Titus' venomous expression.

"Weather is getting worse too, sir," he blundered.

"My gratitude for the report," Titus grunted, "though I was aware," he added for good measure.

With every passing day it was increasingly obvious Jupiter had given the Tempestates his blessing to bring commotion to this miserable province, whenever their fancy struck.

"I'll get your other cloak for you sir," his orderly bumbled.

"Leave it," he barked, "I do not need two wet cloaks."

His man unhooked the heavy woollen garment from the peg. He could tell from the way it was hanging that it was still sodden.

It's not too bad now sir," the orderly lied.

A bright smile of white deceit flashed. He took it from him, felt the dampness, sucked his teeth and fastened it around his neck while his servant flustered like a tradesman attempting a sale to an impossibly picky customer. The lank wool touched his calves and stuck. He flicked it away, picked up his helmet and left.

"I want to eat when I get back," he called over his shoulder, "something hot."

He headed around the back of the principia. The gravel packed paths were pooled with water. He splashed through the flood. It was unavoidable and the grass was equally wet. Up at the Decumana, Arco was attending a bedraggled native. The warrior's spear had been taken from him and one of the guards was fingering twists of trophy hair at the head of the shaft. The hair was too long to have come from a Roman soldier, but the auxiliary tended to keep their hair uncut. The mood seemed a little tense. The native looked up as he got closer and flashed a worried smile at him. The guard straightened to attention.

"Orann," Titus exclaimed, "where is the centurion?"

Arco and the guard performed a rapid reset. Orann's spear was handed back. Orann thrust out the phalera.

"Greetings to Centurion Morenus, Velio Pinneius has the Brigantes spears in front of him. He needs the boar. I am to guide you," he repeated.

"Come with me,"Titus said.

He glanced at Arco. Arco saluted so fast he knew he had been summoned in the nick of time.

"Where is Centurion Morenus?" he asked Arco.

"Parade ground sir," Arco answered.

Titus swept Orann up with a comforting arm around his shoulder and made for the Sinistra gate. Up on the parade ground Morenus took a single moment to examine Velio's disc.

"You can guide me there, now?" he asked Orann.

Orann nodded.

"The centurion sent me to bring you. You must come now. The Brigantes are already attacking him," he begged.

Morenus barked orders. The drilling came to a halt. The centuries reformed. He turned to Titus.

"Get your weapons optio, you are coming with me. Lead the men Orann, I will follow once I have spoken to the camp commander."

His senior centurions stood waiting. Together with Morenus they dripped water like wet crows.

"Velio Pinneius has drawn them out. We march to support him. You will follow this Votadini, he is Velio's man. The Second century will remain here in place of the auxiliary. I'm not leaving the fort unprotected." he ordered.

"We must hurry, Master," Orann pleaded.

"Lead on," Morenus told the First century commander, "I will bring the Uiliocenon ala."

"Morenus?" the centurion of the Second century ventured.

He lifted his palm in pacification.

"I'm taking the auxiliaries. Whatever has been going on up here, Civius and his men can do a bit of proper soldiering. With any luck the Brigantes will solve the problem, one way or another. No arguments Gaius, someone has to stay. This time it is you," he ordered.

Gaius assented with a half salute and turned to order his men.

"Bad country for horses master," Orann said, unasked.

"I think I will decide that, lad," Morenus replied.

"I had to leave my horse," Orann reposted.

The other centurions made faces.

"The ala would be useful but if we can't get them over the hills they will slow us," the centurion of the Third offered.

"Get moving. I will bring them as far as I can. We may need them if the enemy scatters. Civius and his auxiliary will bear the brunt. They fight on foot like the rest of us," Morenus said.

"As you command," the centurions took the order.

The debate was over.

Orann led them, agile as a goat, down the edge of the rear valley where Scribono and Junius Cita had tried to make their escape. He stopped at the foot of the slope while the legionaries slithered and swore their way down in their heavy boots. Morenus held them there until the Delmatarum with Civius and his vexillation standards pushed past them, and his centuries had reassembled in order. Civius had disdained his horse. His face was taut as he marched past Morenus. Orann hoped they were going to march faster than they climbed. He pointed to the north.

"Balls of Dis," Morenus confided to his optio, "he wants us to go up and over the rough. We can't carry shields and pila up this. I thought he was taking us down the valley, not over the top of it. That settles it. We need to find another way. The ala is coming with us. We'll need them to scout ahead if Velio's man came over the tops. He probably doesn't know an alternative route back."

"I'll hurry them on, sir," the optio replied.

"And call them back," he said pointing to the Delmatarum already losing cohesion on the stiff slopes.

"No point in going that way, we need lower ground," he added, "if Centurion Pinneius really has pulled them out of their hiding places this will be the best chance we have to smash their fighting men. We can end the disruption today."

"What if the whole tribe's come out sir? The legate says they have thousands of men," the optio paled.

Morenus put his hand on the younger man's shoulder.

"It's very simple. We kill them one at a time until they've had a guts full and they turn and run. Centurion Pinneius is in trouble. There is no choice about the order," he replied.

"But first we have got to get there. Get Velio's man over here. We need to get him on a horse and get a change of plan. And get me those cavalry," he added.

## Chapter Fifty-two.

## The valley.

Losatas greeted the approaching Carvetii. It was too much to hope they would have brought the standard. He scanned the ranks for sight of it. If it was not in the forefront with the chiefs and high warriors, it was not here. There were hundreds of them, the elite on their horses, the ordinary fighting men following on foot. The Carvetii war chiefs had assembled but there was no sight of the spirit pole. Their chief must have left it safe and secure in his hall. He swallowed his disappointment. His men sat on the soaking ground licking their wounds. The sons of the wolf were not going down without a fight. Their spot was well chosen. The flooding stream in front of them was proving enough of an obstacle to break up the charges. He needed bowmen to finish them off. The Carvetii drew up in a semi-circle and the arm shakes began. It seemed they had their own plans to deal with the Romans.

"Why have you not climbed around the back of them? They are sitting, waiting, right beneath the hill. Spears from the high ground will take them easily"'

A war chief criticised him in front of his men at once.

A growl of mutual antipathy greeted that opinion from behind him. The courtesies between them evaporated. His relayed message about the spirit pole must have had got through to the high chiefs and they had come out to show him they were prepared to hold it. If he wanted it, he would have to take it. He admired their pluck. Not many tribes had the belly to take him on. This was not the time for further debate. They must bend to his will and follow his tactics or there would be a reckoning once these Romans had been slaughtered. He looked back to where the Romans were waiting. They were digging at the water's edge, moving out from behind their slender defence line. Precious little good it was going to do them. He had no intention of letting them finish what they were starting. The snub rankled. He should have seen it for himself.

"Then you take the high ground. Drive them over the stream and we will meet you. Signal me when you are ready and we will attack," he clasped his fingers together in a vice.

*

Velio picked up a spare shield and weighed it for comfort. His shoulder protested, but his arm felt strong. It did not feel a good day to be without a shield. Gallus would have been barking at him if he could have seen him. The new gladius was about to be tested. In the distance it looked like the Brigantes were readying themselves and building up for another strike at his little command. He watched a group split off and begin climbing the slopes off to his right. The rest began their approach once more. This time they were hoarding their energy. They were quieter, less vociferous than earlier.

"I think there are more of them now, sir. If they get the high ground, they'll have us in bad place," Liscus prompted.

Velio went up the slope to get a better look at the situation. Liscus was correct. The Brigantes had been reinforced in significant numbers. An outflanking was clearly what they were planning.

"Liscus, you are going to drive them off before they can get in spear range. You have young legs, take fifteen men and Metius. Get up there ahead of them and stall them. I think you can tell Metius his Carvetii have arrived. Liscus, drive them off and their courage will fail. It will leave them only our front. That stream is still rising. Pray it keeps raining and Morenus is on the way. We need to set those dolabra deep and make sure they don't get washed out. Leave that to me," he said.

Liscus banged out a salute.

"As you command centurion. Metius, bring fourteen men, at the double."

Velio did a swift head count of his reduced numbers. Ribald comments followed Metius and his lads. He cursed himself for the lack of bowmen.

*'Where are you, Morenus?'* he fretted, *'for the love of the Holy Mothers of the Parade Ground, I pray you believed Orann's message.'*

The thought gave him inspiration. He stepped up on a rock.

"Listen to me men. We pray to the Holy Mothers of the Parade Ground precisely for moments like this, don't we? We train like Spartans, day after day, for moments like this, don't we? I call upon Mars Ultor to stand with us today. I ask mighty Jupiter, Thou Best and Greatest, to give us his strength. I pray to the blacksmiths and Vulcan for our swords and shields. We fight for the People and the Senate of Rome. We fight for The Boar, the mighty Twentieth, the Valeria Victrix, the best legion in all her armies. We fight for each other here and now. Your century are the best soldiers Rome has. Show these heathen dogs Rome's mercy to her enemies," he roared.

A huge answering roar greeted his words. It echoed off the hillside. A good omen, a splendid one. He stood down and began straightening his already straightened armour. Plautius risked an exchange of glances with him. There was no more pious a soldier in the century than Plautius. The tesserarius looked up at the black forbidding clouds and the torrents that refused to relent. Something must have amused him. Velio saw him smile to himself as some inner joke tickled him.

"Save you washing when we're done lads," he cackled, "won't be a blood mark on you, mark my words," Plautius promised.

"They're coming on again sir," a voice called.

Velio whirled around looking for Liscus.

"How are they getting on?" he cried to no one in particular.

"I'd like to see that little bastard Metius running after those Carvetii or whatever they are, chasin' them up and down, like a fuckin' goat," another legionary catcalled.

Velio let it go. Liscus and Metius were gaining height. The flanking movement from the enemy had paused as they saw they were going to be checked.

"You just kill the ones in front of you, lad and let Metius worry about what's up there," Plautius burred.

Losatas raised up his spear and began leading his men back to the battlefield. He harangued the Brigantes battle challenge to his warriors and they answered him, chanting it back to him, driving forwards in their wedge formation to the shallows of the flooded stream, down into it, men falling unbalanced, caught out by the sudden step down, dark soil stained water up past their waists and pressed for the far bank of the stream, surging on by weight of numbers.

"Wait for the order," Velio called out.

The dolabra were invisible in the rain and the gushing stream along with a crude tangle of twisted pila. The final twenty implements had been spaced upright in the earth randomly in front of his men. There was a dolabra available for every man in his command. He had not tried the trick before. He had never needed to try it. Plautius had the remaining serviceable pilums in the hands of his best throwers. The Brigantes chant erupted into outright noise. One way or another he knew this was the end of the affair. A verbal wall of pent-up anger and battle rage preceded them. The wedge was now somewhere close to where the near bank should be. Men started tripping over. Velio watched the disruption. It was not enough but it helped. The fallen warriors were trodden under by the mass at their backs. More of them fell. They still came on rising up from the stream. Here and there more of them tripped, victim to the sunken dolabra.

"**Pila now,**" Plautius roared.

The grey volley took them at chest and head height. The slaughter was immense, but the momentum kept them coming over the crumpling bodies. The weapons of dying men caught the legs of their kin.

"Shields up, Fourth Century," Velio bawled, "remember who you are."

The bloodied wedge smashed into the centre of his command. The line buckled backwards. He pulled his shield across the front of a Brigantes who had penetrated the line and chopped him with a short plunge into his side and followed with a downward thrust. The legionary beside him fell two steps forward with a spear in his shoulder. Velio turned to check how Liscus and Metius were faring. Up on the slope behind him a series of hand to hand individual combats had developed but he had not sent enough men to nullify the threat. Spears from warriors were beginning to rain down. Two more men fell to the unseen threat above.

"**Rear rank, form shields in testudo,**" he called.

A semi formation might be enough to give the forward-facing ranks protection. The frontal attack was testing them. It was getting serious. A spear from the hillside skittered forward off an upraised shield and took an oncoming Brigantes in the throat. A joy took his heart at that one unnoticed death.

"**Close ranks,**" he called.

Was there time to blow the whistle and rotate the front line? He took a chance and blew it. The men did it like a drill. The Brigantes looked stunned for a moment thinking the front rank was turning to run.

"Sweetly done lads," he shouted, "now make them pay. Rear rank about face, get those shields up, protect the front."

He stepped into the end of the line as one of his men fell and wafted his left-handed blade at the disorientated warrior who was already expecting glory. He winced at the impact on his weak shield arm, let the other man's shield slide away and jabbed for the throat. The gladius missed the target and slid past his neck. He dragged it back and took him on the reverse stroke, slicing into the unprotected neck. As the Brigantes fell he kicked him away. He caught the look of a warrior, better adorned than most. The man glared unmitigated hatred at him, spitting curses as he pulled his men back. The dolabra in the water were still taking legs and groins.

Plautius had men in the water to despatch them as soon as it was clear the Brigantes were retiring. He hoisted his shield to protect his face and risked another look at Liscus and Metius' separate skirmish. Up there the withdrawal had been seen and the warriors were backing away. He was pleased to see Liscus let them go rather than risk the lives of any more men.

"One more like that and we're fucked, sir, beggin' your permission to speak honestly, sir," Plautius muttered.

"Casualties tesserarius, how many?"

He ignored the advice and counted for himself as Plautius did the rounds. Liscus came bounding down the hill like a fool, sliding the bottom section on his backside as his caligae lost grip. There was not so much as a chuckle at his inelegant arrival.

"How many have you lost. Liscus?" Velio said and kept his question low.

"None, sir, some cuts, but all men still standing," Liscus reported, exultant, "I'm told they are Carvetii," he added.

"So, they have joined together," Velio said.

"I'm not convinced the Carvetii were too interested in losing men," Liscus offered.

"We're down to fifty, sir," Plautius reported, "and the optios of course."

"I want every wounded man who can stand and hold a shield back here facing up at the optio and his men. Prevent any more attacks from up there," Velio gestured, "Liscus, if they show no signs of doing it again, bring your men back down. I need every man here. They will come again from the front, it's only a matter of time. Well done lads, time for water,"he cried out.

## Chapter Fifty-three.

## The estate.

The decurion waited a polite amount time before making his move to leave. Looking about, it was clear to him the pyre for Hanno Glaccus was going to burn for hours. Gallus had dispersed the slaves. All activity ceased for the day. For a recently wounded man the old hastiliarius had taken a robust recovery. Perhaps that was what the death of a good friend did for him. Some men might crumble in self-pity, others strap on their spiritual sword and stand to their particular eagles.

He flicked a glance to the horses and the cart. His men put down their valedictory drinking cups, swallowing the last mouthfuls. He wandered to the edge of the courtyard and gazed out over the vine fields now stripped of fruit. Profusions of coloured flowers bloomed in the sun making the flinty soil a glorious sight. One that could fool the casual observer into thinking all was at peace in Jupiter's universe. He noticed three muscular slaves manoeuvring a wheeled implement from out of one of the barns. He stared at it trying to decide what agricultural task it performed. They turned it to face the distant gateway to the estate. The profile was unmistakeable. The three men fussed around it and stood back, apparently pleased with their efforts. He cleared his throat and coughed. Gallus limped, less noticeably, to his side.

"Citizen Tiomaris, I see you have a scorpion," he murmured.

Gallus held his tongue.

"Strictly speaking, citizens are not permitted to hold military weapons. Veterans may keep their reasonable sidearms with their officer's express permission. A written script should be provided in other circumstances. All legitimate spoils of war, booty, enemy possessions et cetera are exempt," he recited the regulations.

"Indeed, as you say. I was the senior hastiliarius of the legion," Gallus replied.

"I am aware of that, but a scorpion? What do you intend to do with it?" the decurion buzzed.

He feared the answer. Gallus turned and smiled at him, and he felt the genuine friendship of this old soldier.

"It's an old broken one. The lads fixed it up a bit, that is all. It'll do for frightening away the crows. I'm not fond of crows," Gallus stopped smiling.

"The main gate is within its range, I would say," the decurion replied.

"I would say so too. That is exactly what we are going to find out, once you and your men have left my friend. Too many thirsty crows here," Gallus said.

"A word of advice citizen. Just make sure it is only crows that you aim at," he retorted.

Gallus held his arm out to shake. He shook it. Gallus held his arm a fraction longer.

"My gratitude to you and you men for the courtesy to Hanno Glaccus. Bringing him back here and staying. One last favour to ask of you that he would have approved of, I am sure. Don't keep the news of my crow-killer a secret. The more crows who hear, the safer we will all be," he asked.

The decurion doubted that was true, saluted and mounted his horse. The empty cart turned in a circle, laden with gift flasks for the officers at the fort. The axle was no longer creaking.

Bodusio sat on the grass once they had the scorpion in place.

Nahan knelt down, plucking grass stems to chew. Eudo stood with his hand on the front shield of the scorpion, eyeing the departing troopers as they turned out of the gate. It was plain as the hills that from this elevation a bolt would carry to the gateway.

"Lookout, the Old General's coming," Nahan said.

They stood up as Gallus approached. Like the decurion they noticed his limp had been transformed into something more at ease with a normal gait. They saluted him. He nodded and sighted down the scorpion the way Eudo had been doing moments before.

"Within range sir," Eudo called.

Gallus grunted and turned around, chewing his bottom lip.

"If I had the man who killed Hanno Glaccus, I would tie him to that gate down there and let you lads use him for target practice. And once you had hit him with enough bolts, I would give you your freedom to work for me on the estate or leave as you choose," he mused.

"The army will never take us back. We are dishonoured men," Bodusio remarked.

"The army always needs men for the legions. You could enlist without any difficulty. It sounds to me you have given up on the army," he scoffed, "well, I have not given up on you. I am going to make you trusted slaves. You will go with me on all visits to Argentomagus. I will instruct the overseer you are permitted to leave the estate when needed."

He stepped in closer to them. Their faces were keen.

"When they killed my friend Hanno Glaccus, they changed the rules. Up until then, we were happy to let things lie, our plan was to use you three and the scorpion as a threat. We were even prepared to give you swords to fight with if looters came back again in the night. But other than that, we were not going to rock the boat. Just sell our wines and live our days here in the sun and hope the threat was never challenged. That's all gone. My marching days are over, but I want the man who killed my friend tied to that gatepost down there and used for practice. And I want you three to find him and bring him to me," he said.

## Chapter Fifty-four.

## The valley.

In a parallel valley Orann and the cavalry ala found better ground and pounded along, splashing through pools and puddles to bring the news to Morenus. Orann recognised Civius and the Delmatarum in the van, ignored them and rode on to the large cluster of cohort standards to their rear. Morenus had forsaken the privilege of his horse and was marching at the head of his century. The lead decurion of the Uiliocenon cavalry made his report. Morenus kept his gaze on Velio's man for confirmation.

"They are on the far side of this," he jabbed at the hillside, "there is a pathway to the Carvetii strongholds running there and Drapisces hall is over in that direction."

The decurion swung his arm a more south westerly direction.

"Once you make the turn you will be in the valley where the centurion is. There is no other way out except climbing up over the tops," he continued.

"Tell me once more how many men, Brigantes, I mean," Morenus said, waving his fellow centurions to join him.

The trumpeters unslung their instruments. The column readied itself for the predictable sequence of commands that was coming.

"Many Brigantes," Orann replied.

"Only Brigantes?" Morenus probed.

Orann shrugged.

"There were only Brigantes when I left," he answered.

Morenus hoped the young man was not mistaken.

"Civius, you will lead the attack with the Delmatarum. Test their mettle Civius, see if they stand against us. Form your men on a front, two centuries wide, three men deep. Centuries One and Two, Three and Five will form up in the same order behind. The cavalry will remain to the rear. We will wheel in the valley on my command and halt once we are in a favourable position. Give us time to pick our spot. If Centurion Pinneius and the rest of the Fourth are still in there we are going to get them out. I want no prisoners, except their chiefs if we can get them alive. Tell the men," Morenus concluded.

Orann watched as the column reordered into a fighting block, standards and trumpeters, officers all taking their assigned places. The words were low and steady. The cohort waited on its leash, poised and quiet. Unlike Velio, Morenus did not speak to his men. He lifted his sword, called a command and Civius marched off, towing the whole force in his wake. They squelched through the long tussocky drenched grasses, marching over stones without breaking ranks. He could hear the tesserarii and optios calling the lines to straighten and close. He took a place at Morenus' heels. The commander had not given him an instruction and he did not know what else he was supposed to do. Was Morenus finished with his services?

The valley opened up on their left, clumps of trees dotted the line of a stream in full torrent. Civius steered a line past it. Mist and rain hid the tops of the surrounding hills. Up ahead the distant headwall of the valley was faintly visible through the murk. Morenus marched on. The officers' voices got louder as the men struggled with the difficult ground. At last, when the head wall was within three hundred paces, the shapes of enemy warriors materialised in brown and grey-green clusters. He was about to tell Morenus when the centurion reacted.

"Halt," Morenus called out.

The cohort stood in utter silence. Tesserarii aligned erring spaces until it was as perfect in the valley as if it was the Field of Mars outside Rome. The rain sighed as it fell on their heads, into the grass, calling a rustling, sibilant greeting. Titus Vindex tried to quell the pounding in his chest by inspecting the rear line of the First century. Its own optio was halfway down the same rank but for want of something better to do, he followed, wondering what it would be like to have these men under his command instead of the Delmatarum auxiliary. The silence was resolute. He noticed birds calling. Birds singing and the sound of the rain; it was not going to remain peaceful for much longer.

Morenus waited, assessing what he had in front of him. Over the years the enemies of Roman had quailed at the mute faces they faced. No war cries, or curses, nor imprecations to the gods came out of their mouths. It was a day for sword and shield, too wet for bowmen. The spears of the Delmatarum were about to take the sting out of the brunt of what was coming. He spat, wishing he knew better how many Brigantes were concealed in the folds of the ground. It was not too late to change the formation to fighting wedge. He toyed with the thought and rejected it. He wiped his face with the back of his hand.

"Sound, Stand to the Eagles. Let's find out what we have in front of us," he bellowed.

The trumpeters and cornicens shook the water from their instruments, blew a low clearing note, looked at the senior musician, who nodded and burst into the familiar call. It rang out. The effect on the distant warriors was immediate. Morenus stepped forward. Was that a faint cheer as well?

"Did you hear that?" he barked at his leading signifer.

The cohort standard bearer's rich, bearskin cape was blanket-beaded with silvery water droplets. The animal's massive head rested on the top of his helmet, its eye sockets, blank and unseeing, clawed forepaws draped and pinned around his shoulders and down his chest. What little armouring was visible shone with the dullness of fish scales. The skin at the corners of the signifer's eyes creased. The closest he ever came to expressing outright pleasure. Behind him the other four signifers for the centuries nodded agreement. Morenus drew breath from the pit of his stomach.

"Civius, prepare to advance," he ordered, "sound the advance."

The trumpeters ceased blowing the 'Eagles' and broke into the Advance. Civius raised his sword and the Delmatarum garrison stepped forward. Arco gripped spear and shield and shut down the flutter of fear in his belly. There was no time to be afraid now.

*

Velio heard the muted notes of Stand to the Eagles, in the distance. Marcellus came to his side.

"Can you see them?" he asked.

"They are coming. Orann must have got through," Marcellus grinned.

The mens' heads lifted and broke into wry smiles at the sound.

"No, but they're out there and they're close. This damn rain is worse than fog. Give them a cheer lads. It might carry," Velio urged.

A broken raggedy cheer rose from the legionaries. It was not much of a cheer.

"Plautius, reset the dolabra. They might come again one last time and try to finish us off before the cohort arrives," he ordered.

*

Losatas heard the trumpets. A cold horror ripped into his chest. His warriors were tiring. Their spirits were dropping. The little Roman force was defying them with insane courage. He could not believe they were from the same force that had been destroyed on the road.

The old Carvetii chieftain's nerve started buckling before him.

"Not today," he said, "not here. The omens are poor. Their gods have given them strength. My men will not be caught and crushed between them. The gods are not here."

He gestured to the unrelenting sky.

"How are you going to get past them?" Losatas jeered at him

He thrust his arm out toward the cohort emerging from the murk. The Carvetii chief jabbed his spear at the far side of the valley where a screen of trees grew on the lower section of the slopes,.

"That way," he replied.

"Coward," Losatas screamed at him, "I came here for the spirit pole, to stand with you against the Roman dogs," he shouted.

"You came for your own reasons," the Carveti chieftain replied, "I did bring the spirit pole you want so much to taunt them with it. To show them we had taken it before we put them down in the grass like the dogs they are. Not to submit it to you."

"Where is it then?" he shouted.

The Carveti fixed Losatas with a knowing glare. He deserved more respect than this.

"One of my men has it under his cloak, waiting for the right moment. If you show it to the Roman dogs now, while they are still undefeated, they will fight for it. Its spirit will fly to join them. Give them courage. You understand very little about them," he accused.

Losatas felt the words like a slap. This second criticism of him was too much, too insulting.

"You dare to hide it from me? I am Losatas of the Brigantes. You dare to withhold the tribute that is mine by right?" he roared, gripping his sword.

The Carveti snorted.

"The omens are poor, the spirit pole still favours the wolf-soldiers. It is unlucky. I was told to make a sacrifice of it by my druid. I fear that is a mistake, it will bring no good to the Carveti people. The pole is cursed. Perhaps I should let you have it, Losatas. The odds are bad. The Romans are coming in great numbers now," he said.

He called out to a warrior. Losatas could see the concealment beneath the wet cloak.

"Show him," the Carveti chief snorted.

The warrior pulled aside the cloak and the top, decorated part of the standard gleamed in the dull light. The shining, circular phalerae of the century, topped with a gold hand, palm forward. The wood pole was gone. Losatas saw the chop mark where it had been severed.

"You want it, Losatas? Take it and may the gods smile on the Brigantes, our brothers and allies," the Carveti barbed him.

He signed the warrior to relinquish his grasp. Losatas reached out, meeting the man's discomforted look. The man bit his tongue and let go of the signum. Losatas looked at the truncated pole. A swirling joy flooded him filling his belly and his chest, making his heart pump faster. He could not stop himself smiling. A spirit pole: a Roman spirit pole, the greatest of all treasures. Not even the centurion's feathered head would be a suitable match for this. He turned and showed it to his men. Their howl of brute joy matched his own feelings.

"Look, we have it at last," he roared to the sea of faces watching the argument.

"Lord, the sons of the wolf," a voice reminded him.

He made himself calm.

"Guard it well," he said, handing it to a senior warrior to protect.

He turned back to the Carveti chief.

"My thanks. The Brigantes are friends to the Carveti. Forgive my anger, please. Our enemy stands over there," he pointed.

The chief shook his head unconvinced by Losatas' sudden conciliatory tone. His eyes flashed. Losatas saw he was going to have to make a reconciliation for this outright submission. The alliance was too important to be lost over this, no matter how prestigious the prize. He would make it up to the Carveti. There would be trophies today and in return for making this gesture they could take what they wanted. The Carveti chief waved his arm, pulling his own warriors back. They exchanged a final look.

"Live well, Losatas," the old chieftain grunted.

Reconciliation was not going to be easy.

"Live long and well, great chief," he replied.

He turned back to assess the men he had already trapped. A screen of warriors was shadowing the approach of the enemy vanguard. The battle horns were getting closer. His own men responded. He tried to think clearly through the booming noise. Drapisces was dead and he had the spirit pole. He had run out of time to slaughter the small group of trapped Romans. Their relief was now a mere few spears throw away. The Carveti were moving en masse for the trees and a way up out of the valley, fleeing from the oncoming danger. His men were looking to him for courage.

He took another look at Velio's men. They did not look like they wanted to renew the fight. He turned and saw his scouts running back, fear in their faces.

"Many Romans," the first one gasped.

"Good," he crowed, "we will have their heads. Bring the pole," he ordered.

The messenger blurted, "too many Losatas."

The spirit pole put its finger in his ears and blocked the words from his mind. Orgidor was not to be remembered as the only brave warrior in his family.

*

Morenus got a clear view. The Brigantes were massing in an indiscriminate and unco-ordinated mob, boiling themselves up with war whoops, challenges and now battle horns. Over the head of Civius who was now positioned to receive the first onslaught, he glimpsed Velio's command on its low platform. He could not make out Velio, but if he was alive, he would come out and drive in behind the mass soon as he launched his own attack. There was a sudden roar from the Brigantes before they surged forward. Civius got off a volley of pila before they crashed into his men. Out of the corner of his eye a large group of hostile warriors were making a break across the valley for a stance of trees. The enemy was already disintegrating. He took a breath and waited for Civius to drive off the attack or call for help. Every auxiliary lost was saving one of his precious, expensive legionaries. Minutes passed. The Brigantes evidently had the bit between their teeth. The hindmost rank of Civius' men started stepping backwards. It was the tell-tale sign they were about to break. He snorted, they had stood and taken it for longer than he had expected from two centuries, but it still was not very long.

"Forward," he ordered at the top of his voice.

The Brigantes frothed through Civius' lines and turned them into a carnage. The remaining Delmatarum started running back. Civius was cutting warriors down and holding them together as best he might. The Brigantes paused for a moment savouring their victory and then came on at the rush. Morenus stepped back drawing the cohort signifer with him back into the front rank of the First century.

"**Halt. Front rank pila,**" he yelled.

*

Losatas saw Roman javelins flying through the air. Warriors on both sides of him crumpled in screams. He marvelled he had not suffered one too. A second volley smacked into his men. Springing over the soaking tussocks he clashed with the line. The men at his back were with him. The noise of shields meeting shields was everywhere. He stared at the implacable face of a squat, unshaven legionary in front of him. The man spat in his eyes, blinding him. Something hard drove into his knees below the edge of his shield but he hardly felt it. He swung his sword over the rim of the legionary shield and tried to hack down through his skull. A blow to his side took the air from his chest. He could not breathe. The legionary's face was all hatred and aggression. Another blow on the same side put him on his knees. He stared up at the unshaven face poised to strike the third blow, the one that was going to end it.

*'Orgidor, how has it come to this?'* he asked.

*

From his position behind the Brigantes lines Velio saw the beginnings of their great charge. The confused mass of men smashed into Civius' little command. Civius failed to fire a second volley of javelins in time, and they rolled over him, becoming a darting arrow heading to the heart of Morenus' men.

"Do we support sir?" Liscus asked.

He accepted the question and dismissed it with a shake of his head.

"The cohort are fresh and formed up. We are too few to make a difference," he replied.

The cohort trumpets blared in the distance. He screwed up his eyes to be sure.

"I think they're breaking already sir," a legionary ventured.

Velio stared as hard as he could, willing himself the power to detect what the soldier had seen. And then he saw too. Clumps of warriors were breaking for the open bottom land right and left of the fighting. They were cutting and running. The sight of the cohort in battle array was proving too much.

"If Morenus has cavalry support, it'll be a boar hunt," Plautius' dispassionate voice cut through the cheers.

Velio smiled at the pun.

*

Orann walked through the battlefield staring down at the warriors who had died. Were these the same men he had faced up to in the Carvetti chieftain's hall? Was the fierce little druid lying amongst them, the one who wanted him to run?

"Orann,' said Velio.

Orann turned to his name. Velio wrapped him in a great bear hug, held him out and grinned at him.

"Master, I thought I might have come too late. These men run so slowly," he complained.

Velio laughed.

"Well, six hundred men can't run as fast as one. That is true. But you got them here Orann. You got them here in time. You're making a habit of saving my skin."

He clapped Orann on the shoulder once more.

"What a sight, what a sight,' he said.

Brigantes bodies lay strewn across the valley floor. The Carvetii had vanished up into the misty heights before Morenus was finished with the Brigantes. Metius prowled past muttering about the standard being no closer to being found. He laid a hand on Liscus arm to forestall the rebuke. Metius had been a whisker too loud but the tesserarius had a point.

"I must make a report," he told Liscus, "see to the men, I will send a medicus and wound dressers."

He pointing to the middle ground where Morenus was holding a conference with his fellow centurions. The signifers had planted the standards in a circle. They were glancing over to where he stood. Their broad smiles were like sunlight in this miserable place. The rain ceased. A brightness above the clouds suggested the worst of the Tempestates wrath was over. If Morenus stayed true to his usual form, when the back slapping was over, he was going to tell him he had pushed his luck as far as he should. Fortuna had blessed him. The Brigantes had been outnumbered. If it was not the complete victory, it was a thorough warning.

He watched the cohort medicii arrive to tend his walking wounded. The serious ones would have to endure a cart ride to Cantiventi. There was no purpose in taking them to the limited care available at the hill fort. Marcellus had survived intact and was doing the rounds counting the survivors for a report that was going to have to wait for a dryer place than this to be written. He pondered the events of the last few days. If this was his last day on active service, it had been quite something. The new gladius had been a pleasure to use, with its lovely balance and edges sharper than a tavern keeper's tongue. He wanted to fall on his knees and give heartfelt thanks his life was not ending here in utter disgrace and humiliation. It had been a good victory. The attacks on the mines and the convoys, the Iter X itself, now punished. Drapisces was dead. It was time to go and make wine and leave the Fourth century to Liscus, Plautius and Metius. Plautius would make an able optio for Liscus. And Marcellus would become his military secretary. There would be continuity.

*'Wine will have to be drunk, before I go'* he mused, '*sore heads will be the order of the day.'*

And all this dwarfed by the missing standard. It was not a good victory,

*'You are kidding yourself,'* he scorned.

This was far from good. Morenus was wasting no time. He splashed through the stream and went to make his report.

The Assembly horns began blowing. The cohort forming up with the corpses of the Brigantes at their feet. His men rose without bidding and hurried across the stream to their place in the cohort. He waited until they took the line. So few of them now, perhaps a third of what he had led out from Deva for a routine inspection of a hill fort. He waited until they had settled in place and took his place at the front of them. Their faces were contented mixture of weariness and pride. Liscus stood by. Marcellus in lieu of signifer. Morenus did not waste time.

"Soldiers of the First cohort we have retrieved the signum of the Fourth century. All hail to the emperor. Our honour is restored. You can march back to Deva Victrix with your heads up. The Brigantes have been given a sharp lesson and the Carvetii have run away like cowards and dogs."

A huge cheer of delight broke out all around Velio. Liscus thumped his shoulder and retracted his fist before Velio could turn his head.

*'How in Jupiter's name did they get the standard,'* he wondered, *'this is a dream.'*

"I ask Centurion Velio Pinneius to accept and receive back his signum," Morenus called.

Velio got an iron grip of his sudden confusion and marched out with Marcellus at his back. His men began drumming their swords on their shields. The cohort took it up. He halted in front of Morenus and the row of centurions from the other centuries. Civius stood to the side with his eyes fixed to the distant side of the valley. His face was pale and drawn. His surviving men stood in a forlorn row. Perhaps thirty of them. The drumming ceased as if the bandmaster had orchestrated it. They saluted each other. The leading signifer turned to face him with something wrapped in a cloak. The damaged signum lay in the folds, shining and defiant. The skin around the signifer's eyes creased as he held it out to Velio. His mouth was rock hard. Velio took it. The pole had been chopped through with an axe. A single blow most likely. He raised it up.

"**Hail Antoninus Pius,**
**Father of our country,**
**Father to his people,**" he said.

"**Most blessed by Jupiter Optimus Maximus,**" the cohort spoke.

He handed it over to Marcellus. Morenus looked him square in the eyes. There was something in them he found disquieting, almost sneering.

"They always said you were lucky, Velio," he hissed, "but I never thought much of that until today. Good soldiers make their own luck. Hard work and discipline make good luck. Honouring the emperor and the gods makes good luck. But actually getting this back, here."

Morenus broke off, as if words escaped him and shook his head in disbelief.

"Servius Albinius will be relieved. His legion now has all its signa," Velio stuck to neutral, safe ground.

"Indeed centurion, I wish you good fortune when you stand before him and report how you lost it in the first place and disobeyed his direct command to return to Deva. Instead, you come out from Cantiventi, put me in an impossible position that I must support you, and we recover the signum," Morenus replied.

"Do one last thing for me, if you will, centurion. Report the losses from your century. The dead and the wounded. The ones who have paid the price," he added.

Velio decided to take that on the chin, about turned and returned to his broken remnant of a century. The rain had washed the blood from shields and armour as Plautius had promised. He felt the palpable aura of pride and joy rising with the steam off their cloaks. They would mourn their comrades. But Elysium would come to hear the holy signum was safe in the hands of a new signifer. In the rear rank of Morenus' own century Titus Vindex trembled more than he had ever done before.

Arco watched the small ceremony and listened to the joyful voices. The cohort showed no interest in the Delmatarum losses. He could tell by Civius' blank expression that he felt detached from the general celebrations too. One hundred and fifteen casualties out of one hundred and forty-one that had taken the field. He hawked up phlegm and spat. Junius Cita and Scribono had been telling the truth about the legions all along.

## Chapter Fifty-five.

## Argentomagus.

The estate overseer pondered Bodusio. The three Mattiaci were now to be treated as trusted men. From army scum, escaping execution, to slaves, to trusted slaves. They were being careful not to swagger in front of him, but they exuded cheerfulness. After a moment's pause, he decided it was no skin off his nose. In fact, the more trusted men there were on the estate, the better.

'*So be it,*' he thought, '*it makes my life easier.*'

He gave them a nod for no hard feelings and racked his memory for any slight they might harbour against him in the short time they had been here. As far as he could recall there was nothing.

The first waggon load of posca was ready for sale. A light load, Gallus had organised a stall in the forum, to test out local interest and drum up orders. The winemaker was making ready to leave along with the waggon. His part of the contract was fulfilled.

"Take the three of them with you," Gallus ordered the overseer as the waggon was loaded, "they have an errand for me, if there is time."

The overseer shrugged and got on with it. Up front, Bodusio held the reins. Nahan was alongside. Eudo was in the back with the flasks and amphorae. Bodusio cracked the whip and the waggon lurched into motion.

They found a good spot in the forum with some shade, got set up and were soon making sales. The overseer held the money, ticking off his list of every container sold. Gramalcus ambled over and bought a medium sized amphora. He clicked his fingers to his slave to fetch it back home. He stared at Bodusio and Eudo and Nahan in turn. The overseer waited for the acid comment that was bound to coming.

"Enjoy the wine sir," Bodusio forestalled him.

The overseer stopped his counting and poised to step in, but Gramalcus went back to the slave pens rubbing his chin. He did not look happy. The overseer relaxed.

"Carry on," he murmured.

The leather purse was getting heavy with coins. The majority of the wine flasks were gone, snared by local interest and a couple of small amphorae to rivals eager to evaluate the quality. Gallus' winemaker arrived on his horse and tied up by the municipal building. He came to the stall, nodding at the small remaining number of unsold vessels.

"I told you it would be good," he said to the overseer.

"They have to come back regularly and buy before you can brag," the overseer chided in .

But it had gone better than expected. By late afternoon the forum was getting quieter. The wine was gone. He let the Germans pack up the trestle into the waggon.

"A drink, lads?" he offered, "at the tavern," he expanded, feeling happier now that they had had an opportunity to show their true colours.

The three of them had worked hard and been friendly to all the customers. He waited until they were finished and beckoned them to follow.

"If they are slaves they can't drink here," the tavern keeper said, "I'll sell you a flask and they can take it over to the waggon and drink it."

He stood at the door of his hostelry, nodding to the passing citizens. The overseer stared at the self same man who had just taken receipt of six large amphorae from them that very morning.

"They are trusted men, authorised to carry out errands and simple business purchases for their master. You know what 'trusted slave' means, and as you can see, if you care to look, none of them has so much as a hip knife. They are here under my authority," the overseer said.

"These the auxiliary from the front?" an aggrieved voice chipped in, "the ones sent to the slave auction?"

"They can drink out here," the tavern keeper said.

The overseer heard Nahan mutter something to his friends in Mattiaci.

"If you insist," the overseer said.

The tavern keeper was too important a customer to upset over a small thing like this. Gallus would not be amused if he made an issue of it.

"Bloody auxiliaries, I never trusted them in my time. Just one mad druid away from what happened to Varus.

A man pushed past the four of them on his way inside. The innkeeper nodded. The man turned his burly frame. He was well fed and decently dressed: not rich, but an owner of slaves in his own household. The overseer read him like a scroll.

"Once they've turned against the Eagle once you can't ever trust them again. You watch your back my friend. Three to one, understand what I'm saying?" the man pretended friendship.

The overseer looked at the three men Gallus Tiomarus considered trustworthy and decided the conversation had reached a conclusion. No cup of wine was worth this nonsense. He stepped back.

"No hard feelings," the innkeeper said.

The burly man waited with a sly grin flickering on his face. When they turned to go back the waggon five of Durus' off duty auxiliaries were heading in their direction. Nahan, Eudo and Bodusio tensed up.

"Here they are boys," Big Mouth called out, "the ones Gramalcus was on about. The three sent to the slave market for mutiny. I'd have garrotted the lot of 'em, if it was up to me," he stirred.

"Well, it was not up to you," the overseer snapped.

"What did you say?" Big Mouth challenged.

It was a fist fight before the overseer could say more. The legionaries waded in. Bodusio punched the first one so hard he fell in a heap unconscious. The overseer yelled, "stop," once and took a punch himself. Four against five. The innkeeper stood back to watch the fun. Big Mouth dodged into the tavern, his work done. Without a word of command, the Mattiaci punched, kicked and swung, covering each other's back and the overseer's too. The auxiliaries took stock; they were losing the fight. All the pent-up rage and grievances from the Germania limes was knocking them sideways. This was no ordinary brawl. The three auxiliaries were bigger, stronger and out to prove a point. The moment came when knives were the instinct. The moment when it was going to change for the worse. The overseer read it and stepped in, pointing to the unconscious soldier in their midst.

"Take him and fuck off. If you kill one of these slaves you'll pay with your hides to Gallus Tiomaris," he warned.

He spread his arms out to hold Bodusio, Eudo and Nahan back. They obeyed without complaint. They were hardly sweating.

"You," he snapped at the tavern keeper, changing his mind about what Gallus would say, "get wine out here before I let them loose inside. You'll have sawdust for furniture."

The four auxiliaries stared.

He grabbed his opportunity.

"Cups for these lads too. Pax, lads, Pax, honours are even, eh?" he said.

Ten minutes later, Big Mouth scowled when he left the tavern. The overseer flicked a glance to his trusted men. The jug still had wine left in it. The tavern keeper was philosophic.

"Time we were leaving. You lads can finish it for us," he grinned.

Bodusio shook arms with them. Nahan stared at the wine jug licking his lips at the denied treasure it held. They climbed back aboard the waggon. The overseer took the reins.

"We will never find out who killed the General's friend," Bodusio whispered to Nahan.

Nahan looked at him puzzled.

"Why would we want to? We can come here and fight every time we sell wine. Break a few noses, knock out some teeth. Why would you want to spoil that? We can fight the Eighth and get revenge for poor bread and no pay."

"Because the Old General asked us to," Bodusio replied.

"I agree with Nahan. We get fed, the bread is the best. We have a roof over our heads and dry beds. Easy duties and the chance to kick Roman heads. These pigs are never going to accept us Mattiaci as soldiers. They think we are barbarians. That's why we ended up here, Bodusio. It's simple, they don't trust us. We live in caves and eat filth. Good enough to stop a spear and shelter their precious legions, but not much else," Eudo growled.

"We could just kill one of them and bring the master his head in a sack. He will be happy, we get set free," Nahan said.

"Pick a soldier and kill him? We would have to hide the body," Bodusio replied.

Nahan made his habitual, 'who cares?' shrug.

"Why not?" he posed.

Eudo liked it. Bodusio shook his head. The death of a regular after their very public fighting in front of the tavern was a sure way to execution. The overseer turned to look at their animated discussion. They took the hint and started bragging about the fight in 'frontier' Latin. He joined in.

Later they sat by the scorpion out on the grassy bank overlooking the estate road.

"I bet the winemaker knows who did it," Bodusio said, stabbing a twig into the ground.

He did not much like the man.

*Smug Bituriges, never seen an angry man in his life, too busy with his head in the vines and his hand out for payment, when Bacchus did all the work.'*

The red anger surged in his head. It was strange. Now he had said it aloud, the winemaker was perfectly placed to gain from the attempt on Gallus' life and the murder of Hanno Glaccus: he was perfectly placed.

*'Why should I care if Romans kill each other?'* the anger kept flowing.

The sun began its slow, benevolent descent to the horizon. Gallus was out at his gaming table rolling the dice with himself. They watched him for a while. One of the house slaves brought him his cloak and he seemed to shrivel inside it. The slave waved to them as she passed. A wine jug and his favourite drinking cup arrived courtesy of one of the cooks. Bodusio saw the answer to his question was there in front of him. An old soldier, wounded for no good reason except perhaps greed, who had fed them and trusted them. He had rescued them. He pursed his mouth. There were Romans worth his hate: but this man, no, not him.

"If we can't find out who did kill the Old General's friend, and you won't let us kill a soldier as an offering to his spirit, I think we should kill Gramalcus for what he did to us, and make him our offering to Teiws, so he does not forget our names and covers our families with his spear. Pray he allows us to see our homeland again. We have not sacrificed to the gods since we were taken. We should not assume their protection. This is the perfect time. Then we take three horses and make a run for it. I don't think this old boy would chase us too hard. He might even give us food and knives," he laughed.

They smiled with him. Bodusio pulled his thoughts together. It seemed they all felt the same way about Gallus.

"Gramalcus. Now there is a man who really needs a sword in his gut," Eudo countered.

"If we kill him, we have to stay. Old Gallus down there will protect us from the army, if they come knocking, and then if we get away with it, we stay a couple of years and disappear one dark night, when it's all been forgotten," he clicked his fingers.

"Teiws will protect us, or if we have offended hm, he will not," Eudo murmured, "he is father to us all."

Nahan cleared his throat.

"Gramalcus deserves to die. We are agreed? But we can't kill him right now and give his head to Gallus. He only asked us to find out who killed his friend. It will not look right if we give him Gramalcus so soon."

Bodusio snapped his twig.

"Then we kill him one day, when we get him alone, somehow. Not now. It's too obvious. Teiws will be patient. He has waited this long," he paused, "and we keep this to ourselves. The Old General does need to know. We stay here and work for him, bide our time."

Chapter Fifty-six.

Velio took his time. Voccia was huge compared to when he had left Deva Victrix the last time. The summer heat and her condition were making her miserable. The small villa he had taken in the vicus outside Deva was adequate, but the proximity of the fort unsettled him now that he no longer belonged there. He itched to move away and take the road to the coast and the first ship to Gaul. What were Hanno and Gallus be saying about his lateness? The longer he and Voccia delayed the journey, the bigger she would be, and the thought of delaying until next year was too much to bear. She saw his distress.

"I can manage it Velio. But not on a horse. A waggon, can we do that?" she said.

"We can do it in short steps, from mansio to mansio," he replied.

She frowned.

"Mansio?" she asked.

"There are places along the road where we can stay overnight, like taverns. There is no rush, and we can see how you manage," he offered.

"A Votadini girl can manage anything a Roman centurion can throw at her," she teased.

"Well then. I'll buy a suitable waggon and horses and we will make plans," he replied.

"You are sure you want to leave this?" she asked.

He smiled at her concern.

"Voccia, I already have. My time here is over. Gallus and Hanno and I made a plan. You and the baby are part of that now. The sooner we make a start the sooner we can be happy," he smiled.

"We will never come back?" she asked.

"I will need to come back to make agreements with the legions but, Servius has given me our first contract," he said, "are you sure you are happy to leave?" he probed.

"I don't know," she answered, "but you have Gallus and Hanno waiting for you, for us," she corrected herself, "so we must go."

*

Velio pulled on the reins and brought the waggon to a halt. Orann circled back on his horse, still scouting on safe roads, and sat alongside them, stroking the neck of his mare. Voccia stared hot-faced and uncomfortable at the two funeral monuments at the side of the road. He stepped down. Beyond the gravestones the entrance to an estate beckoned up a long gentle incline to soft coloured buildings in the distance. Rows of vines graced the slopes in straight garlands. The faint sound of a dog barking came floating to them on the air. This must be the place. The directions from Argentomagus forum had been explicit.

"Is this it? Is this the place Velio? Who are they?" she asked, pointing.

He did not reply. One must be Priscus. The older looking memorial of the two perhaps? But the other was a mystery? He walked over to the one closest to the entrance. The engraving told him it was indeed Priscus and his wife. The second one, placed to its dextra side was unequivocal.

To the Divine Manes
Hanno Drusus Glaccus Ticinus
Aged Fifty Three
Commander, First Cohort, Twentieth Legion, Valeria Victrix
Faithful to the Emperor in Britannia

His eyes read the words, his brain explained them, his chest tightened in dismay.

"He is dead. Hanno is dead," he repeated.

The divine manes were the spirits of the dead. There was no mistake. This was his tomb. It was a new stone. The inscription was still white from the chisel. He quelled Voccia with gentle, raised hand.

"Something has happened. I only hope Gallus is still alive."

*'It could be any thing,it does not have to be bad.'*

"I can't believe it. After all those years on the wall," he muttered.

Voccia patted his knee.

"I'm sorry darling. He might have died in his sleep," she said, "it's possible," she soothed.

"That's true," he replied.

"Can we get out of this heat now Velio, I am going to burst, I swear,"she pleaded.

He smiled, "of course, not long now."

He picked up the reins and flicked them. Orann dropped to the rear, diplomatic as always. Velio eased the waggon through the gateway and gazed up the long road to the pretty cluster of buildings at the top of the rise. The suspiciously familiar shape of an assault weapon sitting in the sunshine overlooking their approach caught his attention.

"Holy Mothers of the Parade Grounds, it can't be. What in the name of Dis Pater is going on here?" he asked.

Voccia looked at him puzzled. He tried a smile, but it did not work for her. A startled fear crossed her face. He patted her leg the way she had patted him.

"Sorry, my dearest, perhaps it's a memento. Not the sort of thing I expected, that is all," he bluffed.

"Oh," she relaxed a shade, studying his profile.

It had been a long haul down from the coast. She was sick of the waggon and the sight of the horses' backsides. The baby must be coming soon. This could not last much longer. They clip-clopped into the yard.

"Gallus?" Velio called out.

The older man raised his hand in greeting and came limping toward the waggon.

"Swords Pinneius. I am happy to greet you. And Voccia too," he replied.

They shook arms for what seemed to Voccia an eternity, slapping each other on the other arm, inspecting the ravages time had brought to each of them. Then Gallus hugged her like a bear until Velio rescued her. He let go of her and turned his attention to Orann.

"Salve and greetings, lad," he said, "a friend from home?" he asked Voccia.

"You don't remember him?" she asked.

He shook his head and grinned, "old age," he chortled.

"Voccia needs some shade and a drink," Velio said.

Gallus waved to a servant woman and the two of them made their way at Voccia's pace to the sanctuary of the villa. As soon as they were out of sight and earshot Velio turned to Gallus.

"Hanno? The scorpion?" he said.

Gallus showed Velio to his favoured spot and poured him wine.

"I have ill news Velio. Hanno was murdered, nearly a month ago. The estate has enemies. Priscus had enemies and it seems when I bought the place, we took over that contract too," Gallus dared to joke.

"The scorpion, though?" Velio prompted.

"I had a notion it might scare our enemies off. Fat chance, but it helps me sleep better knowing it is here," Gallus replied.

Velio drank the wine and tugged his short, tidy beard.

"Where did you get that limp Gallus?"

Gallus was indestructible. Gallus pushed a wine cup to him.

"You have not heard the half of it Velio. I have three Mattiaci auxiliary, who were condemned to the slavers for trying to stir up mutiny on the Germania limes. Well, they are decent lads, and they are my Praetorian bodyguard. An old scorpion and three Mattiaci. That'll keep the crows off the vines," he cackled.

"Your Praetorian bodyguard. Mithras save us Gallus," Velio tried hard not to laugh but it jolted his chest to hear how low things must have sunk.

"Who killed him, Gallus?" he tried to keep his voice calm.

Gallus went sombre.

"I don't know. One of the local Eighth legion decurions has been quite helpful. Hanno's body was found on the road between here and Argentomagus. He had been stabbed on both sides. Who knows, perhaps he thought he could get back here. Anyway, the decurion's men found him lying on the road. It wasn't the stabbing that killed him, Velio. It was the sword some bastard stuck in his chest twice, we both know what that wound looks like, we've given them plenty of times," Gallus went silent.

"So, it was a soldier?" Velio he spat.

He flexed his hands into fists.

"I never said that, Velio. I said he was finished off with a sword," Gallus said, keeping his voice down.

No good would come of Velio getting himself riled up. Velio shook his head.

"He came through the worst the Caledonii threw at us, Gallus, helped build and defend the wall, and he took a sword here?"

"The Fates play cruel games with us, Velio and then they cut our threads when they grow tired of us, my friend," Gallus said.

"I will find him and kill him," Velio snarled.

Gallus regarded him and raised his cup.

"Be comforted Velio. Hanno died away from the cold and damp he always moaned about. He had time to warm his bones and see the wine come in. Jupiter was merciful," he said.

He swirled his wine, drained it and poured them both more. Velio toyed with the thought of telling Gallus about Scribono's calumny about Hanno. The words were on his lips. He had never lied to his old mentor before, and this was not the time to start doing so. Gallus broke in before he could speak.

"And as for finding and killing the man who did it, I have told my Praetorians I will tie that man to the gatepost down there and they can use him for target practice," Gallus said.

"No, Gallus, I will do that," he replied, "Mithras be my judge."

## Aftermath.

## Argentomagus

The carved letters on Hanno's stone had the sharp cut of the chisel. It was a decent memorial, a nice piece of stone. It was obscene.

It was hard to imagine Hanno lying under there, his face cold and blank within touching distance below the soil. Hanno, veteran of the northern most wall. Commander of the First cohort. The most cunning, astute, adversarial soldier in the garrison of Britannia. The man who had inveigled his way past Servius Albinius to the pinnacle of a military career. And now he was dust.

Velio glanced about. The road was empty. There was no one passing who might look askance at the little scene he was about to enact. No one who might mock, or alternatively simply nod in decency and understanding

He wiped the sudden, guilty, sweat from his forehead with the back of his forearm. He had come to this place expected a fight and then the drawing of swords: the two of them much too old for such foolishness but duty bound to go ahead with it. All on the say-so of a dead traitor: what folly? So many egos and careers at stake. So many men lost in the tides of an emperor's delusion. A line on a map, an arbitrary suggestion of where the empire should end. The implicit permission that no soldier should concern themselves with checking beyond that ink line.

*'I thought we had unfinished business, you and me, Hanno. It seems that it's been finished for me though,'* Velio weighed it up.

Every hot, hard, angry feeling about Hanno that Scribono had managed to unleash was now a sad, forlorn joke. There was no setting right to be done, no explanation or forgiveness between old comrades. It was a joke that Bacchus would have enjoyed, one that dear old Marcus Hirtius, lying dead in his river would have smirked at: the Fates had made fools of each of them.

"It is a funny thing to admit Hanno, but riding here in this heat and dust I realise how much I miss the mornings when the fogs clear. The mists on the river and lakes, like the gods' breath. The wet smell of grass. The mornings that freeze your balls and make you swear just to keep warm. All the things you hated up there," he said.

He drew the gladius Morenus had presented to him.

"They gave this to me, Hanno, for all those years. Mithras knows it is right. Gallus already fancies it. I'll have to watch him. It will be little Velio's one day, when he's old enough to use it. I'm sorry you missed each other. He would have been your shadow. I vow to you, Hanno Drusus Glaccus Ticinus, that one day I will kill the man who murdered you. It will be the last life I take with this sword. I half expected that life might have been yours. Whatever it was you said or did Hanno, it no longer matters."

He gave Hanno the legionary salute and stepped back, sheathing the sword. He blew his cheeks and wiped the sudden, inexplicable moisture in his eyes.

"I must go. Voccia will have finished feeding the little one. She will have a thousand chores for me to do. And Gallus turns more like Servius Albinius with every passing day. Speaking of that old tyrant, you will be pleased to know he has given us a contract to supply the legion with our wine. I told you he was not so bad," he halted.

He had run out of words when there were a thousand things to say. Or perhaps there was not: there would be other visits, he supposed. The story of the signum could wait for another day.

"Hail and Farewell, Hanno," he finished off.

In the distance Trajan was barking. Behind the boundary wall there was a happy mood in the air. He walked up the road. It was going to take time to get used to all of this, but a son, perhaps more than one, who would one day inherit all this, made him feel as content as he could ever recall.

THE END

## Author's Note.

The hill passes and key forts in this story are those of Hardknott, Ambleside and Ravenglass in Cumbria, northwest England. The accepted Roman names for these sites are Mediobogdum, Galeva and Glannaventa respectively. However, when researching this story, I found various sources suggesting these names might not be entirely exact despite their common usage on modern signs and maps. The plethora of Roman sites in the area and the date ranges of occupation make this problematic. This led me to the published work by the late Emeritus Professor of Roman Imperial History at Lancaster University, David Shotter.

I have happily deferred to Professor Shotter's knowledge and adopted the names he proposed for these particular sites. Thus, Galeva fort at Ambleside is my Cantiventi, the hill fort in the Hardknott pass does not actually have a name, and the port at Ravenglass is Iuliocenon.

For completeness, Deva Victrix barracks was situated at Chester. Eburacum was situated at York. Trimontium was situated at Newsteads, Melrose.

Printed in Great Britain
by Amazon

62658560R00261